Praise for *Sunday's Orphan*

Catherine Gentile brings Jim Crow to vivid, heartbreaking life in this tale of a complicated, endearing woman caught between the cruelty of her time and the emerging secrets of her own identity. Compelling, timely, and beautifully written.
–Monica Wood, author of *One In a Million Boy*, *When We Were the Kennedys*, and *Ernie's Ark*

Sunday's Orphan by Catherine Gentile is just plain excellent. Through its acuity of expression, emotional and psychological insight, and the unfolding of characters, it allows us to enter an historical period—the Jim Crow South—that is critical to understand racism today. This is imaginative work that hits home.
–Jeremiah Conway, PhD Professor Emeritus, University of Southern Maine, author of *The Alchemy of Teaching; The Transformation of Lives*

The past is prologue, as Shakespeare once said, and Promise Mears Crawford, protagonist of *Sunday's Orphan*, finds new meaning in that phrase as a twenty-year old in 1930 racially divided Georgia. What begins as simple curiosity quickly turns into a driving pathos as her hidden family history unravels in tandem with her own increasingly complicated present life. Love, a need to belong, and a search for self-identity collide with the bitter reality of Jim Crow racism and a dark history that refuses to go away. Catherine Gentile takes us on a twisting journey where happy endings are at first hard to imagine, but where the human spirit ultimately prevails.
–Jack Trammell, PhD, Chair of Sociology, Criminal Justice, and Human Services Departments, Mount Saint Mary's University

Brace yourself! As soon as you open *Sunday's Orphan*, you will find yourself in a disturbing world—an apparent oasis of interracial harmony surrounded by the threat of the Jim Crow culture of 1930 Georgia. You'll feel the humid heat of the midday sun, smell the farm animals and the smokehouse, and hear the menacing sound of a newcomer whistling "Dixie". Keep going if you like the suspense of a page turner, care to unravel the intricate relationships of intriguing characters, and enjoy masterfully researched and well written prose. But read especially to feel for yourself the forces that shaped the heritage of today's African Americans, as their parents and grandparents emerged from slavery and tried to claim their right to freedom and equality.

- Phyllis Chinlund, MA, MSW, documentary filmmaker, author of *Looking Back from the Gate*.

Sunday’s Orphan

ALSO BY CATHERINE GENTILE

FICTION

Small Lies, A Collection of Short Stories

The Quiet Roar of a Hummingbird

NON-FICTION

The Caregiver's Journey:
Tools, Tips, and Provisions

Sunday's Orphan

A novel

Catherine Gentile

Catherine Gentile
September 2021

BookLocker
Saint Petersburg, Florida

Print ISBN: 978-1-64718-573-2
Epub ISBN: 978-1-64718-574-9
Mobi ISBN: 978-1-64718-575-6

Published by BookLocker.com, Inc., St. Petersburg, Florida.

Printed on acid-free paper.

The characters and events in this book are fictitious. Any similarity to real persons, living or dead, is coincidental and not intended by the author.

BookLocker.com, Inc.
2021

First Edition

Library of Congress Cataloguing in Publication Data
Gentile, Catherine
Sunday's Orphan by Catherine Gentile
Library of Congress Control Number: 2020908729

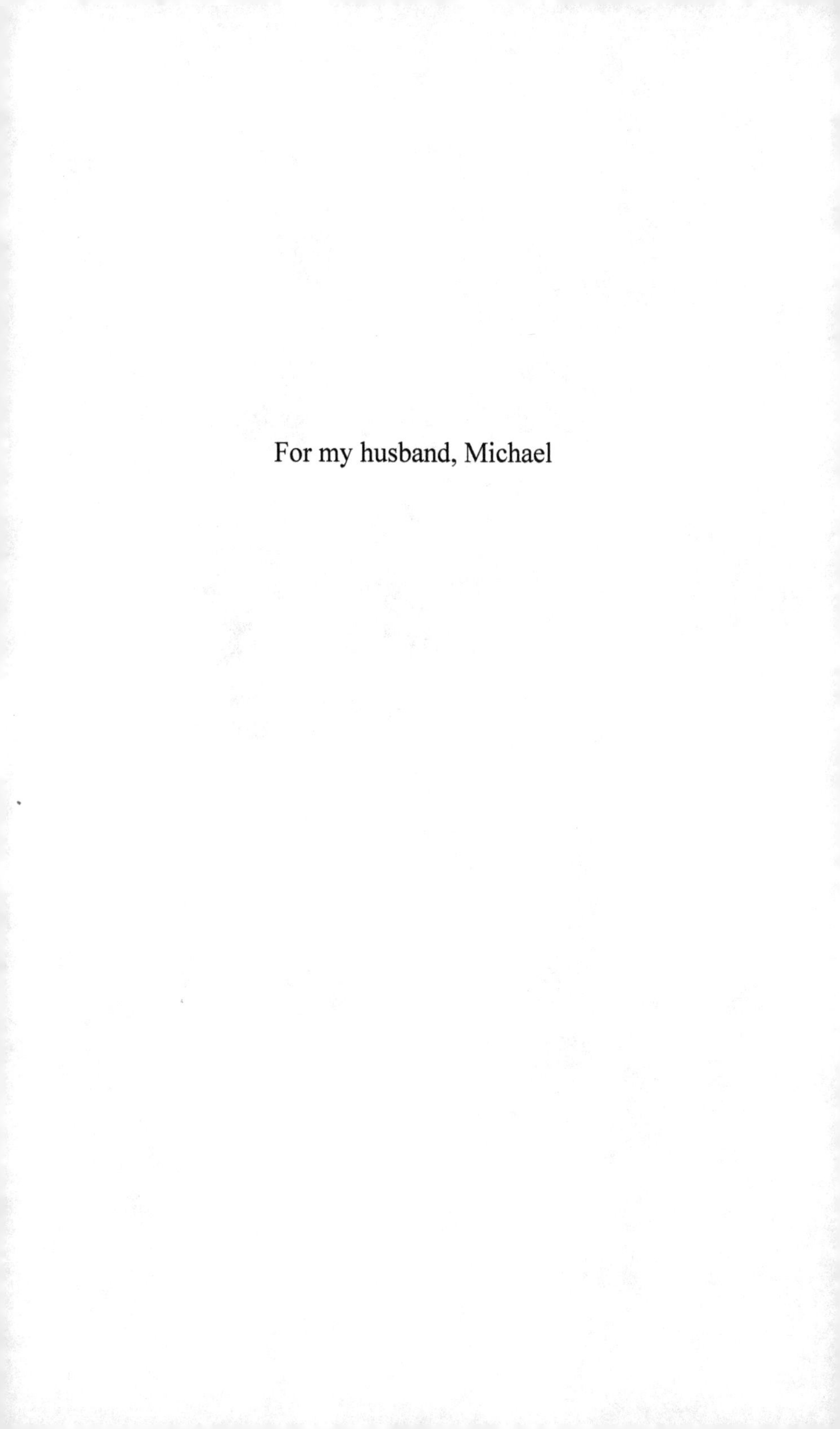

For my husband, Michael

Blue and gray had disappeared from our Southern landscape long before I came into my manhood. Why then, each time I sink my shovel into the soil, do I uncover earth tainted with history's blood? Is there no salve to cleanse our country's festering wounds? I press a handful of crimson earth between my palms, praying it will form one solid ground, but it resists and crumbles. I have no choice but weep.

Taylor Crawford's journal entry,
March 7, 1896

DAY ONE

CHAPTER 1

Death, thou intractable agent,
Just and eternal finale after a life of enduring lies,
You advance doggedly. You arrive too soon.

Taylor Crawford, *My Life in Georgia*, 1929

Promise plunged her shovel into the sandy Georgia soil and splintered the last fence post her Uncle Taylor had hewn, marking the first page of her history since he had died. Etched in her memory was the layout of the property which embodied his life's work. To the north, Taylor's newly dug grave, situated, as he'd requested, alongside the graves of the slaves who had worked this plantation long before he came to own it; to the south, vegetable gardens; to the east, the Cornbread Footpath that meandered through the woods and past the inconspicuous structures housing the farm's workers and their families; and to the west, the pasture dotted with a small barn in which she sheltered animals recovering from a predatory assault. From where she stood within walking distance of Taylor's grave, she could see past the smoke-house and drought-stunted corn plants, over the bean and okra fields to the lean-to beside the small barn. There stood the imposing figure of Fletch Hart, Uncle Taylor's twenty-four-year-old foreman who, after Taylor's passing, had reluctantly agreed to work for her. He looked up from his workbench, where he'd been repairing the latch on a birdcage and, for the first time in the twenty years they'd known one another, made no move to wave or call her name.

Taylor had forewarned her that death rearranges our connections with our loved ones, deceased and living. How right he'd been. Ten weeks ago, she'd inherited his Mearswood Island Plantation, and with it the responsibility to uphold his system of paying the Negro families living here cash wages for working the fifty acres he'd lovingly called his "farm." *I've tethered no one to me or my land,* he'd penned in his treatise, "My Life in Georgia." *I refuse to subscribe to sharecropping, a system laced with elements that create a form of bondage akin to that of its evil twin, slavery.*

He'd bequeathed her the farm and the duty to care for the cadre of loyal workers who, over the years, had become his friends and hers. His insistence on tending to their needs had tarnished the more honorable side of its allure when, upon studying his finances, she'd discovered he'd neglected to set aside the cash needed to finance the inheritances he'd promised each of them.

Judging from the stiffness with which Fletch now approached, head erect and muscled shoulders aligned in starched formality, he was aware of the blow Taylor had dealt his future. Rather than the companionable way in which he usually announced a guest's arrival—"We have company"—he alerted her to the rider coming toward them with, "*You* have a visitor."

Promise peered out from beneath the brim of her sunhat toward the visitor, her longtime friend and, now that she was examining life in an altered light, her only white female friend. Suzanne Peall emerged from the woods on her strawberry roan, riding out from the shade into the unforgiving noonday sun. One hand swabbed her round face with a handkerchief and the other gripped the reins along with the handle of a birdcage which held a baby crow, one of the many rescues she had brought to Promise to heal.

She deposited the cage into Fletch's outstretched hands. Gently, without putting pressure on the bird's splinted wing, he removed it from the confines of the cage it had outgrown and settled it into the larger one he'd made.

Suzanne raised her short leg in a wide unladylike swing and alighted from Emily, the frisky mount Promise had taught her to take charge of. Had this been an ordinary day, Promise would have complimented her on her sturdy jodhpurs and scuffed brogans, for they represented another poke at her father's insistence that his only offspring conduct herself like a true Southern lady. But today, a defiant yet good-natured Suzanne appeared preoccupied.

"Thank goodness this baby bird gave me an excuse to come here," she blurted.

"Hello to you, too," said Promise, scrubbing her dirty hands on her overalls, then gracefully stooping to hug Suzanne. "Let me warn you, I'm poor company. Ask Fletch. I've hardly spoken to him today."

Suzanne's worried hazel eyes squinted up at Fletch, standing two inches taller than Promise's willowy five-foot-six. "Good to see you," she said as he guided his drawknife with strong, confident strokes along a fence post.

As though they were in town, where a Negro man avoided eye contact with a white woman, he averted his eyes. "Sorry to be unsociable, but I'm being careful."

"About what?" asked Promise.

Fletch ran his finger over his curved blade. "Taylor wielded an authority that kept the peace here in Martonsville. We have yet to see if the townsfolk who praised his attempts to unify the races will feel that way now that he's gone. Who knows? They might follow the lead of other towns that have decided there's nothing more entertaining than a community picnic followed by a lynching."

"You have every right to be cautious, Fletch," said Suzanne.

Hearing the indignation in her friend's tone, Promise interrupted, "Don't get Fletch wrong, Suzanne. If your father wasn't such a good sheriff, Negro folks in these parts would fear for their lives, same as those in nearby towns. It's just that being on the outskirts of town, we never saw much of your father. Uncle Taylor had no choice but to act as the law." Her eyes welled.

"Shh, lower your voice," Suzanne whispered, waving in quick nervous movements. "No offense taken. I was talking about Daffron Mears—he's moved back to town. I heard him tell my father he's on his way here. Not for a sympathy call. The man is looking for work."

That moment, the agitated ruffling of a flock of birds caught Promise's attention. As the farm's sentries, the sharp-beaked disapproving crows, mobbed the sky, she followed the lean figure appearing and disappearing among the stands of loblolly pines that bordered her pasture. Flashes of his red clothing bobbed through the underbrush and around the pines. He appeared to have timed his movements, staging his appearance as though he were making a grand entrance to a play, complete with music—a wretched whistling that announced his presence. Sour and off-key, his rendition of "Dixie" made her feel nauseous.

"Doesn't he know he's not welcome here?"

Every inch of Fletch's five-foot-eight frame froze midway through fitting the split-rail fence to its post. He and Suzanne exchanged fretful glances.

"You don't know much about Daffron, do you Promise?" Suzanne asked.

Promise bristled. If there was one thing that had always irked her, it was being left out. Call it an orphan's fear of missing basic knowledge others took for granted, like who her mother might be. "I've heard a few things. So what, exactly, don't I know?"

"It's been twenty years since Daffron lived here, yet to hear people talk, you'd think he'd never left. You've got to be careful, Promise. Keep your distance from Fletch. Don't jostle or brush against him. Daddy says those are unforgivable offenses under Jim Crow law and that Daffron fancies himself its enforcer."

Promise pressed her hands to her sides and raised one forefinger to signal Fletch. Thankfully, he noticed that her forefinger took to circling her thumb knuckle. Judging by his reaction, her tanned freckled face must have blanched whiter than fresh-boiled potato, for while she believed Fletch had as much right as Suzanne to stand by her side, her finger jerked away from her thumb and wagged faster, this time for him to move away. With one imperceptible drop, he slipped his drawknife to the grass and pretended to search for it. Each sweep of his sinewy arm inched him farther from her side.

The necessity of Fletch's moving a respectful two arms' lengths from her while Daffron Mears made his way closer incensed her. Lowering the sack from one hand and fiddle case from the other, he paused to watch the spectacle of a red-tailed hawk abandon its perch at the forest's edge and circle over his head, then took up his whistling, this time louder and more off-key.

The injured baby crow punctuated the heavy air with its squawks. Promise lifted the cage and pressed it to her chest. When the bird had quieted, she set the cage down, scooped it from the pine straw, and fingered the soft spiked feathers jutting from its translucent skin. She cuddled the bird to her lips so Daffron couldn't see them move and said: "I'm not sure what I'm going to do, Fletch, but whatever happens, don't argue, just go along with me. We'll sort everything out later. I promise."

Born wearing a brush-stroke of a smile, he parted his perpetually upturned lips, then clamped them shut. With a sad shake of his head, a reminder that by some vagary of the law a Negro man is forbidden to utter a word in the presence of white women, he resumed his search. He didn't have to explain; the tension of being found alone with two white women rippled across his sculpted face.

Promise stroked the bird's still-downy chest while Suzanne repositioned the splint. Its heart beat faster than hers but not as hard. Small though it was, it seemed to understand since it was unable to fly, there was no place safer than its cage.

Suzanne's comely face tightened into a grimace. "I don't mean to intrude on whatever is going on between you two, but Fletch has a point. We won't know whether the townspeople will maintain the restraint they showed your uncle, or unleash their pet she-devil, home grown Southern bigotry."

Fletch nodded and absently tapped his drawknife against the toe of his brogans. Sawdust exploded from its teeth. "A Negro man unchaperoned with the farm's white mistress is a dangerous—" before he could finish, Promise interrupted.

"What are you two saying? This was never an issue before. Why is it a problem now? Uncle Taylor and I had always worked together with you, Fletch. Everyone on the farm has offered to take on Uncle Taylor's chores, but I can't ask them to do more than they're already doing. Thaddeus is up in the field, harvesting what little corn the drought has left us. Cornelia's fifth pregnancy has left her more exhausted than ever, and I refuse to ask Mother Hart to work in this heat."

Promise pointed behind her at her dismantled fence. "Just when Fletch and I need to take over Taylor's work, a new character enters stage left and interferes. How am I supposed to run this place if Fletch and I need an escort?"

Meanwhile, Daffron meandered through the manure-laden pasture onto the wagon road. Two ruts connected by a mound beneath a canopy of gnarled oak limbs, the road was never intended for strolling. That didn't deter him. He simply adjusted his pace and kept walking. Soon, he stepped from the shade into the sun's white light, arms swaying, pebbles scattering beneath his heels, his wretched whistling the only thing he yielded to the heat of the day.

Behind the pasture in the barnyard, a baby goat abandoned its mother's teat and jumped onto the roof of the hutch, where the rooster chased it away. Cambridge trotted toward the other two horses in the center of the corral and huddled beside them, head up, ears perked, eyes following the stranger.

"You say he's looking for a job?" asked Promise.

Suzanne nodded. "He's in a heap of debt. Needs to earn money, fast."

Promise took a deep breath, the kind that bought her time to gather her thoughts into a cogent whole. "Is that the only reason he's here?"

Suzanne shrugged. "That's what I heard him say."

"Are you sure? Very, very sure?"

"Nothin's dat simple, Miss Promise. The likes of dat man ain't no candidate for a farm like dis. You gots too many of us colored folk livin' long side you." Fletch's lips hardly moved.

Promise locked eyes with Suzanne as though she were talking to her. "I hate it when you use that po' boy talk."

"I gots no choice, Miss Promise."

This from the man who could name every bone and describe every muscle in the human body, argue philosophy, history, and the influence Freud was having on our understanding of the human psyche. She turned her back to him, set the broken bird on its perch, and snapped the latch. "No matter what I decide, no matter how crazy it may seem—from now on, you've got to trust me."

"I always have, Miss Promise, always will."

Ordinarily, this singsong tripped gently from his lips, but this afternoon his voice wavered. She longed to look him square on, study the intensity of his eyes, determine what the uncertainty in his voice was telling her. Instead, she thought about the message Uncle Taylor sent her from the Beyond: S*ear the intruder with your wits, then feign retreat. Let the ensuing confusion disarm him.*

The mishaps she'd endured when she'd struck out on her own over the years taught her to heed her uncle's advice. She decided to capitalize on the scene of two young women spending time together, in hopes it would speak to Daffron of innocence and giggles. She glanced at her friend. Between Suzanne's stricken expression and the pulsing of her own nerves, she longed for a swallow of the corn liquor Suzanne's father hid in his pantry. Setting the stage for her ruse, she draped her arms over the fence by the gate and willed the long fingers on her toughened hands to rest easy. She tilted her head to signal her anticipation of a neighborly exchange—a quick word or a mouthful of gossip. Nothing more.

"Afternoon, sir. Don't believe we've met. I'm Reverend Crawford's niece, Promise."

He eased his sweat-stained fedora back on his head. Graying red curls huddled near his hairline would have had a friendly appeal had his hatband not left an angry crimson imprint. He looked her over. "Ah, so you're the orphan baby he adopted. All grown up now, aren't you? Daffron Mears here."

"What all have you got here?" Ignoring Suzanne and Fletch, he pointed to the cage, then rested his eyes on Promise. "Good of you to save nature's misfits, ma'am." With the confident interest of a hunter stalking his prey, the woman who'd inherited the last fifty-acre parcel of what had been his family's plantation, he watched for her reaction—a start, a twitch, the balling of her fists.

She refused to be goaded and, easing her way around the fence and edging toward him—so much so that he stepped backward—pretended to be perplexed. "Did you happen to see the no trespassing sign marking my property line, sir? Is it still upright?" She envisioned the weathered sign that everyday visitors ignored, and recalled Taylor's insistence that it would one day prove useful.

Daffron lowered his fiddle case, slumped his burlap sack to his feet. "Yes, ma'am, far as I recall."

"Then why didn't you turn back?" She uprooted a tuft of coarse grass with her heel and kicked it in the direction he came from.

Daffron lowered his hat to his thigh. "Apologies, ma'am. Guess I was so busy thinking July's the time of year a woman alone on a farm might need help taking up crops, I missed it. Anyway, here I am to offer my back in exchange for some wages so's I can buy food for my family. Times being hard, work's not easy to come by." His gray eyes wandered toward Fletch and back, then narrowed with coyness. "Unless, of course, your work is spoken for."

Demonstrating a preference for a black man over a white, especially when it came to much-needed employment, was a life-threatening offense here on Martons Island. Were she to lie, Daffron would surely conclude she was favoring a colored over him. Worse yet, he might assume she wanted him gone for fear he'd find that she and Fletch shared another kind of rapport, one that Jim Crow forbade.

Daffron moved closer. She disliked him taking this liberty. She'd overheard Uncle Taylor telling stories of him whanging his way through other farms in other towns, brandishing fear, that most life-sustaining of human emotions. Though deep in her gut she wanted nothing more than to run, she stayed fast, her fingers tightened around an imaginary slingshot, the one Taylor claimed David had used to disarm Goliath.

Fierce thoughts bolted ahead of the logic she was known for, insisting she instill in him a fear of *her* for reasons she had yet to assemble. She wrinkled her nose at his sweet-sour chewing tobacco breath. Once he straightened the round of his shoulders, his faded red shirt hung without a ripple down his trunk, standing head to head with hers.

She read a distress she hadn't expected to see in his speckled gray eyes. Lodged deep within him, a reprehensible injury, the kind she'd observed in beaten horses the townspeople brought to her to care for. Healing broken creatures came naturally to her, although the four-legged variety generally caused others little harm. She wished the same were true of this creature.

Daffron sidled a toe closer. "I'm asking nice, ma'am. Don't force a man to beg."

Of the first lessons she taught a new animal, two fingers pointed in its direction meant "back up." She used a similar gesture with Daffron, except she flicked all her fingers at once. He stepped backward, although as he did he squinted pensively, noting her discomfort. Such a personal observation. So keenly made. She tucked her hands in her pockets and looked in those desolate eyes of his. "You're not sporting the usual cuts, callouses, or blisters found on a working man's hands, sir. That makes me think you don't much care for rough work."

"It's not a matter of caring, ma'am."

She dismissed his injured tone as another manipulation. "Farming takes a lot out of you. Animals require tending. Fences, mending. Tools, sharpening. Then there's hoeing, watering, weeding, picking, staking, replanting, and let's not forget," she smiled innocently at him, "watching for pests."

He shifted uneasily from one foot to the other. "Just when your bones threaten to collapse inside your skin, you've got to pack the produce for market. Anyone works here puts in long hours."

"Time I have, ma'am."

"There's hay to harvest and bale, stables to clean, all of which ruins the strongest backs."

"My back is plenty strong, ma'am."

"Fletch sells the manure for me," her voice was rising. "If you have any ideas about grabbing extra change for yourself..." From the corner of her eye, she caught the tremble of Fletch's hands, the creases and callouses on the fingers she knew so well, and him tucking them into the bib of his overalls. She blinked him out of her view. She had to.

Otherwise she couldn't harden herself to what instinct was driving her to do.

"I got no such ideas, ma'am. Truly. Besides, if you're worried about what your uncle would say—"

"Let's get back to *your* concern, sir. I believe you said you needed food for *your* family." And though this reputed enforcer set her insides to shaking, Uncle Taylor had taught her to stand up to a junkyard dog, especially that of the human variety. His first rule: Show no fear. "Lead with your boldest move, and you will disorient him. Cling to the maxim, 'Truth dwells within paradox,' and the advantage will be yours. View the problem from its inside-out—yes, you'll look like a fool—but, in the end, your wits will save you." It was as though Taylor was standing alongside her, prompting her to stay strong, thrilling and terrifying her at the same time.

Promise drew her overall-clad figure, said to be graceful yet rugged, up tall and spread her feet wide so as to take up more than her share of ground. Good posture and an aura of ownership were basic to entering a pact with the devil.

Suzanne's eyes widened. She reached to grab Promise as though she were a recalcitrant student but shifted to wrapping and unwrapping the reins around her hand. Banishing Promise to the corner of her whites-only schoolroom would not do for the friend who had saved her from the schoolyard bullies of their youth. As senseless as it was to confront Daffron, she couldn't stop herself from nodding in approval.

It was the impetus Promise needed.

"I'll pay no less than what's customary given the times—a meal a day and a share of the crops in exchange for a week's labor, that's the best I can do, no more."

Suzanne clamped her hand over her mouth.

Daffron rubbed his hands together and murmured, "All right," his satisfaction that of a man who'd discerned the final number in the combination of an unyielding lock. Arms at his sides, he seemed to relax for a moment. Then his eyes brightened. He jabbed one thumb in the direction of the smokehouse toward the trail that disappeared into the woods. "It's half a day's walk from here to my house on the other side of town. Mind if I camp back there?"

Fletch's chest rose in a stifled gasp. He stopped himself from speaking, yet Promise read his palms, opened and pleading. Three-hundred-yards at the other end of the trail, Fletch's mother was most likely in her garden, a basket of tender greens pressed to her hip.

"I have someplace closer," Promise blurted. Daffron didn't appear to notice the tone in which she delivered those words, nor her concern that such a living arrangement would frighten the families she cared about. Caught as she was in his inadvertent snare, she dared not put him off. Daffron followed as she pivoted in the opposite direction and pointed past the bend in the wagon road, beyond the last pair of oaks to the large whitewashed barn with the stained tin roof. "You can't see it from here, but there's a shed behind the barn. It's not much."

He leaned his elbow on the fence post Fletch had been repairing and grinned. "It'll do. And don't you fret, I'll do better than my best for you."

Promise's palm tingled with the urge to slap Daffron's elbow clean off her fence. "Store your things, then start picking beans," she said softly as Fletch shuffled off.

Daffron put his finger behind his ear and asked her to speak up. She repeated herself no louder than before. He stepped toward her. His gaze, leadened with hateful assumptions, locked on hers. He started to speak, but she cut him off. “Best get to those beans. Suzanne and I will fetch your bedding.”

She turned to her friend. “Let’s go.”

“Best hurry, your daddy will be looking for you, Cousin Suzanne,” Daffron laughed.

Promise started; Suzanne had never mentioned this.

“Bet you didn’t know she was my cousin twice removed on my daddy’s side, did you Miss Promise? That’ll give you two a chunk to gossip over.”

“Can’t help who I’m related to.”

Moments ago, Suzanne had urged her to stand strong, but now, she resorted to the little girl voice she used with her father. Her friend was so upset, Promise could have taken a bite out of her humiliation. “Makes not a hair of difference,” she said, hugging Suzanne.

An hour earlier, as Promise had worked in her pasture, she’d started to untangle her grief. For a few satisfying moments, the puzzle pieces of her situation emerged, sure as the sky after a rainstorm. She’d thought she was about to come to terms with inheriting a financial mess from Taylor. As she started to restore order to her neglected farm, she had every intention of working out a plan that secured the future Fletch deserved. For a few glistening moments, she felt new as a spring leaf, hopeful and ready to open. Then came Daffron.

CHAPTER 2

The horrible division between our races will be bridged
when men and women of courage
create one race in which to cradle us all.

Taylor Crawford, *My Life in Georgia*, 1929

Promise scooped Emily's reins with one hand and Suzanne's arm with the other and steered her toward her cabin. Decay, the scent by which nature announced the removal of the intractable to make way for the new, wafted through the humid air.

"If Uncle Taylor had left the farm to Andrew Gills, I wouldn't be dealing with Daffron," she said, picturing Andrew, the handsome twenty-one-year-old newspaperman from Boston to whom Uncle Taylor had promised her in marriage. "But as Taylor grew more sickly, he kept changing his mind, waffling between Andrew and me, finally leaving the property to me, the person he referred to as 'his sole relation,' and an adopted one at that."

Suzanne's short legs and wide hips churned faster than they'd ever moved before, causing her face to drip with unladylike perspiration. She spoke in breathless spurts. "But your uncle was so rational. And unusual. Who else encouraged us...to explore...the many aspects...of a problem? He was the one...who taught my students...to develop a logical argument."

"I'm afraid death unraveled a number of things, including Taylor's rationality. I told him I love having the Georgia soil under my feet, and that I didn't want to move to Boston, especially to marry Andrew." Promise stopped, closed her eyes, and sighed.

Suzanne squeezed Promise's hand. "Taylor was lucky. Who else would go along with his schemes? I'm sure he knew you loved him more than a real daughter could."

They climbed the creaky steps to the cabin porch, the massive cypress rounds forming the back wall, a testament to Taylor's desire to create a structure that would outlast insects and intruders of the human variety. "As he was dying, he murmured, 'That man, that man.' When I heard Daffron whistling "Dixie," I began to suspect he was 'that man.' At first I thought that made little sense until I recalled Taylor's maxim, 'Within paradox rests Truth.'"

"What truth can possibly come out of Daffron being here? I never understood what that maxim meant to Taylor, but I understand that you need to be more cautious about your routines. Don't take anything you do or say for granted. Look at your life as though through Daffron's eyes." Suzanne pointed to the kitchen table. "I've been here when Fletch sat at your table, slathering butter on the biscuits his mother had just taken from the oven."

Promise sighed. "That will have to stop," she said, her auburn eyebrows tensing with realization. "He won't be able to spend time on the front porch, reading. Our after-dinner conversations will be out, too."

The screen door creaked as they entered the cabin. Promise searched the piano, the table in her sitting room, wherever Fletch might have scattered his few possessions. She gathered his worn volume of Shakespeare and his anatomy book. On top of them, Taylor's list of chores, which she showed to Suzanne.

"This makes me feel as though he's still here." Penned in his exacting hand, three column headings: *Repair, Rebuild, Replace.* Under the last column, the fence rebuild chore and the date by which the post was to have been restored. Suzanne tilted her head as she always did when she waited to hear more.

"Taylor had little patience with decay, which he fit within the realms of material, spiritual, or racial. After Daffron's performance, Taylor would have recategorized the decayed fence from the material realm to that of 'racial.' But that's not what we're here for." She tapped her foot. "I sure hope I'll be able to..." She quickly removed Taylor's Treatise from a stack of Fletch's bookmarked volumes of Dante, Cicero, and Keats on the quilt chest.

"To what?" asked Suzanne

Without answering, Promise kissed the Treatise's cover and placed it at the far corner of the dinner table. She would return it to Taylor's desk another time, when her heart had stopped aching. She piled Fletch's belongings on the floor while Suzanne checked the fieldstone fireplace for his belongings.

On the mantle beside a clock, a small calendar with today's date, Monday, July fourteenth, 1930. Leaning against Taylor's Bible, Fletch's precious letter from Harvard medical school. Promise jumped to her feet, but before she could reach it, Suzanne had lifted the envelope and was holding it as though it were a hot cinder between her fingertips. Eyes glowing with excitement, she whirled toward Promise. "Is this what I think it is?"

"Put that down!" Promise snapped, immediately regretting having snatched the envelope from her well-meaning friend. "You have no idea what that letter has done to my life," she pleaded, hoping Suzanne would understand. Still, the urge to rant swelled within her. Not wanting to hurt her further, Promise clamped her hand over her mouth. But it was too late; Suzanne's gentle expression had vanished. In its place, a sickening dismay.

Promise gasped. "I am so sorry..." Her emotion had surged, drowning her powers of reasoning. She bit her lip. Uncle Taylor would have been furious. He'd taught her to gain superiority over problems by reasoning her way through them. Emotion be damned, he'd insisted.

But it was too late. Not one to argue, Suzanne did what she'd always done when she became upset—she ran. Promise followed her to the door, but Suzanne, moving like a frightened doe, had mounted Emily and was urging her toward the path into the woods.

She checked to see if Fletch or Daffron had seen Suzanne slam the screen door. Certain they were busy with the fence, she set the books on the floor, lifted the top of the chest and stared into its stained maw. Empty. She'd forgotten: Fletch's mother, whom Taylor reverentially called "Mother Hart," had removed all the bedding, leaving only ragged peels of lining. Promise's hand trembled as she fingered the largest, most brittle curl, then crushed it in her fist. "You fool!" she muttered, lowering Fletch's books into the trunk.

She thought of Fletch, hand resting on the sink, where he often stood, drinking a cup of water and smiling. Draped over the doorknob, the purple bandana she'd sewn for him. She stuffed it in her bedroom out of sight. Given the vow she'd made to Taylor to keep the families on his farm safe, she hid the only thing small enough to fit in her bureau drawer.

Ten weeks earlier, Fletch and his adopted brother, Trivett, had carried Taylor's body out for burial. She'd not opened his bedroom door since. To her surprise, the sour, phlegmy odors of his deterioration had faded. The remaining scents weren't those of death's herbed oils, but those she'd loved of his life: the leather binding on his books; the musty stacks of crumpled paper composing his endless treatise; the plays she had written for his entertainment and his pipe packed with once-fragrant tobacco as though he'd intended to return. But at seventy-six, he'd chosen to share the inner workings of his affairs with his adopted orphan girl and had unceremoniously dumped his life's work into her hands. He'd abandoned her for good. *Within paradox dwells Truth.* Had he considered her that capable? If he'd been here today, would he have glowed with pride?

"I miss you more than I imagined," she whispered, running her hand over his desktop, gently tugging it open. Slat by slat, it rolled upward, its familiar clatter a chorus that sang of his former presence. For a welcome moment, she basked in that comfort. Opening the first tiny drawer, the scent of India ink rose; from the second, the metallic odor of blue-black nibs. As she rummaged through the next few drawers, she pictured Fletch a short while ago, palms open. *Don't abandon me,* they'd pleaded. "I haven't," she said, although, had she been Fletch, alone now with Daffron, she would certainly have felt that way.

The more she worried, the faster she pawed. The tiny compartments went up one side of the desk and down the other. Staring at their railroad-like lines, she couldn't recall what she was looking for. By the time she remembered Daffron needed bedding, she no longer cared what he slept on. She grabbed a torn sheet from her mend pile and hurried out the kitchen door through which Taylor, Fletch, and now

Suzanne had left her. None were blood relations, but they were family. *Within paradox dwells Truth.* A family she loved.

The pathway rounded up behind the smokehouse, past the vegetable gardens, to the shed where Daffron was to stay. She passed between it and the goat shelter and into the barn. Outside, Daffron stood with his back to her, watching Fletch.

A few feet away, Fletch dragged the handles of his drawknife in rigid hacking movements along a fence post. The confident glow of the man who at eighteen had become Taylor's foreman had evaporated. Vigilance now strained his intelligent face. Sweat sucked his sleeveless shirt to his back. He reeked of a scent she'd never known him to give off. She wanted to go to him but stopped. Don't draw attention to him, she told herself. Being Negro is reason enough for those inclined to hate, but a Negro whose father was white...her breath caught in her throat. Don't give in to what you feel, she reminded herself. Stay calm, pretend you're in the corral, and Daffron is nothing but a nuisance of a stallion.

She stepped into the barnyard. Fortified by the high walls of the barn and goat shelter, her voice boomed louder than she intended: "Not much activity from a wanderer in need of a day's wages."

Daffron cocked his head in mock surprise. "Just about to head toward my quarters, Miss Promise." He scooped up his things and whistled "Dixie" haltingly, as though confounded by the complexity of the tune.

"Best put those tools away, Fletch. You need to deliver that manure. And this time, don't let that viper on the other side of town cheat me." She glanced at Fletch's broad forehead, lines of shock issuing from his eyebrows to his widower's peak, and hoped he'd understand her feigned harshness was directed at Daffron.

"Yes, ma'am. Fletch gonna be back first thing tomorrow with your money, Miss Promise." Good, he was playing along. Her relief skidded to a stop when he failed to flicker his eyelids, the secret gesture that meant he was in on whatever game she'd started. He slipped his hat over his glistening forehead, his jaw bearing down on his back teeth. If she reached out, she could dab the round of his cheek. She was that close and that far away.

Forcing herself not to stare as he shuffled off in humiliation through a steaming pile of horse dung, she tightened her arms around the bedding and went after Daffron, who was headed for the shed. This would be the first and last time Fletch would ever need to use such a self-abasing gesture. She would make sure of that. For now, his bogus act of subjection would protect him. This was how it would be. But only for a week.

The noisy summer afternoon had given way to an ominous silence.

Where were her dogs and why hadn't she noticed their absence? She scanned the periphery of the farm, where the cultivated soil deferred to brambled woods. Jasper and Tiv usually alerted her to the presence of intruders. Bluetick coonhounds, they conducted their own chases, yipping as they tracked their prey. Rough-edged grass crackled beneath her footsteps; she missed the commotion that meant her hounds were safe. A chill wormed through her.

When she reached the overgrown mulberry bush beside the shed, Daffron was opening the warped door. A musty odor assailed them. A furry brown spider had spun a lace curtain over the one filthy window. Motionless, yet in plain sight, it waited at the web's edge for its prey. Beneath the windowsill, a rolled mattress rested at the foot of the bed. Bits of hay and black mouse nuggets littered the shelf on the adjacent wall.

Grit on the floorboards crunched beneath Daffron's feet. His creaking filled the room with a menacing noise.

He unrolled the mattress, clouding the air with dust. Absorbed on settling into his new surroundings, he appeared to have forgotten Promise. He pulled his shirt up around his lean middle and swiped the shelf clean. He then removed a photograph of a little girl from his pocket, ran his finger over the child's serious face—she wore the kind of stare that followed you no matter where you moved—and positioned it just so on the shelf.

He placed his oversized sack on the mattress, worked two fingers into the drawstring, and eased it open. Out came a pair of trousers, a collarless white shirt, socks, and drawers. He positioned this tidy bundle on the shelf, aligning it with the edge. He worked with the fastidiousness of a blue jay which, having devoured the robin's speckled-blue eggs, proceeded to make her nest his own. All that remained in the sack was a small protrusion in the bottom right corner. Unremarkably square, Promise guessed he'd brought a tin of tobacco or some similar male comfort.

Daffron squatted beside the bed, lifted the sack's opening, and peered in as if he were a child in search of a much-anticipated gift. He nudged his way inward up to his shoulder and re-emerged, hands cupped, then leaned on his haunches and looked up at her in the doorway. A peculiar smile, wistful and telling, smoothed his scarred chin. For the first time since he'd arrived, he seemed boyish and safe.

Promise let the bedding slide to the floor. "Is it alive?" she asked, surprised by her playfulness.

"In a way." His clamshelled hands opened to reveal a small, carved box.

She clapped her fingers to her mouth. The box's size, its whittled markings, even the miniature wrought-iron hinges were identical to the one her mother had left for her. Although faint, its flowery scent was too powerful to deny. His lips parted in a toothy sneer, as though to say now that he'd penetrated Promise's tough exterior, the rest would be simple.

CHAPTER 3

Tortured thoughts and a sorrowing heart
give rise to unconsidered acts.

Taylor Crawford, *My Life in Georgia,* 1929

Fletch trudged past the vegetable gardens over which he'd painstakingly spread pine straw, never having imagined an afternoon like this, when Daffron Mears' footsteps would tread in those very gardens. He locked his gaze on the cabin in which Taylor once lived. One day not too long ago, he joined Taylor at the dining table, where a cup of tea waited. He reported on the crops that were ready for harvest and the blight ravaging the oats. Taylor sipped his tea and listened thoughtfully.

From the pile of farm journals beside him, he unearthed an article about a farmer who had depended solely on sales of food crops to support his acreage. Between the drought and bank closures, he lost his farm. Pushing his chair back from the table, Taylor said, "Plants, like people, play a part in history. Consider how cotton spawned the cotton gin and with it, slavery. If we are wise, past horrors will help us determine our future course. Which reminds me, best check on the loblolly pines. After this drought is over, we will work to make Mearswood known as a loblolly plantation."

With work to be done before the afternoon's heat set in, Fletch agreed to see if the loblollies were setting seed cones and quickly excused himself. But Taylor was not easily dismissed. "Later we'll discuss the writings of Alex de Tocqueville," he reminded Fletch.

Taylor must have known Daffron would attempt to regain the farm; why else had he repeatedly stressed the need to learn from history's blights? With the inimitable authority of one who lived what he preached, he had redesigned Mearswood Plantation to comfort the lives of its inhabitants. Unlike the original plantation, where people were of such little value that the slave quarters were situated far from the owner's view, Taylor had located his outbuildings as close to his unassuming cabin as possible. The simplicity of its trappings camouflaged his intentions: the inviting porch he shared with a select few; behind it, a wall of thick cypress logs that repelled insects, wintry winds and strangers; and topping it all, a verdant moss-covered roof as fairy-tale-like as his exorbitant plan for Fletch to live in the midst of Boston's welcoming freedom. There, Taylor had assured him, a brilliant black man could study and conduct himself in an educated manner without repercussions—an honor Fletch confessed to being unworthy and desirous of at the same time.

Beyond the bend, the bells on the iceman's wagon jingled along the smooth sections of road and jangled through ruts and over bumps. Ephraim Burns pulled his mules alongside the front porch. The scent of bacon fat wafting from the tin on the outdoor stove brought Fletch's former morning routine to mind. The sun-warmed steps where he would usually sit, breakfast plate balanced on his knees, no longer welcomed him; kitchen door—and best remember to knock.

"Afternoon, Fl-etch."

The sight of another black man reminded him who he was. "Two unequal parts, you got that right. From now on, Burns, we use the back door."

Burns' ready smile collapsed into a frown. "Reverend Crawford never done that to me."

"Takes one person to change things for the worse."

"It's true then, what I heared."

"What was that?"

Burns rolled his cigar to the other side of his mouth and whispered, "Daffron Mears come here."

Fletch glanced at the shed and nodded.

"He's not right in the head, you know. These five years he been up in Tilden, folks say he hung a wagon load of coloreds."

"What else do folks say?"

"They say Daffron come back to Martonsville 'cuz he got business here. Bad business." Fear crept into Burns's cloudy eyes. "If I was you, I be heading elseplaces to work."

Fletch started—he'd planned on doing just that. As much as he wanted to talk about how he needed to earn money for school, the iceman wasn't the man with whom to share confidences. Other than making him the subject of gossip, what good would it do to announce that Taylor had promised Fletch that his alma mater, Harvard University, would make him the finest black country doctor Martons Island would ever know?

"Don't go getting yourself in no trouble." Burns climbed into his wagon. "Me? I knows where I don't belong."

"You can't leave yet. Miss Promise is expecting a delivery."

"*Miss* Promise? You never called her that." He craned his neck. "I don't see him."

"In the shed, with Miss Promise." The epithet caught in Fletch's throat. In the twenty years they'd spent together on the farm—years without once catching a glimpse of Daffron Mears in Martonsville—she'd paid no mind to the differences in their skin colors.

He'd marveled, too, at the sweetness she showed Taylor even as he neglected to help her find her mother. She honored his fear of losing her to her birth parent and respected his reluctance, for she understood what it felt like to be bitten by her own fear of never coming to know her mother. Fletch expected her generous spirit to dampen when her uncle passed on, but hadn't expected her to be overcome by an unreasonableness that set him on edge.

Burns lowered his handcart to Fletch and stepped down from the axle. "Things changin' a mite too fast." He pushed aside just enough canvas to uncover a small ice block, clamped his tongs around it, and lowered it onto the canvas Fletch had spread on the ground. "Hundred pounds for the root cellar, sixty-five for the ice box, right?" Burns asked the same question every week. Without waiting for an answer, he drove his ice pick into a groove and hammered faster than a woodpecker in search of the day's first meal.

Fletch tossed a handful of ice chips into his mouth. As boys, he and his brother hounded Burns until he gave them enough chips to fill two snow cones. If their pursuit drew them too far from Taylor, who had stopped at Latt's store or the blacksmith's, Fletch would search for him. If Taylor strayed farther, Fletch wheezed with panic. How he wished Taylor were alive and well. That he longed for his dead teacher's protection was more than he could bear. He'd read enough about the working of the mind to suspect that his had been stunned by grief. Had he lost the concentration necessary to master the intricacies of the human body, he worried? He feared he was about to fail the man who had treated him like a son.

Burns positioned a wedge and with one blow of his hammer cracked the block in two. He slid the smaller chunk of ice back onto the wagon, slipped into his canvas vest, and hiked the hundred-pound block onto his shoulder. "Back door?" His face wrinkled in disbelief. "You sure?"

"New rules," Fletch said, leading him past the well to the side of the cabin.

Soon as the hickory tree blocked sight of the shed, Burns perked up. "I'll tell you 'bout new rules. You 'member Edgar Jenks, the gimp farmer three towns over? The old man that gone bankrupt? Bank sold his belongings at auction. Before it started, he got his neighbors to promise not to bid, so he could buy his goods back for close to nothin'. But things was so cheap—two dollar for his team of four horses, milk cows for fifty cent each—his neighbors up 'n snatched 'em away."

"I know."

White brows squeezed into a scowl, Burns looked up at Fletch. "You already knowed 'bout Jenks?"

"Not about the auction, about friends spoiling your plans when they think you're about to get a better deal."

Fletch glanced over his shoulder at the pasture and wished they could return to simple problems presented by rotting fence posts. Just last week, he'd showed Promise his letter of acceptance from Harvard University. Her face drooped with the same exhausted seriousness he'd seen on Taylor when the demands of the farm got the better of him.

She told him outright, "Uncle Taylor didn't leave enough money to pay for your schooling and run the farm." She'd never spoken to him in that peevish tone, never while Taylor was alive. Her affectionate voice had welcomed him with every word. He wasn't sure what to make of her bite, nor did he stop to consider his next move. Instead, he reacted.

"One way or the other, I'll make my way to Boston," he'd mistakenly told her, his tone as curt as hers, his thoughts locked on the disgrace of disappointing his dead friend.

***

By the time the inevitability of Taylor's illness had hit Promise square on, she'd not eaten in days and her cheekbones had become unusually prominent. She pulled the chair out from beneath her uncle's desk, snuggled it against his bed, and sat. Despite her tan, she looked pale. Fletch had never seen her this strained. He imagined her mother's ghost—no one knew for sure if she was dead, but he'd planted her firmly in the land beyond—standing in a smoky oval beside her. He handed her a cup of the warm broth his mother had made, hoping she'd make eye contact. The aroma combined with that of freshly washed sheets and Taylor's sour smell.

"This broth will do you good," she said to Taylor. At first, he refused. But when she urged, "Taylor, drink this," he relaxed his jaw enough for her to ease the spoon between his lips and tip its tawny contents into his mouth. The spoon clicked against his teeth as she gentled it out. "Good. Now swallow." Soup dribbled down his chin, his eyelids drooped, and his lips fluttered with raspy snorts. She leaned forward in the waning light and dabbed him clean.

After closing the bedroom door behind her, she absentmindedly placed the cup on Fletch's outstretched fingertips. "This isn't right," she sobbed, bolting from the cabin. The horses in the pasture huddled closer, orbed eyes tracking her, ears twitching in distress.

Fletch followed her dusty trail down the road to the pond. He knelt beside her on the dew-crested grass and stroked her back. Up and down, round and round, firm and gentle, as he'd often done after a strenuous day's work. He expected her to ask him to leave, but she didn't. Long, somber moments passed before Promise shrugged his hands off and propped herself up, face damp, hair in auburn disarray. She sat upright with her back to him until a scrappy pair of ducks splash-landed on the pond.

An angry hurt had hardened the soulfulness within her gray eyes. He shifted slightly, hoping she wouldn't notice the wariness he felt.

She watched the ducks disappear behind the weeds on the far shore, then said, "The night Taylor admitted that my mother was never coming back, my world split in two." She plucked a blade of grass and shredded it. "I was so upset, I couldn't say a word. Not because she wasn't returning—I never believed that—but because I felt that he wasn't telling me the truth. He knew something beyond fearful had happened to her." She turned to Fletch. "I asked him what caused her to leave. Do you know what he said?" Without waiting, she blurted, "He said she had no choice but to go away. It was bad enough that he lied once, then he lied again—he said I would never have to worry, that he'd stay with me forever." Her words crackled with the self-pity that comes from loss.

Taken alone, her words, the product of her long-held grief, confused him. But coupled with her anger, their meaning became clear. Unable to keep Taylor by her side, she wasn't about to let the person she called her "closest friend" get away. She didn't come right out with it, but he understood that should he try to leave for Boston, she'd make his life difficult. Which was exactly what she'd done when she'd hired Daffron. With him around, she knew Fletch would never dream of leaving for school. Not after he'd staged his po' boy act. Not with his mother close by. No, he wasn't about to make Daffron feel like a fool. Not like Promise was doing to him.

***

He flicked at a swarm of flies on Burns's canvas. They blurred and scattered. "Ah, the dark man still has some sway," he murmured, swatting at a pest that had landed on his scarred earlobe.

Burns was busy lowering the block of ice onto the chute at the top of the cellar steps. Fletch tossed him the canvas. He caught it on the toe of his boot, guided the ice into the cellar, and with one practiced motion spread the canvas on the ground. He then unloaded muslin bags filled with meat and butter from a wooden box, positioned the ice in the bottom, replaced the bags, and covered them with a thick layer of sawdust. Yellow wood shavings heavy with dampness dropped to the dirt floor. Behind Burns were shelves dotted with dusty jars of jelly and the peach and plum preserves Fletch's mother and Promise had put up last summer when the harvest was generous, and Fletch reveled in his friend's devotion. Burns tapped the top of the storage box into place and emerged, a musty odor on his clothing. They shuffled in funereal silence toward the kitchen. Burns stood by the plank door, one arm clutching tongs weighted with sixty-five pounds of dripping ice, the other still as a stump. "Knock?" One corner of his mouth curled with incredulity. Fletch nodded. Burns took a deep breath, tapped twice. Seconds passed. The ice dripped.

When no one answered, Fletch reached past him and pushed open the door. "Miss Promise isn't in there."

"Then what you got me knockin' for?" He turned around, pressed the ice to Fletch's shins. "You expect Daffron's gonna be here long?"

Fletch snorted. "Claims his family is going hungry."

"Probably so. Lots of folks in Springdale been standin' in line for food." Inside, Burns lowered the ice into the top of the icebox. He tapped his finger on the wooden counter beside a Mason jar half-filled with sugar. "Soon folks gonna look at sugar and flour like they's gold." Burns waited, no doubt, for Fletch to feed him a handful of details he could pass along during his next delivery.

"Still planning on buying that truck?" Fletch asked.

"Truck?" Burns maneuvered his cigar to the other side of his loose-skinned face and climbed onto the seat of the wagon. "Who got money for a truck? Besides, you ain't got a road good enough to drive one on."

Within minutes, the bells on Burns' wagon jangled into the distance.

Fletch plucked a few blades of grass from alongside the front porch and stuffed them into his mouth. He mashed them into a stringy pulp, swished the juice from side to side, up behind his teeth, and out, just as he'd done when he was a three-year-old, spitting at the men in long scratchy robes, who held his head and forced him to watch his father being lynched.

In the years that followed, Taylor cautioned Fletch against allowing his temper to enslave him. "Apply your energies to more elevated pursuits," he'd admonished.

"I'm trying, Taylor, I'm trying," Fletch murmured as he climbed into his wagon. Today he'd deposited his insignificant life into Promise's hands. Just as she'd hoped. But her hold went only so far. The fear that haunted him since his father died held more sway.

"Get along," Fletch said to his mule, his voice flat. Cassiopeia's steady pulling edged the wagon's steel-rimmed wheels through the remains of the barnyard muck to the dirt road that meandered through Promise's fifty acres. The grassy hump between the wheels fit beneath his wagon and hers but gave others a hard ride; an exclusion he hoped would escape Daffron's notice.

He reached the rise at the far end of the pasture where Taylor was buried and whistled for Cassiopeia to stop. As though he intended to reposition the manure sacks, he turned and looked back at the shed. In a way, he was as responsible for Daffron being here as Promise. Had he followed Taylor's advice and contacted Harvard years earlier, he would have been living so far from here neither Promise or Daffron could have used him as a pawn. Now, he was forced to leave her alone with Daffron. That put her in danger and left him feeling at fault. Contradictions of the human mind are truly mysterious, especially when friends refuse to settle the matters festering between them.

He glanced back at the back of his wagon at the sacks of manure he was supposed to deliver and decided to take a moment to visit his friend. He dropped to the ground and strode, rake in hand, through the tall grass. Clods of earth marked the resting spot for the coffin he'd built for Taylor: five-feet-nine-inches long—an inch taller than his own hard-earned height. He stood in the ragged shade of the pecan tree, tamped the soil, and smoothed gaps that might attract animals. Some folks left the soil and coffin lid loose in the event the person was still alive. Others, out of misplaced compassion, slit their beloved's wrists. Fletch couldn't bring himself to do either; instead, he'd pressed his ear to Taylor's heart and listened until it convinced him of its stillness. Now he was forced to listen to his own.

"Where were you today when we could have used a dose of your railing? Had you heard Promise, you'd scarcely have recognized her, or me, for that matter. You said I'd make a fine doctor. You lulled me into believing I had a place alongside broadminded whites such as you and Promise, so much so that I failed to recognize you as the force that stood between Mearswood and the insanity eating at the South. But Daffron jarred my sleeping brain to wakefulness. Once a black man trusted enough to be known as your Foreman, now an impediment to Promise's safety."

His bitterness disgusted him. "Someday, when I'm a psychiatrist, I'll understand why complaining to a dead man makes me feel better."

He drove his wagon across the property line onto the public road. He flicked the reins, and his mule obliged by hurrying along. Up ahead, a sturdy, long-skirted figure approached. In one hand a basket, as drained of color as she was when her sorrowful memories took hold, and in the other, a jug blue as the sky and just as hopeful. His mother had always moved swiftly, often marching alone at night through the woods to families who'd summoned her to deliver their babies. Today, she was walking faster than usual.

The sight of her straight back, long neck, and halo of gray braids filled him with pride. Determined to reclaim her dignity after his father had been murdered, she'd contained her terror within a seasoned caution. Folks claimed Mother Hart forged fear into a lightning bolt and rode it forward with Fletch and Trivett lashed to its back. "I wish I could do the same as Mam," he murmured.

Mam sucked her bottom lip into a scowl and continued toward him. The wagon's rumbling interrupted her thoughts. She lifted her head and cried out, "Fletch!"

"Where you going, Mam?"

Her panicked hazel eyes told him something was amiss. She planted her foot on the running board, set her things in the wagon bed, and stretched her hand toward his. "Help me," she whimpered. She rarely asked for assistance and never like this.

He slid closer to get a stronger purchase and lifted her beside him. She moaned, a sound originating not from physical pain but a deeper, more wrenching source. "Trivett," was all she could say.

"Something's happened to Trivett?"

Mam steadied herself on the seat. "Got caught helping a white woman," she blurted.

"Where is he?"

"Sheriff hauled him off to jail." With this, her broad freckled cheeks followed her mouth's downward press. "Trivett may not be blood, but he's a son same as you. If Sheriff Peall hurts my boy, he'll answer to me."

"Get along," Fletch called to Cassiopeia. The mule pulled as fast as her load would allow.

"Fletcher William?" This was the first since he'd begged her to call him Fletch that she'd used his given name. She paused, looked straight ahead and said right out loud, "I'm scared." Never after his father's murder or the torching of their home had she talked like this, at least not to Fletch. Witnessing her silent courage had helped him keep his fear boxed tight. Now the seams on that box were coming unglued.

He turned to her, sitting with her head tall, eyes fixed on the horizon. He considered asking her to tell him more but dared not. He didn't want to hear those words again.

CHAPTER 4

To struggle in pursuit of a cause requires vigilance for, if careless, we become the evil we fight.

Taylor Crawford, *My Life in Georgia*, 1929

The faded yet insistent letters on the sign for the *Martonsville Monitor* reflected the town's atmosphere as Fletch drove through the business district. Next door, in the storefront window of Latt's Dry Goods, propped against an off-center pyramid of Clabber Girl Baking Powder, a new misspelled poster beckoned *Special Sale,* WHITS ONLY. Across the street, a notice at Citizens Savings Bank overshadowed the dubious enticement in Mr. Latt's window.

Gathered by the bank's somber locked doors, a crowd read the posting of reduced banking hours, 9:00 – 11:00, MONDAYS ONLY. "They're closing the lid on our coffins," one man muttered. Others nodded and wandered off, their once-confident footsteps drained of swagger. Had Fletch been allowed to stroll this section of Martonsville, his footsteps would have faltered, too. For reasons of a different sort.

He continued past a new red gas pump capped with a circular lamp. Each day around this time its proud owner, Mr. Wiley, balanced his bucket on the top rung of a stepladder and washed the lamp with an oozing soapy sponge. He'd claimed he bought the pump trusting that electricity would one day extend its sagging lines to what Trivett called "this dot of a town." That didn't stop Mr. Wiley from pumping gas, which he often did, using the manual lever. The *Martonsville Monitor* reported him saying, "When these bad times are over, Wiley's will be first in line for the future."

The men working for Mr. Wiley were equally open with their dreams, soulless as they were. Car repair provided a thread that straddled the chasm between past and future. Stooped over an open hood, his wooden leg painted to resemble a furled Confederate flag, Sawtooth Carter was an entrepreneur of dubious renown. His devoted followers gathered at his Road Side Grill, where he was said to make bootlegged beer and liquor available to those like him who worshiped yesterday but held hands with tomorrow.

Beside him, a more humble pair of feet protruded toes-up in a dead man's pose from the underside of a convertible. "Acey, Sheriff's here," called Mr. Wiley. A board on wheels clattered into the daylight and startled sparrows pecking at discarded pumpkin seed hulls. Acey stood, tugged the brim of his grease-speckled cap over his forehead, and waved at the approaching car.

Mr. Wiley grabbed Acey and rushed toward the sheriff, while Sawtooth limped behind. Sheriff Peall's elbow rested on the open passenger-side window of his Model-T Ford. He drummed his fingers on the roof and peered over his knuckles at Fletch and Mother Hart, then said something that made the men's faces harden. They trained their eyes on Fletch and glared.

"I don't like those kinds of stares, no siree, I don't," Mam said.

Fletch hunched in an attempt to appear smaller, but there was no hiding the fact he was higher up in his wagon than the sheriff in his car would ever be. To make matters worse, the small natural upturn at the corners of his mouth made him look as though he thought the sheriff funny. Since Taylor's death, not much about white folks was amusing, and he didn't want the sheriff assuming offense where none was intended. He wanted to urge Cassiopeia to move quickly from the gas station but held her at a pace befitting a black man who meant no harm and had no reason to run.

One gentle shake of the reins and his wagon soon passed the Redemption Baptist Church, where pale ladies in clean dresses and country hats, an occasional bundle in tow, hurried across the street.

"Town's in a jitter today," Fletch said. "You can feel it in the air."

Mam sat still as death on the seat beside him, her evenly pinned gray braids shifting with the sway of the wagon. "Everyone's heard about the arrest," she whispered.

Miss Mattie's Seamstress Shop, the first Negro business on the other side of the church, came into view. Mam gripped the bench, leaned forward and nodded discreetly in the direction of the incident. "There." Her eyes locked on the lacy handkerchief still lying on the uneven section of walkway, where the woman had tripped.

Her voice became indignant: "We both wanted to help for goodness' sake, it was only natural. After all, a woman fell right in front of our eyes. It shouldn't have mattered that she was white, but it does, it always does. I held back, but Trivett..."

She swiped at the air with her fist. "We were walking several feet behind the woman, watching her struggle with her purchases. No sooner did she manage to get one parcel tucked under her elbow than the other slipped away. Next thing we knew, she was shifting her packages from arm to arm across her swollen belly. That brown wrapping paper kept on crinkling and crying as though the babe inside of her was kicking, warning her to slow down, and just as I got to thinking she was about to unleash a storm, she jammed the toe of her shoe, smack-crack against those uneven boards. Oh dear..." Mam clasped her cheeks as though Trivett and the woman were right there on the ground in front of Fletch's wagon.

"All poor Trivett had to hear was 'my baby,' what with his Lizbeth being in the same way, and next thing I knew, there he was, one gentle brown hand steadying the woman and the other helping her up. She was leaning on him and thanking him, telling him she didn't know what she would have done without him. That's when another white woman came along and started beating him off as though he'd been doing the pregnant woman an injustice." By now Mam's hands, folded one atop the other, shook.

Fletch rested his hand on hers, brought them to stillness. She trembled with a silent sob—the same hideous sound she'd made the night the men had dragged his father away—then caught herself and sat upright. "They'd never have arrested Trivett if Taylor were alive."

"Folks like us don't belong in Martonsville anymore."

Mam studied his face. "What are you saying, son? You're not leaving now, are you?"

"Too many bad things are happening."

"You in some trouble I should know about?"

"With Trivett in jail, we're all in trouble. More than you know." He swallowed hard and went on to tell her about Daffron Mears, and how Promise was housing him in the shed.

"One thing at a time. For now, we worry about Trivett." Mam's voice had grown steady and thoughtful, a sure sign she was working up a plan. She worried one wrinkle out of her flowered dress, then started on the next. Only when Jonah, the blacksmith, and Markus, the harness-maker, raised their hands in respectful waves did she stop to return the gesture.

In front of the Negroes-only dry goods store, the most decrepit building in Martonsville junction, a group of men stood in a circle, talking. Charles, a white-haired gentleman, saw them and straightened his shoulders best he could. His companions, all former slave stock, noticed the fix of his eyes and followed. Within seconds, they unbuttoned their circle and formed a line—shoulder to stooped shoulder, one earless, another without a hair to grace his head, another with a melted eyelid—every man stood at attention. It was Mam they were honoring.

Mam, who'd eased their granddaughters' pains when their great-grandchildren were entering this world. Mam, who'd nursed their families with her potions, then taught them to carry their heads high, saying this was a part of the cure. Mam, who insisted surviving with a smile was the most vexing revenge of all, who had, as part of that revenge, reported to Taylor the truth about who in Tacham County fathered whom. Mam, who, now that Taylor was gone, would surely come up with another way to protect them all.

Fletch suspected this was why these men saw fit to part their lips into toothless smiles that gleamed with persistence. Pink was the color of their gummy hope, while his grayed with promises broken, dreams delayed.

The image of their grins accompanied him to the outskirts of town. There, rising in the ominous tower, was the three-story jail. Behind each barred window, a prisoner stood waiting. Fletch searched, hoping he'd see Trivett. They've got him in another part of the jail, he told himself as he urged Cassiopeia into the cool shadows by the fence.

The bricks in this tower had come from a brickworks south of Savannah. Shipped by rail, then hauled one wagon load at a time, they formed the only structure in Martonsville the color of dried blood. To think it had been honored as one of the few jails for Negroes on the East Coast. And thank glorious goodness—this tribute to sweat and perseverance has spared the pious white citizens on Martons Island from the likes of Negro drunks, card cheats, pickpockets, and one unfortunate jazz musician who'd come to the aid of a pregnant white woman.

They entered the door marked Office. The eerie silence of prisoners, forbidden to speak, engulfed them. A deputy sat between two barriers of thick metal bars; one separated him from the prisoners, the other from Fletch and Mam. An arrow pointing to a line painted on the floor directed them to where they should wait. And wait they did.

Telltale scents of confinement, urine and human bowels, baking in who-knows-what-manner of privy, assaulted them as they stood in the barren room. The deputy fluttered his hands in a show of transferring papers from one side of his desk to the other. Other than the release of an occasional sigh, there was no sign of mental activity that should have kept him from inquiring after their needs.

Mam closed her eyes.

"You all right, Mam?"

Her tall solid figure swayed not as one about to faint, but as one reeling with worry. "I feel odd. Maybe some water would help." They glanced at the deputy, who shuffled faster.

Fletch stepped forward until Mam put her hand on his arm. "There's a jug in the wagon." He turned to go outside, and she stopped him once more. "First, find out about Trivett." She was doing what she'd always done, seeing to others' needs before her own, and with this, the feeling returned that she was in charge and all would be well.

Fletch positioned his brogans close to the painted line and peered at the deputy's tan-uniformed back. The deputy burrowed his face in his desk drawer, searched through his papers, and lifted one out. Fletch watched the man's eyes skirr from right to left across the page, saddened that the man couldn't read. Seconds changed into minutes. Fletch dragged his foot across the gritty floor. The deputy refused to look up.

Fletch unbuttoned his overalls and tapped the button against its metal clasp. Still, the deputy ignored him. He took a deep breath and let his words rumble out low and loud as if Mam were hard-of-hearing. "Looks like we gonna be spendin' da night here. I'd best get da quilt outta da wagon."

The deputy jolted upright and rushed to the other side of his desk. "Who you looking for?"

Mam nudged Fletch aside. Her face brightening with hope, she answered in her best you-can-catch-more-flies-with-honey tone. "A fella named Trivett Boyd got himself arrested. We come to see him."

The deputy turned and ran his finger down one of his papers. "He ain't here," he said without bothering to look up.

Mam's face froze. "Where'd they take him?"

"Says here, he's on his way to Savannah to see the judge." The deputy returned to flipping pages. Clearly, he'd said all he intended, but Mam stood there chest rising and falling, jaw grinding, aching for a glimpse of his roster, no doubt wondering if she should chance dashing to that desk of his and grabbing that paper.

Fletch felt her move and grabbed her arm. "We thanks you, sir," he said, and steered her out the door.

Flies buzzed from within the jail, toward Cassiopeia and back. She twitched her ears in one frenzied motion after the other. A puddle of water surrounded her front hooves; the jug lay on its side on top of Mam's blue dishcloth and the simple meal she'd packed for the trip home.

Cassiopeia twisted her neck toward Fletch as if to apologize for not having frightened the culprit away. Ants and flies swarmed over the preserves Mam had smoothed onto her fresh-baked bread. The effect was as crushing as the deputy's illiteracy. Fletch was tempted to go back and accuse the man of toying with his brother's life but couldn't trust his temper.

"That deputy kept us waiting on purpose so some friend of his could do this. He thinks 'cause he's wrapped in white, he's better than us? I won't have this. We've haven't been treated like this in years." Mam's face contorted with pain as though, rather than bread and jam, her spirit had been upended.

On the way home, as Mam slumped against his arm and dozed, Fletch pictured the charred remains of Mam's cabin more than twenty years earlier. He and Trivett were barely three years old when the roar of flames had engulfed their home. After the cinders had cooled, the two of them carried tools to Taylor as he rebuilt that which men in hooded robes had destroyed. Fletch clutched Taylor's hammer to his small chest, reasoning it would help him grow up fast so he could find the men who had lynched his father.

Weeks later, Mam insisted Taylor chop down every tree hefty enough to support even a child's weight. The trees, thick and round, made for the hiding places where Fletch and Trivett played. Trivett cried in protest, and Fletch lent his voice to his brother's cause.

Taylor took them aside. "Your mother doesn't want to lose anyone to a tree again." He felled tree after tree, sawed branches, and chopped trunks into firewood. The boys helped lug the debris far into the woods and watched the sun make its way into the space Taylor and Mam created. Now that space was gone.

CHAPTER 5

Had we recognized the original pustule,
we could have prevented it from becoming inflamed
and, in so doing, averted the festering that
has infected our daily lives.

Taylor Crawford, journal entry, March 7, 1896

Daffron's brother-in-law had a way of taking up space, and that Monday night was no different. Acey propped his head against the flat-chested beauty of a car window and sprawled his legs over the back seat, heels jiggling faster than a dance hall trollop, then shot Daffron one of his cock-assed grins.

A seventeen-year-old tagging along was as pesky as your drawers catching sand—unless you shook them free, those grains festered into a boil. Having forgotten what it was like to idolize an older man with a dubious reputation, Daffron couldn't imagine what had gotten into the kid. Some fool notion made him beg to tag along.

To end the kid's nagging, Daffron had given in that night. That thrilled Acey and infuriated Margaret, who took better care of her baby brother than of him. Now he was sorry. Between family noise, Promise's crazy horse, Cambridge, slamming itself against the barn wall, and her fool dogs' barking, he was building a case of nerves. Times like this he wanted to claw his way out of his skin. Times like this he made mistakes. Bad ones.

He needed to get the hell away from the racket, outside and in. He tapped twice on the roof of the car, waited for Acey to put his feet where they belonged, and opened the door. One thing and one thing alone would bring him back to his God, family, and country-loving self: A good lynching.

"Move the hell over." He got in and slammed the door.

"What'd you do to get those animals going?" Acey asked.

"You'd think their owner would shut them up, wouldn't you? Not a chance."

"I told you you wouldn't like it here."

"Lots of noise for a first-timer." Daffron yanked on Acey's ear lobe, easy at first, then harder, until Acey jerked himself free. He flicked the boy's pimply chin. The pale-haired boy yelped.

Daffron laughed, then clamped a hand on his cousin's meaty shoulder in the front passenger seat. "How you doing, Coop?"

Cooper Peall pressed his shoulder hard against the seat, forcing Daffron to yank his hand free. "How am I doing?" He dragged a handkerchief over his round red face. "I'd sooner march straight to hell than stay at Taylor Crawford's place."

His three-fingered hand eased the sheriff's badge from his chest. As he opened the flap over his shirt pocket, the silver shield of justice caught a beam of soft moonlight and turned it steely. The badge thudded against the inside of his pocket like never before, as though in removing it, he'd unfastened his good sense. That, he feared, was going to cost him. He turned toward Daffron. "Acey's right, what's with you, coming way out here?"

Daffron had had his fill of Cooper's bellyaching and of Cambridge's noise. He cranked the window up. "That stupid horse belongs to Taylor's niece. Soon as it heard your car, damn thing started slamming its stall. One of these days, it's gonna bust that barn to bits."

"She ought to sell it, get one of these babies." The sheriff slapped his palm on the dashboard of his 1927 Tin Lizzie.

Sawtooth caressed the steering wheel with his bony fingers. "It'd be an improvement for sure. Don't need no saddle, don't produce no shit."

Daffron got to thinking about having stumbled earlier that day into Cambridge's stall. The beast had nearly crushed him. He curled his finger around the trigger of the rifle resting on the seat between Acey and him. Next time, he'd have this resting in the crook of his arm. Tonight, he had a more important matter on his mind: his appointment with the fella he'd been waiting years to catch up to. "Get moving, Sawtooth. We got work to do."

The hand brake creaked, then snapped, and the car rolled down the hill. By all rights, tonight was Daffron's turn to drive, to do just what Sawtooth was doing: pressing the ignition switch, working the floor pedal on the left and the throttle on the steering wheel column to make the car go forward. The car sputtered, bucked twice, sent the sheriff smack into the dashboard, and stalled.

Daffron cuffed Sawtooth's shoulder. "I thought you said you knew how to drive. You gotta give it more gas."

Acey hung his arms over the front seat between Sawtooth and Cooper, struck a match, and waited for the flame to settle. Then he pointed at Sawtooth's wooden leg. "Daffron's right, Coop. How's a guy with a peg leg gonna work all those pedals?"

"How am I supposed to drive when the jerk behind me is spitting down my neck?"

The dogs' bawling grew louder. "If you don't get moving, we'll have to deal with the hounds and the owner, and I ain't prepared for that—yet," Daffron said.

Sawtooth restarted the car and switched on the headlamps. "If it weren't for the moon, I wouldn't see a thing. Think it would hurt what's-her-name to light a lantern or two?"

The underside of the car scraped the road, jostling Daffron. "A more backward woman you'll never find. She could care less if the sheriff's car drags like it's got a belly full of worms."

They were rolling past the field where Taylor was buried when the car bounced again. "Go easy! You're gonna rip out the floor," Cooper said.

Two ghostly forms appeared out of nowhere and darted in front of the headlamps. Sawtooth pumped the brake. "Watch out! Don't hit those damn dogs with my car."

"Run 'em over," Daffron said as a rifle shot dinged the bumper, spraying pebbles over the trunk.

"What the hell?" Cooper clutched the back of his seat and twisted around. Sawtooth stepped on the gas and jerked him back.

Acey grabbed the rifle, but Daffron stopped him. "Don't bother. She missed 'cause she wanted to."

"Her aim is dead on, huh? Taylor's doing, no doubt. She was always a feisty one. To think she and my sweet Suzanne are friends." Cooper paused. "She still got no man?"

The lusty alertness in his cousin's eyes added to Daffron's nerves. "Don't get any ideas. I'm saving her for later."

"'Bout time you found yourself a lively one. We weren't sure if your last gal was breathing or not."

"Shut up, Sawtooth." Daffron didn't appreciate Sawtooth airing his exploits in front of his brother-in-law. "Cooper, tell Acey how we run this show. Being we didn't bring our fainting couch, we can't have him swooning."

Daffron turned to Acey. "Seeing a darkie where he belongs can make a man's knees fold. Me?" He thumped his chest. "Makes my little heart sing."

"You mean like..." Acey hammered at an imaginary banjo and began singing: "*My heart's* so *little there ain't room for a dime. Don't mean I'm unhappy, means I ain't got time.*"

The sheriff interrupted. "Listen, this is serious. First, we suit up—Sawtooth got one for you, Acey—then you help me and Sawtooth keep the nigger quiet. Daffron handles the ropes."

Daffron leaned forward. His own kind of lust had penetrated his eyes. "You got the man I wanted?"

"Sure thing. Found him with his mother. My deputy picked him up for laying hands on a white woman. Disgusting, ain't it? A pregnant one at that. Show you how stupid this nigger is..."

The sheriff's voice grew louder, but Daffron had stopped listening. Stupid? The nigger he'd told Cooper to arrest was far from stupid. Word had it he was clever enough to become a doctor. He watched the gray-black shadows blurring past the car window and waited for Cooper to stop blathering. "So, you got that Hart boy, right?"

"The Hart boy?" Acey whimpered.

"No one's talking to you." The kid was already getting squeamish. Daffron folded his arms over his chest. He couldn't believe his ears; twenty minutes into the most important night in his life and his brother-in-law and his cousin were giving him trouble.

"I heard some roving preacher got the town folk riled and hungry for a lynching. You figure on a crowd showing up?" The thought of all those excited eyes watching him slip the rope over a blubbering Fletch made his heart race.

"This will be the town's first lynching in twenty years. You want a riot? I had my deputy tell everyone the nigger was going to Savannah to hang. I'm not in the mood for any commotion." The sheriff turned toward the side window without so much as glancing back.

But Daffron didn't agree. And he didn't like the way his cousin had just shifted in his seat.

CHAPTER 6

What is it in a father that incites him to inflict on his son the hatred that has crawled from his bowels into his very soul?

Taylor Crawford, journal entry, March 7, 1896

The car stopped at the abandoned Hanscom farm outside Martonsville. Wind rustled the pines by the swayback barn. Moonlight seeping through the branches created shadowy ghouls. Daffron was first out of the car and the first to slip on the pine straw. He grabbed hold of the door. Luckily, Acey and the others were gawking out the other window. He knew better than to move quickly on the slick pine needles; that he'd overlooked them annoyed him. He was better than that.

With each step, he ground his heel, crushed his way to the trunk. The scent of pine mixed with the smell of sea air. Despite his nerves, he felt good working in his hometown for a change. He opened the trunk to another of his favorite scents: linseed oil, rancid as the night was sweet.

His white anti-gas suit reminded him of Margaret and her three dresses: one for home, a fancier number for doing her marketing, and her best for church. It'd taken years before he understood how wearing the right clothing made his wife feel.

When he'd begun his work, he settled for a white hood—not that he belonged to the Klan, no siree. No bowing to a headman for him; he'd done plenty of that with his daddy—until the billowy white robes curled around his legs and made him trip. After that, he tried a burlap sack with jagged cuts for his eyes and mouth. That getup startled the darkies all right but set him and the boys to sneezing. That's when Cooper found these suits.

The arms and legs allowed Daffron to move without getting tangled. Better yet, the mask with goggles, gas canister, and a hose that flopped terrified even the dumbest mule. Best of all, one glance and darkies paled. That was perfection. Like tonight would be once he filled his eyes with the soles of Fletch Hart's feet.

Daffron hiked up his suit and fastened the straps around his ankles and wrists. One tug at the zipper resting at his crotch and he closed himself in. He raised the fitted hood over his head and dangled the mask over his wrist, then handed a stiff oiled suit to Acey, who wrinkled his nose. "You're going to look good in this."

"Where'd you get these?"

Daffron pointed to Cooper. "Thank him."

"My daddy was a doughboy in the Great War. He pilfered them, figuring when he got home he'd have to finish fighting the War Between the States. I told him not to bother, we were winning it for him."

Acey flashed a wicked grin and launched his imitation of a fine gentleman. "I must thank him for supplying me with a garment large enough for my God-given endowment."

Had Daffron's daddy been smart enough to hold on to the family plantation, Daffron would have been using that kind of talk for real. "You wish your manhood called for a zipper this big." Daffron tugged his mask over his face and wagged his head, flopping the hose inches from Acey's face.

"Keep your thing to yourself," the boy mumbled, pushing Daffron away.

Sawtooth and Cooper finished zipping their suits and took their places, one to either side of Acey. He smacked his boyish lips. "Klan could take a couple of pointers from us. Wouldn't you say?"

"Put your mask on and shut up. Dumb nigger will take one gander at these getups and think Satan come to claim him."

"Daffron, cut the gab, it's hot as hell in here," Cooper said.

Daffron took the rope from the trunk. He should have expected his cousin would complain. The man fretted like an old lady over any sort of change. "You're going easy with the crowds; I'm going easy, too. No cutting, no burning." Daffron jerked his head in Acey's direction. Having the kid here was giving him the creeps.

Now that he had Fletch Hart, he wanted to get rid of him fast, before anything happened. That way he could get back to Fletch's little sweetie, Promise, and take care of her. Slow and easy. He laid his knife in the box beside his bottle of kerosene and whistled "Dixie" under his breath.

Cooper ripped his mask off. "We never worked that way before. What's got into you, Mears?"

"Tonight's Acey's first lynching. I'm breaking him in slow." Daffron edged closer to the sheriff. "Think about it. If we rough this fella up too bad, Acey'll get all whiny. Then he'll go to Margaret, and I'll hear about how I upset her baby brother. She'll go cold on me. Ice friggin' cold. You *do* know what I'm talking about, don't you Coop?" The sheriff looked away and nodded. "You ain't going to fuss with me about this one are you?"

The sheriff shot Daffron a barbed glance. "Course not."

"Then you just follow my lead."

The four men walked side by side to the barn. "Everything quiet in there, Hobbs?" Cooper asked, his voice muffled.

The deputy lifted his pork chop legs over the barn's threshold. "Until our boy heard your car. Now he's restless. Want me to get him?"

"No use wasting these," Cooper looked down at his suit. "Let's give him a show."

Hobbs held the door for the sheriff. Sawtooth and Acey followed.

Outside, Daffron arranged the rope over his arm, draping loop after loop, until he got to the one that mattered—the one that would do the job. He slid his running knot back and forth. No hesitation. Just the way he liked. Knots had been his daddy's specialty; he'd taught him good. Daffron loosened the loop to the size of Fletch Hart's head.

Any minute now, he'd be rid of the boldest nigger ever squatted on his daddy's plantation. Without him and Taylor around, the others would run off. It was just a matter of time and Mearswood Farm would be his. Then he'd have something worthwhile to leave to his little girl. All he had to do was be patient; that was his rule.

Don't go in after a nigger; niggers come to you—that was another rule. But the scuffling inside the barn made him wish he could join in. If that damned Cooper had hid Fletch anywhere but this lousy barn, he could have. A couple swipes to the nigger's privates would have soothed Daffron's nerves. Tempting as it was, he wasn't going into a barn. Not if he didn't have to.

Barns had space enough for a grown man to lay hands on a young boy, pick him up, and fling him against the walls. Once, twice, maybe a third time depending on how much his pa had been drinking. "Pa, no!" To this day, the terror in his boyish voice echoed in his head whenever he went into a barn, caused a pain made his heart feel like exploding.

Only pain worse came the day his daddy had spotted a pair of young black eyes, peering down at them from the hayloft. For the longest time, Pa stood there without blinking, his gaze fixed on those eyes. Without muttering one little word to the nigger, his old man beat Daffron senseless. The humiliation of that boy's crying stung more than the whip.

Daffron's eyes went fuzzy. He blinked them clear just as Cooper shoved the nigger through the door. He tumbled to Daffron's feet and bit the sand with his bloodied mouth.

Daffron strolled around him, kicking dust on the fine city trousers where his legs were bound. Mighty nice of Fletch to wear his Sunday clothes to his own lynching, but unlikely. Instead of the calm Daffron had been looking forward to, his nerves crackled. He gestured for Acey and Sawtooth to hoist the prisoner to his knees.

Daffron grabbed his chin and squeezed. "My, my. Look at this, y'all. Don't he think he's special." He wedged his fingers between the man's jaws, pressed them open, forced his lips to bulge.

Three heads nodded. Three gas mask hoses quivered.

Daffron jerked the man's face to the side and knocked him to the ground. "You know whose boy this is?" The heads shook.

The fella dragged his knees to his chest and pushed himself away. Once, twice, like a wounded animal. Dust clouds hovered around his torn suit jacket.

Daffron followed one small step after the other, his nerves sizzling. *Fletch would never wear a suit jacket in the middle of the week.*

Once the man backed himself to the barn, Daffron turned to the others. "This man's daddy was a white boy. Why else would he think he's entitled to touch a white woman. Ain't that so?" Daffron pressed his mask to the man's face. The fella's eyes opened wide as his swollen eyelids allowed. He'd waited a long time to have this nigger inches from his face, squirming. Daffron kicked him, then headed to the far side of the barn.

From beneath the oak tree, he called to Hobbs, "We got a proper bench for this fine gentleman?" Hobbs froze. Something was wrong; he shouldn't have to remind Hobbs. "Where's the bench?" Hobbs waddled to his truck.

Daffron looked at the branch high off the ground, plenty strong and covered with resurrection ferns. How fitting. One easy toss and the rope cut the air, curled over the branch, jittered for a few delicious seconds, and gentled to a stop. The noose dropped open, a hungry mouth begging for a meal.

Daffron had been practicing for this lynching since the day Taylor stole Mearswood out from under him. With every knot tied, every toss pitched, he savored the satisfaction he'd finally get from striking back at Taylor Crawford. And the best part? This was just the beginning. He didn't give a damn that no one could see him behind his mask; he grinned wide and mean.

"You got a name, boy?" Daffron moved toward Sawtooth, hauling the man to his feet.

"Trivett, sir." The nigger sucked blood and snot into his nose.

"Trivett?"

"Boyd, sir. Trivett Boyd, sir." He lowered his chin.

"You're lying." And why wouldn't he? Daffron's eyes darted from the sniveling man to the sheriff and back.

He searched for Fletch Hart's features through the blood and swelling: thin lips, the kind you wanted to slap because they turned upward into a grin even when he was serious, and a wide forehead with an arrowhead of hair dipping into the middle of his drum-tight skin.

But this fella's lips ballooned, and not from his beating. Then there was the matter of the space between his two bloody front teeth. Fletch had no such space. And this man lacked the worried rail-track separating Fletch's brows. As Daffron stared eye to swollen eye, it occurred to him this man and he were damn near the same height. Had this been Fletch, he'd be looking up: that nigger was close to six-foot tall. He hardened his gaze at the man with the small face and large full lips.

A double-cross! Fists clenched, he spun at Cooper.

Cooper shook his head and shrugged: "Hobbs saw Mother Hart and figured who else but Fletch would be with her?"

Damned if he'd let Coop see him this furious. Daffron forced his voice to stay so calm only a fool would miss the anger rivering beneath. "Anyone call you TB?"

"No, sir, not that I recall." The man's eyes were watering.

"You're supposed to be Fletch Hart, you know that, boy?"

Trivett lifted his head. "Fletch, sir?" He looked confused.

"Seems the deputy here made a mistake. A big one." Daffron glared at Hobbs. "You're the boy that that Hart woman adopted. The one plays jazz music. Am I right, boy?"

"Yes, sir." Trivett glanced at the tree and back in Daffron's direction. His panicked expression returned.

"This fella's a damned good trumpet player. How about him playing a tune in honor of our little get-together? What do you think, Coop?"

Cooper looked at Hobbs. "He didn't have no instrument when we picked him up," Hobbs said.

"You mean to tell me he left his instrument behind when he was taking care of that white woman?" Daffron snickered from behind his mask. "You think he might have hoped to play a few tunes at our very own Grand Mitreanna Hotel on the off chance he might steal a good paying job from a local white boy?"

Because there was no good reason to wait for an answer, Daffron walloped him in the gut and watched him crumble. There, that felt better.

Daffron caught sight of Acey, caving as if his stomach had just been slugged. The boy's shoulders slumped. Daffron knew this would happen. The little jerk.

Cooper pushed Sawtooth toward Acey.

"Stand up straight," Sawtooth hissed, jagging his elbow into Acey's side. He motioned with his head toward Cooper, who nodded.

"I'm okay, Coop, honest," Acey mumbled. "I'm good, real good. I'll show you." He pulled his shoulders back, walked to Daffron's side, and kicked the nigger, who curled in on himself with a yelp. Acey glanced back at Cooper, nodding for a second time. Acey kicked him again. Blood from the side of the man's mouth drizzled to the ground. Acey stepped on the limp musical notes on the man's tie and slid the toe of his work boot towards his throat. "Now play for us."

Somewhere from in the woods, an owl screamed. Trivett started.

"You know what it means when an owl screeches?" Daffron asked.

"Yes, sir. Means someone's about to die."

"Give me the name of a song, Trivett."

Trivett took a long breath and released it with a shudder. "I can't think of none, sir."

Daffron motioned for Acey to come along side. "You decide what Trivett should hear."

Acey opened his eyes wide, thumped his white-suited chest with his thumb. "Me?"

"Go on, pretend you're making up a fancy little song like you sing for your sister." Daffron watched his brother-in-law's eyes dart toward the bushes and back. He was searching the brambles for a tune. Fool!

Acey cleared his throat. His voice drizzled, off-key and pathetic. "*'Bout to visit heaven/ died de home soon/ 'Bout to see yer mama/ died de home soon /Joy's a calling Trivett/ died de home soon/Died he, died he, died he home soon.*"

Sawtooth poked Trivett's back, started him walking toward the tree. The binding around Trivett's ankles forced him into small shaky steps. Acey glanced from Trivett's feet to Sawtooth's mask and back.

Sawtooth looked at Daffron, waiting under the tree, grabbed Acey, and pushed him to the other side of Trivett. They fell into step with Acey's mangled song, *"'Bout to see yer mama, died de home soon,"* sung slower, in time with Trivett's shuffling.

Their bungling disgusted Daffron. His most important lynching and they'd botched it. It was Cooper Peall's fault; who knows what he told his fat deputy. Knowing Hobbs, he'd probably been thinking more about his next sandwich than the man he snatched off the street. Then there was Sawtooth's crappy driving and being shot at. And Acey's girlish stomach.

But he never thought Cooper would double-cross him. Never. He should have known something was wrong when Cooper didn't scare up a crowd. Now he wouldn't even have the town's tongue wagging to look forward to. And this

Trivett fella—the way he stared straight through to the other side of his noose—gave Daffron the jitters.

Sweat drained down his face and stung his eyes. He needed time to cool down. He wanted a good whiff of this man's fear. Without the smell of fear, what little satisfaction he'd squeeze from this hanging would disappear. Evaporate. With all the trouble it took to do away with a nigger, he expected something in return: panting, sweating, the kind of out-of-control that seized him whenever he forced himself onto a sweet black thing. All the scratching and spitting—he liked when a darkie fought hard—that's when it was best.

Daffron ripped off his mask and moved closer to see if he could get a quiver out of the nigger, but he was still as fawn in the brush. "You that willing to just lay down and die? Well, you ain't helping no one," he whispered through his teeth, "'cause when I get hold of Fletch Hart, he ain't gonna have it as easy as you."

Daffron followed the nigger's gaze to the brambles. There in the spotty moonlight, two eyes peered back at him, eyes like the ones in the hayloft when he was a boy. He blinked and looked again. Nothing. They were gone.

Trivett was drawing in long slow breaths; the fool was preparing himself to die. Daffron moved closer; Trivett started to pant. Ah, that was better. He slipped the noose over Trivett's spongy sweating head and helped him mount the bench.

By this time, a fine calm was usually coming over Daffron, one that slowed his breathing, made him feel nothing existed except him and what he was doing away with. Afterward, for a few perfect moments, he was free; nothing could touch him. Not his father's whip. Not that boy's eyes staring down at him from the loft. Not the indignity of his daddy's farm being overrun with niggers like this one.

Trivett's ignorant pride infuriated him. He whispered his father's words, "Stupid boy!" and kicked the bench from under the tree.

Trivett's fancy trousers flapped in mid-air. His torso jerked and twisted with such fierceness the moss hanging alongside him trembled. Leaves on the lynching branch clawed at the night. Trivett pumped his legs up an invisible staircase, creating a breeze that seared Daffron's face. Trivett gasped once, twice, then stopped running. His head slumped to his chest. Limp and motionless, his bowels let loose, splattering Daffron's white suit.

Fire! That's what it felt like. Daffron thought he'd caught fire. He wiped Trivett's leavings off on his legs and smirked; Fletch Hart would never be this brave.

CHAPTER 7

Walk side by side with your sorrow and, with time,
it will become your friend.

Taylor Crawford, journal entry, August 10, 1910
On the first anniversary of Will Hart's death

A live oak, carpeted with lichen and hairy ferns, bore down on Fletch during his dream. Not with the leg-crushing, rib-cracking impact he associated with the falling of a tree, but with a mesmerizing weight that coaxed the air from his lungs. The tree spoke, offering him a gift, freedom from pain. He accepted. His breathing became effortless, pleasantly shallow, restful. He tried to move, but with his arms pinned to his sides, he couldn't muster the strength. His Adam's apple froze, and saliva trickled from the corner of his mouth. His knees tensed beneath the leaves' funereal rustle.

So inviting was this descent from life that he welcomed this vision, greeting it warmly, until a figure, ancient and ghostly, hovered inches from his face. It breathed the smell of earth and pungent herbs into his nostrils. The tree's massive weight lifted from Fletch's body. Air flooded his lungs. He swallowed.

"You were about to join Trivett," Crossover Casner, the herbalist capable of sensing death long before it arrived, said, his near-blind eyes reflecting the stark moonlight. Fletch swung his feet over the edge of his bed, sunk his elbows into his thighs: three years old again, tears spilled from his cheeks.

"You know they hung Trivett." The ancient humpbacked herbalist posed his question as a statement.

"I suspected. You've seen him?"

"Out by Hanscom's barn."

Fletch envisioned the rope hanging from the only tree large enough to support a man's weight and thought his heart would stop beating.

Savannah? So, the deputy *had* lied about Trivett going there for trial. Fletch punched himself hard on the thigh. He should have known. Niggers don't get trials. Dear God, he wished he'd gone looking for him.

He laced his brogans and hurried out to the barn. Dead? Trivett's easy smile, his full cheeks, the softness in his eyes when he'd said he was going to be a father. Gone? "Am I dreaming this, too?"

Inside the barn, a crushing darkness. Fletch removed Cassiopeia's collar from the hook opposite her stall, lowered it to his feet, and rested its oval weight against his shins. An insistent fury pulsed through his limbs. Had it been daylight, he would have hacked weeds until his arms ached.

Instead, he grabbed hold of inside the collar with both hands, stepped into the center of the barn, and dragged it round and round until he gagged on the dust. Gasping for air brought him closer to Trivett. He pushed himself to spin harder, faster. Inch by inch, the collar lifted into the air, and as it did, he leaned back. Its undulating movements hurled dizzying accusations: Coward. You left him.

Fletch's feet skimmed the slick hay-strewn ground, and he tumbled into Cassiopeia's stall, where she kicked him and brayed. He agreed with what she was telling him: You were his friend, you should have saved him.

Crossover hobbled to Fletch's side between him and the mule. Cassiopeia quieted. Leaning forward, humpback pressed to his cheek, Crossover offered Fletch a hand. Fletch squeezed it and righted himself. Then it struck him: Lizbeth. He looked at the herbalist and mouthed her name. "No one's told her," was all the ancient said.

Most likely the last time Lizbeth had seen her husband, she and Trivett were by their bed, the half-formed mound of their child wedged between them. His leather grip was packed with enough clothing to get him through a week's visit with Fletch. Lizbeth had taken his shirts from their dresser and folded them into tidy squares. She handed him the pile. Placed lovingly in its center, the gold pin she'd given him on their wedding day. Fletch leaned his forehead into his palm, pressed his fingers to his throbbing head and closed his eyes.

***

By the time they arrived at Hanscom's barn, scalloped clouds had edged out the moonlight. Crossover struck a match on his thumbnail, held it until it burned evenly, then touched it to Fletch's lantern. The kerosene burst into a mustard glow. To their left, the barn's weary boards bowed in brittle frowns. Night's chorus of whirring bats, snarling raccoons, and the rustling of a lone leopard cat disappeared. A hallowed silence prevailed.

Beyond the wagon, a shroud of sooty darkness. Crossover tried to lift the lantern over his head but could raise it only as high as his humped shoulders allowed. He handed it to Fletch.

“Damn you to hell,” Fletch shouted as the wire handle singed his callused fingers. He was about to blow out the flame when Crossover, hair drooped in steely waves, rested his hand on Fletch’s arm and held him in his steady gaze.

Drawing on Crossover’s wordless strength, Fletch stepped up onto the wagon seat and thrust his arm above his head. The lantern hissed from fifteen feet in the air. Darkness alongside the barn receded into shadows: the leafy outline of a tree, branches in juxtaposing rounds, equally weighted except one.

He hanged disfigured and limp, robbed of the liveliness he was known for. His stillness so stunned Fletch that for one joyous awful moment, he presumed Crossover had been mistaken, that this body belonged to another poor soul, not his adopted brother. His friend.

The branch swayed, and the rope rotated to display a brutally swollen mouth. The telltale space between Trivett’s front teeth gaped in undeniable proof. Fletch gasped. He imagined the horror that consumed Trivett’s final moments, the prayers he’d uttered, the persons Trivett had thought of: Lizbeth, and the baby he would never hold, Mam, even him.

A spasm rippled Fletch’s throat and threatened to explode into sobs. Crossover’s quiet voice distracted him: “Drive under the tree so we can cut him down.”

Cassiopeia flicked her ears in the direction of Fletch’s hoarse commands as she aligned the wagon seat directly beneath Trivett. Fletch unsheathed his knife and, drawing his lips back, clenched the blade with his teeth. The frigid steel shot a wave of pain upward into his head. He positioned himself on the wagon seat, where he should have been hours ago—beside his brother.

The blade worked of its own accord, making an incision above the irrevocable precision of the hangman’s knot, slicing through fiber after fiber. Fletch’s other arm knew enough to hold Trivett around his chest. Trivett had let go of his insides. The stench seeped from his wet trousers to Fletch's, up his damp thigh into his heart.

He clung to the body while he sawed, stopping only to swipe at the occasional mosquito that dared interfere. Trivett's head wobbled like a child's broken toy, obstructing Fletch's blurry vision. He wanted to say something to his brother, but his words abandoned him, just as he'd abandoned Trivett. His lips brushed Trivett's still-warm cheek, tasted his salty fear, and scorched it into memory.

As he was about to cut through the rope's last strands, he glanced down at Crossover, bracing his short legs in the wagon bed, reaching upward best he could. "Careful, or he'll land hard," the ancient said.

Fletch agreed, once was enough.

Trivett's boot heels scraped the wagon as Fletch clutched him, and Crossover unbuttoned the dead man's trousers, tugged them down his legs, and tossed them into the dust. Fletch lowered the body flat onto the wagon bed and couldn't bring himself to let go.

Crossover loosened the knot from Trivett's bruised neck. "No use Lizbeth seeing him like this." He soaked a rag in a powerful-smelling emulsion, and gently wiped one of Trivett's legs, turned the brown-stained rag in on itself, and cleaned the other.

An owl landed in Trivett's death tree and chanted, *Hoo!Hoo!*

Crossover stepped over Trivett's feet and pattered along the edge of the wagon bed until he was close enough to land his fingers on Fletch's cheeks. "You've got to let him go, or he'll never rest easy."

Images of his father, face bloodied and eyes swollen, being pried from his mother's arms flooded Fletch. His arms went limp, just as his mother's had, and he let Crossover take what was no longer his.

Crossover worked in the light of the lantern, first closing Trivett's eyes on the world that had turned on him, then wrapping a strip of white cloth under his jaw, around his head. A kinder, less exacting knot eased Trivett's jaw into place and lessened his agonized expression. When he'd finished, Crossover touched Fletch's arm once more. "Ready to move on?"

Fletch heaved himself to his feet. The tree from his dream pressed down on his shoulders with its excruciating weight, and he wobbled. The night was closing in on him, suctioning air from his lungs, threatening them with collapse, until Crossover's call released him from his trance.

"Spirits have been aroused," was all Crossover said, then motioned for Fletch to grab hold of Mam's old quilt.

As they covered the body, the sounds of Fletch's breathing softened. Crossover stroked the tired fabric, patches snipped from Fletch's grandmam's faded dresses. "T'was your grandmama welcomed him into the beyond."

"I'm not surprised. She fried corn cakes for us when we were no higher than the stockings rolled at her knees. Trivett's always had extra sugar on them." His words rose untainted by the anger roiling inside.

They settled themselves on the wagon seat, and Fletch clicked Cassiopeia away from the hanging tree. She moved forward without her usual lurch, gentle yet eager to leave this place behind. But Fletch wasn't.

He let her pull them past the barn and handed Crossover the reins, "In case you have to move her." He groped under the wagon seat for his shovel and ax.

Layers of leaves beneath Trivett's tree crackled with the crush of Fletch's footfall. He jammed his shovel through the earth's parched crust into its soft sandy guts. With animal swiftness, he scooped out a resting place for Trivett's trousers. Before burying them, he searched the pockets for Trivett's small gold pin. Their flannel lining warmed his hand like a glove. Other than the handkerchief Trivett always carried, his pockets were empty.

Yesterday morning while he and Fletch sipped coffee, Trivett had fastened his pin to his collar. But moments ago when Fletch held him in his arms, it was missing. He pinched the trouser pockets once more, hoping that snagged in a corner he'd feel the golden replica of Trivett's trumpet. Finding nothing, he dropped to his knees and sifted through a pile of dirt, fingering pebbles, shells, twigs—anything small enough to be Trivet's pin—and cast them aside. Still nothing. He shoveled the sand over the trousers and tamped: gone, gone, gone.

Fletch twisted his wrists back and forth along the ax's smooth wooden handle. His chest surged with heat that seared his shoulders and arms. Within seconds, he drove the ax head into the hanging tree, landing it with a jolt. He tugged and rocked to work the head free, pulled back, and sunk the blade six inches above his first insult. He was moving faster. The ax head rounded his shoulder. The energy in his coiled muscles added to the ax's momentum, then erupted, releasing itself once more. Chunk by chunk, he gouged a hideous wound into the tree's flesh.

With each swing, he tried to picture Trivett's killer. "Tell me the name of the man who tied that knot," he hissed, his words exploding in a spray of spit. Other than sending a shock of a vibration up his arm, the ax's bite mocked him with its nameless reply.

He dropped the ax and leaned all his weight against the tottering tree. Branches from the live oak snagged those of nearby trees, tearing them loose. Birds squawked and fluttered. The trunk cracked.

He tilted with the tree and pushed until the trunk upended itself with a thunderous snap. The ground trembled. A terrible quaking, this time of *his* doing.

DAY TWO

CHAPTER 8

Fear is our most crippling malady.

Taylor Crawford, *My Life in Georgia*, 1929

Dawn brushed its gauzy fingertips over the day as Fletch woke Promise and told her about Trivett. "Crossover and I just delivered his body to Lizbeth," he said, choking on his tears.

"Poor Lizbeth," Promise murmured, "What about Mother Hart? Does she know?"

He closed his eyes and nodded. "The moment she heard, she collapsed," he said, his voice spasming. "Crossover is with her, spoon-feeding her strong tea."

Promise had heard rumors about innocent people in other counties being hanged but never anyone close. Trivett was her first. Thoughts of his life snatched in such a soul-shredding way set her head a spin. She imagined his first glimpse of the slack oval that formed the noose, the knot pulsing with every jerk of the rope, his tittering between life and beyond, his whispered good-byes, a final prayer rushing from his lips.

During those minutes, she hoped he had unleashed on his attackers whatever meanness he had to give.

Truth was, this man existed only to delight others. Even during Taylor's funeral, Trivett's churchy rhythms erupted into fits of mournful jazz that set everyone swaying. And when those weeping had wailed themselves dry, Trivett's trumpet took over and cried for them.

Promise wiped her eyes on the sleeve of her nightgown. "How could something like this happen here in Martonsville? Uncle Taylor wouldn't have allowed it," she said.

Fletch gently touched her head. "I need to get to work before Daffron finds me here. Just remember to keep going, or you'll freeze sure as a duck that stops swimming in winter."

She didn't know which was worse, the sense of devastation that filled her small bedroom or the pain in Fletch's eyes. "I'll do my best," she said, burying her head in her hands and listening as Fletch left for the barn.

When she opened her eyes, she found her uncle's shadow, weeping at the foot of her bed. Frightened but curious, she gathered her nightgown around her knees and crept closer. The shadow writhed in a fearsome manner, most certainly over Trivett. She pulled on her overalls, bolted through the front door, and slammed it behind her. From the safety of the front porch, she peeked through the window, but by then, her uncle's shadow had vanished. Her heart pounded with the realization that the dead suffer this kind of horror along with the living. *Oh, Taylor, what are you trying to tell me?*

What was happening to her? She'd lost Taylor and with a nod of her head had betrayed Fletch's trust. Now Trivett was dead. She missed the life she'd never questioned, the freedom from lynching that Taylor's misguided idealism had brokered. Had he been right, she wondered? Was coercion, however subtle, the only way to bring people together? She shivered as she headed for the barn, though she barely noticed for the heaviness rooting through her. A heaviness she could only describe as fear.

***

Fletch pounded nails with a frightening fierceness. Not one to hold onto her tears when someone else was in distress, Promise's eyes welled. As much as she disliked Andrew's having manipulated her into completing this project for him, the stalls he insisted on gave Fletch a place to unload his grief.

The memory of Andrew's boorishness as she stood by Taylor's grave, sprinkling earth over his body, added another element to her worries. "Please, Promise," he'd said, fumbling with her hand, "I'm paying a king's ransom to board my horses. As soon as this is over, work on the barn."

She glanced at the roll of bills he'd folded her fingers around and turned slowly toward him.

"I'm sorry to bring up business at this sad time," he whispered.

Unsure whether the flush heating her face was born of disbelief or revulsion, she nodded slightly. Had he mistaken her for a servant girl, or is this the way he intended to speak with her when she became his wife? "When I get back to normal," was the most she could bring herself to say.

Fletch's pounding came to a startling halt. Grabbing another fist full of nails, he blurted, "Taylor worked to keep men like Trivett and me alive, and within hours we destroyed his legacy. Chewed it and spit it into the wind. What happened to the decency he worked so hard to create?"

"Taylor taught us to look beyond the obvious, to root out the paradox behind events, but —" she couldn't bring herself to say that in hiring Daffron, she had unlocked the door to Trivett's murder. Was she responsible for re-introducing hate into Martonsville? Her insides shivered at the thought. She dismissed this possibility. It was more than she could bear.

The barn's horsey smells combined with the aroma of freshly milled lumber. Beneath the archway to the new stalls, perched over three sawhorses, was a board in need of trimming. Promise grabbed the saw, carved a groove over the line Fletch had drawn, and forced the tool back and forth. The rusty steel squealed, then jammed; she yanked back. The blade buckled, broke loose and forced her into a step as ungainly as the one she'd taken with Daffron.

Fitting the blade back into the groove, she tried again, but Trivett, Fletch, and Taylor occupied her thoughts; the saw jumped and landed hard, gouging out a new and different trough. As she tore into the wood, it occurred to her that Fletch was right: Trivett's murder had destroyed the boundaries Taylor had established. Unless she rebuilt those boundaries, no one would be safe. Her head throbbed with the responsibility this would entail. Would this destroy her, too? Would she devolve into a version of her uncle, consumed by the mantra of "*Repair, Rebuild, Replace*?" If so, would she come to know which of the three ingredients had enabled him to keep Daffron Mears out of their lives?

Fletch's hammering shook the barn. Hay needles from the loft rained on her shoulders and hair. He removed a nail from between his teeth and positioned it on a board. "Are you all right?" she called. The crash of metal upon unforgiving metal said more than his most eloquent words. She took his deafening noise as a measure of his misery.

Thinking more deeply, she found his warning to "keep going" reassuring, for if he hadn't been afloat, he would never have tried to console her. They shared this similarity, a lifelong refusal to let the other be undone. If during a keen game of chess Fletch won, he'd bow to receive the pebble-encrusted victor's crown she readied for his head. Then, with the graciousness of a prince, he'd raise her arm high in the air, above the surface of defeat. Before this business with Daffron was over, she'd do the same for him. By then, she'd repair the damage she'd caused, and he'd forgive her for dismantling his position as foreman, for pretending she didn't care. For now, directing this saw back and forth through the mangled wood was all the comfort she could offer. As she considered how she might set things right a faint trembling rippled beneath her soles.

Outside, Cambridge raced around the tulip trees in the middle of the pasture, his coarse mane flopping, hooves spewing sandy tufts of grass. He galloped along the fence to its far edge and back. Overhead, crows circled and screeched in alarm. Bird by bird, they settled in the trees seaming the pasture to the road.

Promise squinted against the morning brightness. In the distance, a monotonous chugging. Cambridge's frenzy meant more than she cared to admit—he sensed the return of the carload of men who had terrified him last night and Daffron with it. What else could go wrong today?

Grabbing Cambridge's lead, she stooped between the fence rails and headed across the pasture. Her horse-training trinity—stay calm, walk slow, go easy—drummed in her mind and reminded her not to let her mash of feelings overwhelm her; if she lost control, Cambridge would, too.

He arched his ears toward her, then, glancing at the approaching car, flattened them to his head and pressed himself against the fence farthest from the road. "Don't move, sweet boy," she crooned, hoping to calm him before he panicked. The last time a car approached, he'd broken through the fence and speared himself on a split rail. "You're going to be all right. Easy does it," she murmured, talking her way toward him. His velvety nostrils pulsed. His sides heaved in quick shallow breaths. Like Fletch, his wild glare blamed her for yet another terror.

If Cambridge weren't so upset, she'd have gone for her rifle. But she couldn't chance leaving him. Didn't want him to confuse her attempt to protect him with abandonment; Fletch, who'd never forgotten his father's death, had done enough of that for them both. Cambridge shifted from side to side. Close enough to touch his nose, she relaxed her arms so as not to startle him. "We're going to be all right, you wait and see," she said, for her benefit as much as his. She eased herself aside his head, where he didn't have to strain to see her, and waited.

After a few long moments passed, she stroked his neck, using the firm movements he loved. He stepped closer and, when the car churned past, shifted. Though it wasn't the same car as last night's, it was a car. With one practiced movement, she slipped his halter over his head and led him toward the northwestern woods farthest from the road on which Andrew Gills steered with one hand and waved madly with the other. The muscles in her neck knotted with fury. "What is *he* doing here?" she blurted in one huge exasperated breath.

Beside the oblivious Andrew, his sister, Ellen, cupped one gloved hand above her eyes and waved gently with the other. Promise's scalp contorted with what was becoming an excruciating headache.

Then she recalled that Ellen had written this past May, apologizing for having missed Taylor's funeral. *Between the demands of my high school students and preparations for my speech at the Anti-Lynching Conference in Atlanta this summer, life has been merciless. Andrew and I will arrive at*

Mearswood Farm the second week of July, as usual. We considered staying at the Grand Mitreanna Resort, as Mother and Daddy had while we children stayed with you and your uncle, but Andrew was anxious to spend as much time as possible with you. I hope this won't be a hardship so soon after your uncle's death. After having lost our dear parents two years ago, I know how much you must miss your uncle. He was a very fine man.

Promise's finger circled her thumb knuckle; she'd forgotten that Ellen was instrumental in starting the Boston chapter of the Anti-Lynching League. What would news of Trivett do to the woman who, after witnessing a baby's birth, labeled it "too visceral for words"? Ellen's description of Taylor as a 'very fine man' made Promise cringe.

Andrew had echoed his sister's admiration in the article that had warmed his newspaper's readers to Taylor's experiences in Georgia. In it, he'd described Taylor's despair after failing to save a black child from the hangman's noose. That Ellen and Andrew had joined forces with Taylor to rail about hanging seemed more than a matter of political convenience. What the inseparable team would expect now that Taylor and Trivett were dead, she could not yet say. But Andrew's tendency to seek his sister's approval in matters large and small troubled her more than she cared to admit. Were she to honor Taylor's demand that she marry Andrew, would their union be of man and wife, or that of man, wife, and sister-in-law? Was this the type of complication her uncle had envisioned for her life?

At Ellen's urging, Andrew had written a series of articles about Taylor, a Bostonian and graduate of Harvard's School of Divinity, who'd been dismissed from its ranks of professors for proposing the unification of the races. But it was Ellen's suggestion that he focus on stories describing

Taylor's subsequent life on Martons Island, where he had tested his utopian social designs, that launched Andrew's fledgling newspaper from obscurity into a respected political vehicle. One that supported the anti-lynching laws Ellen and her group proposed. The paper attracted youthful readers, those like Andrew who shared a fascination in anything remotely unusual. This inclination temporarily freed him from his sister's dominating influence, which irritated her and further fueled his devotion to Taylor and, Promise surmised, his interest in her.

His collections of early typewriters, old Scribner's magazines, and posters advertising Havana cigars supplied Promise with her best clues as to why he'd agreed to marry a Southern country girl like her. The entire circumstance behind Taylor arranging this marriage was unusual, and that was exotic enough to capture Andrew's attention. But there was something else, something more fundamental that appealed to the businessman in Andrew: each of his collections held enormous future value. Apparently, he thought she did, too.

Irritated by "all things Andrew," Promise led Cambridge deep into the woods toward the marsh, where Andrew would never venture. Birds whistled and trilled to the steady rhythms of Cambridge's hooves. Moss, in the form of old man's beard, fluttered from sweetgum boughs and whisked across their path. When the noise from Andrew's car engine had faded, she stopped to rest by the edge of the marsh, where cypress trees poked skeletal knees through the ground. Along the far shore, reflections of cottony clouds quivered on the water. Cambridge munched the tips from a mound of grass.

Had this been their usual summer visit, Promise would have looked forward to riding with Ellen along these very pathways. Ellen was an accomplished rider, much more so than Andrew, who would do anything to avoid sitting on a horse's back. Promise wasn't sure what bothered him more: being outdone by his sister or by the horse that had tossed him into a thicket. As confusing as things were, having Ellen here was a gift in itself.

She rode Cambridge toward the farm and stopped by the edge of the woods. From where she was seated high on his back, she glimpsed Andrew's shiny black automobile, the sun glinting off its hood. Andrew must have already dusted his precious auto, as was his habit upon arriving. Hers entailed settling Cambridge in the pasture before joining her guests. She needed to settle, too.

CHAPTER 9

The wisest of men defers to the consequences
of an ill-considered thought.

Taylor Crawford, *My Life in Georgia,* 1929

After many summer visits, Andrew and Ellen were accustomed to Cambridge's skittishness. Promise took comfort knowing they would unpack, Andrew in Taylor's room and Ellen in hers. With just two bedrooms and one large room that served as kitchen and sitting room, the cabin was far from the elegant spaciousness of their four-story brownstone. For Andrew, the draw of spending time with Taylor on Mearswood Farm overpowered the inconveniences of kerosene lanterns, pumping water, and midnight visits to the privy. For Ellen, staying here was a combination of good sportsmanship and her iron-forged sense of family duty.

Although this wasn't the best time to have guests, Promise resolved to make them comfortable. "Andrew? Ellen?" she called from the sitting room, where suitcases had been haphazardly deposited.

The doors to the bedrooms, one on either side of the fireplace, opened and the three of them singsonged each other's names. Wilted from the heat, nattily dressed Andrew—a few pounds heavier than when she'd seen him at Taylor's funeral—and ever stylish Ellen hugged Promise, chattering all the while about their trip. With the bray of their accents filling the room, Promise recalled how Taylor's had ripened with Georgian softness. How she wished he were here.

"Hey, give us some privacy, will you?" Andrew brushed his tawny hair from his forehead and wedged his once-athletic body between the women. He was about to kiss Promise when he touched her damp cheek. "I'm so ill-mannered. I should have written to apologize for leaving so early after Taylor's funeral." He followed her eyes to the upright piano. "It's Taylor, isn't it?"

"He always looked forward to having you here." Her glance returned to the piano, where the sheet music Trivett had given Taylor rested, dusty and untouched. "There's more." As much as she'd intended to let them settle in before sharing the disturbing news, she flooded the room with Trivett's story.

"A hanging? That's unheard of in Martonsville. Taylor would be furious. Where did it happen? Who was there? Any witnesses?" Andrew's square theatrical face contorted with outrage as his reaction rose with the tide of his reporter's curiosity.

As usual, he neglected to ask her how all this made her feel. Taylor had dismissed Andrew's inability to console as the characteristic coldness of a life-long city dweller, but that didn't help: his selfishness irked her more than ever.

By the time Promise finished filling in the details for Andrew, the color had drained from Ellen's cheeks. She pulled out a chair from under the table and sank into it. "Your uncle must be writhing in his grave, not to mention what you must be going through." Thank goodness, Ellen more than made up for her brother's thoughtlessness.

But the lovely woman who'd always assured her, "Don't worry, you'll find your mother," stared past her as though she wasn't there. She'd done this before when they gathered with her friends in Boston. At first, Promise had wondered if she'd said something to embarrass her until it occurred to her that Ellen's behavior was that of one who'd suffered some disgrace. Over what, she dared not guess.

Glancing through the window toward Taylor's grave site, she blurted, "Was Duchess here when you came in?"

Andrew rested his hand on her shoulder. "She was with Windsor. Better yet, my horse remembered me. Is that so bad?"

His usual jovial tone returned, a bit too readily for Promise. "That's not what I meant. My new farmhand took Duchess to the market this morning. If she's back, Daffron is back. That's what's bothering me."

"I'm sorry, I'm not sure I understand..." Andrew drew his brows into a thin line. "Banks are closing, and people are losing their jobs. Are you telling me the farm is doing so well you can afford to hire a farmhand?" His voice had a frayed, possessive tone she did not deserve. Yes, Andrew controlled the farm's finances—Taylor had orchestrated that—but apparently he'd forgotten that Mearswood belonged to her.

"Nothing's happened to Fletch, has it?" he added in a breathless afterthought she resented.

"Fletch, Mother Hart, we're all upset. What's worse, Fletch and Daffron don't get along. If I had known Daffron..."

The more Promise said, the deeper the lines on Ellen's forehead. Ellen caught Andrew's eye, pointed her chin toward the door and, without making an effort to hide her distress, mouthed, "*I'm scared, let's go.*"

Panic surged through Promise. *No, not now.* As he was about to respond, she interrupted. "Do me a favor, Andrew? Daffron's probably out in the barn with Fletch. Make sure Fletch is all right. I'll be there soon as I give Ellen something comfortable to wear."

***

The morning shade, a gift from the hickory tree outside Promise's bedroom window, had surrendered to the afternoon heat. Ellen took longer than usual slipping out of her clothing and pulling Promise's overalls over her small city hips. Finally, she inched the straps onto her shoulders. Her painted fingertips fumbled with the crude metal clasps, and by the time she finished buttoning the last button, the strap had already fallen off her shoulder. She scooped a kerchief from the floor and handed it to Promise, her frightened little girl eyes locking onto Promise's.

Without thinking, Promise took the kerchief and was about to reassure her when Ellen cut her off: "Please. Enough about these awful doings, no more!" She paused as though attempting to compose herself, then blurted, "Tie these stupid straps together, will you?"

Promise's fist tightened around the kerchief. Heat surged up her neck and fanned over her sunburned cheeks. Her temples throbbed with self-reproach. Taylor would have used the word, 'hubris'—her belief that the same bravado she flaunted before the horses she'd tamed would strike fear in a man like Daffron. She raised the kerchief, dotted with a burst of brown stars against a buttery background, holding it at arm's length as though it was a critter the dogs had dragged in. "Where did you get this?" she asked, immediately regretting her accusatory tone.

Bristling, Ellen pointed at the foot of the bed. "Your dog, Jasper, dropped it there." Jerking her head in the other direction, she swept her now limp high-styled haircut from the side of her face. "Why? Isn't it yours?"

"That belonged to my mother." Her hand gently tapped her heart. "I keep it in a special place."

"Maybe Mother Hart borrowed it." Ellen's voice had softened.

Promise shook her head. Her own mother had given this to Mother Hart for helping deliver Promise. Other than the carved wooden box like the one Daffron had with him—a coincidence she had yet to understand—it was the only thing of value her mother had owned. She brought the scarf to her face. An indescribable ache tightened her chest. "Not without asking, Mother Hart would never," she murmured.

Ellen picked at a chip in her nail polish. "I hope you don't think I—" she stopped. Her brown eyes flashed hurt, then anger. The floor squealed as she moved to the other side of the room.

Promise raked her fingers through her disheveled hair. Strands of auburn waves came free like her tongue. She pursed her lips. *What am I doing? Alone with Ellen for the first time in months, and instead of weeping, we're fighting. I can do better.* "Of course you didn't take that scarf."

She put her arm around her. "Don't mind me. So much has happened. I feel like a fool. Up until now, I've lived in a make-believe world. I never understood why Taylor stopped me from looking for my mother. It's as though he didn't want me..." Her voice trailed off, and for a moment she felt like a little girl again, crouched on the servant's stairwell of Ellen's home, sketching Mrs. Gills as she braided Ellen's hair, envying every tuck and tug to her daughter's head. Mrs. Gills' humming accompanied the frantic scratching of

Promise's pencil. When she'd finished, she studied her rendition of the strong fingers and trimmed pink nails of a grown woman, her best drawing yet of all she longed for: her very own mother.

Ellen turned and took her by the shoulders. "I wish I could tell you losing a parent—a mother, an adoptive uncle—gets better as time goes by, but it doesn't. You fit your life around losing them. It changes and so will you. You're going to get married, lots of things will be different, understand?" Her brown eyes came alive with the promise of their future as sisters-in-law.

Overwhelmed by this kindness, Promise couldn't bring herself to speak. She went to her bureau drawer, selected her best green ribbon, and slipped it beneath Ellen's shoulder straps.

Ellen inspected the vision of her country self in the splotched mirror. "I've been meaning to have that resilvered," Promise said.

"Don't bother, you'll have plenty of mirrors once you move to Boston. By the way," Ellen's eyes twinkled, "Andrew hopes you'll choose a date for your wedding."

She gathered her slip and stockings from the floor and chatted the way she often did when she was apologizing. "We'll have plenty of time to talk about that."

But Promise had stopped listening; she was thinking about Daffron. Had he gone through her bureau while she was walking Cambridge? How else would her mother's scarf have made its way from beneath her underclothes into Jasper's mouth? How would he have known that she kept her mother's scarf there? If he hadn't been in her cabin during the day, the only other time he could have entered was last night. The possibility took her breath away.

Why, oh why had she taken him on for a whole week? She should have offered the man a few hours of work, maybe less. Perhaps if she explained that she'd checked her ledger and found that the farm wasn't making money enough for his wages, he would accept a bushel of food and go on his way.

Even so, Daffron would peg Fletch as the favored Negro, then drive that peg straight through his heart. There was no doubt about it—her closest friend was in danger, and it was all her doing. One of them, Fletch or Daffron, needed to leave Mearswood. Soon.

CHAPTER 10

Never underestimate the prowess of a madman, for every act he undertakes is the product of thought distorted and pushed to its extreme.

Taylor Crawford, *My Life in Georgia*, 1929

Andrew removed his shirt and hung it on the tree limb, then mopped his forehead with his handkerchief. Southern heat was more suffocating than he'd remembered. He entered the old section of the barn that his mentor, Taylor, had built. Pausing to let his eyes adjust to the shadowed light, smells of horses, manure, and fresh lumber assailed him along with the cacophony of dueling hammers.

He followed the incessant racket past empty stalls draped with aging tack to a partially built stall, where Fletch wielded his hammer, one angry blow after the other. At the adjacent stall stood Promise's new worry, Daffron. Shorter than Fletch, he held a fraction of his muscular girth or his intensity. Something about this lean graying man drove Fletch to pound in staccato bursts that ranged from feverishly competitive to downright unruly. His grunting charged the air with foreboding.

Reaching into a canvas sack for a handful of nails, Fletch glanced at Andrew, then turned away. Andrew sensed it unwise to speak to his friend. There'd be no handshaking, greetings, or exchanges of recent happenings. And, if Andrew's reporter's instincts bore out, later this evening neither of them would sit, as in summers past, on Promise's porch with the chessboard sandwiched between them. He had yet to understand the details of whatever was happening between these two men, but he was certain of one thing—something untoward was unfolding.

Of the horse barns Andrew had visited recently, Fletch's carpentry was the most masterful: skillful, artistic, flawless. Concerned that the original wall would sag once he cut through it, Fletch had chiseled grooves in the old beam and shaped new timbers, one on either side, to support the entryway. Yet now he was acting as though he'd never held a hammer. He bent nail after nail, yanking and tossing them into the aisle that separated him from Daffron. With each toss, Daffron shrieked with glee. Apparently, they were locked in an impromptu competition, with Fletch insuring that Daffron emerged the victor.

The smells, the dust, the atmosphere filled Andrew's head; he pulled out his handkerchief and sneezed. Once, twice, three times. Daffron turned toward him and blinked as though a bright light had just flashed. Ignoring Andrew, he sauntered up to Fletch. "You done wasting Miss Promise's nails? Cause she doesn't want you working on her stalls anymore. She said I'm to finish them." One lie at a time, his voice rose to a screech. The man was losing control.

The wall trembled as Fletch's hammer crashed into it and bounced, stopping dead in the sand at Andrew's feet. The loathing in Fletch's eyes terrified Andrew. Usually self-possessed, this gentle, accomplished man reeled with disgust at being disgorged by the underling. Fletch roiled past, unaware that he'd just clipped Andrew's shoulder.

Daffron started toward Andrew, then stopped and planted his feet in a steadying stance. "Best damned thing happened so far today, him going off like that. Got himself all huffy 'cause I called him 'Sandy the Sandman.'" His breath fouled the air with the aftermath of drink.

He examined Andrew from head to toe. "You look like the kind goes to the Grand Mitreanna Hotel. You ever seen him build one of his sand castles? Tall as a house. Fancy, too. Real entertaining to watch. Enough so's he ought to stay there, not here, not in this barn, not where I'm working." As though it were his creation, he pointed to the beam joining the new section of the barn with the old.

"That's a handsome piece of craftsmanship, wouldn't you say?" Andrew said, hoping to ease the man into a less volatile topic.

"Craftsmanship? Easy for you to say. You have no idea what goes on between men in a barn." Daffron sidled closer.

"You're probably right about that. I spend a fair amount of time in barns with horses and their owners, but I'm no expert about the best way to build the structure itself. I suppose disagreements can happen—"

"Can't stand being in the barn with his kind, you know what I mean? Seeing him leave makes me wondrous happy." Daffron slapped the wall behind him. "Ought to be a law against allowing niggers in barns."

Suddenly, Daffron's bravado shriveled. His sun-beaten face paled. His chest moved in quick panicked breaths. At first, Andrew believed Daffron's heart was failing. The man slid heels-first down the wall. A dust cloud veiled his haunches. His hands clawed at the ground, grabbing as if handles, one to each side, awaited him. He drew his knees to his ears and hung his head.

Andrew tiptoed in an arc around him and positioned himself at the farthest point. The sense of intruding on this, the most profound of human nakedness, resurrected the revulsion he'd experienced when, during his first year as a journalist, he'd visited hospitals for the chronically insane. If he hadn't spent considerable time touring these, he wouldn't have known what to make of this scene.

He'd not stumbled upon a dying heart, but the revival of some reprehensible memory. He recalled how the staff's uneasiness aggravated a patient's volatility, and how doctors in long white coats made cautious efforts to speak to their patients in reassuring tones. Andrew tried to imitate them: "Mr. Mears? Mr. Mears, are you all right?"

"Mr. Mears?" Without raising his head, Daffron repeated the inquiry, prolonging the pronunciation of his name, chanting it with an increasingly mocking intonation as though trying to recall a person from the past.

Andrew backed away.

Face flushed purple, neck muscles tightened and straining, Daffron glared at Andrew. "MR. MEARS? Mr. Mears will always be my father, and don't you forget it," he bellowed. Doves flew from the rafters, agitated wings whirring. With that, he fled.

Andrew gasped. That's it, he thought, leaving the barn in search of Promise, I have to know how on earth she came to have this desperately sick man on her farm. On his way to retrieve his shirt, Daffron sauntered out from behind the barn, tapping tobacco from a pouch into a cigarette paper.

With practiced, albeit trembling, movements, he licked and rolled the paper onto the opposing edge. A perfect union. Not a thread of tobacco protruded from either end of his cigarette. His work had a certain artistry of which he seemed proud. After admiring it, he turned to Andrew. "Smoke?" Andrew shook his head. Daffron slipped the cigarette between his yellowed fingers and glanced at Andrew's unstained hands. "Didn't think so."

Andrew took his words as a warning, one he chose to respect. He imagined how he appeared to Daffron. Between his new paunch, the fine hairs protruding from the neckline of his sleeveless undershirt and those on his blanched arms, he must have seemed physically inept. He slipped his shirt from the branch and quickly put it on.

Daffron's satisfaction had faded into a scowl. He stared at the dark wavy stains that had penetrated the pale Italian leather on Andrew's shoes. From there, he worked his way up Andrew's seersucker trousers. Then, as Andrew fastened the buttons on his shirt, Daffron perused its fine fabric. Not a flicker rippled his bland disinterest until he looked up at Andrew's eyeglasses. He tilted his head and studied them. Coated with sawdust, they must have looked ridiculous. Andrew took them off and rubbed them on his sleeve.

"You always wear those spectacles?"

"Can't see a thing if I don't." Andrew regretted revealing this tidbit. He adjusted the piece across the bridge of his nose and secured the thin gold frames behind his ears, not that that would do much if Daffron chose to rip them off.

"My little girl can't find her words. Think they'd help her?" He reached for Andrew's glasses.

With a quick swipe of his arm, Andrew warded him off. "If she has trouble seeing they will."

Daffron glowered for a moment, then turned toward the pasture, where the women were tending the horses. Some hurtful thought shadowed his eyes. Andrew leaned, just slightly, to get a better look. Daffron flinched. His expression shifted into a foxy alertness.

Good grief, this man is no bumpkin, thought Andrew, drawing back. The wily bastard wants something else.

In that regard, they were alike. The imperious scowl Ellen wore when she'd shredded the letter he'd written to Promise came to mind. "You'll not send this," she said. "If Mother and Daddy were still alive, they'd be ashamed. Dishonored. You made a promise to Taylor, and I'll see that you keep it." Ellen could be uncomfortably direct, especially when she was right.

After his first fiancée—the Boston beauty Promise and Taylor knew nothing about—had returned his engagement ring, his sister had warned him not to commit to anything with Promise, not until he'd recovered his senses. But he refused to listen. Later, Andrew considered jilting Promise but decided this move would ruin him. Whether or not he was thinking clearly, he identified one thing for certain: marrying Promise was central to his future success, and that depended on the inheritance his parents had left in Ellen's control—the inheritance, should he renege on Promise, she'd threatened to sever.

A sour lime smell rose from the powder he'd doused himself with after this morning's bath. Daffron stared at the damp circles under Andrew's arms and snickered. Andrew hadn't intended to acknowledge the man's observation but couldn't stop himself. "I've had enough of this heat. I'm going to the cabin."

"Hold a minute. I have something to show you."

Andrew rolled his shirtsleeves and despite his misgivings waited for Daffron to return from the shed. With the new section of stalls tucked familiarly against the side of the barn, the old structure looked uneasy. Rather than creak as most barns do, it whimpered.

Daffron returned with a couple of old photographs and handed them to Andrew. "Mearswood Plantation when my daddy still owned the place." He spoke the word "plantation" as though the photograph exuded grandeur.

So that's what brought this fella here, Andrew thought as he studied the photos. The manor house, if you could call it that, was nothing more than a small building with a large covered porch surrounding the front and sides. Compared to the photograph of the servants' quarters, Daffron's father's home was palatial, although neither building was remarkable.

What did impress him was the forlorn expression on the Negro man and woman posed in their tattered clothing, exhausted hopelessness creasing their delicate faces.

Daffron pointed to the man and woman. "They weren't slaves if that's why you're screwing up your face." Then he sneered, "But if my daddy had had his way, they would of been."

That did it. Daffron was clearly interfering with the business of the farm, which Andrew was supposed to oversee. He dropped his jaw and was about to tell him to pack his things and clear out when a voice asked, "Pa?"

Daffron froze. "Pa?" the little voice whined again. A child stood squinting into the afternoon haze. She wandered sleepily down the path from the shed, twirling a shock of long wheat-colored hair.

The scorn melted from Daffron's face. He dropped to his knees and felt the child's forehead with the back of his hand. She'd smeared dirt on her face, down the front of a shirt, over her protruding belly. "You're not hot like this morning. You feeling better?"

The little girl nodded, her round face solemn.

"Want a drink of water?" Another nod.

"Pa will get it for you, Beatie. You're gonna be okay, you'll see."

Daffron rested on his heels and twisted toward Andrew. "Mind getting her a cup of water?" His tone became remarkably humble. "And something to eat?" He sucked in a mouthful of air and tightened his belly like a man waiting for the kick he deserved. His eyes widened with fear. He grabbed his daughter, scrambled to his feet, and backed off so fast he almost tripped.

Promise and Ellen walked the horses up the path and stopped within a few feet of Daffron and Beatie. The child scrambled into her father's arms, yelping as though she'd been walloped. Andrew's chestnut horse, Windsor, shifted nervously. Promise put two fingers up.

Morgans were Andrew's favorite breed, and Windsor one of the most elegant Morgans he owned. Andrew watched with satisfaction as Windsor, quick to master Promise's signals, backed half-dozen paces from them. Curious, Cambridge cocked his head to one side then the other.

The child screamed again, louder and more terrified. Daffron loosened her arms from around his neck, then patted her back.

The louder the child cried, the more Promise gawked. Andrew tapped the hand in which she gripped the leather lead. She shifted it to her other hand. He sighed. "For God's sake, Promise, take the horses away."

"Good idea," she murmured, and handed the lead to Ellen.

The little girl straightened in Daffron's arms and opened and closed her fists, with their tiny fingers attached by bands of gossamer skin from her palms to her knuckles, in a baby-like wave. Other than at the circus in the hall of freaks, Andrew had never seen webbed fingers like the child's. He wasn't alone; equally intrigued, Promise stared.

Daffron sheltered the child's hands in his and brought them to his lips. She shrieked with delight, and Daffron kissed her fingers again.

"Is this who I think she is?" Promise's question landed innocently enough.

"Miss Promise, this here's Beatrice Margaret Mears. We call her Beatie." Daffron jiggled Beatie, who rewarded him with a delighted giggle.

"I helped Mother Hart deliver Beatie, but I didn't realize..."

Absorbed by Beatie pointing at the ground, Daffron stopped listening and set her down. She took a few determined steps, watched Ellen and the horses down by the cabin, then scurried back to his knees. "Her ma's sick, couldn't take care of her today."

"What's wrong with her?"

Daffron gazed in the other direction. "Don't know. This morning when I got to the market, my brother-in-law, Acey, told me I'd best get home. By the time I got there, I found Beatie's ma lying in bed, staring at the ceiling, eyes spooked like Crossover Casner just paid her a visit. Beatie was out in the yard, naked."

"Did you give Margaret something to make her feel better?" Promise asked.

"Margaret?" Daffron echoed, as if unfamiliar with his wife's name. "Acey's taking care of her, don't you fret."

"Listen, Promise," Andrew interrupted, "the little girl hasn't eaten. Could you get something for her to eat, and some water, too?"

Beatie grabbed Andrew's legs, gathered a fistful of seersucker in each hand, looked up and beamed. A smile mushroomed on his face. She giggled and headed toward Promise, standing statue-still.

Beatie stood, arms dangling at her sides, staring up at her. Promise squatted. Neither moved. Then Beatie leaped forward, clamped her hands on Promise's cheeks and laughed. Promise peeled Beatie's hands away and held them.

"How old are you?"

"She's almost four," Daffron answered.

"Do you like soft peaches?" The child pulled her hands free and scratched her arm. "How about milk? Soft peaches and milk? That's what I ate when I was your age." Promise waited, and when Beatie didn't answer, stood.

"That would suit her just fine," Daffron said.

"How'd she get to be so shy?"

"Other than to say 'Pa,' she doesn't talk."

"A mute," Andrew murmured.

Fists clenched, Daffron headed toward Andrew. "You calling her stupid?"

Promise stepped in front of Daffron. "That's another way of saying what you just told us."

"You sure?"

"As sure as I know Beatie wants a bowl of peaches."

Andrew sighed. Promise's words had pulled the thorn from the lion's paw. Daffron's face went slack, thank God.

Andrew joined Daffron and Beatie and followed Promise past the gardens towards her cabin. A snake glided from the rock on which it had been sunning and slithered into the tall grass on the knoll. Beatie pulled to a stop and pointed. Crows swooped from the tree limbs, caw-cawing a warning before they arrived at the porch, where an injured baby crow watched from its cage.

Promise squatted beside Beatie. "What happened to her arms?"

"Heat rash," Daffron said.

"That rash is oozing, and that's not good. I'll give her something to eat, then get a salve for her arms." Before Daffron could say anything more, Promise got up and walked to the cabin. Alone.

With Promise's auburn hair coming undone beneath her straw hat, and her blue blouse luffing in the breeze she created, Andrew couldn't help but admire her big-hearted, annoying brand of beauty. And if there was one man he didn't want around, it was Daffron. For obvious reasons and more.

CHAPTER 11

Small towns produce small answers,
and Martonsville is no exception.

Taylor Crawford, journal entry, August 10, 1909
On the occasion of Will Hart's death

Cooper settled himself on the topmost step of the porch—what Aville Louise called their veranda—and clamped two fingers of his three-fingered hand around the Lucky Strikes in his shirt pocket. The wrapper rustled its way out from behind the crush of his badge. Having something soft between his lips soothed him until an annoying strand of tobacco stuck to his tongue. Pppt. He half-spit, half blew air. A foamy wad of tobacco landed on Aville Louise's prize azalea.

The morning after a lynching, Cooper liked to recollect the tempting creatures he'd come to know over the years, their beds hopelessly rumpled, legs intertwined, them squeezing him just the way he liked. It helped him relax. Women, sweet women, oh how he loved them. Plump as a hen or lean as a walking stick, long as they were inclined to find him enjoyable, he was more than willing to indulge their fancies.

Yes, siree. The thought set his divining stick to throbbing in the manliest way.

Women were his downfall, that he had to admit. For the longest time, he couldn't bring himself to keep his distance no matter how much trouble they brought him. A dog is what he'd been, picking up on a bitch's heat, needing to have it, surly till he claimed it. Was a time when the more he had, the more he wanted. Didn't give a donkey's rump if anyone knew, neither.

Till one night, twenty-one years back, he was at Paula Jean Winston's house, and Daffron, that bastard, showed up with Mrs. Aville Louise Peall in tow. They leaned their elbows on Paula Jean's windowsill and got themselves an eyeful of his pasty round ass pumping away.

Goddamn that Daffron, Cooper thought, stretching his legs down to the step closest to the dirt. His cousin was nothing but trouble, been so ever since he was a gruntling.

Aville Louise fussed so about Paula Jean being one of the women in her sewing circle, she forced Cooper into striking a deal. But only after she'd called him a cur, told him he was worthless, companionship-wise, especially when it came to helping her make a baby. "Of the two," she brushed a fly away, "I want a baby more."

She suggested adoption, but Cooper, whose hamper overflowed with problems a husband tended not to discuss with his wife, wasn't drawn to the notion of taking on someone else's. Till Aville Louise gave him the choice of a baby or a visit to the local attorney. Wouldn't look proper for the sheriff of Martonsville to be without a wife, he decided.

Lucky for him, Mother Hart, that nigger lady who had her nose everywhere—from places chewing gum gets stuck to places it'll never go—knew of two babies-in-the-making who'd soon need a home. One would be white through and through, and the other, his. "Well…" Mother Hart hesitated, "there's no telling what color a baby with a mixed mama and white man might be until I see the size of its God's mark, then I'll know for sure."

The notion of having a child of his own stirred something in Cooper. Something he hadn't expected. "Find out for me, will you?" He posed his question in his most gentlemanly tone, hoping Mother Hart wouldn't find a blue spot anchoring his baby's tailbone to a darkie's lot.

He made like Aville Louise's arthritis was acting up again, complicating her early pregnancy. 'Poor thing can hardly move' is what he'd told Deputy Hobbs when he pronounced him acting sheriff, and he and the Mrs. moved out West for a while. Or so he let everyone think.

In fact, they stayed with Aville Louise's cousin in Alabama for the next six months until the baby was born. No need telling Aville Louise this baby was his now, was there? Especially when the child was one of those unusual creatures come sliding out of her golden brown mama covered in rose petals 'n cream.

Unaware he was within listening distance of their bedroom window, Cooper's newly married neighbors had come together on the private side of their curtains with groans that were just now dissolving. He envied the peaceful snores that soon followed. He took a long drag from his cigarette, held it, then let the foggy smoke seep from his nostrils.

Always took him a while to get over a lynching, and this one was no different.

The magnolia in the middle of his front lawn shivered in the morning breeze. He'd planted that tree the year his Suzanne was born, same year he'd started terrorizing niggers with Daffron up Tilden way. Anything to keep Daffron out of Martonsville.

He sighed. He'd gladly made a whore of himself—anything to keep Jim Crow the hell away from his baby girl. But last night he'd driven a crack in his reputation as the toughest sheriff on Georgia's coast and that bothered him. All because of Daffron. Now that was a shame.

Hanging a man who was about to become a father was another shame. Oh hell, what difference did it make, doing away with one nigger instead of another? Cooper reckoned his name and the word "decent" had never tumbled together in anyone's mouth, and he certainly wasn't one to deceive himself with this brand of lie. Though, if the sloshing in his gut was a sign, there was hope for him yet.

"Psst, Coop," a voice whispered.

The sheriff jumped up, pistol in hand. "Who's there?"

Out from behind the roses of the charmin' young thing next door came Acey, his grease-stained Wiley's gas station shirt unbuttoned.

"What's got into you, sneaking up like that?" the sheriff asked, relaxing his hold on his gun. "Almost got yourself blown up."

Acey could barely catch his breath. "It's Margaret. Got home last night and found her throwing her insides out. Couldn't get her to stop."

"She got a fever?" Not that the sheriff knew what to do about Acey's sister, but that was the question Aville Louise asked when their Suzanne was feeling poorly.

"She's all lathered up. Worse than any fever I ever seen." He threw himself onto the step and dropped his head into his hands.

Cooper looked at Acey's wavy uncombed hair and stifled an impulse to reach down and ruffle it. Funny, he'd never before paid much attention to Acey's sandy hair, a shade lighter than Suzanne's. *Don't know what's come over me.*

He squatted, smelled the boy's sour breath. "You sure it isn't you been sick?"

"Once. Only once, on the way over here. I got to thinking about that man we hanged. Felt sorry for him, is all. Don't think I'll ever forget his eyes. They were kind, don't you think, Coop?"

Cooper sat beside Acey and put a hand on his damp shoulder. "Forget that nigger. You got to stop thinking like an old woman. Kind or no, his troubles are over."

"He's gonna haunt me, Coop, I just know it. Matter of fact, he's started already."

"How's that?"

"If it weren't for us hanging him, Margaret wouldn't be home retching."

"You didn't tell her, did you?" The sheriff eyed him, but Acey shook his head, stared back with a hollowness that left the sheriff feeling sorry for the kid.

The blue-eyed boy's puppy-worship had gone, drubbed the first time he'd seen Daffron at work. Damned pity, thought Cooper, realizing how much he'd lapped up Acey's shadowing him, ogling his every move, begging to include him on the hanging circuit.

At first, Daffron would hear none of it, said he was just a kid though Acey was almost eighteen. Old enough to see Daffron for what he is: Trouble, mean filthy trouble.

"Wait here, Acey. I'll get something for Margaret." Cooper opened the screen door slowly to avoid its creaking. But creak it did, loud as any circus barker. He poked his head in, listened for Aville Louise or Suzanne stirring. Other than the soft padding of his wife moving about upstairs, no one greeted him.

He mushed across Aville Louise's soft oriental carpet—part of an inheritance that left them more well-to-do than most and turned Daffron greener than moldy cheese—over its swirling border of reds and blues—the colors of Acey's troubled eyes— through a pattern of green and black paisley that reminded him of Trivett dangling on that limb, and onto the safety of Aville Louise's green hallway runner.

The kitchen was emptier than usual. His wife had given the woman who came every morning to help her with the house the day off. Pleasant woman, with creamy cocoa-colored skin. Dignified, not in a haughty way, but with a quiet sureness, the kind Suzanne had when she gathered the children around her in her schoolhouse.

If Mother Hart hadn't told him Suzanne's real mama had died, he'd have thought Aville Louise's cleaning woman... Cooper reached for the bottle behind the flour on the bottom shelf in the pantry and sighed.

Aville Louise hated that the sheriff of Martonsville kept bootlegged liquor in her pantry. "Imagine what people would say if they found out," she'd scolded.

Imagine. Goddamn. There was so much the townsfolk could imagine. If only Aville Louise knew. He poured some amber liquid into an empty canning jar and clamped the lid. Put it in a limp sack and drew the string, gathering the cloth into a nice tight pucker.

"Give Margaret a tablespoon of this," Cooper told Acey, who sat propped against the banister, knees clutched to his chest. Cooper liked that he sounded smart as Doc Hovner. "Once every three hours," he added.

Acey scurried to his feet. The puppy-worship had returned to his eyes.

"Don't make so much noise," Cooper said, one hand cradling the bottom of the sack, the other gripping the jar's hard mouth. He gave the package to Acey. Maybe its hardness would rub off on the boy, just a little. Enough to jump-start him into manhood.

"Thanks, Coop. If this doesn't help her, nothing will." Acey took the sack and loped off through the neighbor's yard, past the mulberry tree, shirt-tails rising and falling like a heron about to fly.

Cooper lit one more cigarette. His head throbbed; Daffron's staying at Taylor's old place made him nervous. What was his wretched cousin up to? Though he claimed he intended to get his granddaddy's farm back, Daffron wasn't stupid; he knew damn well Taylor Crawford would never have bought the place if the sale hadn't been on the up and up.

Losing his inheritance had riled Daffron, but it wasn't Taylor's fault Daffron's old man was a drunk who'd wager his crippled grandmother if and when he found a sucker willing to take the gamble. Cooper had given it to Daffron straight: "Gambling fever's what pushed your old man to auction off the plantation, not any of Taylor's finagling."

Daffron never forgave him for siding with Taylor. For marrying better. For driving him out of Martonsville. For being smarter. When Daffron locked him in one of his stony stares, Cooper swore he could chew on the man's hate.

That's why Daffron's cozying himself close to Mother Hart's house made him uneasy as a newborn colt with a snout full of bobcat. If Daffron sniffed out the truth about Suzanne's birth, Cooper's life here would be over. What would Suzanne say? What would Aville Louise do?

He gazed at the wicker furniture and potted flowers on her veranda, reminded himself to slow down, think right. Far as he could tell, Mother Hart never lifted her skirt hem to show one ruffle of his secret. Didn't suspect she would neither, no matter what.

White boy Daffron, on the other hand, was the one he didn't trust. The hideous jumpiness that curled his innards when he heard banging on his door in the middle of the night returned. Nope, he'd be damned if he'd take a chance on Daffron finding out about his Suzanne.

He took one last pull on his cigarette, flicked it on the lawn and watched it burn. He knew what Daffron would do to Suzanne and him if he found out she was part colored; he'd seen him cut, carve, burn his victims, then laugh when they thrashed and pleaded and finally fainted from the horror of it all. Then, only then did Daffron call for smelling salts—the man liked his victims awake.

Cooper shivered as only a father could. No way he'd allow that to happen to his daughter. The folks in Whispering Willows had been after Suzanne to open a school for them. He'd have to find a whopper of an excuse to get her to leave her beloved school.

When he did, he'd visit her often, and on the way back, he'd pay his respects to the big-breasted darling lives on the outskirts of town. Cooper sighed. He had that plentiful feeling in his groin again; women brought out the best in his thinking. With Suzanne safe, he would take care of Daffron Mears. He didn't know how just yet, but he would figure it out, he was sure. He scratched his stubble with a matchstick and headed inside. Maybe Aville Louise was feeling frisky.

CHAPTER 12

A mind at war with its heart is one of
nature's most destructive of forces.

Taylor Crawford, *My Life in Georgia*, 1929

Years earlier, hours before Mother Hart gave birth to Fletcher William, she asked her husband, Will, to move the chairs from the porch of their small cabin to the grassy patch at the bottom of the steps. When he'd done so, he gently said, "I've set the chairs in the grass." Too uncomfortable to sleep through the relentless Georgian heat, she sat there gazing at the stars. Will dozed fitfully beside her until she roused him with, "It's time." Will left the chairs in the grass, so after Fletch had been born, she could sit there late at night nursing their infant son.

She loved that story so much she repeated it many times to her friends, who adopted Will's words as their greeting when they came for her. As soon as she heard a frantic father babbling about chairs, she grabbed her birthing bag and rushed to help his baby join the world. But this mournful July afternoon when Thaddeus's son, Randolph Hayes, shouted his news: "The chairs are in the grass," Mother Hart opened her eyes and stared at the ceiling. The more he yelled, the harder it was to pry herself out of bed.

***

What a sorry time to be born, she thought as Fletch stood, outstretched hand ready should she need steadying. She placed her hand in her son's and crawled down from the wagon. When did I start needing him like he once needed me, she asked herself.

"You think your dizziness is a touch of the fever, Mam?"

"Fever?" she repeated absently. "This is worse."

Fletch scowled with what she recognized as concern. Her insistence on being here disturbed him as much as the flimsy excuse he'd given for abandoning his work on Promise's barn worried her. He'd offered to get Promise to come to Thaddeus' home in her place, but she'd refused. Not that Promise wasn't good; she was gentle with the mothers and quick to learn.

Mother had taught her about midwifery, except how to keep the neediness from her eyes when a new baby nursed. Mother was all too familiar with that emptiness. After she'd lost the only man she ever loved, she refused to come undone, not while young Fletch and Trivett were watching. Instead, she tightened her fist around her dignity, forced her face into a tattered smile, and showed them how to live with an aching heart.

Determined to help her boys grow up outside the shadow of their father's murder, she pretended to set it aside so they would do likewise. Unfortunately, that crippled them when it came to understanding what was happening to her now. Pride, hers and theirs, had deprived them of a cleansing slog through grief's swamp. Worse yet, holding back had fooled them into believing she was so strong nothing could touch her.

For a while, even she had believed it, until early this morning when she learned of Trivett's murder. Fletch didn't have to tell her: as soon as she read the horror in his eyes memories exploded to life and with them the urge to unravel. That was her third such urge, her third such denial.

"You sure you're feeling all right, Mam? It's not too late to get Promise." Fletch leaned forward, ready to do her bidding.

"The bruises on your brother's neck are still fresh, and you're going to chance being seen with a white woman? That's the most foolish thing ever come out your mouth, Fletcher William. Stay away from Promise."

No matter how often he had insisted his dealings with Promise were nothing compared to the attraction that had lured his white father to her, Mam narrowed her eyes into slits and accused him of lying. Of course, she was right.

Since reading Dr. Freud, who maintained though a person is outwardly unaware of the consequences of her acts nothing happened by chance, Fletch had come to the conclusion that his escapade with Promise and yesterday's lapse in her judgment were linked by way of retribution.

Still, he understood his mother's worry. She would do anything to keep him from the horror that ended his father and Trivett's lives. Had it not been for Mam's incessant warnings, and Taylor's intrusion into the hours he'd spent alone with Promise, their attraction to one another would have become deeper and more painful. For the most part, fear, self-preservation, and guilt worked against that.

Shame clouded the golden flecks in his brown eyes, and she chided herself for lashing him with her pain. She was about to say more when he put his fingers to his lips and pointed to the back of the wagon.

There in the wagon bed, Randolph Hayes, the handsome lad who had summoned her, lay curled in an earth-brown ball. Annoyed at having bared her emotions in his presence, she was about to caution against repeating her words when his lips fluttered with soft snores. Thank goodness. She'd convinced Fletch the next few hours would be trying enough for Thaddeus and Cornelia; this wasn't the time to tell them.

Randolph's three sisters burst from behind the cabin through a flutter of hens and chicks. "Mother Hart," they called in unison.

"Since when are you wearing your Sunday dresses for play?" was the first thing out of her mouth.

No sooner had she finished than the middle girl, Wenda buried her face in her sister's chest and cried, "But we're having a birthday party for Ma's new baby."

Fletch put a gentle hand on her arm. "You sure you don't want me to get Promise?"

The cabin door opened and closed with the exaggerated caution she'd seen folks use when a beloved had just died. She swept her free hand to hush her son.

"Thought I told you to play quiet till I rang the bell," Thaddeus said to the children as he trudged down the steps toward Mother. His eyes were rimmed in red, the lines around his serious mouth deeper, more tired than usual. "Cornelia was up all the night. First she wanted to walk, then she wanted me to rub her feet and sing to her. When she told me to stop, my heart got to racing. Then she asked me to sing again. She wasn't like this with our other babies."

Mother Hart eyed the bloodstains on his shirt. "What's happened?"

He looked down at his chest. "Oh, that," he stammered. "Cornelia...she was twitching this way and that..." He sniffled. "I was so tired, and the knife was so dull, only thing it pierced was…" He raised his finger with its angry gash. "I was rushing to slice peaches for Cornelia to suck on."

Mother Hart's sigh turned into a whistle. "That's better than what I thought you were getting around to." She patted the back of Fletch's protective hand and gently removed it from her arm. "After I check on Cornelia, I'll brew my best tea. Cornelia, the baby, Thaddeus' finger, everything and everyone is going to be fine." She borrowed the mantra she'd relied on when her boys were young.

"Make sure Thaddeus drinks his tea, you understand, Fletch?"

He nodded same as he would have any other day, but there was no getting past his scrutiny. Not when she was talking this fast.

She turned towards the children. "Lilly, go get overalls for you and your sisters."

"But Ma doesn't want us inside."

"Us is not going inside, you are."

She pulled the drawstring on her birthing bag tight enough to keep its contents from spilling and slipped it over her arm. The stained deerskin bag nudged her thigh just as Trivett had when he was small. For a moment, his sweaty little boy smell filled her nostrils. She breathed deeply, then eased his spirit by assuring it, "A little one is coming to fill your space."

The cabin with its large gathering area and two bedrooms resembled hers. The table to which Thaddeus had added a section each time another baby was born filled the center of the room. On the cook stove, a simmering kettle gave off mare's tails of steam that floated over the counter, where a pile of hacked peach pits rested by Thaddeus' knife.

Pale muslin light shone through the curtains by Cornelia and Thaddeus' bed. "Don't know as it'll be much longer,

Phua," a weary voice said from the bed. Mother Hart smiled. Cornelia was one of the few who still called her by the name her mother had given her.

The front door creaked open. Rooting sounds came from the next room. Cornelia lifted her damp head from her pillow. "I told Thaddeus to keep the children outdoors."

Mother stuffed a worn edge under the braided rug and went into the next room. "Got all three pairs of overalls, Lilly?"

Lilly raised her denim-filled arms. "Tell Mama we're going to make ash cakes for the party."

"That's a sweet child."

The children's bedroom had small beds built out from the walls, one above the other, two on one side, two on the other with room for two more on the inside wall. A hand-sewn doll with one missing leg fell from beneath Lilly's arm. Mother picked it up. "Oh, that's for Mama to hold until she gets her new baby."

"I'll be sure to give it to her," Mother said, setting the doll by her birthing bag. Lilly skipped across the porch singing, "No, sir," to her father's question about having seen her mother.

Mother wrapped a dishcloth around the handle of the iron kettle and lifted it from the back of the stove. Steam drifting toward the open window over the sink coated the cold pump with a rash of tears. She wished she'd thanked Lilly for setting the water to boil. She could have reassured Thaddeus about Cornelia, too. How could she have been so thoughtless?

She filled four cups with water and added fifteen drops of St. John's wort to hers. In Cornelia's cup, she swirled dried peach leaves for her favorite tea. Later, if Cornelia's pain demanded it, she'd add a few drops of skullcap and, if her own pain threatened to undo her, she'd take skullcap, too.

She then recited a passage from the Bible as she always did before delivering a child into the world. "The leaves of the trees were for the healing of the midwife." She glanced out the open window to see if anyone had heard her mistake, then repeated the passage. "The leaves of the trees were for the healing of nations."

A voice from deep within her cautioned: Trivett's death is hobbling your memory.

She'd gotten on after her husband's murder, but this time she doubted she'd be able to move forward, not after having lost the little boy they'd adopted. In failing to protect their son, she'd failed her husband's trust. And though Trivett was a grown man, she'd failed him, too. It wasn't until she heard Fletch's soft voice that she remembered she'd promised to make the men tea. She dropped a slice of ginger into their cups and added one for herself; she could use some soothing, too.

Thaddeus and Fletcher sat at the bottom of the stairs facing one another, a checkerboard balanced on their knees. The sun shone in Thaddeus' eyes. His scowl made her edgier.

"How's Cornelia?" Thaddeus asked, his eyes brimming with suspicion.

"Fletcher, get my ax from the wagon."

The wooden checkers scattered.

"You sure Cornelia's all right?" Thaddeus fretted.

Mother summoned her surest voice. "She will be."

CHAPTER 13

How does the Creator, in all his wisdom, deem to share this gift we call life with mankind who believe justice entails extinguishing its glow?

Taylor Crawford, journal entry, April 30, 1910

When Mother Hart returned, Cornelia was kneeling by the bed, back arched, face pressed to the mattress. The baby hung low inside her. Mother set the cups—St. John's wort to the left and peach tea to the right—on the night table. She bent aside Cornelia and slipped the ax out from under her elbow. "I'm gonna ease the pressure."

Cornelia winced and looked away. "Hurry."

A groan, then the hollow thud of the ax scraping across the floorboards. An ax under the bed cuts the pain of birthing. And of grief.

Mother straddled Cornelia's bare legs and slid her hands down her muscular back, over her once-indented waist to the fleshy round of her hips. She'd taught Cornelia to take charge of her pain, to work it by rocking her hips, panting softly, and whispering after every breath.

"Conversing with the pain eases it into behaving," Cornelia said after she'd relaxed.

At one time I believed that, but not anymore, Mother thought, removing her hands from Cornelia, massaging the tightness knotting her own forehead. Others, who'd begged her to stop the agony of their womanhood being forced wider than they imagined possible, were able to concentrate after she'd convinced them of the power of their pain: "Without it, you'd abandon the task nature set out for you to do."

Her words held true if the hurt was lightning quick and no bigger than a teardrop. When it wasn't, she drowned their pain with potent herb teas, the same ones she drank to quiet memories of Will's death. Problem was, her pain had stretched her so far, it threatened to turn her heart inside out, render her incapable of attending to the dangerous job she had yet to complete.

Cornelia groaned. "This one's giving me trouble, Phua. This baby's wrong, I can feel it."

"You need the slop pot before you settle?"

Cornelia nodded. Mother fetched the enamel pot from beneath the night table. "Just put it on the floor," Cornelia said.

When she finished peeing, she crawled to the foot of the bed and sat her backside on the clean muslin sheets she'd put down for this very purpose. Mother propped her neck and shoulders with pillows. When she'd made Cornelia as comfortable as any woman in the birthing way could be, she washed her hands in the tub Thaddeus had placed at the foot of the bed. "We'll use curly dock oil to help that child slide out easy."

She wiped the yellow oil around her close-cut nails, fingers, and palms. When they were soft as new butter, she scooped a hint more and rubbed it in small firm circles over Cornelia's opening.

"That's nice, Phua, so nice." Seconds later, her face twisted with pain.

Mother Hart pushed herself up from her knees, gathered her skirt, and joined Cornelia, lying there as God, with Thaddeus' help, had created her—darkened nipples and swollen breasts resting on her rounded belly, the mark of her connection with her own mother flattened into a reminder of what once was. She held a lavender compress to Cornelia's forehead and waited until the pain had done its work. When it had passed, she returned to the foot of the bed.

Cornelia lifted her head, her face scribbled with worry.

"Another pain, Cornelia?"

She dropped back into her flattened pillow.

"Try this tea, it will help you relax." Mother Hart supported her head with one hand and was about to reach for the cup when the next pain overpowered Cornelia.

"Ah," she cried.

Mother Hart climbed on the bed and worked her legs under Cornelia's shoulders. Cornelia puffed her cheeks, forced her peachy breath out slowly, then as the pain worsened, in quick little bellows. When it was over, she rested her head against Mother. Cornelia's hair, freed from the knot atop her head, covered Mother's chest with damp black waves like Will's had when they'd laid his limp body in her arms.

She slid her hands along Cornelia's narrow honey-colored face, humming same as she'd done for Will. His tortures had left his beautiful face wet and contorted like Cornelia's. She stroked her damp cheeks, hummed a little more, then stroked and hummed some more. No matter how sweetly she hummed or how fast she stroked, there was no bringing Will back. This she knew. She told her hands to stop stroking Cornelia, but they moved faster.

"Phua, enough." Cornelia looked up, her brown eyelashes touching her eyebrows, her face a muddy mix of annoyance and strain that suddenly lightened with recognition. "I've lost my water, Phua. I want to push." Her gaze became fixed; she'd taken to concentrating.

Mother scrambled off the bed and searched her birthing bag. *Where did I put my twine? Why didn't I check my bag before I left home?* She tossed her notebook, scissors, bandages, towels, and soap aside. *My twine's gone missing.* She lifted her scissors and dropped them, did the same with her other things, then rummaged through them once more, just in case.

She ran to the front door, yanked it open, and hollered, "Fletcher, baby's coming, and I can't find the twine to tie it off with. Look in the wagon. Hurry!"

Cornelia's screaming ended with a grunt each time she pushed. Missing twine was all Mother Hart could think about. "What will Cornelia say when she hears the midwife lost her twine?" she mumbled, her mouth erupting into a maniacal grin. "Without it, Daffron can't hang our baby boys," she announced.

Cornelia had stopped pushing and was panting. "Phua, what's happening to you? Why are you talking nonsense?" Her worried voice, her woman's smells brought Mother back.

She peered at Cornelia's opening. There, waiting to get out, not a soft wet head, but skin that had no business showing itself first. Mother Hart splashed water over her hands and scrubbed them good. "With this water, I cleanse my thoughts of demons," she prayed, dipping her hands in the basin and bringing them up to dry.

She rubbed them with oil and slid her fingers between Cornelia and the baby. Though its slippery sack formed a thin barrier between her and its arm, the smallest of fingertips wiggled within her grasp. "It's spreading my bones apart," cried Cornelia.

Extending the baby's arm, Mother eased the hand through its satiny caul, past its head, and out into the world. Cornelia pushed. The back of the shoulder followed with the head tucked close. The little body slipped into Mother's large waiting hands.

The boy child glistened in the afternoon light, flopped silently until, struck by the change he'd just endured, he wailed. Mucus drained from his nose and mouth as she placed him, attached by his still throbbing cord, face down on his mother's breast. At this, his first encounter with the touch of another human, the poor newborn flinched.

And why shouldn't he? The blue splotch on his behind, a mere spill of God's ink, was a reminder to all dark babies that they were like his own son, condemned to be different from the start. A cruel joke, thought Mother, as if between now and the next few hours, weeks, months, or years—whenever that mark disappeared—his life wouldn't be complicated enough.

Cornelia counted his fingers and toes, then ran her fingertip over his sweet brown forehead, pushed his damp down this way and that, and covered his face with teary soft kisses.

The curls of his pearly gray cord would pulse a few minutes more. It smelled of iron much like the earth during a spring rain.

Mother sloshed water in the basin as she cleaned Cornelia, who'd not torn an inch, then the baby. She hummed the same lullaby she'd hummed for her little boys, one her own, and Trivett, the one God sent to her to care for. She folded one hand over the other to keep them from shaking and swallowed hard.

"Rest, both of you," she said, lowering the sheet over them and leaving to answer the knock on the door.

Through the haze of the screen, she eyed the twine in Fletch's palm. "Tell Will he has another fine son," she told him, mistakenly repeating the name her own mother had called out after Fletcher had been born.

Fletch winced. "Mam? You feeling poorly again?"

Seeing the shock on her son's face brought back the oddity of her words. "Can't help it if the past drops in at a time like this, now can I?" She stroked his chin, took the sack from his hand and added, "I'm fine, truly."

Thaddeus had set the checkerboard aside and was standing to hug his children. "What will you name your fine boy?" she asked.

"Cornelia and I...we were thinking of Whittling."

Mother thought for a moment. "Whittling," she repeated. "Because he looks like a shaving that escaped the hanging tree." She took in Thaddeus' shock, then closed the door.

"Barbed talk isn't like her. Something's nettled her mind," she overheard him say. Much to her relief, the good man understood.

She paused by the bed: the baby had fallen asleep, and Cornelia was concentrating. "Good," Mother murmured, pushing the curtains aside and tossing the bloody water out the window. Then she slipped the basin under Cornelia. Within minutes, the dark red bumps of the second birth quivered against the white enamel. Mother checked to make sure everything had been emptied.

After a few minutes, the cord went still. She lowered it into the basin and placed it alongside the baby. She tied the twine into a slipknot, eased it close to the baby, and prayed silently: *Let this be the only rope you'll ever know.* With Cornelia's other babies, she'd waited a full hour for the second birth to stop pulsing before separating it. Today, she cut this baby free.

Outside, Thaddeus carried a small peach tree in a bucket to the hole he'd dug hours earlier. As he'd done for each of his children, he would plant the sapling along with the afterbirth in hopes the youngest child would never know hunger. "Is this what you're waiting for?" Mother asked, handing Thaddeus the basin. The happy sound of the children scurrying into the cabin after their father was her answer.

Fletcher took the basin and set it on the chair. "I do believe Whittling has led me to a decision I've been avoiding," she told him.

"Have you made yourself a promise, Mam?"

"I have, Fletcher William, I have."

"Are you going to tell me what it is?"

A glimmer of happiness, the likes of which she hadn't observed since Taylor died, shone in her son's gentle eyes. His face glowed as though he pictured her engaged in a worthwhile deed, an act that would change them all for the better. He'd guessed both right and wrong.

Before she could answer, Thaddeus and Lilly came out of the cabin, he wearing a soft smile, carrying Mother's belongings, Lilly concentrating on the contents of a small basket pressed to her chest. "Mama says we need to save our ash cakes till Whittling grows his teeth."

"I agree with your mama. How's Cornelia?" Mother asked Thaddeus.

"She told me what you done for her and our baby. I'm grateful, Phua." He nodded to Lilly, who handed her the basket.

"No need to pay me. You and Cornelia are like family." Mother counted five speckled eggs in a bed of hay.

"T'ain't much, one for each baby. I'd give you more if I had 'em to give."

"Five should make a fine supper."

The baby started crying, a robust, healthy sound. Thaddeus listened and as he did, handed the birthing bag to Fletch and the ax to Mother Hart. "You'll be needing this," he said.

So somber was his tone that Mother Hart was certain he'd guessed her vengeful vow. She caught the startled recognition in Fletcher's eyes and averted hers. "Go, Thaddeus, see to your family."

While Fletch hitched Cassiopeia to the wagon, Mother hoisted herself onto the seat, positioned the ax under her foot, arranged her skirt, and settled the basket in her lap. Fatigue, heavier than a rain-drenched cloak, settled on her. She sighed; she'd set out to be strong, and that's what she'd done. Barely.

As Fletch climbed beside her, she prayed her sanity would serve her enough to fulfill her vow. She wedged the basket between her hip and the side of the seat farthest from her son, where he wouldn't see two of her eggs lay broken and oozing.

CHAPTER 14

Bridged by anger, soothing words cease to flow.

Taylor Crawford, journal entry, August 10, 1909
On the occasion of Will Hart's death

"Here it is," Promise said, easing her way outdoors as she balanced a bowl brimming with milk and peaches and the child-sized spoon that she'd once used. Sprawled on the lowest step, legs stretched before him, Daffron twisted toward the porch where she tapped her foot in a gritty one-two-get-up-here rhythm.

She ignored his grinning familiarity and fixed her eyes on Beatie. The child had interrupted her game of gathering twigs from around her father's feet to scrub at the rash collaring her neck.

Neither Andrew, perched nearby on the railing nor Ellen, seated below him on the bench, knees tucked to her chest in an unlikely girlish pose, took their eyes from Promise. "Daffron, you've got two seconds to get up here," Promise said.

"Just trying to get you to have some fun like my Beatie here," he said, his forefinger running along the confident protrusion of his lower lip.

"Keep in mind who hired whom."

He scurried up the steps, placed a hand on either side of the bowl and tried to turn, but Promise held fast. His face lit with startled surprise.

"Sorry, Daffron, I must have missed your polite acknowledgment of which one of us is boss here."

His back stiffened. "I'll remember, Miss Promise. I sure will," he mumbled.

Before he could place the bowl in Beatie's lap, she jumped up, grabbed a fistful of peaches, and mushed them into her mouth. She chewed greedily and swallowed, milk dribbling from her chin. Her eyes, large plum-colored spheres surrounded by fine yellow lashes, dwarfed her small round face. She raised her spoon to Promise and giggled the kind of giggle little girls make when sharing secrets. The child reached for her. Her face was dirty, fingers webbed, and her arms crawled with rash, but her spunk and porcelain beauty enchanted Promise.

Which wasn't lost on Daffron, who absorbed this attraction with narrow-eyed satisfaction. Had his wife, Margaret, not become ill, Promise suspected that he would have conjured up another excuse to bring his little girl here. The child served as his shield—a sweet distraction that deterred Promise from telling him to leave. Sure enough, he was using Beatie as bait.

Even so, Promise couldn't help but return Beatie's smile. That the little girl had taken to her so readily warmed her heart. Whether she was flattering herself made no difference. Although robbing Beatie's attention from her father clearly mattered. What else could have made him so surly?

Daffron tucked the spoon into his daughter's fist. "Show everyone you know how to eat proper." She ignored his prompt a defiant moment longer—enough for her audience to revel in the aggravation she was causing him—then plunged the spoon into the bowl.

Promise planted herself inches from Daffron's feet, where her shadow reclaimed the stairway. "That rash needs tending. I can't chance Beatie spreading her infection to my animals." Edginess wasn't like her, but his taking advantage of his daughter disgusted her. And the child—well, there was more to her than the rash; the little girl's vulnerability unsettled her, so much so she wanted Beatie in sight, where she could keep her from... She dared not guess what.

Well looky here, Daffron's smirk seemed to say, I finally got a rise out of the lady. "Give it a day or two more, it'll go away," he said, turning away.

"Before putting Beatie to bed, you're going to give her a bath. First, heat a tub of water until it's lukewarm. Not hot, you hear? Lukewarm. Then lather her up good with this." Promise pulled a bar of oatmeal soap from her pocket and tossed it at him. "It'll help dry those sores. In the meantime, Ellen and I will get her a salve."

Daffron caught the soap. "Where—," he started to say when Ellen squeezed past him.

"You're leaving?" Andrew's panicked question.

By the time the women reached the edge of the woods, Ellen's eyes glowed with intensity, and her usually soft voice took on that thin, squeaky quality that meant she was upset. "I'd go anywhere to get away from that man." She grabbed Promise's arms and twirled her to face her head on. "Tell me, what is he doing here?"

"Staying within eyesight."

"What's that supposed to mean?"

Promise twisted herself free. "He and I have business."

"Business? What kind of business?"

The woman wouldn't let up. Her we-up-North-know-better-than-you-down-South attitude had surfaced. Promise recalled prickly political discussions in Boston when she diffused an issue with an abrupt change of topic. But this barrage had a targeted quality, as though Ellen, who'd never paid much mind to whether or not the farm flourished, actually cared. Promise wasn't sure what to think. "It's personal business."

"Personal? What could be personal with the likes of that man?"

Promise picked up a twig and began stripping it of its bark. "If you must know, Daffron claims he was acquainted with my mama." Admitting this awful truth brought a shiver of relief. That he had had a connection to her mother, however remote, ignited long-held possibilities of learning about the mother she'd never met. Daffron had unwittingly released something in her she hadn't fully understood: She would do anything, absolutely anything, for a glimpse into her mother's life.

But Ellen persisted. "Your mother? How?"

Promise questioned the wisdom of sharing her precious morsels, but talking about her mother brought her to life, as though she might turn and find her standing there, arms wide open. "He knew her when she was a girl of fifteen, playing piano for the Baptists in town. Every once a while he'd buy her a cola."

"Even so, is that worth having him here? And that child?"

"What else was I supposed to do? Do you have any idea what might happen if I let him think I'm afraid of him?"

Ellen eyed her appraisingly. "But he does scare you, right?"

Promise nodded. "More than you know."

"I still don't understand. Why do you care what he thinks?"

"Because he's got it in his head that I'll tremble the minute his shadow crosses mine, and I refuse to oblige him."

Ellen slipped an arm around her waist. "I'm afraid that doesn't make sense, not to me at least."

"Lots of things don't make sense."

As they walked along the root-studded path to Mother Hart's cabin, Promise's thoughts drifted to the woman who would set whatever she was working on aside and listen—no questions asked, no judgments rendered—whenever she fretted that her mother might be gone for good. She realized she hadn't seen her since she'd tried to comfort her over Trivett. She'd meant to look in on her earlier. Then it hit her: Neither of them would see Trivett again. Her eyes welled.

Ellen rubbed her arm. "Hey, are you all right?"

"I miss—"

"Fletch?"

Embarrassed at Ellen's insight, she found herself agreeing: she missed Fletch more than she liked to admit—his ready availability, the comfort of knowing he was nearby, the ease with which they talked about almost everything. She'd taken their unfettered life for granted, until yesterday.

"The last couple days have been hard on him. I hope he understands I had to hire Daffron. I had no choice. If I hadn't, he would have accused Fletch of taking a job that belonged to a white man." Ellen wrinkled her face in confusion. "To put it simply, if I keep Daffron busy, he won't have time to bother Fletch."

"That's what Andrew has been saying—you think more about Fletch than about him."

Promise didn't care for the direction this conversation was taking.

"When you work with someone from dawn to dusk, that person tends to absorb your thoughts." She shrugged. "It's natural. But that will have to change if I'm going to marry Andrew, won't it?"

"You don't sound sure."

"Would you be? The marriage was Taylor's idea. He knew I'd balk, so he waited till he was on his deathbed to ask me to honor his memory by marrying Andrew. That's when he told me that he and Andrew had been exchanging letters about the topic of our marriage for quite some time—without saying a word to me. I felt like a horse, trapped in the middle of a shabby trade. Taylor should have spoken to me first. Instead, he gave me no time to object. He knew this marriage would take me from everyone I love, but he arranged it anyway. Above all, it'll make it harder for me to find my mother. I'll never forgive him for that."

"For which, waiting until last minute or the marriage?"

Promise bristled; what was it with Ellen and this marriage? Her thoughts raced back over the letters she'd sent her. Usually, they were about the people and events on the farm, although now she wondered if, in a bout of foolish anger, she'd mentioned the horrible incident with Fletch?

Her heart pounded as she recalled Taylor the winter before he'd taken ill, walking in on her and Fletch, skin to skin in the barn. Sensing his presence, Fletch scrambled to his feet, shoved one leg into his overalls, and hobbled half-naked past Taylor in the doorway, swiping at him with his hat, hissing, "You were the one I trusted."

Despite what he'd thought he'd witnessed in the shadowy barn, their urges had gone unsatisfied. With Fletch's back to Taylor, he couldn't have seen Fletch's passion melt. Even now, her face burned with embarrassment. The humiliation of it all. Worse yet, he'd accused Fletch of stealing his trust—not his niece, but his trust. That cut deepest, more than him seeing their naked passion, than his unexpected outrage, than being abandoned, again.

Brokenhearted, she added Fletch to her list of those she'd lost, those who should have been a part of her life: a mother, father, and a lover.

That evening, when Mother Hart joined them in the cabin to make their supper, Taylor insisted over Promise's tearful protests that he tell her, right then and there. As naked as she'd been in the barn with Taylor, now clothed with her offense fully exposed, she felt more naked than ever. For she'd done the unconscionable—endangered Fletch's life. She braced herself for the humiliation, which she fully deserved, and, not sensing the outrage she'd expected from Mother Hart, turned toward Taylor, who nodded in Mother's direction.

Promise took a shaky breath and forced herself to absorb the anguish in Mother Hart's eyes. "I always thought I was plenty smart, that I could sort out complications, but standing here right now, I'm not sure what I know and don't know, other than I could have done Fletch unforgivable harm and that my thoughtlessness has caused you hideous pain." Her words hit the air, and Mother Hart withdrew her gaze to the floor. Without uttering a word, Mother agreed that yes, she'd chanced putting Fletch's life at risk, and that she had disturbed Mother's memories, most likely of Will Hart's horrific murder.

She drew her shoulders up to her ears and her jaw dropped open. "I'm sorry...so very sorry...I should never have let things go that far." She searched Mother's eyelids for a flicker, her hand to wipe the perspiration dotting her upper lip, for a sign that her generous heart was softening. But she stood, stone still. Just as she was about to go on, Mother interrupted.

"You're some headstrong all right, Miss Promise Mears Crawford, always have been, and no one is about to say you've done right. But my foolish Fletch is as much to blame as you. My boy should have known better...he was by my side the night they took his father...he witnessed the devil's handiwork." She paused, giving her words time to swell with intensity, then peered into Promise's eyes. "You do you understand what I'm driving at, don't you, Promise? Women like us can be tricked into making way for the devil's handiwork, into unlocking hatred's doors, kicking them wide open." She broke her gaze, and took a deep breath, as though to rein in anything hurtful she might mistakenly say.

From then on, Mother measured her words, relegated them to the realm of the necessary. Without the closeness Promise once took for granted, she seemed to no longer exist in Mother's eyes. Someone else had died...this time it was her.

In studying Ellen's questioning eyes, she knew without a doubt that she would never, never have shared anything so personal with her. She barely allowed herself to dwell on such moments and wouldn't think of putting them in writing for Ellen. The need to keep Fletch from harm rose more urgently than ever; she made silence her gift to him in hopes it would make up for never having given him the fullness of the gift she'd once meant as his.

Ellen gnawed her lip. "I'm sorry, I still don't understand why you hired Daffron."

What more could she say? Ellen didn't know that Daffron's father had lashed his young wrists to a tack post, loosened the leather traces, and whipped him senseless. All for being lazy. There was no point in explaining further, of telling Ellen that hours earlier in a fit of anger, she'd planned to deal with Daffron by breaking his spirit as though he were nothing more than an unruly mule. Fortunately, his daughter had clamped her tiny fingers against Promise's face, inadvertently reminding her of her own desperate longing for a father. That's when she realized the man she intended to harm was the father Beatie loved.

CHAPTER 15

Just as the assurance of freedom is a country's most significant offering to its citizens, so, too, the assurance of sanity is the mind's greatest gift to its spirit.

Taylor Crawford, *My Life in Georgia*, 1929

To stand in Mother Hart's herb gardens was to bathe in magic. Beds of swaying echinacea cones, dutiful lavender, and furry-leafed sage. Bees and butterflies in yellow and black uniforms, waltzing with flower after flower. Hummingbirds hovering, darting, gathering evening meals. The gentle order refreshed and soothed.

Not so this evening. Uprooted clumps of broken-stemmed tansy had been scattered along the path. Floated in water, the tiny gold button flowers gave off a foul odor that kept pests away. Mother Hart never wasted a blossom no matter how small. Every part of every plant had its purpose. If she didn't grind it into tinctures or poultices, she saved the seeds and returned the stalks to the soil. Such was the life-to-death-to-life force among the colorful amaranth globes, papery chamomile, and lobed hyssop. Now that was gone. The earth had been gashed. Beauty banished.

A covered walkway connected Mother's cabin to her summer kitchen. Wilted remains of herbs and flowers lay heaped on the table across from the cook stove. Disorder was unlike Mother Hart. Promise exchanged worried glances with Ellen.

"Mother Hart?" Not hearing her stir, Promise broke into a run. Within seconds, slippery pine needles along the path brought her down. She scrambled to her feet and called again louder, dreading what she would find. "Mother Hart?" An ominous rumbling answered.

By the time she reached the summer kitchen, the lid on the pot was spitting a boiling infusion into the air. She wrapped a dishtowel around the handle and lifted the lid; a bitter cloud escaped. Dark droplets collected on the wall. She yanked the pot from the stove and slid it onto a warped metal slab. The stack of aging catalogs on which it was perched wobbled dangerously. She steadied it and turned to find Mother Hart looking slump-shouldered and crazy mean.

Wisps of gray hair snaked from her braids over her breasts. Tatters of garden debris streaked her white nightgown, the garment she'd been wearing early this morning.

"I made that for Trivett's wife, poor Lizbeth," Mother said, her fingers white from pressing against her folded arms. "Herbs and oats for the melancholy that's sure to come once she hears what they did to him. I know, believe me." She brought her hands to her face and massaged her graying eyebrows. "It might set in tonight or later, but it'll roost for sure. And when it does, she'll learn the full meaning of torment."

"I'm worried about her, too." Promise's voice caught in her throat.

"Oh, sweet Jesus, I prayed they'd leave him be. But men in white hoods don't tend to work that way, now do they?" Her question seethed flat and dark as her stove. She stared as if in a trance, her right arm on her breast, chin cupped in her palm, the veins along the back of her hand twitching.

Edging closer, Ellen stepped on a pile of dried twigs.

Suddenly alert, Mother glanced past Ellen. "I raised Trivett like he was my own sweet baby," she murmured, searching the woods as though she might spot him, fishin' pole in one hand, a string of shimmering sunnies in the other.

Finger to her lips, Promise signaled Ellen to keep silent. "Is there anything I can do to help?" Ellen's voice wavered.

Mother Hart grabbed the railing and shrieked. "White girl, was you one of them?" Her eyes flashed, and a banshee-like fury scorched the air.

Ellen backed into a rock at the edge of the borage bed and fell. "Of course not," she whimpered, propping herself up from within the jumble of cracked plants.

"You're in need of a good holding," Promise said, borrowing the words this big-hearted woman had often whispered to her. She'd not dared so much as brush against her since Taylor wedged uneasiness between them, but now she touched her hands lightly to Mother's trembling shoulders and, lest she provoked her beyond repair, held her at a cautious distance. The moments passed long and slow, weighted by the changes taking hold of Mother.

At last, Mother relaxed, just slightly, enough for Promise to draw her close. Breathing her scent, a mix of oatmeal soap and pungent potions, she pressed her face to Mother's damp back and chanted, "Hush, Phua, hush," but Mother trembled more. Promise worried she was losing her to grief.

Mouth clamped, full freckled cheeks drawn into a frown, Mother shook herself free. An unholy calm was taking hold.

She studied Promise's wet face. "Why this boy?" she stammered, her lips quivering. "Why now?" She stretched her arms and thrashed the air with her fists. "Wasn't hanging my Will enough? Why again?"

Ellen waved. Promise shook her head, hoping to ward her off, but Ellen persisted, tentatively at first, then more frantically. Finally, she shouted, "Promise, the stove!" Gray smoke was seeping from the oven door.

Mother Hart beat Promise to the stove and whisked the dishtowel from the floor. "My cornbread," she moaned, yanking the door open. "Ruined, everything's ruined." She grabbed the smoking skillet and swung it to the hot pad on the table. The weight of the cast iron set the table's tired wooden legs to swaying. Smoldering edges framed the bread, now a mass of blackened crust. "That was for your supper." Mother pointed to a screened dome; beneath it, a platter of fried chicken.

"We'll cut away the burn and eat it anyway," Ellen said with a doubtful smile.

Mother shuffled toward her cabin, flicking her wrist. "Do whatever you please."

Promise followed, her footsteps sadly inconsequential. When Mother had closed the door to her room, Promise invited Ellen into the cabin. "Why don't you come in? I'm going to make her a cup of tea—the one she drinks that calms her."

"No, thank you," Ellen said, her voice strangely soft and thin, "I'll wait here." She picked absently at the dried bark on the outside cabin wall. The healthy reddish coloring she'd gained from spending the afternoon outdoors had faded. She tugged at the buckles on her borrowed overalls. They smelled of horses, hay, her tired cologne.

No doubt about it, Mother's outburst was having an effect. Exactly what Promise dared not guess. Ellen scrubbed at invisible grime hidden deep within her pores. A thought smoldered, sure as Mother's oven: Ellen abhorred the rural South, didn't like having to accompany Andrew. Never had. Life on Mearswood Farm was too real, too soiled, too close to the concerns she and her like-minded friends discussed over the delicate clatter of teacups returning to their saucers.

"Are you sure you won't come in?" Saturated with the quiet, ladylike politeness Mother Hart had always insisted upon, Promise's words hung heavy between them. Far from polite, she was putting Ellen to the test.

She spoke as she would to a pony that was about to buck. "Mother didn't mean what she said. Come in." She held the door open with one arm and beckoned Ellen with the other, then thought about pulling back, but too late. Splayed as she was, she'd left herself open.

Sizing up the situation, Ellen looked away. Her voice, reedy as Promise had ever heard it, trembled with humiliation and, dare she say it? Shame. "You don't understand. How can I bring myself to go into Mother's house when I've refused to have a Negro woman in mine?"

In her letters, she'd described the tensions within Boston's Anti-Lynching League and her refusal to allow a group of Negro women to attend an important meeting she'd hosted in her home. Intent on exposing a "commonly held falsehood"—that white women needed protection from Negro men—she argued that the group best suited to evoke the public's sympathy consisted exclusively of white women. In her return letter, Promise had criticized her logic, saying it made little sense when the Mother Harts of the world had more to lose. Being one who chewed forever on the slightest criticism, Ellen had not forgotten.

Her eyes took on a blue aloofness. She folded her arms across her chest. "I can't." She broke from Promise's incredulous gaze. "Besides, if I compromise the point of view I urged others to adopt, I couldn't live with myself. You see, I'm a lot like your uncle—when I take a position on an issue, I stake my reputation on that stand."

The image of Taylor in the barn after Fletch had fled intruded on Promise's thoughts. "Even if your stand is wrong?" With each passing moment, the screen door grew heavier, the rust more enmeshed in its fibers. "Andrew will wonder what's taking us so long. Why don't you head back? I'll be along later." And without waiting, Promise let the door snap shut.

CHAPTER 16

In my heart's darkness lurks my truest self.

Taylor's journal entry: August 15, 1909

Ellen refused to leave Mother Hart's unescorted. She clung to Promise's arm and sulked all the way back to the cabin. "The night animals are more frightened of you," Promise said, in an attempt to reassure her that a family of raccoons meant her no harm. She spoke gently about how Ellen's thinking worked against her. "It makes no sense to try to pass a law against lynching and, at the same time, prevent Negro women who are profoundly affected by this horror from joining your fight. Don't you see? You're gagging them with a different kind of rope. One that is just as disrespectful."

Not a flicker of understanding crossed Ellen's face. Only, "That's the rule—no Negroes." The lantern from Promise's cabin glimmered through the trees, and Ellen stomped off, slamming finality in the face of remorse.

A hickory leaf strayed past Promise, grazed the lid on Mother's cast-iron skillet and drifted to the ground. She peeled the underside of her arm from the sticky pan and shifted it to her other side. Her damp skin, hair, and stained overalls smelled of singed cornbread. The only thing to escape charring was hidden inside, where it was still raw.

She climbed the steps to the porch and peered through the window into the kitchen just as the platter in Ellen's hand slipped and crashed onto the counter by the sink. Ignoring the mess, Ellen pumped water, then flipped the huge bar of soap between her greasy hands, scrubbed, lathered, rinsed, and started over. Like the fastidious raccoons that had frightened her, once wasn't clean enough.

Hunched over the table, the first three buttons of his shirt open, shirtsleeves rolled as far up as his arms allowed, Andrew was thoroughly engrossed in writing his first installment in a series about Taylor. Oblivious to the noise, he read what he'd written, scratched out a line, and wrote more.

By the time he finished, Ellen was hovering at his shoulder. "You startled me," he said, stuffing his papers into a pile and setting them aside. He twisted in his chair, blocking his work from her view.

But Ellen paid not a horse's whinny of attention. Instead, she recounted Mother Hart's outburst. "Something awful happened to her, her mind went," she leaned into Andrew's face and snapped her fingers, "like that."

Andrew studied his sister, no doubt wondering what she wasn't telling him. Whatever misery it entailed, she'd allowed it to push her into taking the words of a grief-stricken woman personally. He refrained from pointing out the implausibility of Mother Hart calling anyone, much less Ellen, a racist.

What can I do to help?" he asked quietly.

Ellen crouched in front of him. "This place is about to erupt, I can feel it. We need to leave. Please. First thing tomorrow."

He blinked in reply. Ellen tapped his knee, and when he didn't answer, she lowered her eyes and touched her fingertips to her brother's shoulder. Andrew didn't respond.

Moved by Ellen's vulnerability and puzzled by Andrew's aloofness, a heaviness settled within Promise. Unlike any feeling she'd known, she struggled to put a name to its soggy presence. She searched the legions of words Taylor had strutted out whenever they played word games. Only one came to mind: Sadness. Deceptively simple, a pedestrian choice, her childish word captured the pall this evening had left behind: Sadness, immense and profound.

Promise stepped onto the threshold of the kitchen, her heart tightening with an unfamiliar fatigue. Not the exhaustion that consumes after a day of mending fences and relents with a night's rest, but the kind powerful enough to drain an uplifting memory of its joy. She closed the door behind her with a brisk click that interrupted the uneasy stillness.

Andrew and Ellen watched in silence as she walked past the glimmering wafers of mica wedged within the fireplace's milky quartz—mementos of Taylor's spare time pursuits in New England before he'd been drawn to this place—past the twin rockers he'd made before complications had marred their lives. She was within a yard of Ellen when Andrew sloughed his sister's hand off his shoulder and leaned toward her. Oddly pleased, Ellen flashed a knowing smile at Promise and stepped aside.

Promise was about to set the skillet of cornbread on the table when Ellen took it saying, "Here, let me help."

Promise shot her a curious scowl. Was this an apology? Breathless, awkward, but an apology nonetheless?

Ellen turned to her brother. "Hungry?"

Neither Andrew nor Promise answered. The kerosene burned unevenly in the lantern, adding a dark twist of smoke to the dense air. Ellen rifled through the cabinet for a knife. She sliced the cornbread in half, in half again, and again, mashing it into pieces.

Promise eased into the middle of the room and, as though Ellen were a skittish pony, lowered her hands to her sides. "Try not to be angry with Mother Hart. Her outburst was my fault, not hers. I should have known better than to bring you there so soon after Trivett." She kept her voice soft and calm. "Imagine how Mother feels." Ellen fixed her eyes on the clock. "Trivett was like a son to her. And his death...his death marks the beginning of something we've all been afraid of..." She searched Ellen's face for a glimmer of understanding and, finding none, went on, "Take Mother's outburst as an act of grief. After all, first she lost her husband, then—"

Andrew bolted out of the chair, jarring the table, causing the lantern to skid dangerously close to its edge. "For the love of decency, what is going on between you two?"

"Let's see." Promise tugged one finger at a time, beginning with her smallest and weakest. "First my Uncle Taylor died. Then the work on the farm got ahead of me, so I hired a drifter named Daffron." Her chest tightened. "He chased Fletch, the only person besides me who knows how this place works, off," this wasn't entirely true, but she made it sound as though she believed it, "then Trivett got in trouble..." She yanked her index finger for effect. "And when I went to Mother Hart's," she was getting awfully loud, "she was inconsolable because the man she'd raised since he was a nose taller than his trumpet had been hanged."

Reminded of her own selfish act and its impact on Mother, she stopped short of asking Andrew if he and his sister thought of anyone other than themselves. She swept her arms open: "Which should I have informed you of first?"

Ellen marched across the room to the cabinet, removed plates, and stacked them with forks, knives, and a handful of frayed napkins. "We'll have dinner on this side of the table," she announced as though she hadn't heard a word of Promise's litany. She slipped past Andrew and the sewing machine draped with the lavender wedding dress fabric and offered Promise a plate.

Promise closed her fingers around it and lowered it to her side. For a quick second, that chunk of pottery weighed more than the skillet. Was this an apology? If she was making amends, Promise would have to offer something in return. Nothing direct, just a few quiet, forgiving words. "Aren't you going to eat?"

"I'm going to bed." The weariness in Ellen's tone was threaded with remorse. If she hadn't folded her arms across her chest, Promise would have gladly believed her.

"You're exhausted. Sleep will do you good," Andrew said, piling two chicken legs, a breast, and a wing on a plate beside a crumbled mound of charred cornbread.

He waited for Ellen to close the bedroom door behind her, then picked up a drumstick and tore off a mouthful of chicken. "Tension isn't good for anyone," were his garbled words. He closed his eyes for a long second and chewed. His face glowed with ecstasy.

Promise had forgotten Mangy-Mannered Charlie, the game they'd played as children. Whenever Mrs. Gills left the room, Mangy-Mannered Charlie offset the rigor of her insistence on perfect manners. If Mrs. Gills caught them chewing with their mouths open or, worse yet, heard Andrew belch, they blamed Charlie. Foolishness provided relief then and now.

She nodded in appreciation—Andrew was trying to make a bad night better. He ripped off another chunk of meat and chewed, licking and smacking his lips. "Ellen's missing all the fun," he mumbled.

Promise forced a smile. "Country air has a way of making you ravenous." She stared out the window at the darkness. "What about Daffron and Beatie? If I put a plate together, will you bring it to them?"

"I forgot to tell you that I gave Daffron whatever was in the icebox. Cheese, a piece of meat, green beans, the rest of the milk, a few slices of bread. He said that would do just fine."

"And Beatie? Was there enough for her?"

"Daffron seemed to think so." Andrew wiped his hands on his napkin. "He's dangerous, Promise. Downright explosive if you ask me. You ought to tell him to pack his things tomorrow or the day after at the latest. Blame it on me. Tell him you didn't know I was coming, and now that I'm here to help you won't need him."

"Daffron worries me, too, Andrew." He reached for her hand and gave it an affectionate squeeze. "But you're right—I didn't ask you." So suddenly did he release her that he reminded her of a little boy, who'd just had his knuckles slapped.

"I'm sorry for," he nodded toward the bedroom door, "everything."

Although his bid to reclaim his dignity didn't fit his words, it hummed with an uncomfortable sincerity. One she was too exhausted to question. They'd had enough wrangling for one evening. She was his hostess and his friend. A truce was in order. "Let's see what you've been working on," she said wearily.

Pushing his plate aside, he spread the papers he'd hidden from Ellen out between them. "If we're going to make this farm profitable, we'll need to make a few changes."

She cringed; it was the first time he'd spoken of what "we" were going to do. And with such confidence. Too much so. It didn't sit well with her for many reasons, finances being one.

Shortly before Taylor had taken ill, Promise assumed responsibility for the farm's finances, successfully managing to pay the bills and keep the farm going. The week before he died, he shocked her by announcing that she would inherit the farm and marry Andrew who would assume responsibility for its finances. "He has a head for business," was his meager explanation.

"You realize that with this I'm nothing more than part of a business deal? There was a lot more she wanted to say, but she clamped her mouth shut. Had she continued, the questions marching through her mind would voice the anger seething within her: He could trust her when it was convenient but not forever? Was this oddly configured arrangement his idea of a wedding gift that would bind she and Andrew together? Or was Taylor shoving back at her for winning Fletch's affections? What was his point? Why didn't he just hand Andrew the deed to Mearswood?

Now she wondered if he had.

CHAPTER 17

The tendency to struggle is inherent in human nature; living in harmony is our greatest challenge.

Taylor Crawford, *My Life in Georgia*

Promise dragged the oversized captain's chair out from under the table and sat beside Andrew. After burying Uncle Taylor, she'd been the first to sit here. In a voice so loud that mourners paying their respects could hear, Mother Hart said, "You're in Taylor's chair. That means you've taken over as rightful owner of the farm." The significance of those words was not lost on Promise; Mother had pronounced her the farm's heiress and crowned her with the duty that once belonged to Taylor alone. Now she had to act on Mother's words. Just as important, she had to keep Fletch safe without resorting to her uncle's manipulative ways.

She locked eyes with Andrew. "I don't have money for extras. If you hadn't paid for the wood for the new stalls, I wouldn't have been able to build them."

He waved a page scrawled with figures in her face. "That's just what I wanted to talk about. Horses. Racehorses, to be exact." He lowered his head, his hair hiding his eyes as he shuffled through the sketches he'd drawn of the farm. He spread them, one more elaborate than the next over the table, sliding the most accurate portrayal of the farm as it now existed farthest away. He pointed to a large rendition of his new paddocks, shook his hair out of his eyes, looked up and beamed.

He followed the horses, watched the races, and hobnobbed with the breeders and jockeys, so his desire to raise racehorses did not surprise her. Careful to restrain the annoyance welling within her, she softened her voice. "And this will become a racetrack?" She mashed her forefinger on the oval where her pastures had been and noted his erasure marks.

He nodded.

"Racehorses are the prima donnas of the horse world. They take special care and feed. Right now, we grow barely enough hay for our horses. And I make just enough money to buy grain. You're saying you want to change all that?"

"I've bought and sold my share of businesses. We can do this quite nicely, you know."

His words flowed with a cock-sure attitude that made her warier than ever. He was treating her as though she were part of his reading public, choosing his words with great care, applying his ability to persuade on her, a manipulation she resented.

Of course, the farm needed some changes; she, too, had been thinking about improvements and about borrowing money for them. Then she'd read—in Andrew's newspaper of all places—that some banks had failed and others had stopped loaning funds. That's when she put such risky notions aside. She planted her hands on the arms of the captain's chair and drew herself up tall. "You're talking about hiring staff, jockeys, trainers, and managers. Where will the money come from?"

"From people like myself, who avoided banks that were loaning themselves out of business."

This wasn't even close to what she had in mind. She'd planned to rebuild the cabins dotting her property: Thaddeus and Cornelia needed bedrooms for their children. Mother Hart had been putting off repairing her roof. And they weren't the only folks in need.

"I was saving this for a wedding present, but since you asked," he took hold of her fingers, his aristocratic face bright with excitement, "I've organized a few investors, classmates from Harvard who are interested in the farm. We've come up with a plan. We'll start small, clear the remainder of Taylor's acreage so we can grow more hay. After we sell a few horses or better yet, once they win a few purses, we'll be in a position to buy hay from other farmers. By then, we'll be able to expand our operation, build a full complement of paddocks plus exercise grounds. Maybe even buy more land." Out of breath, he paused, clearly fatigued after brandishing a mouth full of first-person pronouns. It was the most self-serving wedding gift ever described.

"Listen, Promise, you and I share a number of inclinations. You're absorbed by this farm and its animals, and I'm interested in building a horse business. We'll join our talents." He tapped her knuckles. "We'll make this work. You'll see."

"And what about the people who've been living on the land you intend to clear?" The bed in the next room creaked. Promise's voice dropped to a fierce whisper. "Where are they going to go?"

He waved his hand dismissively, then reached for another drumstick. "We'll find them a place."

She'd heard enough. "You know better than to come up with a scheme like this. Uncle Taylor bought this farm so those families would have a place to live. Nothing's changed, other than all that deep admiration you insisted you held for him."

"This conversation and the way we speak to one another straight on is the reason Taylor thought we'd make a good match." Mangy-Mannered Charlie, talking with his mouth full was no longer amusing. He swallowed. "Now that I think of it, I tend to agree. Telling another person what's on your mind has got to be..." he paused to study her face, "more considerate than getting information second hand."

Considerate? Promise pushed her chair as far from his as possible, stood, and brought her unused dish to the sink. Opening the porch door carefully, so as not to wake Ellen, she found the kettle on the summer cook stove still warm enough to wash the dishes. Inside, she poured the water and soap flakes into an enamel tub and stirred until the foam climbed the side of the sink and onto the counter. She would wash those that were dirty and those that a good scrubbing would never clean.

"Excuse me," she said, whisking the remaining dishes along with the lantern from the table. "I need this." She took a few steps and turned around. The light cast her shadow up the wall to the ceiling. "As long as we're talking about the farm there's something else you need to know."

"Tell me."

"I'm not the only owner."

He drew his weight forward and flattened his hands on the table as if he was about to leap over it. "Wait a minute. Just what do you mean?"

She paused a few seconds, long enough to assure herself that revealing this secret would cause no harm. "Uncle Taylor didn't buy the farm alone. He had a partner, Fletch's father, Will Hart. After Will had been killed, his half of the property went to his widow, Mother Hart. Because it was illegal to have a black woman's name on the deed, when Taylor decided to leave the farm to me, he specified her as my partner." Apparently, Taylor had not shared this little piece with Andrew.

There, she'd settled that problem. She set the lantern on the counter by the sink. Accompanied by a chorus of cleaning noises—the creak of the cabinet door, the muffled transfer of leftover chicken from the platter to a small plate, the rapid *click-click, click-click* of the icebox door opening and closing—she tidied the evening's mess. She swished suds over each greasy dish, then watched the dirty water whirl down the drain and disappear. By the time the last bubble burst, she felt she'd finished more than the dishes.

For a while, Andrew sat slumped at the table, his head in his hands. Then, he looked up, clutched his pencil and started scribbling figures down the edge of one paper onto the next. An unsettled feeling came over Promise. "Why didn't Taylor tell me about this before?" he asked no one in particular.

At last, he set the pencil aside and pushed himself from the table. "Where's the dish towel?" he asked, sounding once again like his relentlessly cheery self. Promise nodded to the drying rack by the stove.

He removed Mother's platter and folded the towel around it. "It'll take some doing, but we could buy her out." He set her dish down with a determined clatter. Promise forgot to breathe.

They bumped into one another so often as she went from the counter to the cabinet that she finally planted her hands on his shoulders and positioned him aside. She'd never encountered this problem with Uncle Taylor, who knew enough to mirror her movements so they would work smoothly together. Thoughts of marrying someone unwilling to notice how the other person moved in her surroundings were as disturbing as Andrew's plan to upend the farm.

Until now, she'd avoided setting a date for the wedding, but as Andrew's shoulder clipped hers again, she questioned the wisdom of honoring Taylor's last wish. The annoyance of doing dishes together was minor compared to living with Andrew or his plan, she reasoned. Where her thoughts would lead, she wasn't ready to say, but she knew for certain that she'd added Andrew to her list of problems.

She opened the cabinet and caught sight of another stack of papers piled carelessly on the chair: Taylor's Treatise. Andrew had gone into Uncle Taylor's desk!

"How could you?" she demanded, slapping the dishrag into a ball and hurling it at his chest.

Snatching it from the air, he jerked it to his side. "I told you I was writing about him for the paper."

She peered through his glasses at his muddy eyes. "Mentioning the assignment gave you the right to snoop?" Andrew broke her gaze and started pacing; shifting their argument to Taylor's papers distressed him more than anything that had happened that evening. She wondered why.

"I'd hardly call that snooping. Taylor said I could read his work whenever I wanted. I've never had to ask—"

"Things have changed. And so have I."

CHAPTER 18

Life poses sufficient challenges without compounding it with false constructions.

Taylor Crawford, journal entry, April 10, 1929
On Promise's nineteenth birthday

That evening, Promise had unhorsed everyone she touched: first, Mother Hart, then Ellen, and now Andrew. She seated herself as far from him as a round table would allow. He needed breathing room, and so did she. Besides, if she sat too close, he'd think she was gloating. Left to his thoughts, she hoped he would realize he'd stepped outside the comfort of his corral.

Andrew lowered his face to his palms and scrubbed his eyes.

Seeing the portrait of cockiness succumb to the jitters filled her with another dose of guilt. What had triggered her newfound talent for reducing people to their most fragile? Was it the farm? Had she absorbed Taylor's single-minded determination to plant blacks and whites in the same garden regardless of the cost? Was that it? Was she becoming a replica of her uncle, someone who loved family and friends immensely but not as much as his own dream? She feared she'd lost sight of her plan to do better; that she'd forgotten the way back to her corral.

A loud squeal of fiddle music interrupted her brooding.

Andrew pressed his nose to the screen and turned back into the parlor with a shrug.

"It's a fiddle," she whispered, noting the screen's crisscrossed impression on his nose.

He stopped scratching at the mosquito bite he'd already reduced to bleeding. "The air's so dense, the sound could have come from miles away."

"That's Daffron—he's like his music, appears out of nowhere."

Andrew edged his way across the room and seated himself in Taylor's rocking chair. "Quite the rogue, that one. How's the saying go? Even the devil can make music?"

"You mean, 'even the devil can quote scripture?'" She forced a smile. "Thanks for trying to make me laugh." He nodded wearily.

Poor man. She'd been overbearing, and it exhausted them both. She rekindled her resolve to do better, for Andrew's sake as well as hers.

She imagined the prayer a forthright minister would utter during a ceremony that combined Andrew's high-handed ways with hers: "Dear sisters and brothers. We have come together to unite two sets of failings in marriage." Now there was a formula for misery. Sure as the sun rises in the east, marriage would end whatever remained of their longstanding friendship. That didn't fit her notion of doing better, of becoming a person like Mother Hart.

Keeping the promise Andrew had made to Taylor had to be as difficult for him as for her. Worry etched its way beneath the rim of his glasses and trudged over the arc of his cheekbones toward his hairline. Even the square of his shoulders sagged as he rocked in time with Daffron's music.

Suddenly he stopped. The floorboards groaned as he rose to his feet, closed the window by the table, then lowered each of the remaining windows with a decisive push.

Promise worried he was about to rekindle their argument. "What are you doing?"

His gallows walk reminded her of Mother Hart's on the wretched occasion of delivering a lifeless babe. "I'm sorry, I had no right to go through Taylor's papers. They're not his anymore. They belong to you." He spoke rapidly, spraying saliva. "But since I have, there's something you should see." He raked his hair from his forehead and, lowering his hand, struck the edge of his glasses.

Promise rearranged the gold frames on the bridge of his nose, "If you lose these, you won't be able to talk."

She'd used the same conciliatory tone with Taylor when he begged her not to argue with him about marrying Andrew. So she stopped herself from asking her two-faced old uncle why she should marry a man she didn't love; she simply agreed to his demand. She expected him to say how surprised he was, but he outfoxed her one last time by drifting to sleep, leaving her with this, his most disturbing puzzle.

He'd planned to exit that way, she was sure of it. Configuring a problem and letting her work it out had been his way of teaching her to think for herself. But had he really cared, wouldn't having a husband she loved and who loved her be equally important? Nothing made sense.

Except that Taylor had loved games. When she was a child, he'd write a word on a piece of paper, cut it into individual letters and leave them jumbled on the counter. Every morning brought a new jumble for her to decipher and add to the previous day's solution. By the end of a week, she'd link the words into a sentence, usually a delightful suggestion like, *Let's ride into town for a Nehi Cola.*

Perhaps Andrew had found another of Taylor's jumbles. Unraveled, it would release them from their engagement, expose it for what it was, another game, an all-important test of their loyalty. She settled into her rocker. "What do you want to show me?"

"I had it here somewhere." He rustled through his stack of paper.

She closed her eyes and listened to Daffron's now muted playing. "Why did you shut the windows?"

"If we can hear Daffron, he can hear us. Who knows, he was probably listening to me ramble on about my plans for the farm when all along I should have been asking about our plans."

"Oh," was all she could think to say, feeling at once petty and small in her great big chair.

She glanced at the mantle and wished Andrew would hurry so she could check on Mother. "Have you found what you're looking for?"

With his palm supporting a solitary document, he presented her with a fragile yellow sheet of paper.

She squinted at it and pointed toward the clock. "Hand me my glasses, please."

Once they were square on her nose, the familiar tiny scrawl came into focus. A hint of Taylor's tobacco—as much a writing tool as his pen—drifted upward. After he'd written a few sentences, he would lean back in his chair, cradle the bowl of his pipe and let the smoke swirl his thoughts. Minutes passed before he would reach out from this cloud, dip his pen into a pot of India ink, and, tapping the nib twice, call his thoughts to order. She could almost hear his pen scratching as he wrote:

My dear Promise.

I have known many a grown man who could handle a horse admirably, but few possess your ability to hold yourself in check when confronted with an animal's agitation. A kicking horse provokes fear and provides the less thoughtful man with reason to whip the animal into submission and, worse yet, break its spirit.

So it was with great pride I watched you train today, working as you did to understand what that horse was telling you with its kick, the only language it could offer. And though you weigh not a tenth of that horse's weight, you were proud and confident, using every ounce of your being to fullest advantage, first earning that horse's trust, then taking that stubborn animal one small step after the other, until it was ready to accept your lead. And doing so in such a way as made sense to the beast.

If only I had your patience, the same confidence you display in your ability to reach such a difficult student. Years with students more intransigent than your four-legged variety have dissipated the ideals I once held as absolute. Therefore, what I'm about to tell you may not make much sense. It makes little sense to me sometimes.

I've watched you transfer your guileless observations to those around you, judging people not by superficial notions such as the color of their skin but on their trueness and kindness of spirit. For this I am proud and grateful; my daughter, the only child born to me, has not been stricken with the malignancy that has turned so many generations of Southerners bitter and hateful.

She took her first breath since she'd begun reading. "I'm not sure I understand," she murmured, then continued.

Were I to live my life over, I would think long and hard before giving life to a child who would grow up in the midst of such disharmony. Lord knows I have spent my days trying to dispel it. In buying this farm, I had hoped to create a world in which black and white could live without fear. Life as we know it poses sufficient challenges without compounding it with false constructions.

When you find this, you will be understandably dismayed by my deception. In the years you have known me, I have sought to conduct myself as a rational man and, having never failed you as such, my dearest hope is for you to trust that the force behind my concealment was grave, indeed.

Never forget, the words we have so often exchanged in the language I have shared with you and no one else, for they will never change, regardless of what has transpired between us: roytal lliw saywal velo somierp.

Taylor Crawford, April 10, 1929
Promise's nineteenth birthday

She pictured Taylor a year ago when she'd just turned nineteen, his eyes a healthy ocean-blue, smiling with love that had, during earlier seasons, insulated her from the realization that he preached one set of ideals and lived another. Those were their happiest times.

She fingered the rip beside his name at the edge of the journal page and wished she could repair this damage. Wasn't that what he was doing right here, above his signature? He had been a proud father. Hers. How could she have been so wrong about him? She dropped her head to her chest. Oh God, how she wished she'd known.

"Why didn't Taylor tell me?" she demanded of Andrew.

He lowered himself to his knees in front of her. "What should I say? I'm sorry you had a great man for a father only he's dead, and you've just found out?"

When she looked up, her face burned. "You've read this."

"I wish I hadn't. Believe me, I can only imagine how intrusive—"

"Please..." She turned away. She was working hard to absorb Taylor's confession, she didn't need another. "Forces? Which forces was he talking about?" she slapped her fingertips across Taylor's words.

Andrew's face grew taut. He said nothing.

She lowered her eyes to the page and skimmed line by line, until she reached the words, my child, then returned to the first paragraph and reread it all. She had to be sure Taylor was referring to her. No one but her. Andrew lingered by her shoulder, snuffing in and out, while water dripped from the pump into the granite sink. Outside, insects droned, and the fiddler played once more, soulful and off-key. All seemed to have known. All except her.

Her thoughts tumbled and nicked one another with sharp opposing edges. Sweet, bitter. Happy, furious. Sure, uncertain. Belief, disbelief. She wished Taylor were here, his lanky figure towering over her so she could ask if he'd intended his letter to repair, to rebuild, or to replace her orphaned history? Or all three? Guided by Mother Hart's oft-repeated cautions, she'd conducted herself as Taylor's guest, singing out "please" and "thank you," waiting during meals for him to urge her to take another morsel, trying not to ask for more. If what he claimed was true, that all was paradox, did this paradox now define her, and, if so, how would her future life unfold?

The other day, after she told the story of Taylor's having woken to Jasper, chewing on his beard, the familiar ache, a pressure she hadn't been able to relieve, lessened. She laughed, thinking she'd crossed the threshold of her grief. Never did she suspect where that rough-hewn plank would lead her.

She let her uncle's—no, her father's journal page drift to the floor, far from ink-blurring tears. What kind of man would listen to a child's plea to help her find her "real father" and not say a word? How could she have mistaken Taylor for a man of principle, demanding, consistent, compassionate to a fault?

She moved the toe of her brogan in persistent little taps. Something was missing. The letter didn't make sense. Taylor gloried in playing games, speaking in riddles, regaling her with mind-bending problems. His letter was too straightforward; it wasn't the whole story. There was more; there had to be. She pushed on the arms of the rocker, stepped away from its vacant motion, and headed toward the kitchen door.

Andrew trailed. "Promise, are you all right?"

"I'm going to check on Mother Hart."

"I'll come with you." His voice was as worried as she was confused.

She pointed to the floor as if he were one of her dogs, "No. Stay," then, as she dashed out the kitchen door, added, "Please."

Once her feet hit the pathway to Mother Hart's cabin, she searched the trees for her favorite moths. Larger than bats, soundless and still, they blended with the bark. Unless you were directed to look, you would have never suspected they existed. Just like her. Is that what Taylor had wanted? Her heart raced as she considered this clue to the puzzle she had become. Not paying attention, she tripped on the remains of a rotting tree stump and plunged into layers of decaying leaves.

Disturbed, they released a scent, musty as old lies, decrepit as their tattered remains.

What would become of memories of the hours she and Taylor had spent together each evening after supper on the front porch? After he packed his fragrant pipe, he'd taught her what she'd come to understand as a vital lesson: to reclaim the scattered tobacco and wedge the filaments into the near-to-brimming bowl so everything would fit as it was intended. What of those memories? How would she catalog them without the anchor of "uncle?" Would they drift into nothingness?

More importantly, what would become of the feelings she'd held for him? Gratitude? Annoyance? Fondness? All had been forged into the many-faceted love she'd reserved for the man who, taking trepidation in hand, had adopted a homeless orphan. Not the coward who'd waited until he'd gone to claim her as his own.

CHAPTER 19

When confronted with a question that perplexes,
I probe relentlessly, refashioning my query
until the truth emerges rumpled yet intact.

Taylor Crawford, journal entry, April 15, 1929

Promise pressed her nose to the door of Mother Hart's cabin and called her name. "Stopped by to see if you needed anything." Silence. She reached for the latch and found the door partially open. The possibility of Mam padding around in her distressed state instead of resting in bed added another worry to Promise's untidy life. She listened once more and hearing nothing, checked the barn to see if Fletch had returned from work. Despite the hopeful ghost of a moon that lit the decimated gardens, summer kitchen, and privy, Cassiopeia's stall was empty.

Promise trudged back to the porch, rapped twice on the doorjamb. Fearful of what she would find, she tiptoed in. "Hello? Anyone home?" Nothing, no sound other than her breathing. A brown jug crammed with wilted flowers on cracked stems—the remains she'd salvaged from this afternoon's rampage—sat on the long plank table in the middle of the kitchen. Benches huddled against the table's legs were a sure sign Fletch hadn't returned; if he had, the one closest the stove would have been askew. Behind the table, floor-to-ceiling shelves lined with jars, some tall, others round brimmed with seed pods, roots, and powders except one, Mother's favorite tea, St. John's wort. The jar lay on its side, its sedating powers scattered along the shelf.

In the sitting room, locked in a squat that spread her floor-length white nightgown into a small tent, Mother Hart swiped her hands repeatedly beneath her divan. Her broad face registered a disturbed concentration. Promise let a few seconds pass before interrupting with, "Lose something?"

"Solace," Mother intoned like a hollow bell. She reached for the armchair, the sunken mate to her worn blue divan, and patted the torn leather cover on her Bible. "Without my spectacles, I'll find no solace."

Promise knelt with her face to the floor. The lantern's smoky chimney diffused its light, making her search impossible. She reached under the divan and tried to push the spring out of the way. Wedged between the floor and a broken spring, the glasses wouldn't budge. Must have been quite a force, a hard kick, perhaps, that jammed them there. "I'll need the broom handle," she told Mother, who'd seated herself on the chair.

"Out on the porch."

The door creaked open. She grabbed the broom and, in swinging around, sent two empty buckets clattering down a small incline and up against a tree. All night-music stopped. Moments later, as if in response to the conductor's cue, the wary insects resumed their hymns.

When she returned, Mother's face was bundled in distress. "It's not like you to make so much noise. Something troubling you?"

Promise envisioned the tear in the journal page she'd just read and recalled the many times Taylor, dissatisfied with the slightest imperfection, would recopy a document. He had too much respect for the written word to tolerate an inexact word, blurred ink, or a damaged sheet of paper. A marred journal entry was unlike him. The more she thought about what he'd written and how he'd written it, the less she trusted it.

If anyone would understand Taylor's intention, it was Mother. Promise ached to ask her about it. Instead, she busied herself retrieving Mother's glasses, first pushing with too much force, then pulling. Finally, she dragged them out and dropped them in Mother's outstretched palm. "Seems whatever I touch, breaks."

"Don't be foolish." Mother gathered a handful of white nightgown from around her waist and lowered her spectacles into the soft fabric. She straightened the bent frames and rubbed the lenses clean. Her face relaxed some as she slipped the rounded ear pieces into place. For the first time since Promise had arrived, Mother looked her in the face. "Seeing clearly is the first step toward solace."

Which was why Taylor's journal confession didn't ring true. A demanding author, it was unlike him to leave a torn page for her to find. Besides being uncharacteristic, it was too easy. He'd taught her that simplicity in human affairs camouflaged delicate and often painful underpinnings, and was therefore rightfully suspect. He'd intended his journal entry as a clue, his peculiar way of urging her to look beyond the obvious. All is paradox. She had an inkling he wanted her to know who her real parents were. Or are.

Despite her best intentions to avoid the subject, the pressure that had been building within her released and, like an unruly filly escaping its corral, galloping into the wind, air streaming into her lungs, she couldn't stop. She started telling

Mother about Andrew finding information that was none of his business. Little by little, the events leading to the discovery of Taylor's journal slipped out. She stopped short of repeating his claim to be her father.

"Did my Fletcher say how long it would take him to deliver that manure? Because if he's not on his way home, we have lots more to worry about than some tired old piece of writing."

"I promised myself I wouldn't ask this, but it's like a baby ready and waiting to be born. I can hold back by squeezing until I turn purple as sunrise, but it's going to come just the same. Nature says so."

"Then ask your question."

"What was it like for Taylor to adopt a baby when he wasn't married?" This wasn't what she wanted to know, not exactly, but it eased her into talking about her parents.

Mother took to massaging her lips with her fingertips. Her unblinking eyes were wary yet curious. She hesitated, then leaned forward. Her penetrating expression made Promise squirm. "Fletch is usually settling Cassiopeia in by now." She glanced at the window. "You found my glasses, you wouldn't happen to know where my son disappeared to?"

"He's delivering manure, then he's off to the Mitreanna. You said yourself." Promise hadn't meant to brush her question aside. Go gently, she chided herself. "There was no mistaking the writing, I read it for myself." She prattled on, hoping to get Mother to respond. But she didn't. She sighed, "If only Andrew had minded his own business." Seconds passed, awkward, silent.

"What did you read?"

Mother's unexpected casualness caught her off guard. She braced herself, ready for the room to collapse faster than a hayfield in a downpour. "Taylor said he was my father."

"Andrew wouldn't be a good newspaperman if he didn't mind others' affairs." Mother squinted thoughtfully, then moaned. "Dear Lord, let these tired ears hear old Cassiopeia's hooves and the rattle of Fletch's wagon wheels pressing along our dirt road."

"You're not surprised then."

Mother placed her hands palms-up in her lap as if to prove she wasn't hiding a thing. "How can I be? I deliver everyone's babies. I always ask the name of the father." She made a writing motion in the air. "I have to, for my records." Mother became impatient; if there was one thing she preached about midwifery, it was the importance of keeping confidences.

"You knew? All these years, and you never told me?"

"I deliver, Promise. I don't tell."

"But I asked you about my parents. Many times. Over and over." Her words slid out curdled as yellow milk.

"What folks choose to tell is their affair, not mine. That's the vow I made when I became a midwife. I've never broken it, until now."

Another more accusing thought occurred to Promise. "Did Taylor know you knew?"

Mother stared with an intensity Promise had never before seen. "Taylor stayed by that girl's side from the moment he found she was pregnant, till the hour she handed him her baby girl. Now he's dead, and it's easy to be angry with him. He did a brave thing taking you in."

"Then why didn't he admit he was my father?"

She shook her head. "Who knows? Maybe he came to love the girl and didn't want to embarrass her. I agreed to keep house for him, to teach you the womanly things he knew nothing about. He paid me a handsome wage, helped me keep my boys and me together. I repaid him by limiting my questions to household matters. That's how I showed my gratitude for his kindness. You'd do well to do likewise."

The annoyance in Mother's voice upset Promise. She hadn't expected a rebuke, just as she hadn't intended this conversation to happen. Not now, not tonight. But the urge to learn the truth rose so fast she couldn't stop herself from another question that had been bothering her all afternoon, "What do you know about Daffron Mears?" His name crashed into the room.

Mother stood. Promise braced herself, this time for a throttling. "You're confusing me, child. Weren't you asking about Taylor? What's Daffron got to do with him?"

"That's what I'm asking."

"Taylor went out of his way to keep Daffron out of Martonsville."

She ignored Mother's unspoken accusation. "Is there more?"

"Anyone's lived on Martons Island knows the Mears family—they're a hateful lot. Always have been. He did us all a favor by chasing Daffron off."

"I heard Daffron was cruel to women, especially Negro women. That's what I heard." Promise couldn't believe the accusation lying within her words. The possibility of Daffron and Mother Hart hadn't occurred to her before—not that she was aware of—but that didn't stop a shapeless suspicion from latching onto her thoughts and tearing through its camouflage.

The awful hurt in Mother's eyes told Promise she understood exactly what she was alluding to.

Mother blinked hard. "Why are you talking to me like this? Life landed you a chunk you didn't expect, and you're handing it off to me? Is that what you think I deserve?" Her voice cracked. No matter how fast she blinked, tears dribbled down her cheeks.

Mother stopped, and with one hard breath composed herself, then reached for her lantern. "I have to excuse myself. Time to find that solace I was telling you about. Lord knows I need it."

The urge to throw herself in Mother's path hit her harder than a wave on a storm tide. Don't go. You're the only one who can tell me who I am. She wanted to fall to her knees, grab Mother's ankles and beg, but she knew better. Mother, who'd always espoused the virtue of self-control, would find Promise repulsive.

Mother's long braids swayed across the back of her nightgown. She passed through the sitting room into her bedroom and with a flick of her wrist closed her door.

Promise stood at the edge of the small sitting room. After adjusting to the moonlight, her eyes settled on the bowed top of Mother's old steamer trunk. As children, she and Fletch had made rubbings of the tooled leather, marveled at the wonder of pointed oak leaves, twigs and acorns appearing beneath their stubby blue crayons. Oak strips held ornate molded tin panels in place from front to back across the bow. Beneath those strips rested a moonfaced steel lock. Had her little fingers the power of wrought iron skeleton keys, she would have unfastened that lock many times over. But Mother kept the contents of the trunk from her sure as she'd done tonight with her thoughts.

How foolish she'd been; she'd expected answers to appear as magically as her rubbings otherwise, why would she have asked so brazenly about Daffron? She studied the thick skin on her hands and wondered if her heart, once kind, had grown calluses, too. She turned her palms over as Mother had done when as a child she'd badgered her about the trunk being locked. "I have to keep my birthing supplies far from small soiled hands," she'd said. But that didn't stop her from spying through the window as Mother hid her birthing books at the bottom of her trunk.

She tiptoed toward the trunk. Was the birthing book that contained her birth date—Sunday, April 10, 1910—bound in dull gray canvas? Ordinary gingham? Leather perhaps? Since little hands were now large, perhaps Mother no longer locked her trunk. Promise bowed low before this magical piece of furniture, the vault that held the secrets of her birth. Blue moonlight shone on the lock, now smaller, the steel chillier, its keyhole darker than she recalled. But one thing remained the same—it was still locked.

CHAPTER 20

Mercy, uncrowned potentate, you who have the power to elevate mere humans to extraordinary, help me translate one of mankind's most despicable acts. Mollify it with an understanding that propels me to mold evil into good. Guide me to overcome the grief that desiccates my spirit.

Taylor Crawford, journal entry, August 10, 1909
On the occasion of Will Hart's death

Had this been any other night, the panicked rapping at her kitchen door wouldn't have terrified her, but circumstances being what they were, Mother flung her feet over the edge of the bed, shoved her arms into her bathrobe, and wished she'd propped her rifle nearby. More rapping, the quick start-and-stop rhythm of a woodpecker, not the incessant banging of a husband whose pregnant wife was in need. She knotted her frayed sash and poked her head into Fletch's room, hoping he'd slipped in sometime between her restless dozing and bouts of worry. His tidy bed had yet to be disturbed. Good Lord, first news of Trivett's death, then Promise's prying, now Fletch. Let him be safe at the Mitreanna, Lord, please, she prayed as she pattered through the kitchen and yanked the door open.

Acey Baldwin's eyes widened round as her best supper platter and were so startled, she thought she'd mistakenly grabbed her rifle from its resting place behind the door and pointed it at his snuffling nose. He dragged the back of his wrist across his gleaming forehead. "You scared the bejesus out of me, Mother Hart."

"Something happen to my Fletcher?"

"Fletcher?" he repeated as though this was the first he'd heard the name.

"You come to tell me about Trivett, then?"

Acey's jaw dropped. "Trivett?" his voice quivered.

"You didn't hear? They hanged him last night."

Acey worked his fingers up the front of his stained shirt, past the fob of thread that once held a button, to his throat. "That's awful." A shiver rippled down his neck to his shoulders. "Just awful." He babbled something about Margaret being sick these past two nights. "But don't worry. I shouldn't have bothered you, I wasn't thinking. I'll try Cooper's tonic again. Maybe it'll make Margaret feel better." He turned to go.

Mother watched him slink past what was left of her gardens. He stopped at the remains of a stooped flower head and set it upright against its stake. She put her hand over her heart; if only someone like Acey had come along when Trivett had been in trouble, he'd be with us still, she thought.

"Wait," she called out, and when he protested about disturbing her "at a time like this," she claimed tending to Margaret's illness would do her good. "Trick my mind into thinking about someone else's troubles for a change."

Besides, she hated hearing he was involved with Cooper Peall, though the sheriff was the only white person other than

Margaret to show a whiff of interest in that boy. Margaret's caring for her brother made sense, but the sheriff—now there was a man she didn't trust.

Acey scrambled to the porch and clutched the railings like they were gunnels on a lifeboat. "Really? I would have brought Margaret with me, only she's too sick to travel." He ran the back of his hand under his nose and swallowed hard. "She's dying," he added weakly.

"I'll see what I can do for her." Mother put her hand on his shoulder—something she'd done many times before—never expecting him to flinch. The poor boy looked flustered. She took in his pimply chin, disheveled hair, and worried eyes. She had a fondness for orphaned boys. She gave him a biscuit and told him to wait in the kitchen. Her Trivett wouldn't mind if she helped Acey. After all, Acey needed a mother, too.

She dressed quickly, removed her birthing book from her bag, and hid the record of who belonged to whom in her trunk. She'd memorized most combinations like Lawrence and Pamibel Baldwin, who'd brought Margaret into this world and, four years later, sweet little Acey.

Though Pamibel ran off long before Lawrence died, she'd taught Margaret survival was a matter of lying and doing whatever the drunken old man wanted. That Margaret survived her parents' influence buoyed Mother's hopes for her, until the violet-eyed beauty hitched up with Daffron Mears. The seventeen-year-old girl put off marrying him for a while until pregnancy rendered the exchange of vows a necessity. Now she was sick. Most likely, of him.

***

Ocean breezes wafted over the bluffs to the eastern side of Margaret's withered corner of the world. Mother wrapped herself in her sweater and held her breath against the stench. "From the privy," Acey murmured by way of explanation. Streams of silver-gray fog twisted around the pilings beneath Margaret's house, giving it a ghostly appearance. Mildew splotched its warped clapboards, and shutters dangled in sorry half-frowns aside the windows that framed the front door.

Off in the darkness, restless waves crashed and withdrew. Acey stopped the wagon alongside a solitary loblolly pine. Mother looked up into the whorl of scaly limbs. Trivett had been hung on a tree this size, she decided as she steadied herself on Acey's clammy hand and stepped down from the wagon into the warm sand.

Even before Acey opened the door, the telltale odor of neglect leached from the house. With a sweep of his arm, he cleared a spot on the kitchen table for his lantern. Jagged-edged tin cans clattered to the floor and rolled past crates of empty green bottles that waited for who knows what. Mother picked up an empty box of Brown's Mule Chewing Tobacco and pushed it into the overflowing trash bin.

The bedroom smelled worse than a slop pot. On the floor, a figure lay on a stained mattress, knees pulled tight to its chest. A hand ventured out from beneath a tumble of yellow hair and curled its fingers over the edge of the bed. A bucket frothy with vomit and a tumbler of clear liquid were within reach. "I tried to give her a drink," Acey said.

Grains of sand bit into her knees as Mother lowered herself beside the mattress. "Margaret? This is Mother Hart. Acey's asked me to help you."

No answer. Mother's hand burrowed through the yellow tangle toward Margaret's damp forehead. A musty odor rose from her sweaty hair. "How long you been like this?"

Margaret fixed her eyes on Mother's, then, seeing Acey, signaled her brother to go away. "He's bringing it on again."

She made a churning gesture over her middle, dropped her head into the bucket Mother set beside her and heaved, long and dry.

"Bring this and the slop jar out behind the privy and bury it." Mother handed sniffling Acey the bucket. He took the handle with one hand, lantern with the other.

"I offered to empty it, only she wouldn't let me," he whined, his neck craned away from the stench.

"Acey?" He glanced at Mother Hart from the corner of his eye. "Leave the lantern here."

He set it down and hurried off as fast as he could without sloshing.

Mother waited for the door to slam, then asked Margaret, "Why wouldn't you let him empty the bucket? Most likely 'twas the smell made you retch."

"Because it made him gag. Once he started, I did too."

"But he was willing to do anything to help you. Maybe you were looking for a reason to keep him away. Has something happened, Margaret?"

Margaret's gaze traveled from Mother's eyes to the window. "He kept asking if he was making me feel better. A blind man could tell I was too sick to answer."

Mother moved the lantern to the side of the bed and picked up the Mason jar nearby. "What's this?" She lifted the wire handle securing the glass lid and sniffed.

"Homegrown liquor." Margaret pressed her head deeper into the pillow. "From Cooper Peall."

Mother scowled. "Do tell. Sheriff Peall and bootleg liquor. What a surprise. Has Acey been drinking this? Is that why he's acting so strange?"

"He tried to give me a mouthful. I spit it out." Margaret dropped her limp hand over the front of her dress. "Got it all over me."

Mother raised the wick on the lantern, until smoke rose from the chimney, then lowered it so that it gave off a smooth even light. Unmasked by the glare, a pair of fist-sized holes glowered from within the wall. Margaret's bedroom was as sparse as the kitchen was cluttered. On the other side of the mattress was a shabby bureau and beside it, low enough for a child, hung a small oval mirror. In the corner, in a wooden wagon sat a rag doll with large button eyes and a stitched red smile. Mother sighed; she still wanted the little girl fate had denied her. "Any chance you're expecting?"

"Just finished bleeding."

Mother removed a jar from her birthing bag, unscrewed the lid, and took out a few spearmint leaves. "Chew these, they'll ease your stomach, make your mouth taste better." As she placed them on Margaret's pale tongue, she eyed the trail of newly crusted scabs on Margaret's thin arms. Between those, her torn dress, and the leaves clinging to the rickrack decoration on her pockets, she looked as if she'd tumbled headlong into brambles. Mother shook her head.

This was one kind of tumbling, but the real fall happened when Pamibel abandoned her family. Had times been different, Mother would have adopted little Margaret rather than let her fall prey to Daffron Mears, almost fifteen years her senior. Mother gently brushed Margaret's hair from her face. She was the first baby she'd delivered after losing Will Hart.

For a long while after his death, she'd confined herself to Taylor's house, where she and the boys stayed while he rebuilt theirs. Every morning, she forced herself out of bed. It wasn't until she held Margaret Baldwin, squirming and floppy, that she realized her place was among the living. But during the endless hours preceding that child's birth, she would have gladly joined Will in the land of the dead.

***

Will's whiteness had taunted the Fates who first struck Daisy, their brown-spotted dog with legs so short and ears so long that Phua—she had yet to be named "Mother Hart"—had to wash them every day after they'd drooped in her food pan. One night, she woke to find their quilt damp with salt air and crawled to the window by their bed to close it. Something was amiss. She checked the boys in the next room and, finding them asleep, climbed back into bed. As usual, Daisy lay there between her and Will. She patted her rump, then scrambled to her knees, hand muffling the scream reeling between her stomach and lungs.

By that time, she'd woken Will. "Sweet Jesus, she's dead," he said. Gathering the cord that had been pulled so tight it burrowed into her neck, he wrapped the quilt around Daisy's body. "Shh," he whispered, kissing her eyes, "You'll wake the boys." He rocked her until her sobs ebbed into a ruffled silence. The meaning of Daisy's murder was clear.

"This is a warning. You have to leave, Will. Go away. Now." She broke into a whimper only he could hear.

He slipped into his pants and brogans and lifted Daisy's body. "We'll talk about it in the morning."

"Where are you going?"

"To bury her."

"What if the person who did this is still out there?"

"This is a coward's work. Cowards always run."

Quiet though his words were, they failed to convince her. Phua had hoped her family would never be forced to act on the plan she'd made after the birth of Fletch, her mixed-race baby. Other families had traveled west; they could escape there, too. Her mind darted from how to wake Fletcher and Trivett without alarming them, to wondering about the dangers of traveling, to worrying about Will alone in the woods. Her chest felt weighted. Her head ached.

Galloping horses sent vibrations through the earth up into their floor. Its trembling reminded her of Will and Taylor, racing one another through the woods. But the pounding of these hooves sent a message—not of brotherly playfulness caught in the challenge of who would reach the barn first—but of hunters stalking their prey. The pounding grew into an insistent rumbling. With it, the shouts of men, aroused and angry, burning holes in the night with their torches.

Fletcher called Trivett. "Wake-up. Ghost-riders." Ghost-riders? The thought of Will alone out there left Phua breathless.

She hauled her trunk filled with supplies out the front door, where the stink of lathered men and horses engulfed her. Faceless men draped in burlap robes dragged Will to the nearest tree. Trance-like, she followed until someone shoved her out of the way.

Faster than a snake's strike, they snuffed the life from Will's tortured eyes. The only thing that kept her from screaming, "take me too" was the terrified clutch of his boys. Moments later, flames roared through their home.

Pregnant with Margaret, Pamibel pulled up in her wagon, lumbered down, then guided Fletcher and Trivett away from the confusion. She wrapped them in blankets and pressed their heads to her breast, while Phua cradled Will's body. Phua had never forgotten Pamibel's decency; she was the only person, other than Taylor, who'd bothered with them that night.

When Pamibel was ready to deliver, Phua agreed to assist the woman who'd taken pity on her. Several years later, Pamibel told her she had had no cause to hold Will's whiteness against her and, from the numbers of white ladies who called upon Phua for her services, others felt the same. That was when little Margaret first called her, "Mother Hart."

***

Margaret's murmuring brought Mother's attention back to the room. She inspected the slash across Margaret's cheek. "Lordy, child, where did you get that? Was this Daffron's doing? Trouble goes hand in glove with that man."

She soaked a wad of cotton with antiseptic and dabbed the wound. Margaret winced as her brother entered the room with the empty bucket.

"I washed it clean," he announced. "How's Margaret?"

"Her stomach has quieted some."

Acey put his hand on the wall and leaned his head on his arm. "She gonna be all right?"

"Don't you go getting sick, too," Mother pretended to scold. "Margaret needs some fresh water." She handed him a tumbler. When he did nothing, she looked up, "Acey?" He took it and hurried from the room.

"Your brother's not himself. Something happen to him?"

"Got himself a mouthful of life last night—a taste too big to chew." Margaret may as well have spit the words on the floor.

Mother thought of Trivett—she couldn't believe Acey was involved in anything like that. "Acey?" She fell back on her haunches, too stunned to say more.

Margaret put her hand on Mother's. "First time with a woman," she whispered.

Acey, no bigger than a stunted cornstalk, with a woman? When her boys had fluttered into manhood, it showed in their eyes, their strut. Mother scowled. "You sure? Who?"

Margaret rolled her eyes and started coughing. "He must of bungled her good. She threw him out, hurt him some awful." She turned on her side, hands clutching her stomach.

"You gonna be sick again?" Mother dragged the bucket closer.

"No, but if you hadn't been so good at birthing babies, I wouldn't be here now, would I?"

Mother studied Margaret's twisted face, then glanced at the rag doll in the corner. "Shh. That's no way to talk. Little Beatie needs you." She put her hand under Margaret's head and fed her a spoonful of dark sweet liquid. "Here, try this. I use it when I can't sleep." She dabbed at the liquid dribbling down Margaret's chin, then smoothed ointment over her face and arms.

She pulled a sheet from the bottom drawer of the bureau and was covering Margaret with it when Acey returned. "She's going to be thirsty when she wakes. Set the water by the bed." Acey held his nose and nodded. "I know," Mother said as she opened the windows over the rag doll, "The smell won't go away." She checked Margaret once more and motioned for them to leave.

***

Silent foggy tears dripped from the moss on the loblolly pine. Mother looked past the tree at the spray of stars surrounding the moon and scowled. Yes, the loblolly against the sky was beautiful, but if she had her wish, every tree solid enough to hold a man's weight would come down long before it did anyone harm.

Rank as the night air was, it smelled better than Margaret's room. "Needs help," she said, glancing back at Margaret's blighted house.

"Daffron built it for Margaret and Beatie."

"You'd think he'd care for it, 'specially the privy." Little more than an oversized birdhouse, the roofed rectangle gave off an odor ten times its size.

"I give Margaret my pay. After she buys food, there's nothing left for lye, so we live with the stench."

"When we get to my place, I'll give you a cup of lye. No, you're going to need two."

For the first time that night, Acey's little boy sweetness returned. She was about to pat his cheek when his expression soured. He grabbed hold of the tree trunk and, surrendering or doing homage, Mother couldn't tell which, he bowed, then unexpectedly spewed. Mother whirled around in time to catch Margaret moving away from the window.

CHAPTER 21

Despite history's ruthless tutelage, generation after generation has failed to acknowledge that desperate people inflict suffering on those least deserving of punishment.

Taylor Crawford, *My Life in Georgia*, 1929

To Daffron, a can of kerosene had always been an easy thing to carry, but tonight the coiled handle felt like it was about to bite. Ordinarily, he'd have charmed Acey into doing this job, but he couldn't risk the kid getting mush-kneed again. Too bad, because Acey just about wagged himself foolish whenever he took him aside for one of their private talks. "I'll teach you to be my right-hand man," he'd told him.

But the wilting wallop Acey had planted in that Trivett fella's gut was proof enough: he could trust none other than himself to do this job. Already Cooper, the only man he'd ever really trusted, had stomped all over his plan to hang Fletch Hart.

Did Cooper think he'd missed the cozy way he and his deputy stood by the barn, comparing notes? Come to think of it, nothing was bedeviling about last night's stunt. Cooper never had much regard for his plan to reclaim his daddy's plantation—what was left of it, that is. Too bad he'd made the mistake of telling Cooper how much that high and mighty Fletch reminded him of the nigger boy who'd hidden in the hayloft while ol' daddy Mears beat him senseless. There was no denying the fact: Cooper had botched his homecoming hanging on purpose. And he was going to pay.

Daffron's footsteps crunched noisily as he crossed the pebbled schoolyard to the whitewashed school. This had been Cooper's doing, all of it, starting with the day he'd convinced the teacher with the wobbly voice to retire. Soon after, Cooper saw to it that his daughter, Suzanne, was awarded the job. To celebrate, he talked folks into building a new school, twenty-eight by fifty-six, a one-story structure he'd designed. When he donated the wooded acre lot ten minutes from his house, townspeople cheered.

Charlie Hinks from Sunrise Farm north of Martonsville junction dug the well, and Martin Turner, the father of two sets of twins who'd be attending the school, built privies fifteen yards southeast of it—one for the boys, another for the girls. Even Taylor Crawford put his back into the education of the children of Martonsville, although everyone suspected the moment Promise had her first playground spat, he would pull his precious niece out of public school and teach her himself. Which is precisely what he'd done. Men who adopted other people's offspring could be fussy as cats.

Along with the land and lumber, Cooper had donated the windows for the school. He didn't want his Suzanne to catch a chill from winter drafts or suffer through an Indian summer without a lick of cooling ventilation. Daffron stood by the brick pilings, looking up at those windows: six panes over six with double-hung sashes. His moonlit shadow against the horizontal wooden siding gazed back. Cooper had built the school for the kids but mostly for his Suzanne, the only female he'd ever given a snake's slither about.

He ran his fingertips over the schoolhouse's wooden siding and kicked the door open. He hated doing this to family, but his cousin Cooper had been a fool to double-cross him. Times like this the best way to get Cooper's attention was through Suzanne. Daffron clicked his tongue in disgust. His cousin was downright disappointing. A family embarrassment.

The rusty threads on the kerosene can ground against one another as he unscrewed the cap. He splashed the gurgling fury over floorboards and onto the fancy wrought iron legs on a student desk where not a scratch or an initial had been carved. Cooper had told him if the kids so much as nicked the desks he'd bought, Suzanne promised to send them into mosquito-infested woods to fell and lumber the very trees they'd need to build new desks. "Suzanne is like her daddy," Cooper had told him, "loves her job more than anything else."

Daffron knew how it felt to live for one thing alone. He fingered the head of a kitchen match, the small rough surface powerful enough to light a lamp, cook a meal, or destroy a dream. Framed photographs on the wall behind Suzanne's desk caught his eye. Suzanne's students, all of them. He lifted the pictures from their nails, placed one over the other, and positioned a crude portrait of Suzanne, painted by one of her students, on top. He capped the pile with the book Cooper had bought Suzanne after they'd hung a couple of niggers in Tilden—*Poems of Emily Dickinson-Second Series*—and, arranging them to look like a vandal-thief got scared and dropped his booty, stashed them in the woods.

Beside a rotting stump, he dropped the red handkerchief he'd lifted from Cooper's automobile. Cooper had taken the dirty rag from Pucker Face Francis Dobles a few weeks back after the goofy kid had been puppy-dogging his daughter to the point of scaring her. Pucker Face had so wanted Suzanne to notice him. Let her, and the rest of this nigger-infested town think this was his doing.

Everyone would fall for this trick. Everyone but Cooper. He'd get the message, an unfriendly reminder: Don't screw with Daffron Mears.

A strange calm, a gift he hadn't expected, filled him. He sighed as he dropped the lit match in the kerosene. Without looking back, he tore through the woods. Within the next half-hour, the townsfolk would tumble, shovels in hand, out their front doors, and he had to make it look like he'd never left Mearswood Farm.

CHAPTER 22

Lies, housed in the hell of good intentions,
reveal themselves in the flames of deceit.

Taylor Crawford, journal entry, April 10, 1910

One hell of a crowd. Whites to one side, Negroes to the other. All had roused themselves to see what was going on. The fire, whooshing up the walls of the school, hissed and roared with a deafening fury. Pressed in the crooks of their mamas' arms, howling babies covered their tiny ears with their hands. Women with their hair wrapped in curling rags wept.

The mayor, who'd been elected because Cooper and his deputies counted the ballots, was a short nervous man whose hairy bowed legs showed from the tops of his sockless shoes to the hem of his nightshirt. Unselfconscious, he bounced from person to person, consoling mothers and fathers, reassuring them that "Yes, of course, we'll build another school."

Drought had taken its toll on the fire pond behind the school. Within fifteen minutes, the flames were so close that shovel-wielding men fighting the fire couldn't stay at the well long enough to draw its meager water. Racked with coughing fits, they withdrew, taking with them suffocated hopes for their children's futures.

"Let it burn," Cooper ordered the flummoxed deputy as he tried to explain what Cooper could see with his own damned eyes.

"But Coop, it's the school," Deputy Hobbs said, his voice hoarse from the choking night air.

"Keep everyone back," Cooper snapped as though the destruction of his daughter's school didn't trouble him a lick. Citizen safety had to sound like his only concern. Trying to keep his rage in check, he dug the fingers on his good hand into his palm. "What's the matter with those people? Get them out of the woods." He was screaming now. Goddamn, he meant it. "Out of the woods," he repeated. "Tell them, Hobbs. Move!" The deputy padded along, careful not to step out of his slippers.

Cooper couldn't wait. He stomped off, unlaced boots pounding, hand on his holster, just in case. "Everyone to the north side of the fire," he hollered, jerking his arm and three-fingered hand in the direction he wanted his neighbors to go.

They shuffled along, stopping to glance back at the fire and him repeatedly flicking his wrist, a display that made him look like he was shaking off a fistful of shit. Prompted by the premonition that something more than the fire was terribly wrong, he elbowed them aside.

***

Suzanne stared in horror at the flaming pyre. Aville Louise wrapped an arm around her daughter's waist and was drawing her in close when Suzanne burst from her side. "My rabbit's in there," she screamed, darting toward the fire, arms pumping, sky-blue bathrobe flapping.

"Cooper!" Aville Louise shouted, but Sheriff Cooper Peall, occupied with everyone else's safety didn't hear her but then, did he ever?

"Stop. We'll buy another rabbit. Don't..." Aville Louise yelled against the fire's raging. Screaming, "Suzanne!" she hiked her nightgown and robe to her knees and ran after her, rampaging toward the schoolhouse.

Her face dripped, arms tingled, her nightgown clung to her back. Her lungs ached from yelling for Suzanne to forget that rabbit. Her panting seemed louder than all the turmoil combined until a deafening crack shook the ground. Explosions followed one after the other. Windows thundered through the air.

Glass rained. Sheets, shards, sparkling sharp slivers chased Aville Louise. Shoulders humped, arms protecting her head, she scrambled toward Suzanne's sky-blue figure at the far edge of the fire.

Neighbors bolted past, making what should have been a short dash to the other side of the schoolyard near to impossible. Aville Louise caught a glimpse of her daughter being snatched from the path of flying glass. She stopped to yell to her and was jostled, turned around, and carried off in a stampede. By the time she got her bearings, she'd lost sight of Suzanne.

She stepped onto a tree stump. Able to see outlines of smoky faces from her new vantage point, she scanned, starting at the far end of the remnants of the school and worked outward. A tall, thin man was bending over someone on the ground. Not Suzanne, Aville Louise assured herself as the person lying there wore white. Selfishly relieved, her chest tightened with a new dread. What if Suzanne had made her way into the schoolhouse?

As she got down from her lookout, Mrs. Latt tugged at her sleeve and asked if she'd seen Mr. Latt. "No, no I'm sorry," Aville Louise said, hating herself for pushing past her. "But keep looking, he's here somewhere," she added, shielding her eyes from spits of glowing wood and sizzling ash, straining to relocate Suzanne.

By the time she reached the other side of the schoolyard, rumors had already started: Mr. Wiley's son found a red handkerchief along with photographs that had been in the schoolhouse... The handkerchief belonged to the Dobles boy, the one they call Pucker Face... Sheriff Peall sent his deputy to arrest him... The sheriff won't sleep until he finds him... Too bad for that Dobles boy, he's in trouble now...

A tall scar-faced young man was tucking a bathrobe like Suzanne's around the person lying at his knees. "She's cut bad, but she's gonna be all right," he said, his voice scorched and raspy.

She couldn't bring herself to speak; 'dear God,' she mouthed, dropping to the ground beside her baby.

Aville Louise didn't cry until she caught sight of her husband coming toward them. As she pieced the scene together, she wasn't sure what frightened her more: her daughter's insane sprint towards the flames, the explosions, the drama of this young man's brave interference with Suzanne's dash—his leap into the air, lanky legs flapping like a heron's as he tackled Suzanne, snatching her from sure disaster—or the shard of glass protruding from her daughter's once-flawless cheek.

***

Suzanne's hands fluttered around the shard, approached and withdrew in waves of repulsed motion. She started to lick her lips to dampen them so she could speak but stopped when she realized they were coated with blood. "Help me," Cooper heard her whimper as he glowered at his wife.

He lightly touched Aville Louise's elbow to move her aside so he could take over when panic, an overwhelming hysteria he'd never before experienced, brought him to his knees. Suzanne's injury bore down on him. Her unbelieving eyes, her startled mouth, and that wound... He could barely look at it. He fought back the surge of bile in his gullet and forced himself to lower his eyes to that jagged glass.

He took his daughter's sticky hands and silenced them within his. His face settled into the brittle mask of calm. "Dr. Hovner is on his way." He studied her for signs of pain. Shock had set in. "Don't talk, lie still." With this, her writhing stopped and his started.

"Aville Louise, can you see Dr. Hovner?" He followed his wife's pokey movements as she wiped her eyes and searched figures huddled within shrouds of smoke.

"Aville?" He hadn't meant to use his worst husband's voice, but it rushed out: Impatient. Demanding. Loaded. Silently accusing her: You don't understand this brand of terror. How can you when you're not Suzanne's real mother?

"I'm looking, I don't see him," she said in a voice that let him know he ought not to be so cruel.

He hated when she talked to him like that. A string of thoughts assembled in his mind like good deputies, ready to do his bidding. Other than vent his frustration, setting them lose would serve no purpose. Besides, he didn't want to upset Suzanne.

This isn't a fatal wound, he reminded himself, although he worried she would have to live with a permanent reminder of the fear that had goaded him these past twenty-one years—a vicious scar, the kind Daffron Mears seared into the faces of niggers, poor folk who for no reason other than the color of their skin became his victims.

Cooper had watched nigger-hating men whose lynching activities had the holier-than-y'all quality of the housewife who scrubs every corner of her home with good strong bleach. Daffron was different. It wasn't niggers haunted him; it was another demon.

He hadn't been the one to explain this to Cooper, Suzanne's Negro mama had. Seems her little brother had been hiding in the barn when Daffron's father whooped him limp. The old man knew a pair of nigger eyes was watching, and he made sure Daffron knew. Later, Daffron told the nigger boy he'd kill his father before he let him pound him again. But his father was bigger and meaner and just to remind him, he beat Daffron a lot.

Beatings fertilized a boy's wish to get back at his father into a man's desire to kill. From first light to the end of day, Daffron imagined himself choking the life out of his old man. But his father one-upped him one last time—he went and died in his sleep. That made Daffron even angrier. Only thing helped him forget his old man was killing niggers. To quell the fire searing his gut, he told Cooper he planned to do away with every last nigger in Georgia.

Suzanne groaned. "Goddamn it, run and find Doc Hovner," Cooper snarled at the fellow gawking over his shoulder.

As the tall, thin figure loped off, Cooper glanced at Aville's adoring face and realized what had happened: if not for that fellow, his precious daughter wouldn't be alive.

CHAPTER 23

Flotsam weights truth and holds it beneath the storm's unruly surf until, contrary to that which nature would have us expect, truth gentles its way to the surface and beckons with a gasp.

Taylor Crawford, *My Life in Georgia*, 1929

"Margaret still sick or are you here for the lye?" Mother Hart said. "The stink won't go away unless you pour the entire jar into the privy."

Acey didn't care about lye. How could he? With pictures of the school sizzling in his brain, he wasn't worried about the stench from his privy. He looked up at Mother Hart, waiting for him to answer. No, he mouthed, swallowing to make his voice return.

"Did you see the fireball in the sky? It was the school, going up quicker than fireworks on the Fourth of July." He spread his arms wide over his head to show her how the smoke had billowed. There was plenty more he would have said, but he clamped his mouth shut. No way could he chance telling her that seeing Daffron set that fire scared him more than watching him hang Trivett. Most likely he didn't need to say much. That he'd caught a gander of hell had to be written plain as the soot on his face.

Mother leaned her head against the doorjamb. "Dear Lord, what else can go wrong tonight? The news would have reached me soon enough, I may as well hear it from you. But that's not why you came back, is it?"

Acey couldn't recall. Not exactly. Looking at his mule and wagon brought some pictures to mind. Earlier tonight after he left Mother Hart off, he was almost home when he remembered the lye. He turned the wagon around and, on his way back, stopped to pee. Thinking a fox was rustling in the woods, he peeked from around a big old pine to find Daffron, shoving something into the brush. He almost called, "Hey," but thought better of it.

Instead, he climbed the pine and watched Daffron head toward the school. And that's when things got real strange. Seconds later—whoosh.

Acey leaned forward to get a better look, to make sure the figure silhouetted against the flames was really Daffron Mears, and nearly tumbled from the tree. He wrapped his arms around the sappy branch and hung on tight. If he stayed that way, maybe his stomach would stop churning. Maybe he'd see the man down there wasn't his brother-in-law but the devil wearing his brogans.

The flames grew hotter by the minute, sucked the sweet salt smells from the air, and sent sweat draining down Acey's neck. He didn't know what to do next until his mule started braying. Last time she'd been near a bonfire, she got so spooked, she up and ran off. He hurried back to her, cupping his hands, one to each side of his face, so the fire wouldn't hurt his eyes. He tied the kerchief Margaret had left in the wagon around the mule's eyes and led her down the road.

By the time he made his way around to the school, folks were running back and forth, yelling and hollering. Cooper stood by the dried-out fire pond, shouting orders, his face burning redder than the fire. Daffron was nowhere in sight.

That's what confused Acey the most. Made him think maybe he'd seen the devil and not Daffron Mears at all. "Devil plays tricks on people's minds," his mother used to warn. Anyway, here he was in front of the only person left who could make things better, trying like hell to remember the message he was supposed to give her. Finally, he blurted the best his memory could serve, "Sheriff told me to fetch you."

"I've smelled a fire for some time now," Mother Hart said. Her gaze followed the milky smoke swallowing the trees. A set of lines appeared across the bridge of her nose. "Somebody hurt?"

Acey nodded and plucked a pine needle from his hair—so, his memory hadn't been singed after all. "Suzanne Peall—she got hit with glass."

Within minutes, Mother Hart was arranging herself on the wagon bench beside him. He placed the jar of lye she handed him out of the way. "Thanks." He shook his head, "Can't say that lye will do much. The stink's worse than you know."

***

Cooper Peall paced across his front porch, the glow from his cigarette traveling up and down, back and forth. His toe caught the edge of his wife's favorite wicker rocker and almost yanked him to his knees. Quick as a cat he recovered his balance, kicked the chair and created a satisfying clatter. He paused to listen for nervous pattering overhead across Suzanne's bedroom floor. Sure enough, a drum roll of footsteps later, Aville Louise poked her head out the window.

"Must you make so much noise?" she demanded in a hoarse whisper. Cooper pressed his haunches to the railing and looked up.

"Sorry," he murmured. His awkward position made it difficult to see the strain of her neck, the clench of her teeth but then, he didn't need to. He'd witnessed them many times before.

"How long does it take that Acey to wake Doc Hovner? Doc never sleeps that sound," he grumbled, smoke from his mouth adding to the smoldering that had settled over the town.

He rubbed the sweat dripping from his chin onto his reeking shirtsleeve. He clamped his cigarette between his front teeth and brushed bits of soot from his khaki uniform, smudging it from his collar to his pocket. "Shit," he muttered, jamming his fingers against the badge in his pocket.

A gray arch of ashes dangled from his lips. He flicked his cigarette, then pinned the badge on his chest, where it belonged. In plain view. Don't know why I didn't think to slap this on when I went down to the school, was his innocent thought. You know damn well, replied its more honest twin.

"About time," Cooper snarled when Acey's wagon came rolling down the lane with Mother Hart seated where the doc should have been.

Acey hopped from the wagon, rushed up the steps.

Cooper poked him in the chest. "Where's Doc Hovner?"

"Doc Hovner?" Acey aped. "This lady's better. She's a real healer."

Cooper felt his face flush with anger. First the fire, then Suzanne, now this. Acey glanced at the sheriff's fists opening and closing and hopped out of arm's reach. But Cooper dragged him close enough to kiss the blindfolded lady on his badge. "Aville Louise is gonna have a fit when she sees..." He paused, his eyes tracing the birdlike silhouette in the doorway from the hem of the ruffled nightgown upward along the bloodstained folds of her pink bathrobe to her annoyed olive green eyes.

"The doctor's here? Thank goodness." A mother's worried voice. "The bleeding..." she choked on her words, then caught hold of herself. "Suzanne can't wait any longer."

Acey brightened. "She ain't a doctor, ma'am, she's better. You should have seen what she did for Margaret. I thought she was going to die until..."

"Shut up, Acey." Cooper pushed him aside. "Acey fetched Mother Hart by mistake. He was just leaving to get Doc Hovner. Weren't you?"

Acey looked from Aville Louise to Cooper. "What about Mother Hart?" he blurted. They glanced at her, hands folded over the bag on her lap, back straight as a new blade of grass.

Cooper picked up the wicker rocker and carried it to the bottom of the steps. "She can sit here, while you fetch the doc, then you can bring her home."

Aville Louise stepped out from behind the screen door, put her hand on Cooper's shoulder and gently, firmly moved him aside. She crossed the veranda to the stairs and paused on the first step until the ball of her foot lighted on the one below.

With her back to him, she raised her face to Mother Hart and lowered her voice into the private womanly tones that infuriated Cooper. "I'd be forever grateful, Mother Hart, if you'd see to my daughter."

"I'm here to do my best, ma'am."

Aville Louise murmured in relief as she stretched out her arms and swished down the steps.

"If you please, ma'am, Promise would want to be here with Miss Suzanne. Besides, I imagine I will need her help."

"Of course. Acey can get her. Here, let me help you with your bag."

Mother hesitated. "I'd be grateful," was all she said as the bag moved from one mother's hands to another's.

Cooper glared at Mother Hart, who made no eye contact with him. Instead, she trained her eyes on his wife's ruffle and followed her past the men into what he'd come to think of as Aville Louise's home. He couldn't say for sure but, if the opportunity for a wager were to appear, he'd have placed his hard-earned coin on the glimmer of a smile cracking Acey Baldwin's chops.

CHAPTER 24

When a wife cracks open her husband's lies and places them, slithering and gelatinous, onto a platter for both to see, he has little choice but to succumb to the scrambling his misdeeds have perpetuated.

Taylor Crawford, undated journal entry

Suzanne's jewelry box bedroom was lined with petal-soft carpeting, walls that danced with meadow flowers, and frilly drapes the color of the creamy satin bedspread spilling over the foot of her bed. Beside it on the floor, a blue chenille bathrobe caked with drying blood. Accustomed as she was to the smells of a woman giving birth, the violent scent of injury stole Mother's breath.

She arranged the drawstring on her bag, so it gaped wide on the straight-backed velvet chair by Suzanne's bed. With jars, bandages, scissors, towels, and soap in clear view, she slipped into her apron and buttoned it secure. After setting a fresh basin of hot water on the nightstand, Aville Louise hurried to the other side of the bed and lifted the kerosene lantern.

Had it not been for the telltale shard of glass protruding from the pale cheek, Mother would have worried about intruding on Miss Suzanne's sleep, for her eyes were closed, lips gathered in a gentle pucker from which she breathed in and out. "I gave her a few drops of sedative, something Cooper keeps downstairs in the pantry," Aville Louise explained.

"We'll have to wake her," Mother said, removing from her bag the manufactured bandages Promise had brought from Boston and cutting small triangles into them. "Best let Miss Suzanne know what's happening."

Aville Louise seemed puzzled. "She was so upset, I hate to wake her."

Mother dipped her hands in the basin and scrubbed with one of the soap cakes she and Promise had made last summer. Flecked with citrus skin, its fresh smell wafted upward on threads of steam. "I can't take a chance on her moving while I work on her." After washing, she asked Aville Louise for a clean pan of hot water. "And if Sheriff Peall is free, perhaps he could join us."

Disapproving wrinkles formed at the corners of Aville Louise's small mouth. "But we're handling the situation quite well."

"We'll need an extra pair of hands until Promise gets here." Mother's words helped move her along.

By the time she and the sheriff returned, Mother Hart was dabbing golden antiseptic liquid around the injury, taking special care to stay away from the wound itself. Suzanne groaned and rocked her head slightly.

The sheriff positioned himself opposite Mother. The scent of smoke from the fire along with his cigarette breath made her queasy. "How is she?"

Mother dabbed over and around the shard. "If she'd been hit an inch higher, she'd have lost her eye, so I'd say she's lucky." She pretended not to see Cooper Peall shiver.

"I suppose you're right, though I hate to think..."

Suzanne groaned again. "We'd best get to work. Hold her head steady, Sheriff." Mother Hart locked her eyes on his and asked for Mrs. Peall.

"Aville Louise. Call me Aville Louise."

Cooper glanced in amazement at his wife. He took a breath. Mother suspected he was about to correct her until he looked into her eyes and realized there was no need—whatever transpired in this room would never see the light of day.

"Yes, ma'am, Aville Louise, see if you can wake Miss Suzanne. Gentle now."

Nudging her husband closer to the headboard carved with cherubs, she placed her hand on Suzanne's shoulder. "Suzanne? Open your eyes, Mother Hart is here to help us." A groan. The flutter of lashes.

"You're going to be all right, Miss Suzanne. I'll go easy, but this is going to sting." As Mother dabbed closer to the wound, Suzanne pulled herself deeper into the pillow. "Hold her firm."

Cooper worked his fingers beneath his daughter's hair, stiff with dried blood, and pressed his palms to the sides of her head.

As Mother Hart sprinkled a white powder on Suzanne's cheek, she explained that this "blood blocker" would keep her from bleeding once the glass was removed. She dipped her long dark fingers into the white powder she'd poured on a towel, raised her chin and nodded first at him, then focused on Aville Louise, who waited for her unspoken signal.

Now, Mother blinked. Her white-tipped fingers lifted the glass out and away and, within the same movement, edged one side of Suzanne's torn cheek toward its mate all the while talking to Suzanne in a low steady voice. One so reassuring that Suzanne lay still without her father's help.

Cooper relaxed his grip and stepped back, but not before Mother read the rejection smarting in his eyes.

"Daddy?" Suzanne murmured for her father for the first time since Mother Hart had arrived. "Daddy, don't go. Stay with me, Daddy." He stared at her dry pale lips and swallowed hard.

Aville Louise waited. And when her husband didn't answer, she spoke for him. "He's right here, baby, helping Mother Hart is all. That's why he can't talk now."

Mother Hart ignored the tension festering between Aville Louise and her husband and hoped, when Promise arrived, she would have the good sense to ignore their rift. Delicately, as if matching lines within the intricate plaid of a fine dress and joining them without a hint of a seam, she secured sections of Suzanne's face with the bandages she had shaped.

With luck, there'd be no scarring. She promised to leave a cream that would ease the chance of a disfiguring line. "I give it to all the new mothers. Helps their bellies and other places repair good as new."

***

Aville Louise didn't care to think about which "other places" Mother Hart was referring to. Matter of fact, she avoided the topic of birthing altogether even though twenty-one years earlier, after she'd returned from Alabama with her bundle of sweetness in the crook of her arm, she recited (in hushed ladylike tones, of course) the birthing story she'd concocted to any lady friend who dared ask.

She did what her husband insisted she do—create a story to cover her "inadequacy" as Cooper so indelicately put it. She'd listened carefully to other women's stories, then picked out a labor pain here, a rip there, and pieced together her very own quilt of lies.

By now, Mother Hart had positioned two triangle-shaped bandages bridged by a strong but narrow rectangle onto Suzanne's cheek. The white powder made the bleeding stop, just as she had promised. And that horrid chunk of glass lay on a towel.

Aville Louise dropped her handkerchief over the glass, cupped her fingers into a claw, and whisked it from her daughter's bed. When she looked up, her husband was walking away. "Where are you going?"

"That's got to be Acey," Cooper said, brushing aside a ruffled curtain to peer out the window. "Can't see with all the smoke. Looks like the doc's with him."

He resumed his position by Suzanne's side and took hold of her little finger. She tried to draw her full lips into a smile, which made her wince. "Don't move, rest," he said.

"Sorry you had to come out so late, but everything is under control," Aville Louise said to Doc Hovner, standing in the bedroom doorway. She glanced at Mother Hart, twisting lids onto her jars and placing them in her bag, and back towards the doctor. "I suppose Acey told you what happened?"

The doctor was confused. "Acey? No, Francis here," he pointed over his shoulder and down the hallway, "told me Suzanne was heading into the burning schoolhouse when he tackled her. I understand she's been cut rather badly by flying debris."

Cooper came forward and shook the doc's hand. "Glass, she caught a chunk of glass just as the windows exploded. Appreciate your coming. Did I hear you say Francis?"

Aville Louise stepped in front of her husband, took the doctor's arm and guided him toward the bed. "We were fortunate Mrs. Hart was available to assist us. Suzanne was losing a fearful amount of blood. Thank goodness, Mrs. Hart stopped the bleeding and—"

"I'll have a look," the doc said, setting his black grip on the velvet chair as Mother lowered her deerskin bag to the floor.

The left half of Suzanne's face from her lower eyelid to the edge of her mouth was dressed, bandaged, and taped. Doc Hovner adjusted his glasses. "How are you feeling, Suzanne?"

"Like my head is the size of a termite's nest."

The doc wiggled his silver whiskers into a smile. "Headache?" he asked, gently fingering Mother Hart's tidy bandage.

"No, just feeling bruised like the time I fell off the swing."

He passed four oversized fingers in front of her eyes. "How many?"

"Seventy-two?"

A flicker of distress flashed, then melted from his tired eyes. "After that, how many?" She raised four fingertips. He glanced sideways at her mother. "Nothing's damaged her sense of humor."

"No," Aville Louise said, releasing a grateful sigh and putting her hand on the doctor's arm to stop him from peeling back the bandage Mrs. Hart had so carefully applied. He looked surprised at her boldness, the audacity of her touching him.

Aville Louise faced him. "The work was flawless, from cleaning the wound to piecing the flesh together to dressing it. I watched the entire operation." She thought of her husband's accident—the stumped finger the doctor had left him with and how, when she complained of the dangling tag of skin, those large, awkward hands of his fumbled as he clipped the skin and stitched the remains in place—and shuddered.

Doc Hovner cleared his throat, sank his hands in his pockets. "Then why, my dear lady, did that young man drag me from my bed?"

She glanced at Suzanne's eyes weighted with sleep. "Shh," she brought her finger to her lips. "What if I brought her to your office, soon as she's up and about? You could check her then."

The doctor raised his bushy eyebrows. "Fine," he sighed and reached for his grip. "Perhaps Francis can take me home?"

Just then, Cooper grabbed hold of the doorjamb and pivoted into the hallway. "My deputy's been looking for you," he hissed.

Sounds of a scuffle sent Aville Louise scurrying. "What on earth are you doing, Cooper? If that young man hadn't caught Suzanne, we'd be picking her remains out of the schoolhouse because that's where she was headed. Right into that goddamned fire." Aville Louise was screeching, and while she'd been known to shout, she'd never, in all the years she'd spent with Cooper, sworn.

Cooper tightened his grip on Pucker Face's arm. "If it hadn't been for you, young man, we'd still have a school."

Aville Louise blanched. Doc Hovner inched forward. Mother Hart craned her neck. Suzanne's eyes jerked open.

The front door slammed, and Promise rushed up the steps.

Deputy Hobbs followed, slippers slapping. "Someone said they saw Pucker Face at the Doc's, but when I went there..." The deputy's jaw dropped.

"Bring him to the jail. Lock all the doors and stay with him. And be sure to arm yourself. Townsfolk are feeling nastier than hornets in fall, threatening to lynch the bastard who started the fire."

Hobbs' bleary eyes just about popped from their sockets. "They're gonna hang Pucker Face?" With that, the boy slid down the wall and dropped his head between his knees.

"Not if you do your job."

"Got him," the deputy said, pulling the boy to his feet and handcuffing him behind his back. "Wouldn't happen to have a rag, would you?"

The sheriff gave Aville Louise a look that sent her scurrying for the clean cloth Mother Hart had folded and left on the nightstand. She motioned for Promise to join her.

Suzanne's eyes questioned her mother.

Not now, she mouthed, guiding Promise to the foot of the bed beside Mother Hart. "You have a visitor," Aville Louise said and, rag in hand turned toward the hallway.

"Suzanne, what happened?" Promise said, lurching toward her friend.

Mother Hart grabbed Promise's forearm, whirled her around.

"Is she going to be all right?" Promise barely whispered. "Who would do something like this? Who?" she demanded, her glistening eyes darting back and forth between Suzanne and Mother Hart.

Mother Hart took Promise's chin in her fingertips. Stroking her cheek, she pushed the teardrops aside and willed her to calmness.

It was the first time Mother Hart had touched her since Taylor told her about the episode in the barn. Promise locked eyes on Mother's. "I'm sorry, I was harsh...I didn't mean to be cruel," she started apologizing for having treated Mother unkindly and, realizing this was hardly the time, took a breath. "I mean, is Suzanne in pain?"

Without waiting for a reply, she gently ran her hand along the side of the bed, to her friend's shoulder. "Don't worry, Suzanne. Mother Hart heals everyone she touches. I'm glad she's here for you."

***

The sheriff took the rag from Aville Louise and handed it to Hobbs, who tied it around Pucker Face's eyes. "Got any rope in that damn wagon of yours?" Cooper yelled.

Aville Louise, the doctor, Mother Hart, the boy, Hobbs, even Promise gasped. Cooper rolled his eyes in disgust. "I'm going to tie his feet to the bench in the wagon."

Aville Louise sighed in relief and out of the same relief, rushed to her husband's side and put her hand on his arm. "I'm not going anywhere," he said, grabbing hold of the blindfolded boy and leading him down the stairs.

Aville Louise stood there, struggling with her thoughts when Pucker Face jerked his head around. "I'd never hurt Miss Peall. No one loves a woman would do anything like that. You believe me, don't you, Mrs. Peall?" He scanned the air with his chin, searching for her reply.

"She's got nothing to say to you," the sheriff grumbled as he and his deputy dragged the boy outside.

But the sheriff had spoken out of turn, thought Aville Louise as she fingered the penny in her bathrobe pocket. If she were asked to hand that penny to the most honest man standing there—the arrogant doctor, the bleary-eyed deputy, the lanky lad, or the man wearing the badge—she wouldn't hesitate. She'd march down those steps and tuck that penny into Pucker Face's hand.

DAY THREE

CHAPTER 25

I have a multitude of reasons for keeping fearful details about Daffron Mears from Promise, foremost of which is her safety.

Taylor Crawford, journal entry, July 21, 1925

Promise arrived at her farm and found Duchess at the fence by Cambridge's stall. She walked her to her stall at the other end of the barn and, waiting for her to settle, slumped on a bale of hay. Soon, she fell into a deep, disturbing sleep and dreamed she was surrounded by coyotes. Their snarling seemed so real, she opened her eyes with a start, her heart racing. She rushed out of the barn to find the smoke-lined sky had capped the mist and stopped it from dispersing.

Other than insects, nothing stirred. Silence blanketed the early morning. No screaming crows flapping from tree to tree, no screeching rooster claiming his territory, no boisterous romping dogs. Come to think of it, Promise hadn't heard the dogs since she'd returned from Suzanne's. By now, Jasper and Tiv would usually create a ruckus in the henhouse, poke their heads under the lean-to and annoy the goats. Afterward, they'd scare the ducks from the pond, lap up a long drink of water, and race back to the horses' stalls.

Ordinarily, their absence wasn't disturbing, but in the aftermath of the fire, the air reeked. She worried they'd gone searching for the source of this acrid smell. After snooping among the chars, perhaps they'd been injured and had taken to hiding. Creatures suffering the aftereffects of a fright often refuse to leave their shelter, which was how she'd felt last night when she was alone with her horses in the barn.

She walked through the ashen fog that lingered in low spots along the ground, planting round-toed footprints in the soot. As she headed for the cabin, she hoped Andrew would still be asleep. But there he was in his bathrobe on the front porch, handkerchief pressed to his nose, pacing. Seeing her, he leaned over the railing and whispered one frantic question after the other. "What happened? Where's the smoke coming from? Was it arson? Did the sheriff find the culprit?"

Exhausted, Promise answered with as few words as possible.

He took her by her shoulders, "What about you, are you okay?"

She nodded, told him about Suzanne's injury, then said, "Please, Andrew, I need to find my dogs."

"But, Suzanne. Is she going to be all right?" he asked as she hurried down the steps.

She fingered a petal of ash and watched it disintegrate. "She lost her precious school. I'm afraid her heart is in cinders."

***

Promise whistled for the dogs. The drone of insects became louder and more insistent as she neared the pond's looming cattails. She crossed the wagon road and headed toward the old orchard by Taylor's grave, whisked past the quiet busyness of the beehives through the grayness past her herb garden, around the listing privy to the back of her cabin. Limp muslin curtains in both bedroom windows had been drawn, as only city-dwellers would think to do.

There was no sign of Mother Hart, starting breakfast on the summer stove. Though hours had passed since reading Taylor's journal, she had yet to make peace with the revelation that had turned her life into a lie, what Taylor had defined as an insidious act that undermines a person's honor and harms the community. To which she added, "And makes her once-solid ground slippery."

She stepped carefully past the motionless swing on the hickory tree, the moss-covered springhouse, sooty vegetable garden, beyond the smokehouse to the gate at the farthest end of the hay field. On her way back, she whistled two notes, one high the other low, and waited for foggy fingers to carry them to her dogs. Had they been anywhere on the farm, they would have heard her and she, them. Dread, a lurking sense that reached beyond missing pets, crept through her.

"Jasper! Tiv!" Not a yip or bark.

She wandered past Taylor's grave. Upturned clumps of weeds marked a patch of ground long as her arm and five times as wide. Beside it, flies, the first to appear after anything died, crawled over one another, circled upward, and returned to a puddle of blood. "Oh, God, no." She grabbed a stick and waved it. A cloud of flies rose only to reappear when he stopped.

Though Taylor had slaughtered farm animals for food, he'd ended their lives swiftly, mercifully and buried their entrails out of respect and the need to keep vermin away. Not so here. Something destructive had happened. The possibilities sickened her.

She tossed the stick beside the buzzing swarm and headed towards the herb garden, around the cabin, and onto the front porch. Her nightmare was beginning to make sense. The coyotes. The howling. Something had been killed. Something she loved. “Tiv? Jasper? Please come home,” she whispered.

The small rug by the cabin door lay bunched into a lumpy nest, the kind Tiv and Jasper had snuggled into as puppies, head to head, tail to tail in a circle of bluetick fur. She squatted beside her shivering dog and patted it gently. “Where’s Tiv?” Jasper’s brush-stroked white eyebrows shifted from her to the floor and back. He whined.

“I buried it best I could in the dark.”

Startled, she lowered her hand to the porch floor to keep her balance. Jasper growled. “What did you bury?”

Daffron whipped his hat from his matted hair. “What’s its name, the other dog.”

“Tiv?” she said weakly. She wanted to ask what had happened and why he hadn’t come looking for her, but couldn’t speak. All she could think of was Tiv’s cold nose, waking her in the morning.

“Like I said, it was smoky-dark. I could just about see.”

She scowled. “Early on, the moon was so bright, I could have read by it.”

“I’m talking later, before dawn. By then, smoke from who-knows-where blew in thick and low. If you don’t like where she’s buried, I’ll move her, Miss Promise. You just say the word.”

Her stomach roiled. “Get the vet. He should be on his way into town by now.”

Daffron paled. “You want him to look at that dog?”

"Duchess is sick," she snapped, sinking to the steps. Just then, Jasper poked his head at her elbow. She raised her arm to let him in and pulled him close, breathed the woodsy smell of his fur.

Daffron looked genuinely distressed. "How am I going to get into town? Walking will take an awful long time," he brightened when he heard the rumble of wagon wheels and turned toward the road, "unless I borrow Fletch's wagon."

Fletch drove past them to the barn, then trudged back to the porch.

Covering her mouth so she wouldn't gag, Promise said, "You heard about the schoolhouse?"

Fletch nodded.

"Bet you haven't heard about Tiv—she's gone," Daffron blurted. "Dead," he added.

Fletch trained his eyes on Jasper.

"There's more. Duchess hasn't eaten in two days. I'm sending Daffron for the vet."

"I'm going to need a lift into town." Daffron glared at Fletch. "Don't know if you recall, but Cambridge and me don't get along."

"My fifty-seven-year-old mother walks when my mule isn't around."

Daffron glanced at Cassiopeia and gave Fletch a sly smile. "Now, that's good thinkin'. You don't mind if I use your mule and wagon then, do you?"

Promise wiped her cheeks. "Take Windsor. Fletch will saddle him for you." Daffron looked horrified. "Don't worry, he rides real gentle."

"What about my Beatie? I can't take her all the way into town on horseback, she's too little for that, and besides, she's sick."

"She can stay with me." Her words dropped hard as stones, and though she didn't mean to imply the child might come to some harm if he didn't get back and soon, if that's what was going through his ugly head, then fine.

He hesitated. "That's asking a lot, Miss Promise."

Footsteps in the kitchen and the swish of water being pumped drew Promise's attention. "Mother Hart is fixing breakfast. Soon as Beatie wakes, I'll give her something to eat. Now hurry."

After Daffron had gone, Fletch came out of the barn, shovel pressed to his shoulder, his eyebrows kneaded in thought. "Where did Daffron find Tiv?" he asked quietly.

"Near Taylor's grave."

"What was Daffron doing down there?"

She shrugged. "Walking, roaming. Who knows why he does the things he does?"

"Show me."

***

They walked down the road, her hand occasionally brushing his. He stopped and shook his head as though waking from a frightening dream. "I'm not sure what it is about that man, but when he's around, I feel helpless, like a little boy." The drum-tight skin across his forehead wrinkled with concern. "He's nothing but—"

"There," she wasn't interested in having him repeat Taylor's take on Daffron Mears.

But Fletch insisted on being heard. "When Daffron came whistling out from the woods the other day, you know the first thing I wanted to do?"

He peered down at her with such a distant look that she wasn't sure he saw her.

She hadn't been alone with him since Daffron arrived, and she wanted to make sure he understood that she'd hired Daffron to make him think they had nothing to hide. And that she'd knowingly kicked dirt at Taylor's platitudes about keeping Daffron clear of Mearswood. But that wasn't the point. Most of all, she wanted to tell him she had proof that Taylor had been a liar.

Fletch focused on the ridge on which Daffron had first appeared. "I never in my life felt inclined to kill a man, never. The minute I heard that whistling, before I saw the man's face, something inside me told me to drop my drawknife. If I hadn't, I swear I would have used it on him." He whispered, "Shameful thing is, I wish I had." He swiped his thumb across his throat and let his fist fall limp at his side.

"Fletch? What's the matter? You've never talked like that before."

He doubled over as though he'd been kicked in the stomach. Beads of sweat erupted over his face. She stepped closer. He put his hand out and twisted his head in the other direction. "There's no telling if he's watching from the woods. Make like I'm getting sick from the sight of this grave. That'll please him just fine."

"You're scaring me, Fletcher William. Answer me, or I'll throw my arms around you, right now. Fletch? I'm coming closer."

"I don't know for sure. Something about his whistling. Whenever I think about it, I have a hard time keeping myself from going after that man. Putting him someplace final." He picked up the shovel and tapped on the freshly turned earth. Flies scattered.

"Did you get a look before Daffron buried her?" His voice had hardened.

Her eyes brimmed. "No," she whispered.

"I'm going to see for myself."

"You're going to dig her up?"

He nodded, "Have to."

"What for?" She waited and when he didn't answer, headed for the pasture. "No need to be rude," she grumbled.

***

Cambridge stopped munching on a tuft of grass and came toward her, his massive shoulders swaying with an overgrown schoolboy's swagger. "How's my best boy?" He lowered his head and nuzzled her. "Did you hear about Tiv? How about Suzanne?" He whinnied. "I don't know what Jasper will do without her. Don't know what Suzanne will do when she hears."

She rubbed her cheek along his smooth jawbone, patted his beamy neck and recalled the morning of her sixteenth birthday when Uncle Taylor had gone off with his aging horse and returned with Cambridge and Duchess. That afternoon, Fletch, Mother Hart, and Suzanne stopped by with a basket. In it, two puppies, Tiv and Jasper, each wearing a yellow ribbon. "You grew up with Tiv, didn't you, fella?" Cambridge pressed his soft black lips to her neck.

"Down." He heaved a sigh and folded his legs beneath him. This had been the second command she'd taught him after "Stop." Cambridge watched her reach for the brush on the fence post. She stroked with one hand and brushed with the other, moving in a smooth rhythm from his shoulder down his ribcage over his heart and back again, stopping only to wipe away her tears.

She reached over Cambridge's haunch and looked up to find Fletch, face contorted, shovel clenched in one hand, Tiv's bloody collar in the other. "Tiv got caught in a trap."

She swallowed hard. "I don't allow trapping on my land. No one's been here, except Daffron." Her voice trailed off.

"Promise, send Daffron away before anything else happens." Fletch had never given her an order before this.

"What are you saying?"

"Someone killed Tiv with a noose."

Promise felt queasy. She dropped to her knees and sunk her fingers through the ashes and grassy sand into the earth. Fletch ran his finger over the top of her head and shuffled away, each footstep bursting with ash.

The farther he walked, the more clouded the distance between them. When the ash settled, she could see his shirt in the horses' water trough, where it floated in a bloody bubble. He stood half-naked, water rushing down his forearms. No matter how hard he scrubbed, Tiv's collar would always be ruined.

CHAPTER 26

Gripped by fear,
the righteous man analyzes its causes,
formulates a plan and seasons it with bluster.

Taylor Crawford, journal entry, June 10, 1910

No one knew for sure who had left this piece of damask, presumably in payment for delivering a baby, on Mother Hart's porch. She'd hemmed it by hand and used it as a tablecloth that she lent to her neighbors for the special occasions dotting their lives. Twenty years of birthdays, weddings, funerals, and a smattering of mounded stitches, repairs Mother had made to keep the mice chews from unraveling, had relegated the tablecloth to the realm of everyday.

Promise caught one rectangular end before it slid off the edge of the table's round surface, out of Mother's reach. Without lifting her eyes from her breakfast preparations, Mother rearranged the once lustrous flower pattern and coaxed the limp cloth to hang as gracefully as it could, then smoothed its wrinkles. From the looks of her quick, smart movements, she'd decided to grab hold of her grief and take charge of the day.

After landing another swipe at a remaining wrinkle, she removed the butter from the icebox and positioned it in the middle of the table along with the pair of church-hall salt and pepper shakers she treated like the queen's silver. She looked up to find Promise, leaning against the counter. "Eggs need cleaning," she said.

Still trying to absorb the fire, Suzanne's injury, and Fletch's discovery, Promise wrapped her hand around the cold handle and pumped as though a solitary act could cleanse the world of its barbarity. Water gushed over the morning collection of eggs, soaking her and sending torrents of feather-caked manure down the drain. She loaded the speckled beauties in a round-bottom basket and set it on the counter.

"Mind what's about to happen." Mother pointed to the glistening contents of the listing basket about to tumble to the floor.

Promise rearranged the eggs, and the basket recovered its balance. Sometimes that's all it took.

"Heard anything more about the fire?" Mother asked. Not a vestige of displeasure from last night's conversation reverberated in her tone or the pleasant way she arranged her smile though, truth be known, it was too fixed, too calm for the morning after their own blaze.

"Horses smelled it before I did. They were restless all night."

Mother picked a piece of straw from Promise's hair.

Relieved to reconnect in private, Promise welcomed her touch.

"Is that why you slept in the barn?"

She glanced toward her bedroom, where Ellen was sleeping.

Mother raised her eyebrows, gave a knowing nod. "Schoolhouse is gone, not a board left behind," she said, taking a few spoons from the cupboard.

Promise sank into a chair. "Who would do such a thing to Suzanne?"

"Don't worry, she'll heal with hardly a scar, I made sure of that."

Promise leaned her cheek on the hand Mother had placed on her shoulder. "You don't know how relieved I was to see you at Suzanne's bedside. I wish you'd been able to save Tiv."

Mother whirled around and faced her. "Something happened to Tiv?"

And while she told her everything, except Fletch's horrid discovery, Mother's intense gaze traveled to the front window in the direction of the shed.

"You think he started the fire? Why would he do that?"

"We've had one sorrow after another since Daffron came back."

Promise had to agree. "He seems to plunge his finger into every pie he sees. Claims he knew my mama, too."

Spoons clattered to the floor. "That man wouldn't recognize his own mama if she spit on him, never mind someone else's. Don't you believe a word, you hear?"

"That doesn't explain how he got hold of a box like the one my mama left me. You recall," she pressed her index fingers and thumbs into a rectangular shape, "yea small, carved, with a tiny latch?" Expecting Mother's easy recognition, she looked up to find her fumbling with the spoons, madly scrubbing one after the other with her apron.

"Course I remember," was all she said.

The door to Taylor's bedroom creaked open. "Trivett, Suzanne, the schoolhouse, your dog. What next?" was Andrew's distraught question. Raking his hair, he added, "I overheard everything from the other side of the door."

Before Promise could reply, the door on the other side of the fireplace inched open. Andrew took a deep breath. Mother and Promise exchanged wary looks. Ellen emerged in a blue short-sleeved dress that hung scandalously short, an inch below her knees. Her silk stockings gleamed, accenting her elegant heels and the thin leather straps snaking her ankles. Her short dark hair had been brushed shiny. On each side of her tight square jawbone rested a large brown spit of a curl that pointed to her red lips.

"It's not going to be a dressy kind of day," Andrew said, giving his sister her morning hug.

Promise added a quick, "You look nice, Ellen," and brushed past her into the bedroom where the bed had yet to be made. Powder puffs, hairbrushes, and a box of hairpins cluttered the bureau. Promise opened the top drawer and rooted around. She located her mother's white box and rushed out, accidentally bumping Ellen, who had yet to release her pose.

She grabbed hold of Ellen's elbow, steadying her. "Sorry." One whiff of her flowery cologne and she sneezed. Ellen didn't offer a sniff of a comment.

Mother and Andrew shifted their gazes toward Promise. Ellen scowled, clearly displeased at losing the spotlight. "I'm supposed to look in on Beatie," Promise explained, sliding her hand over her pocket and hurrying out the front door.

***

She found Beatie in the shed asleep, curled on the mattress, her thin, wheat-colored hair matted with sweat. One tiny hand clutched a threadbare pink blanket to her chin. Promise touched Beatie's damp forehead. Her muteness reminded her of her own childhood ailment: born with her tongue rooted to the floor of her mouth, it thickened her words into an unintelligible stew. Taylor had often asked her to repeat herself, causing her to choose between being misunderstood or doing without the assistance she needed—a button she couldn't reach or the letter she wanted him to mail to her lost mother.

She tiptoed across the room, trying to avoid the floorboards that creaked. She stopped and, seeing Beatie's eyes closed, hurried to the shelf. There, plain as the ash-filled sky, Daffron's white box.

She took her mother's from her pocket and held it alongside. Her mother's was a quarter of an inch wider and deeper but the wrought-iron latch and the carving—a hummingbird hovering over a welcoming morning glory—were identical. Her heart raced. Could Daffron really have known her mama? Might Taylor have written his confession to deter her from this discovery?

How insane, she thought, dismissing the notion. For this trick to work, he would have had to gain Mother Hart's cooperation. That's where her hypothesis flagged. Taylor wasn't beyond castrating the truth to suit his purposes, while Mother had always gone out of her way to keep it intact.

She tucked her mother's box into her pocket and held Daffron's with both hands. For some foolish reason, she expected it to be heavy. She flipped it over. From inside, a soft thud. She rapped her forehead with her knuckle. Why hadn't she checked before rattling it? If anything were broken, Daffron would know she'd been snooping. She wiped the sweat trickling down her temple, eased the box right side up, then gingerly lifted the latch. Face down on the velvet-lined interior was a tiny gold pin. Her mother's jewelry, perhaps?

She didn't think so. Mother Hart had described her as "shameful poor," someone who couldn't afford a pin like this with a locking clasp and delicate chain. She chewed her lip and considered the possibility that it might have been a lover's gift. She was about to pick up the pin when a voice shattered the silence.

She flipped the pin over and drew a startled breath. "No, oh no," was all she could manage to say. Snapping the lid shut she returned the box to the shelf, unwilling to believe what she'd seen. A lover's gift for sure, but not her mother's. It was the miniature trumpet Lizbeth had given Trivett on their wedding day. The pin he'd worn every day since.

Her hands suddenly felt dirty. She scrubbed her fingernails with imaginary soap and rubbed her palms together. The voice called again louder. "Pa?" Tiny rash-covered arms reached for her.

"Got you." Promise lifted the child, blanket and all, and ran from the shed. Beatie's arms tightened around her neck and her heart. Her orphan's vulnerability reacted fiercely—over-reacted as Fletch would have reminded her—to protect this small discounted child. She'd do anything to keep Beatie from harm. Anything.

"You're going to be all right, you hear?" She whispered into the child's musty hair. "You're with me, you're safe." And for a second she believed it until it occurred to her that none of them—Fletch, Mother Hart, Thaddeus and Cornelia and their children—were safe. Not even Beatie.

***

Promise set Beatie down by the swing on the hickory tree. The child chose a couple of hickory nuts and handed them to her, then ran to the front porch.

Promise steadied herself against the outside wall—ancient cypress planks Taylor had chosen because they'd never rot. Now she understood why Taylor had railed against Daffron whenever he tried to slink into Martonsville. Unreasonable as it seemed back then, Taylor's reaction was finally clear. To think she'd argued in favor of letting Daffron come home to visit Margaret after she'd given birth to Beatie. Her cheeks flushed with humiliation. She glanced down at Beatie, hands on her pale knees, squatting in front of the bird's cage, one wounded youngster to another.

Promise filled an eyedropper with food and lowered it into the bird's open beak. Beatie snuggled beside her. The crow swallowed greedily. Beatie's eyes widened. "Ready to give Peggy more breakfast?"

Beatie's lips parted into a wondrous smile. Right then and there, Promise knew she was right in deciding she'd do whatever it would take to keep that wonder intact.

"Lordy goodness, what have we here?" Smelling of fresh bacon, Mother Hart came outdoors, sat on the bench, and rested her elbows on her knees. "Haven't seen this little one since we delivered her. She looks just like Margaret when she was her age."

Mother reached for the child's chin, moved it from one side to the other. "Have you done anything for that rash?"

Too unnerved to speak, Promise shook her head.

Mother leaned forward, eye-level with Beatie. "Does it itch something fierce?"

"She doesn't say much, other than 'Pa.'"

"Acey told me she used to talk a streak." Mother clicked her tongue. "There's a reason a little one gives up on language. I have my birthing bag. Let's see if I have something in there for that rash." Beatie looked at Mother and pointed to the bird, now settled happily on its perch. "I watched you handle that bird gentle as can be. Someday you'll be like Promise, and all the animals will tell you their secrets."

"Here you go," Andrew said, opening the door and handing Mother the deerskin bag. Seeing her surprised reaction, he grimaced. "I was eavesdropping, again."

"Helpful hands and vigilant ears are always welcome." She set her bag on the bench, worked the drawstring open, and rummaged through its contents.

Seconds later, she showed Beatie a jar of golden salve and explained that after she washed, Promise would dab cream on that rash and make it better. "Sure is nice to have a little girl in the house again. Later when I get back, I'll bake you a peach pie with a crumbly crust, the kind Promise liked when she was your age." She rubbed her tummy. "And you can help. Would you like that?" The child clapped her hands.

Promise stepped aside to give Mother space to kneel by the cage.

Placing one hand on Mother's shoulder and the other on Beatie's, Andrew squeezed in. From solid to paunchy to miniature, they fit together neat as a New England stone wall.

Within Mother's birthing bag, the orderly arrangement of cord, compresses, salves, and a gaggle of purple threads caught Promise's eye. The ribbon, in particular, stood out, a ripe plum begging to be picked.

As Mother lowered her head beside Andrew's, Promise eased the ribbon from Mother's bag. Tied to the faded satin was the key to her trunk. Promise slipped the cool wrought iron deep into her pocket and drifted inside. After all, Beatie needed a basin of warm water and a chunk of soap, and she needed answers.

Promise glanced through the kitchen window—Mother was following her. Her smile had lost its buoyancy, her theatrics its drama. Yet Promise was pleased, oddly thrilled with what she'd done.

Mother started sorting through the heap of fabric by the sewing machine while Promise joined the others. Gently, ever so gently, she washed and dried Beatie's face. "We don't want to irritate that rash, do we?" She lifted her wet chin. "Oops, forgot a spot." Promise feigned a laugh. "All clean, you can open."

Beatie mouthed the words, "all clean."

"You keep trying, you'll be talking soon."

"Look what I found. Remember this, Promise?" Mother Hart stood in the doorway, holding up the long-sleeved dress with the ruffled hem she'd made when Promise was little. "Do you think Beatie would like to wear this?"

Promise rolled her eyes toward the child. "What do you think, Beatie?" She loved the feel of her name, deep and perky and round as a handful of fresh-picked peas.

Beatie answered with a smile. Promise swabbed the golden salve over Beatie's rash and slipped the dress over her head. The sleeves were too long, the waist too low. The yellow flowered ruffles reached her toes. Promise looked back at Mother Hart and wrinkled her nose.

Mother came down the steps, tilted her head to one side and studied the dress for a moment. "That little extra gives her room to grow. Besides, it won't aggravate her rash." She tilted her head to the other side." Hem's easy enough to take up. For now, she can roll up the sleeves. What do you think, Miss Beatie, do you like your new dress?"

She didn't answer. She was busily bunching the sleeves in her fists. When she'd finished, she raised her arms to show Mother.

"You've made yourself mittens, and that'll do just fine."

Just then, Jasper raised his head. His sleek blue fur twitched from the top of his neck down over his shoulders. He perked his ears. Alert, yet more alone than ever, Jasper was like the sky without its sun. A growl rumbled in his throat. He jumped to his feet, then chased down the road, barking.

"Beatie, your daddy's here," Promise said with a shiver. Beatie turned towards Daffron.

Promise's thoughts turned to Duchess. "What happened to the vet?"

Daffron leaned forward in the saddle. "What happened to my little girl?"

Promise's fingers tightened around the railing. She asked again, exaggerating each word as if he were hard of hearing. "Did you talk to the vet?"

He punched out the crown of his felt hat and repositioned it jauntily on his head.

"What did the vet say about Duchess?"

He pulled on the reins. Windsor stopped and began munching the grass. He patted the horse.

Promise chose the largest hickory nut from those Beatie had deposited on the bench and closed it in her fist.

"Goodness, Miss Promise, you get yourself all aggravated, you're gonna burst into flames, right before our eyes."

She forced herself to look at him. Bluster is the best cure for fear, she reminded herself as she headed straight for him. "Why won't you answer me?"

She took a firm hold of the edge of the saddle and squinted up at him. "I'll ask one last time. If I don't get a helpful answer, I'm going to wedge this," she showed him the nut with its rock-hard husk, "under Windsor's saddle. He'll give you a ride like you've never had before." She paused to let her words take effect. "Let's try again. Did you speak to the vet?"

He glared long and icy. "The vet had another emergency. Won't be in Martonsville till tomorrow."

She stamped the ground. "I can't believe it. Are you sure?"

But he wasn't listening. His eyes bulged with rage. He stared at Beatie, standing on the porch railing while Andrew held her waist.

Sleeves bunched in her fists, Beatie extended her arms out by her sides and stepped as though she were balancing on a tightrope. Between the yellow ointment streaked over her face and that oversized dress, she looked like a clown. Not that that mattered to her. She waved to her father and laughed.

"Who do you think you are, tying my little girl's hands like that?" Daffron bellowed.

The glee drained from Beatie's face. She turned and flung her arms around Andrew's neck.

"Who said you could touch my girl?"

Andrew set her down. Jasper snarled. Beatie froze.

Daffron swung his leg over the saddle horn and dropped to the ground. A burst of dust clouded his boots. He stomped up the steps to the porch, his ash-colored eyes stalking Andrew. "I don't want you near her, you hear? Get away."

Andrew spun around, feet in a boxer's stance, arms tensed, fists ready to stave off a punch. "Her hands aren't tied. Never were."

"You leave my daughter alone." Spit showered from his mouth and landed on Andrew's. Daffron smirked.

Andrew wiped his mouth with the back of his hand. Daffron whipped his fist back and was about to launch a punch when Beatie poked her hands through the ends of her sleeves. "No, Pa, look, Beatie's hands."

So the child could speak! More importantly, she'd bartered her speech for the grateful surprise that registered on her father's face and stunned him into dropping his fists.

"Here you go," Andrew said, handing Beatie over to Daffron, then mopping his face with his handkerchief.

As though Daffron was holding a precious piece of heirloom china, he moved slowly down the porch steps. "Did you have fun while Pa was gone? Tell Pa what you did." He jiggled her up and down, urging her to speak.

She gazed sadly into her father's eyes, placed her fingers over his lips, and lapsed into silence.

CHAPTER 27

Truth, like justice, makes its appearance when least expected.

Taylor Crawford, journal entry, January 11, 1930

Opened, Mother Hart's trunk brimmed with a tidiness that would have been reassuring had this been an ordinary visit. Today, however, the inside of the trunk took on the artfulness Promise had observed in Boston's finest storefronts, where meticulously dressed mannequins stole shoppers' attention from the disorder of daily life.

She, too, had allowed herself to succumb to distractions. Her suspicion that Taylor's journal entry was a mere crack in his window display continued to grow. With it, the painful realization of how thoroughly she'd trusted him. Betrayal, she was beginning to understand, created an irreconcilable hurt.

The penetrating scent of bleach rose from deep within the trunk. Reluctant to place Mother's clean supplies on the floor, she sorted through them a few at a time. She handled Mother's soaps more gingerly than this morning's eggs. Promise raised a tiny cake to her face and sniffed. Covered in pale blue from the quilt Mother had sewn for Trivett's baby, it smelled fresh as a newborn. Were she to damage it, Mother would never forgive her, understandably so.

Reaching for a ledger with a mottled blue cover, she whispered prayers, promises of the changes she would make if it would please, oh please unlock the secrets of her birth. Her hands trembled as she thumbed through pages of births she'd attended. Not what she wanted.

She tried replacing each item exactly as she'd found it but worried when Mother opened her trunk, she'd know that Promise had violated the fragile trust she had been trying to rebuild. Mother's trunk, their lives—she'd made a mess of both. But for now, she couldn't stop pawing through Mother's things.

The muted morning light made it impossible to see the bottom of the trunk. Promise pulled herself to her knees and swept her hand in broad, swishing movements. Shoulder-deep in birthing supplies, she reached into the back corner. A book-like object more compact than the other ledgers jammed against her fingertips. She whisked out a book with a tooled leather binding. Bumpy leaves and ridged vines identical to the design Taylor had worked into the top of Mother's trunk graced the cover. Promise settled cross-legged on the floor. As she opened it, the binding crackled. She warned herself not to expect much, but her hopes had already leaped wildly out of sync.

The topmost corner of the first page was golden-edged and rippled, most likely from Mother's wet fingertip. Its reverse side, the second page, was joined to the third. She slid her finger upward from the opening at the bottom and edged her way toward the top.

Page two opened to Mother's tiny curlicued letters—a series of formulas for tinctures. Pressing her hands to her inner thighs, she studied the handwriting. Why would a woman with hands as large as Mother's loop her letters so tightly? Surely, she had knotted secrets into her e's and o's.

Promise flipped page after page of recipes. At last, she came to a psalm Mother had copied from David: *Lord, don't be angry and rebuke me! Don't punish me in your anger! I am worn out, O Lord; have pity on me! Give me strength; I am thoroughly exhausted, and my whole being is deeply troubled. How long, O Lord, will you wait to help me?*

The same despair that had found David gnawed at her hopes. She considered returning the book to its dark corner, where it could no longer tease, but an irrepressible longing urged her on. She turned the page.

Tucked within the hand-stitched spine, a downy white feather pressed against a curl of silky auburn hair. Hers? Her heart somersaulted. She turned the page and read greedily:

The birth: pains rapid, labor quick, lasting only a few hours as common with a third baby. I delivered her myself in Taylor's bed, where she'd been planted. Taylor, waiting with his ear pressed against the other side of the door, kept asking if I wanted one of the women from town to help. After a while, when I could no longer spare my energy, I stopped reminding him that that wouldn't do. We'd decided against taking such a chance. That, after what had happened to Will, it would be unsafe for a mixed baby, or for us. Besides, if a midwife couldn't deliver her own baby, who could?

Thank the good Lord, the child came fast, slipping out onto the feather pillow I'd stitched for just this purpose. Lord knows I wanted her first landing to be soft; beyond that, there would be no telling. But at this moment, as my sweet baby girl nurses, I'll write what I wish I were free to shout to all of Georgia: on this Sunday, April 10, 1910, in Martonsville,

Georgia, a girl baby was born to Phua Semra Hart and Taylor Lowe Crawford.

Promise clamped her fingers to her lips and groaned. The journal slid from her lap. Mother Hart, her mother? Fletch her half-brother? Could it be? She stared for a long inside-out moment, her mind unwilling to move forward.

Turning her head slowly from side to side, she caressed the outside of the journal, read its bumps and ripples like a person robbed of the gift of sight. Although April 10, 1910, was her birth date, and it seemed likely she was the baby girl Mother had written about, something was amiss.

When her scheme of rummaging through this trunk first occurred to her, she'd envisioned a ledger page with columns that listed her birth date, the names of her parents, and her given name. After years of living a lie, her orphan's dream of seeing her birth documented same as everyone else's bobbed more stubbornly than ever.

Repair, rebuild, replace, that's what Taylor had insisted upon. That's what she was doing, especially the 'replace' part. Whether or not she deserved it, no longer made a difference. She wanted to see her name, spelled in big proud letters, alongside those of her parents. To some, this might seem childish, a trifling thing to demand, but without this anthill of proof, she would never be sure she was theirs. "A baby girl" would not do.

The journal rested at her crossed ankles. She picked it up and read on:

Other than the warmth of my two boys, this baby girl is the first joy I've known since my Will Hart was murdered a year ago. What was formed out of excruciating sorrow has become my consolation and joy. One day, while she was at my breast, I created a story about a woman who had wandered into town, gave birth, and left her baby behind.

This wasn't an unusual occurrence; it happened every once in a while. Taylor agreed we needed to explain the child's appearance. He also agreed to raise her, but first, he insisted I ask around to see if anyone wanted an orphan girl. (I checked, but only with those who could scarcely afford to feed their families, who would surely decline.) Taylor's misgivings about his ability to do justice to a little girl disappeared when I reminded him the devil himself couldn't keep me from her.

Taylor is as taken with the child as I am and, one of these days, I'm sure I'll convince him to adopt her and give her his name. Oh, he'll have a lot to say about the senselessness of adopting his flesh and blood, but eventually, he'll come to accept my reasoning. I know because seconds after our baby girl was born, he swore he'd do everything he could to make up for being away when Will needed him most. I joined him by vowing to help keep her safe. I didn't shed a tear, not a drop, (not in front of Taylor) though a pain more searing than childbirth ripped through me. For, in the end, I'd promised to live apart from my child.

A birth date and talk of keeping a baby girl safe. If she were this baby, wouldn't new confidence quell the orphan's emptiness she'd carried in her belly all these years? Wouldn't she know relief from the sense that she'd been abandoned? Was that asking too much?

Days after Taylor died, she complained to Mother Hart about feeling abandoned, first by her mother and then by him. Despite the chasm that had distanced them, Mother's lips curved into a slight but knowing smile, the kind you share with someone who carries the same hurt as you. "The day will come when you make the hard choice to love someone, to offer care that goes beyond a barnyard romp." Promise winced; Mother was talking about Fletch. "The smallest acts of goodwill toward that person will fill you, help ease your pain. You'll see." Caressing Promise's chin, Mother added, "This thing you're looking for happens drop by drop. It's hard to describe. You'll know you found it when that cave inside your heart feels full."

Promise doubted the cave within her heart would ever fill. She bent the journal backward—gently, oh so gently—and combed the remaining pages for a more satisfying entry. Toward the back, a small envelope had been wedged within the binding. First a feather and a lock of hair, now this. What was it about tightly sewn bindings that invited this kind of tucking?

On the back of the envelope, in Taylor's firm hand:

Born to Phua S. Hart and Taylor L. Crawford, a girl child, Promise Mears Crawford, on Sunday, April 10, 1910. Phua argued for naming her Orphana Sunday, but I felt it too telling. I mentioned the possibility of an unusual name inciting curiosity about the child's identity, and she relented. Promise is the name we agreed upon because she is the embodiment of our hearts' deepest convictions and, more importantly, our gift to the future.

She gazed out the window. Her mind pulsed. Minutes dissolved into shards and carried her into hours. The past few days blurred, dreamlike. One turn of an envelope had released the truth. Its fresh scent filled her lungs and rushed into her hungry heart. Now she knew! The information surged within her.

She read her name aloud, "Promise Mears Crawford." Taylor must have given this envelope to Mother, to her Mother, shortly after he'd adopted her.

She recalled the boys at school pinning their favorite taunt, "Lynch man, Daffron Mears, was your ol' pa," on whomever they disliked. The day they taunted her with this, she ran home, dress torn, lip swollen, and, in a bout of raging humiliation, scribbled 'MEARS, MEARS, MEARS' on the essay Taylor had recently finished. The following week, Taylor presented her with a legal document that attached his name to hers. All this time, she'd assumed her brawling had triggered her adoption.

She paused. An unsettling thought—of Daffron, his white box, and its ghoulish contents—intruded. Her insides tightened. She wouldn't be satisfied until she understood what Daffron had to do with all this. She worked her finger beneath the envelope's flap. Inside, small raggedy-edged squares of paper. On each, a single letter penned in Taylor's hand, just as he'd done when he'd created the word games they'd played when she was young. She'd participated in his puzzle intrigues then, but now, she wanted much more than a game.

Throughout the years, her suspicions had surfaced like a ball, popping up from the underside of one wave only to be swallowed by the next. Now, she understood why Taylor and Mother's quiet closeness reminded her of the oneness Cornelia and Thaddeus shared. A sacred force caressed Taylor and Mother with an invisible power that elevated their everyday comings and goings into extraordinary acts.

Adoption had wrapped her within a legal entity and made her obvious, a person with nothing to hide. Just as she had done with Fletch when Daffron appeared, Taylor and Mother

Hart had swept her along in plain sight and in doing so had hidden her from view. All is paradox.

She should have gushed with gratitude. A simple blush of thanks would do, for had Taylor and Mother breathed a hint of her identity she might not have survived, would never have had the opportunity to wrench her story from the innards of a dried-out leather trunk. White-robed murderers might have removed the problem of Taylor and Mother, just as they'd done with Will Hart. Her face grew warm with humiliation—she'd been utterly naïve!

Mother's harping about Promise showing her gratitude to Taylor for all he'd done for her was beginning to make sense, yet the feeling that there was more to her story loomed huge as a rogue wave. There was no denying it—Taylor and Mother had lied, again and again. No wonder they'd gone easy on her after she'd been found in the barn with Fletch; they were as much at fault as she! Their deception burrowed into the soul of the belief Taylor had taught her: color, as the sole distinction between the races, was as artificial a construction as man in his most depraved state could create.

Anger pulsed so vengefully within her that she imagined feeding Andrew details for an article entitled, "Paradox in Paradise: Taylor's Deception."

Her reactions shocked her. Exhausted, she leaned on her elbows and perused Mother's belongings. They'd become as untidy as her thoughts, fragile and too unformed to allow for the thanks she ought to feel. Without gratitude, she could not voice her thanks. Without thanks, she remained as empty as ever. She tried to mouth the word, thanks, but her lips wouldn't move. She wasn't ready. Not yet. Not when she wished she'd left Mother's key in her birthing bag, where yesterday's secret would never have become today's burden.

Did Fletch know? Promise's face heated with shame. She recalled the way Mother tended to drown her in the details of the conversations he'd had with every young lady, "Negro, of course," she'd usually add. Never had Promise suspected the reason Mother had encouraged Fletch to pursue his own kind. She'd admired Mother's ability to distract women from their pain; how could she not have realized that Mother had been doing that with her?

And what about Taylor? The rage with which he reacted to finding Fletch with her in the barn now made sense. To think her father had seen her in the hay with her half... Her face flushed. She couldn't say the word. She felt lightheaded. Embarrassed. Humiliated all over again. Taylor and Mother had seen how she felt about Fletch, yet they let her make a fool of herself.

Had they entrusted you with the truth, would you have felt less betrayed, she asked herself? She wished she were ready to say.

CHAPTER 28

Blessed are the surreptitious
for their offspring will survive.

Taylor Crawford, journal, October 16, 1920

Mother Hart stood inside her kitchen door, peering from beneath the brim of her hat, head cocked toward the ominous rustling in the other room. Soundlessly, she reached for her broom. Precious little protection unless the hook protruding from the end of the handle landed in the intruder's eye. Breathe, she reminded herself. She placed her hat on the counter and inched her way into the sitting room. Her trunk's steel-rimmed maw gaped, exposing her birthing supplies and ledgers. *If so much as one small bar of soap has been stolen, I don't know as I'll be able to keep control of my shattered self,* she thought.

She gripped the broom club like and hid aside her bedroom door. The intruder moaned. A bedroom escapade, here, in this house? Incredulous as it seemed, she wondered, who? She peeked around the corner. In front of her dresser mirror a woman stood, pivoting on one foot, then the other. Slender in her nakedness, Promise twisted her tanned shoulders, ran her hand over the tight curve of her pale backside and glanced up into Mother's wild-eyed stare.

A dread stronger than Mother's fear of a love-struck thief came over her. Of the two, the thief would have been the simpler fight. She was about to unleash a scolding when her attention shifted to the floor: overturned brogans, threadbare socks, a sluff of overalls, an inside-out blouse peeled off without unbuttoning, wadded underclothes and beyond them—oh dear.

She dried her clammy palms on her skirt and picked her way toward her journal. The night she and Taylor had created Promise, he retrieved this from under his creaky bed and presented it to her. Now, his hand-fashioned book weighed more than she remembered.

Since the day she'd handed Taylor her baby girl, placed her forever into his arms, Mother had dreamed of the moment she and her daughter would snuggle on the divan, sharing the comfortable warmth of their bodies. Bathed in evening's softness, Mother and Taylor would gentle Promise through the circumstances of her birth. In return, their daughter would marvel at her parents' love. Mother looked in the mirror and studied her own reflection, fully clothed, yet as naked as Promise. And foolishly armed. She leaned the broom against the wall. Unable to find the words to bridge their awkward silence, she blurted, "Mind telling me what you're doing?"

"Looking for my God's mark. You could have told me."

Mother ignored the bite those words held. Fierce talk was nothing more than hurt's fragile mask. "God took his mark back long before your legs held you upright."

She whisked Promise's hands from her hips and turned her daughter's backside toward the mirror. "Here's where it was." Her finger rested on the flat space above Promise's buttocks between two small dimples. Not a telltale birthmark or freckle remained. The way Mother glowed, you'd think she'd bleached out the blue mark Negro babies are born with. "Your mark was the size of a pea."

Promise scrubbed the place where the spot had been. Their hazel eyes met in the mirror; Promise blushed with relief.

Mother quickly looked away, but Promise, always observant, had read her hurt. She hadn't meant to flinch when the daughter she'd cared for from afar made no effort to contain her relief, but what else could she do? She focused on the tan line encircling the tops of Promise's arms, camouflaged in paleness. The remaining portion, deeply tanned and sprinkled with freckles, edged closer to the truth. She sighed. Bittersweet as Promise's disillusionment was, it was honest, the very quality she'd nurtured. Besides, why would any sensible child, cloaked in white skin, find joy in shouldering a black woman's troubles?

The speech she'd assembled as she went about her chores, praying its flow would ease the confusion surrounding the last twenty years, refused to come together. Now, when she needed those words most, they hitched up their fancy skirts and fled. Her mouth went dry and just as well. She didn't want the rage poking at the back of her throat to rumble into accusations about the misguided hospitality that had hastened Trivett's entrance into the great beyond, not to mention the danger it presented to Fletch. Though Promise had been insufferable lately, she deserved better. From the way she was slapping her clothes on, she thought so, too.

She could hardly blame her daughter. Proud as she'd been of what she'd made of her own life, Mother would have jumped with relief at the gift of not having to deal with that which her own parents had unwittingly forced on her. How different life would have been if she'd been white, free to marry Will Hart, live life in the open, and confer whiteness on Fletch so he'd never fear the ignorance that drove men like Daffron Mears. But that was not what the good Lord had in mind for her.

Mother drifted back into the sitting room and lowered herself to the divan. Twenty years earlier, sitting in this very spot, untroubled by what her daughter would one day think, she'd written her most private thoughts in her journal. Truth be known, she'd chronicled her secrets—most of them—in anticipation of a day such as this.

She squelched an ironic smile. Withholding the last and most troubling secret struck her as diabolical. Especially now that her daughter had plucked a few feathers of truth, she'd hunt until she ferreted out both wings of that sorry angel. Once Promise grabbed onto that possibility she would never ease up; in that, she resembled her mama. But what her daughter had no way of knowing was, when protecting those she loved, her mama's stubbornness surpassed all.

A breeze ruffled her simple white curtains, filling the room with the scent of spirits come to witness her unholy confession. Promise came out of the bedroom buttoning her overalls. "How long were you watching me?" Her voice had taken on a stony impatience, the kind that keeps a loved one from venturing close in, where who-knows-what might happen.

No answer. She repeated her question.

Mother shrugged as though nothing had happened. Had anyone looked in on this encounter, they would assume two women were having one of those easygoing conversations friends tend to share on a lazy summer afternoon. But behind Mother's casual gesture, a more virulent thought: All these years living side by side and the child blames me for the tricks life unloaded. She cautioned herself against lashing out—hush, Phua. Anxiety brings out your less charitable aspects.

Worried that Promise wouldn't appreciate the gravity of having Negro blood in her veins, she wished her daughter would take hold of her senses and leave for Boston. Now. As much as she hated to lose her, she remained committed to Promise marrying Andrew, a union in which she'd live unhappily but safely ever after.

Mother raised her eyebrows in answer to Promise's question, "You mean how long have I been waiting for this to happen?"

"How long, then?"

"A painful long time."

"What brought you back?"

"I forgot something for Cornelia's baby."

"What?"

"I stitched little Whittling a stuffed horse, same as the one I made you."

Promise glanced at the divan, chair, the small table in-between. "I didn't notice a horse. Where is it?"

"On the kitchen table, out in plain view—" she lifted her journal, "like most of what you just read."

Promise walked away. The thorny twig on her untied bootlaces scratched across the floor and stopped in the kitchen. Mother listened to the sudden stillness: Promise was fingering the stuffed toy. A chill blanketed her with its suffocating realization: she'd lost the trust her girl baby had placed in her, those innocent threads a child tends to stitch its loved one in. Promise had started picking at them shortly after Taylor had found her and Fletch in the barn. Now, mending was out of the question.

"When I was little, I pretended you were my mama. Wearing the dress you made me for Sunday church, I'd bite my tongue to keep from telling everyone, 'My mama sewed this' for fear they'd call me a liar. Why did you hide this from me? Didn't you think I could keep a secret?" Coming from that big empty kitchen, her voice wobbled close to breaking. Beneath it, the frayed ticking of a countdown nearing its end.

Mother waited, hoping Promise would sit with her on the divan. When this didn't happen, she spoke. "It wasn't you we were worried about, it was the times. Taylor fostered your natural curiosity, said you had a right to ask as many questions as you liked, that you were as smart as Fletch and deserving of whatever education he could offer. I argued your curiosity would lead to crossroads too frightening to imagine, but Taylor insisted you and Fletch and Trivett be taught the same way. He wanted to give you a chance you wouldn't ordinarily have."

"A chance?"

"To be white."

The twig scraped the floor. Promise was pacing. "Lofty, wasn't he? Too bad he lived a lie. I was his lie and yours. Why didn't you stop him? You heard me complain about not having a real mother and father."

Mother moved to the doorway separating the sitting room from the kitchen. "There's many a gulf between what we want and what we can have."

"You haven't answered my question."

"Twenty years is answer enough. Do you think I would have put my sons at risk if I didn't love you? They murdered Will, then Trivett. Don't fool yourself into believing they aren't after Fletch and won't go after you, should they find out. Do you have any idea how it feels to know I couldn't protect those I love?" Her voice crackled with anger: at Taylor for experimenting with people's lives, at Daffron for what he'd done to her and her family, and at Promise for being more persistent than wise.

Promise pulled the carved white box from her pocket. "What about this?"

"Small things have a way of interfering with our vision."

"Not seeing is one thing, but you told me my mother left this for me." A tiny noise jumped from her throat and fell like a bird shot from the sky. "I thought she was dead."

Mother moved toward her, arms opened and ready to wrap them around her baby girl.

"Liar," Promise murmured.

Mother spun into the sitting room, sank to her knees and began rifling through her trunk.

"That's the end of our conversation? You're not going to say more?"

"I have plenty to say." Mother nodded in the direction of the divan. "Sit."

Stunned by her forcefulness, Promise backed into the divan. Seated, she crossed one arm over the other, folding what little dignity remained to her chest.

Mother pushed herself up, then motioned for Promise to open her fist. Promise knew which hand she meant but unfolded the free one instead. Mother shook her head and pointed to the fist clamped around the carved box. Promise leaned forward, placed her elbow on her knee and slowly did as she was told. Mother removed the box from her daughter's palm and set it on hers, alongside its twin.

"So there was more than one box."

"Taylor carved them. Years later, when I was carrying you, I set one aside for you." Mother traced the hummingbird feeding at the flower atop Promise's box. "I was never one to tell lies. Keeping secrets is one thing, lying is another. I told you the truth: this was a gift from your mother." She gripped

Promise's chin. "Everything I told you about your mother was true. Every last word."

"You said she left Martonsville and was never seen again." Hard words, but gentle.

A shiny film covered Mother's eyes. "Yes. The minute I handed you over to Taylor, a part of my heart disappeared. Taylor was the first to notice."

Before Mother knew what was happening, Promise threw her arms around her and hugged her tight as could be, squeezed the air out of her poor lungs, covered her sweaty face with kisses. As though to make up for every heartbeat she'd missed during the years she hadn't recognized Mother, she pressed, eager and greedy at the same time.

Mother longed to hug and kiss her back, to give her daughter the contact she craved, but something warned her against sharing whatever strength she had left. Closing her eyes, she pictured Will and Trivett, faceless bodies dangling from ropes, feet grabbing for stairways that weren't there. A warning from beyond the grave was nothing to trifle with.

"Poor sweet child," was all she could say as she pried Promise's arms from her neck, then held her at arm's length until she understood this wasn't what her mama wanted.

When she handed Promise a handkerchief, Promise did what any daughter would do—wiped her nose and sniffed herself dry. Her shoulders shuddered like a body seconds before dying. She sniffled a few times more, inched farther away and stopped.

Mother sighed; she'd regained the distance she needed.

A terrible rushing sound flooded the room—the dead, returning to the other side. Will and Trivett had finished what they came to do. Promise's hazel eyes brightened with recognition—she'd heard their noise, too.

Mother understood what was coming and welcomed her daughter's questions without a flinch of anger.

"I don't want to whine, and I hate to carry on after all that's happened, but for years that foolish box was all I had of you. I packed my hopes in there. If you don't mind, I have to ask again: I have a box, you have one, and Daffron has a third. Is that right?" Promise's voice held the ring of kindness that accompanies long-held love.

"Taylor carved them. He meant them to stand for the three of us, Will and Taylor and me. We were like water in a pitcher, that's how inseparable we were. He married Will and me, you know."

Littered with dust motes, a ray of sunshine rested on the trunk's disarray. "You never told me that."

"I thought once Will and Taylor got a taste of living with honest-to-goodness nigger-haters, they'd head back north where they belonged. But Will wanted me to marry him, and I refused to leave Georgia, so he stayed. That's when this farm came up at auction, and Taylor and Will bought it. If I had refused to marry Will, none of this would have happened. But we were young and oh so full of ourselves." Memory's smile played on her lips.

Promise frowned. "Like someone else we know."

Mother's eyes softened. "At first, Will lived at Taylor's and sneaked over to my cabin at night. We were terrified by what we'd done—even Taylor. But when the boys came along, Will insisted we live as a family." She gazed out the window. Her face hardened. "That was our big mistake."

Neither of them spoke. Mother fiddled with their white boxes, placing one on top of the other, then arranging them side by side in her trunk. For a moment, even the birds outside her windows went silent.

Promise gathered her hair, pulled it to the back of her neck, knotted and unknotted it. "I'm not sure about all this," she blurted. "You still haven't explained how Daffron got the third box."

"Oh, that." She lowered herself to the divan, rubbed her forehead and thought for a moment. "He must have stolen it." She looked down at the floor, hoping she didn't sound as though she'd just figured this out.

"That's it? That's too easy. So far nothing you've told me has been easy. Why should Daffron be any different? You see why I'm having trouble?" Promise waited a few seconds, and when Mother didn't answer, threw her hands in the air. "You always told me I had the gift of good sense. You taught me to listen to my gift. Here I am, listening, and all I hear is the thrum of, 'there's more, more.' Don't you see? I want to believe you, but can't. Not yet. Not until the thrumming stops."

She was halfway through the kitchen when Mother said, "With all this talk about Daffron, I thought you'd have asked why you carry his name."

Promise pivoted and hurried back to her side. "You're not going to tell me I'm related to him, are you?"

Mother took the envelope with Promise's birth information from her journal and removed the torn yellow squares. "You see these?"

Once again a little girl staring at a jumble, Promise sat beside her.

Mother lifted each square by the corner and ordered the letters on her palm: S-E- M-R-A. "Do you know what this spells?"

Promise flicked her wrist dismissively. "Another of Taylor's games."

Mother handed her the letters and flipped to the back of her journal to the page on which she'd written her name: Phua Semra Hart.

"Oh, I'd forgotten. That's your given name."

"I didn't want to call attention to you, so I stopped using it." Breaking into a gentle smile, she rearranged the letters in Promise's palm: First M followed by E and A, then R and S, and eased them together to form MEARS, a common name.

A little girl's gasp. "You named me after you."

"I wanted to give you my name without letting the world know. Taylor found a way. He always did."

That moment, more than any other, Mother saw that her daughter ached to join the legions of little girls who made their mamas' every word their own. Yet Promise was holding back, trying the idea on for size. It was clear, her newfound blackness made this new arrangement a breath too tight for comfort.

Descending into a childish pout, she slumped against the divan. "I wish I could believe you," she leaned forward and cupped her hands beneath Mother's, "but you're trying to distract me so I'll forget about this." She dropped Mother's hands and reached for her carved white box.

Mother pulled herself up straight. "I've already told you about that, Promise Mears Crawford. Now you're being stubborn. Downright pigheaded stubborn."

"Then it's true. The third box is the key to everything. How did Daffron get it?"

"You're pushing too hard, Promise, making me angry. Real angry." She pounded the air with her fist. "No orphan in her right mind refuses to believe her mama once she finds her."

"No mama in her right mind refuses to tell her daughter the truth once she's no longer a child." She stood, eyeing

Mother as though she were a stranger who refused to return the treasure she'd run off with. "There's more to your story, I'm sure. If you won't tell me, I'll ask Daffron. He'll tell me."

Mothers breath whistled its way out. "Don't you say a word to that man. You hear?" she snapped.

Promise pressed her nose to Mother's. "Then tell me."

Mother dabbed at the sweat along her hairline. Staring into the past, her head whirred. "It was the middle of the night, and I was getting ready to run away with Will and the boys. I thought I was gathering the things we'd need to start a new life—important things like seeds and medicines and warm clothing—but I grabbed these boxes instead." She moved her hand up and down as if trying to determine the boxes' weight.

"I was afraid. More scared than I'd ever been. Something awful was going to happen. I sensed it the minute Will left our bed to bury the dog. All I could think about was getting the boys out of there. I shoved the boxes into my pockets and grabbed their little hands. That's when I must have dropped the third box... The one Daffron took before setting our house on fire."

"Daffron was there? You had a dog?"

"Daisy—she belonged to the boys."

"What happened to her?"

"Someone killed her. Left her on our bed while we were sleeping." They locked eyes. Mother whispered, "I suspect it was Daffron."

"He's the one killed Tiv," Promise gasped. "Daffron's got to go."

As she headed for the door, Mother feared her daughter was about to do something reckless. Sensing Taylor's presence in the room calmed her. Remind her to think first, she prayed, lunging for Promise's arm. "Don't say a word. Leave things as they are. I'll figure something out."

Promise rubbed her neck and scowled. She turned to leave, and Mother pressed her carved box into her daughter's hand. "Keep this. It was your mother's way of telling you she cherished you from the moment you grabbed hold in her womb. She loved you then, she loves you still. No matter what happens from here on in, you remember that."

Promise took the box and tried to work herself free. But Mother tightened her grip. "Anyone asks why your eyes are so red, you say we had an awful fight, you hear? Not a word about me being your mother, about how Daffron got that box, about him killing Daisy. Not to anyone. Especially Fletch."

"Fletch doesn't know Daffron killed his father, does he?"

Mother hadn't said as much, but she could tell from Promise's expression; Promise understood it was so. Her eyes hardened with purpose as she moved her head from one side to the other and landed a gentle finger on Promise's lips. "Silence has kept us alive these many years, and you're going to keep it that way. Do as your mother says, you hear?"

CHAPTER 29

Diversion, serendipitous blessing from above,
Be thou the key that transports mankind
Beyond events that threaten the heart of its humanity.

Taylor Crawford, journal entry, April 10, 1910

That afternoon, Fletch eased Cassiopeia to a halt at the entrance to what had been Mam's gardens. Bastions of her devotion to healing, they no longer existed. In their place, mutilated stems, mashed blossoms, mangled beds. Scabs of war. Such was his reaction last night when he'd first seen the flower beds, when he'd first questioned her about the devastation.

As he added a stack of "tea wood"—enough shaved wood to heat a cup of water for the St. John's wort tea Mam had been drinking too much of—to Mam's kitchen stove and struck a match, he couldn't help bringing up the topic again. "Any new thoughts on who might have ruined your gardens?"

But Mam kept to her story, insisted that she'd come home from Aville Louise's to find the mess. And that the devil himself had wormed his way from hell to leave his calling card, destruction. "Don't!" she blurted when he suggested that he get Sheriff Peal, then dropped her voice, "He's occupied with Suzanne and the aftermath of the fire."

While he guided her to her favored place on the bench by the table, she rambled on about Acey and the sheriff and Aville Louise and Suzanne and Pucker Face and Doc Hovner. Her simple cotton dress was as rumpled as her thoughts. And the dignified gray braids she usually pinned neatly around her head drooped over the round of her once-proud shoulders. He watched her intently as she went on, stopping only to gulp her tea. By the time she'd finished, her story had a beginning, middle, and an end that made sense, but he understood it for what it was—an attempt to distract him from her unraveling.

"Sounds like Aville Louise is indebted to you," he said when she'd finished. "The fire and Suzanne's injury were awful, and so was the damage to your gardens."

She took in a wobbly breath and let it out slowly. "Awful, yes," she sounded exhausted, "you cannot imagine." She fussed with the dishtowel he'd left on the table, folding it in half again and again, until it fought back when she tried to flatten it into another fold.

"Are you sure you didn't have anything to do with what happened in your gardens?"

Still bearing down on the dishtowel, she glared at him. "Course not."

Had she been telling the truth, she would have dropped the matter. Instead, she protested more vehemently: "I have no inkling of who ripped out my healing herbs." She waved a dismissive hand, as she often did when she'd had enough of his antics. "I have no enemies among the folk I've helped in Martonsville. None among the babies I've delivered into their mother's arms. And those few infants who failed to survive? Their parents thanked me for helping them mourn their loss, for showing them how to get on with their tattered lives." She jutted her chin at him. "I know, Fletcher William, how to go forward and pretend everything will be just fine." She turned from him and acted as though she was about to sneeze into her handkerchief when, in fact, she was drying her eyes.

A mere three days since Trivett's death, Fletch wished he didn't need to introduce another sorrow into his mother's life. In an attempt to determine how committed she was to living with the threat of lynchings, he had suggested they were no longer welcome in Martonsville. Her insistence on remaining in Georgia when it had stolen so much from her troubled him. If he could convince her that having her with him in Boston would help him complete his studies more quickly, perhaps she would agree to leave this place. Certainly, staying together would be an enticement. Ashamed at his plotting, he edged from his mother toward the kitchen counter. No longer straightforward, he'd become the type of man he disdained.

Mam began emptying the contents of her birthing bag onto the table. She started the ritual of getting ready to clean her scissors, inventory, and replenish her supplies. It was her duty as a midwife to have her birthing bag "charged" for her next call, she'd often said. The normality of the scene buoyed Fletch's spirits; perhaps she wasn't as unglued as he suspected.

One by one, she removed jars of herbed oils, positioning them with the soft thud of chess pieces. Without turning, she said, "Smells as though that shirt of yours could do with a good washing. Take it off and set it in my laundry basket. I'll get to it shortly."

Her composure took him aback. *Maybe Mam is herself again.* Encouraged, he grabbed the bottom of his shirt and was about to follow her order. Wanting to test his assumption, he stopped, then sauntered around the table to get a better look at her.

Dark pockets puffed beneath her half-closed eyes, now fixed on a small roll of bandages. The smell of bleach wafted through her fingertips. She gathered as much material in her right hand as her fingers could manage, gripped the bulk of the roll in her left, and dropped the material from her right hand into a heap. She repeated this aimless activity, bunching and gathering until she could hold no more, then blinked upward toward Fletch, hazel eyes glazed with sorrow.

Clearly, this wasn't the time to discuss his plan. He lowered himself to the bench opposite her, his thoughts leaping between his Boston plan and needing to leave shortly for his job at the Mitreanna Hotel. With a clattering sweep of his arm, he pushed her jars aside. Gently taking her hands in his, he loosened her startled grip from what was left of the bandage roll.

Mam fixed her eyes on his and took in his furrowed brow. She listened as he laid out his plan for them to escape Georgia, then disengaged her fingers from his. "You want me to spend what could well be the rest of my life up North?" she asked. "I've always been a strong woman, but these past few days..." She studied the grown man, offering to bind himself to a failed woman who'd been unable to keep her husband and her adopted son from harm.

"You will never understand, but from the moment a woman conceives, she forsakes her life, puts it in danger so her child can be born. When at last that mother folds that baby into her arms, her womb sets to shrinking while her heart swells with the urge to shelter that new creature. So fierce is this love that the bravest of women recognizes when she must allow another more capable person to protect her baby from dangers seen and unseen. I don't know how else to explain this to you, Fletch, but the first time I held baby Trivett, I could taste his birth mother's trust. Having failed to protect him, how can I abandon his wife and his baby-to-be? Think, Fletch, think. While you're at it, consider where your old mother's heart resides."

Fletch hadn't expected her vehemence. He hadn't meant to make this exquisite woman uncomfortable; he just plain forgot. Forgot his place in this life. Forgot to mold himself to what others expected, needed, wanted. He owed so much to the women in his life, women he cared about, that from now on he intended to mind how he spoke. He needed to do this and more to keep from further harming Mam and Lizbeth, who grieved over Trivett, and Promise, his most forthright critic. Still, he'd thought Mam would be more concerned about what might happen to him. He slid his hand to his neck and massaged his throat.

"Fletcher William, are you in some trouble you're not telling me about?" It was the second time in three days she'd asked him this. The second time he'd sidestepped the truth.

He gazed out the window at the remains of Mam's gardens. There was a lot to what she said. Maybe they were all in trouble. Why else would Taylor have extracted any number of promises from those around him: Promise to marry Andrew Gills; Mam to continue to cook and keep house for Promise; Fletch to return to Martons Island after completing his medical training. And who knows how many other hands he had forced? What if the persons who'd murdered his father and Trivett were, in some convoluted way, involved in Taylor's bundle of promises?

His disorganized thoughts skittered back to his father's hanging, to being forced to watch him gulp his last breaths. Other blacks whose families had been hanged never mentioned a bystander's eyelids being pried open the way his had been. No doubt, he'd been targeted because his father was white. Targeted but not killed. Might there have been a person, related in some way or not, who had witnessed Trivett's hanging? If so, what would it take to get him to identify the hangman? His mind would have continued to swirl through this muddled logic had he not felt Mam's eyes on him. "Look at what's been happening, Mam. It's dangerous here."

"It'll become more dangerous if people like us run away."

He flinched. She'd seen through what he'd hoped would sound like a selfless proposal.

"You've never been that kind of man. Don't change," she gently begged. "No matter how bad the situation."

He drove his hand into his pocket and fiddled with Tiv's collar. "I'll admit, going to Boston isn't a perfect solution. It would be a compromise, but it would keep us safe." Without thinking, he withdrew Tiv's damp collar from his pocket and placed it on the table.

His mother reached for the bloodstained collar. "I forgot about Tiv..." She ran her midwife's fingers, conversant with bloodstains of every size and duration, over her perfectly spaced stitches. "I made this for her," she said, pushing the bench out from the table, scraping it hard and loud. She rushed out the door, down the steps, and into her garden. Fletch followed.

Spreading her feet wide, she planted her hands on her hips and inspected the debris. "It's time, Fletch. Time for me to set everything right." Her voice was frightfully soft. "Bring me my shovel, will you, Fletch?"

"Yes, Mam," he said, taking Cassiopeia by the lead and trudging toward the barn. There was no point pursuing the matter further.

CHAPTER 30

Storms strengthen the resolve of those blessed with the foolishness of intractable courage.

Taylor Crawford, *My Life in Georgia*, 1929

That morning Promise had been a white woman free to come and go as she pleased. If she wished, she could make her purchases in the shops in the white section of town, although she rarely did so. She conducted her banking during regular posted hours, never considered waiting for the single hour set aside for Negroes. In the train station, she sipped from the white water fountain and, after boarding, took a seat in the section clearly marked Whites Only. The thought of keeping people in separate pens had sickened her then. Now, as she rounded the corner to the front of her cabin, where Andrew was waiting on the porch, indignation welled up in her so insistently, she could barely breathe.

"I didn't know where you'd gone." Andrew's concern seemed genuine.

"I needed something from Mother's." She glanced at the small suitcase by his feet. "You've decided to go with Ellen."

"Just overnight. I left my other grip in Taylor's room. Hope you don't mind. Ellen plans to stay with friends in Savannah until she finishes her work. She'll be more comfortable in the city."

Promise couldn't help but smirk. "With all that's happened, I can't blame her for wanting to get away from here."

"I suppose that's some of it, but don't forget she's got all those meetings to prepare for, and that important speech she has to deliver. A speech about anti-lynching laws." The more he said, the less convinced he sounded.

"I've got a question for you." She wandered away from the cabin, far from the shed so neither Ellen or Daffron would overhear. At the smokehouse, she turned and faced Andrew. "Are you ready?"

"If this is about raising racehorses, I'm—"

She put her hand over his mouth. "This isn't about you, it's about me."

The slightest scowl clouded his pleasant features, then faded. Fingertips arched, his hand hovered protectively to his heart, then flitted down his shirt and landed on a cracked button.

Promise took a deep breath: "Would you still marry me if I told you I'm a Negro?" It was the first she'd described herself as she truly was. She sounded as though she was referring to a stranger she'd just encountered. Someone she was determined to get to know.

"What?" He drew his aristocratic brows together and peered at her from behind his glasses. He seemed so genuinely astounded that she wished she'd been gentler.

He took her hands, turned them palm-side-up, and inspected them. He turned them over and fingered the blue of her veins, pinks of her fingernails, the pure whites of her moons. His mouth quivered. He threw his head back and laughed long, then gave way to breathless hoots.

"For a second there—you—really had me. You're funny, Promise—very funny." He was gasping for air. "I knew you'd get—back at me—for my Mangy Charlie act. But I never thought—"

"You think I'm joking?" She tingled with the impulse to slap him into seriousness, but realized as he stared as though she had two heads, that she *had* slapped him, hard. Did she expect him to react with a congratulatory hug? Why wouldn't he be dumbfounded, just as she had been? As she continued to be. Trouble was, Andrew found humor where there none was intended. She crossed her arms. "For glory's sake, say something."

"That's ridiculous," he said, dismissing her with a shake of his head. And when she pursed her lips, he lowered his shoulders and chewed on the stew she'd just shoveled into his mouth. "Tell me more," he said, his voice uncharacteristically stern.

After she'd finished telling him about reading Mother's journal and how Mother said it was all true, she said, "The pieces to my puzzle are falling into place."

"Isn't this what you've wanted? It's not like you have a disease or something. It's who you are."

His voice sang with a logic that comforted until she realized he'd skirted her question. And she said so.

He looked confused. "I feel like I'm supposed to apologize, but I'm not sure about what."

She couldn't bring herself to restate the matter so abruptly. Throughout her life, she'd wrestled with her orphanhood, with having been deprived of her identity. More recently, she'd struggled with the burden of an unexpected identity, that of plantation owner. Then there was the probability she would assume an unwelcomed identity, that of Andrew's wife. Now, as she moved into the person she really was, Mother Hart's daughter, she wanted to unwrap the trappings of that gift slowly, so she could gentle herself into its complexities. So she rephrased her question, made it sound as though they'd known all along that one day they would decide to end their engagement. "Now that you know, should we still get married?"

"You're being absurd, absolutely absurd." He wrapped her in his arms and planted a kiss on her forehead, then eased her away. His speckled brown eyes glistened with disappointment or schemes in the making, she couldn't tell which. The disdain beneath his laughing response to her most serious question continued to reverberate through her thoughts. She recalled watching a snake devour a frog: its fragile bones snapped and, after a while, it gave up its pointless struggle. She reminded herself, she was the princess in search of a prince. She wasn't the frog.

The door slammed. Ellen dragged one of her suitcases onto the porch, then called her brother, stretching his name into two long loud syllables, "An—drew."

He raised his eyebrows in exasperation. "Coming," was all he said, moving toward Ellen.

Promise stepped in front of him and took hold of his shoulders. "It's time to reconsider," she said softly.

They walked along, chatting quietly. At the porch, he said, "I'd better help Ellen get the rest of her things."

"Before you go, I have a suggestion." As Promise whispered in his ear, she could feel him nodding in agreement.

"That's it then. We have a plan," Andrew said, backing away from her one hurried step after the other.

"Not a word of this to her or anyone. Hear?" She repeated her mother's warning, the one she'd pretended not to understand. "Give me ten minutes to lead Cambridge into the woods, then you can start the car."

"That should be about right. It'll take ten minutes to get my sister's trunks situated. We'll talk more about this tomorrow." He kissed her full on the lips, long and slow. As his taste faded, she knew he'd never do that again.

Hours after Andrew and Ellen had gone, and she'd mucked the stalls and spread fresh hay, she returned to her cabin. An eerie quiet had settled there. She checked her bedroom to see if Ellen had left anything behind. Other than an untidy bed and stray hairpins on the bureau, there wasn't a trace.

She went into the room where Andrew was staying. Not a wrinkle in the quilt. Not a sock on the floor. The room looked just as it had before he'd arrived. She peeked under the bed. Opened the chiffonier. Nothing. He'd taken his large leather grip.

CHAPTER 31

An inch over the boundary is an inch too far when it comes to Daffron Mears.

Taylor Crawford, journal entry, July 4, 1922

Daffron had been tapping at Promise's door for some time now, and his knuckles were turning red. He was about to rattle the screen door and, if need be, her with it. He'd been waiting twenty years for this day; who could blame him, the son who was to have inherited this farm, for being shy on patience? He cleared his throat. He wanted the speech he was about to deliver to enter the world on a quiet breath, one that would make her think he was turning himself inside out for her.

At last, she showed up on the other side of the screen door. He tipped his hat. "Miss Promise..." he hesitated, real timid like, "I'm here to apologize for this morning. Beatie's giving me what for in front of Mr. Andrew," he hung his head, "—well, I guess it got to me."

Staring at the gritty porch, he waited for her offer of consolation. When it wasn't forthcoming, he went on: "I figured if I tried being a good pa that once Beatie saw fit to use her words again, she'd say something extra fine just for me." He rubbed the left side of his chest to show how much Beatie's slight hurt.

Promise joined him on the porch, her pretty face screwed into a hard knot that made it clear she wasn't bothering a hair's lick to hold back her true feelings. Between the effort he was putting into playacting, and her little display, he felt downright put out. What had happened to the morsel of forgiveness he'd been expecting? A word of pity, a sympathetic smile, something more womanly.

Since he'd started working here, she'd tucked her smiles in her deepest pocket like they were precious five-dollar bills. And the understanding smiles she'd just about drowned that nigger, Fletch, in? She'd buried them, too. Never, in all the years he was supposed to have been living in Tilden, did Missy Promise catch sight of him in the woods, spying on her. But he'd been up there, in and around the underbrush, checking up on what her boy, Fletch, was doing to the farm that was by rights his. If only she knew how much he hated having a grown black boy working his daddy's farm, then she'd be more careful not to vex him so.

He wasn't prone to wasting his time, figuring what chewed at a woman's thoughts. Yet, standing within arm's grab of this young beauty, he took the flicker of kindness that just flashed in those hazel eyes of hers to mean he was getting to her. Time, he decided, to introduce his next act.

Anyway, I'm guessing this belongs to you, Miss Promise." Draped over his arm, her old dress. Promise's eyes clouded with displeasure at the return of her gift, which pleased him immensely.

He paid no mind to her bristling as he pressed the dress against his chest and fumbled to button it, and with it the struggle he'd just had with Beatie. His feisty little girl had refused to remove the dress and, hugging the skirt to her waist, wrapped the yellow flowered fabric in her stubborn little fists. He'd done what any father would do—threatened to shred the nuisance of a frock to rags.

After fastening the last button, he edged closer to Promise. He'd made a substantial wager with himself—one of those five-dollar bills he'd imagined Promise tucking away—and waited to see how far he'd have to go before her eyes darkened with the respect he, Mearswood's soon-to-be-declared owner, was due.

"Bet there was a time when you looked right sweet in this. It's a shame it's a tad too big for my little girl," he said, shrugging apologetically. He folded the dress in half and handed it to her.

He extended his arm and was about to deposit the dress in her outstretched hand when Promise sent her gaze downward to the carpet on which Tiv once slept. She stiffened. The revulsion curdling her face told him she knew who had killed her stupid dog.

As he released the dress, her hand went limp, dropped to her thigh, and bounced.

She might as well have struck him for the way he gasped. The meager spark of humanity that Beatie had ignited in him just snuffed itself out. His face turned sour. He welcomed this loss and feared it, for once he kissed good-bye what little good simmered within him, he could no longer hold himself in check; he would commit acts unbecoming a righteous man.

He squared his chest into a posture that quartered no disagreement. Intent on creating a distraction to overshadow his reaction, he forged on. "Beatie and I were in the shed having ourselves a little conversation. We figured this would be a good time to show our thanks for your taking Beatie in.

I'll come right out with it—we were hoping you'll come with us to get something to eat."

Her appalled expression thrilled him. After we dine, he thought, I'll put on a lynching you'll never forget. He eyed her; he was familiar with her type—she would plead and bargain and finally bury her head in her hands so she wouldn't have to live with the picture of Fletch gulping his last breath. But he wasn't arranging this show so she could close her eyes, no siree; he'd make sure they were open when he slipped a noose over Fletch's head. That thrilled him more.

***

On his way to the Mitreanna late that afternoon, it occurred to Fletch that the half-mile-wide ribbon that the Mears River had chewed to form Martons Island wasn't shaped like a teardrop as he'd once thought. Slithering snakelike around the island, the Mears River more aptly resembled a noose.

Fletch twisted toward the back of his wagon and pictured Trivett's body lying there. The same frightening stillness that had replaced his father's gentle movements had smothered Trivett's. The leap from life to death had been so chaotic for his father and so unfathomable for Fletch that he'd forgotten all but a few fragments until Trivett had died. Oddly, he remembered describing his father's death as "itchy."

Taylor had allowed it was entirely plausible for a little boy to connect death with an unpleasant scratchiness. In a way, it was. Fletch was only three when his father was murdered, and to this day, more than twenty years later, itchy was the word that most aptly captured that night.

Nothing so benignly childlike had imposed itself on the memory of Trivett's death. From the moment the tree in Fletch's dream had almost crushed him until he'd placed Trivett's remains between two candles in Lizbeth's sitting room, every thought and sensation had been weighted with foreboding.

***

Daffron savored watching Promise shift from one leg to the other. Between the brew of his thoughts and her becoming this unnerved, his confidence bloomed showier than violets in spring. "My friend Sawtooth owns the Roadhouse Grill. He lets me eat for free, so that's where we'll go."

"Is Beatie still talking?" Promise rubbed her finger in slow circles around her thumb knuckle.

He made it his business to observe every last thing around him, including her nervous thumb-rubbing habit. Early on in his young life, he'd taught himself to stay alert. He had to. If he caught a spark of oncoming fury—the twitch of his old man's eye, the grind of his jaw, the flex of his hand—he'd sidestep a head wallop. Otherwise, his old man would have killed him for sure.

Daffron forced a grin, then glanced at the space along the road where Andrew's car had been parked. "You're alone, ain't that so, Promise?" No longer Miss Promise, his employer, he'd reduced her to his equal. His smile deepened.

She rubbed even faster, turning her knuckle an angry red. "What about Beatie? What else did she say?"

"My Beatie was talking just fine," his eyes narrowed, "till I made her give this back." He worked the toe of his boot under the dress that had landed at their feet and flicked it her way, same as she'd done with that tuft of grass the day he'd arrived.

She stepped over the dress to the bench. The baby crow was making a god-awful noise in its cage. She unfastened the lid from its food jar and began popping feed into the bird's oversized mouth. "One winter when I was up North I noticed a tree during a snowstorm. I had no cause to think about that tree until the snow outlined the twisted snarl of its inner branches and the gaping wound within it. Took a storm to make me wonder about things we keep hidden from view. And since you got here, Daffron, I've seen more inner branches than I thought possible. Makes me believe I best stay home."

"Suit yourself." He stomped down the stairs onto the path.

"Fencing at the far end of the pasture needs repair," she called.

He stopped without turning, "That's nigger's work," and went on.

"What did you say?"

"It's a shame you don't want to come, 'cause after we eat, we're going to stop by the Mitreanna to watch Fletch's show."

***

The closer Fletch traveled to the Mitreanna, the redder the wounded sky. A gust of northeast wind delivered the unmistakable stench of rotting flesh. Facing it square on, his breath lodged in his throat.

Off in the woods, a mass of pulsing blue-black feathers, the monster he'd observed many times. Gruesome gobbling sounds added a macabre chorus to the spectacle of a half-dozen or more buzzards, feasting on a deer carcass. The putrid odor wasn't from the remains of the protruding fawn-colored legs but from the buzzards themselves.

Fletch tugged repeatedly on the reins, but Cassiopeia refused to draw closer. He couldn't blame her. He watched from a distance as the buzzards' bloody maws ripped at evidence of the deer's elegant existence. Leftovers, sinew-laced bones, would mark its life as insignificant. No doubt, his was a similar fate.

"Let's go." Cassiopeia lunged forward. As the wagon moved steadily toward the Mitreanna, a premonition that he'd never return to Martons Island preyed on him.

***

Daffron registered Promise's footsteps pounding down the stairs with a smirk. He turned so she would be sure to see him dawn his most heinous grin. "If you want to make Beatie happy, you'll join us for supper. After all, a fella's got to show his thanks for someone taking a shine to his little girl. Ain't that right, Promise?" That was the second time he'd called her Promise.

Her fingers tightened around the jar. He edged closer. She steeled herself, most likely so's she wouldn't panic. "What are you getting at?"

"I'm talking about helping you decide which frilly dress you're going to wear when you come with me and Beatie tonight." He could feel his craziest look taking hold of him. Fearful thoughts arose in his mind, twisting it and him, changing him into a man possessed.

He sidled over, eased his arm around her waist and squeezed. "Bet you're a sight prettier than Miss Ellen when you get yourself all fancied up."

"Wits be damned," she murmured, "sometimes a good elbow to the ribs..." she landed her elbow with a grunt, "works just as well."

Rubbing his side, he followed her toward the cabin. "Being the faithful type doesn't mean you can't be social. And don't pretend you're all cozy with Mr. Andrew because, for folks about to get themselves married, you two been doing a lot of scrapping."

She whipped around, sloshing the crow's feed over her hand.

"Amazing what a fella can learn by passing an open window." He winked real cunning like. He was breathing hard.

That invincible feeling he craved was returning. His eyes sparked with a fury that would get him into the mood to hang Fletcher-boy Hart. What he described as "his frenzy" was coming on. Soon he would churn with capacities beyond everyone else's, including his stupid cousin, the sheriff, who'd tried to trick him into believing his deputy couldn't tell one nigger from the next. What hogwash!

He intended to apply his routine, step by step. He kept it the same no matter whom he preyed on, although he would later admit to Promise that he'd added the school fire to celebrate his permanent return to his hometown. But tonight would be his most satisfying evening. To prepare himself, he'd turned the town inside out by slapping it with its first lynching in twenty years and, because doing away with an animal stimulated his killer's juices, had strangled that stupid dog, Tiv. Then, he set himself to riling its owner, one hell of a smart-alecky woman.

Watching her grow quiet—the most ladylike he'd seen her behave—swelled him with superiority, over her and everyone he'd ever known, including his father. "The voices in my head told me I was better than the best of the rest," was how he would later put it.

For the time being, he focused on Promise's baby crow. "Take that young crow you fuss with. Jays would have pecked the scrawny thing to bits if you hadn't stashed it in a cage. I hate people messing up the South's natural order." He leaned against the porch rail and watched Promise dry the dripping jar of bird food on her overalls. "I'd best take that jar before you dump it."

Before she could move away, he was beside her, running his finger down a strand of hair that had fallen over her cheek and tucking it behind her ear. The terror registering on her face pleased him in the most satisfying way. She jerked his hand from her face. Anyone else would have found her little fit provoking. Fact was, it helped him grow calmer than ever. He was beyond insult. Nothing could touch him now.

CHAPTER 32

Solutions to complex problems
rarely appear amidst frenzied action;
the capable man tempers his impulse to act
with a reasoned period of waiting.

Taylor Crawford, *My Life in Georgia*, 1929

Fletch squatted by the berm of oyster shells at the edge of Mears River Road and inspected the wattle he'd built to secure it. The vertical logs on either end and its hickory-woven boughs were intact, except for two that had been chewed through. A mixture of earth and crushed shells from the other side of the berm poured like salt through the gap.

Left alone, water lapping at the breach would gnaw at the road and create a gully deep enough to catch Cassiopeia's hoof and break her leg. The image of Daffron, smirking if Fletch had to shoot his loyal mule, sent him stomping into the woods. The man had exacted enough ruin; Fletch wasn't about to hand him the opportunity to hurt another creature. He worried he was becoming like Mam, unraveled. Why else would he consider destroying a man he'd just met?

He removed a couple of boughs from a hickory tree, stripped them, returned to the wattle, and wove them in one by one. Between the narrow swath left for the second bough and the earth that oozed through the remaining gap, weaving the last bough was close to impossible. Cupping his hands, he scooped water from the inlet onto the soil and stirred it into a paste. Only Mam's finest herbal remedy would have stopped the hemorrhaging faster.

The repair brought satisfaction, but the dearth of a plan to get rid of Daffron left him with little to celebrate. He clicked his tongue, and Cassiopeia swept him toward the wooden bridge that would take him off Martons Island onto the wagon path.

A decaying scent wafted from the warm moist ground. Usually, the humidity's press didn't bother him, but late that afternoon it prompted worries of being drawn from the island on which he'd been born to which he would never return.

Without an inheritance from Taylor, he had no choice but to work until he accumulated the funds he needed. If he added tonight's earnings to his savings, he could barely pay for the first part of his schooling. Perhaps he should find a better paying job in Atlanta. Could this be another aspect of his premonition? That if he lived to become a doctor, he'd be forced to leave the island long before going off to school? How could this be when his exile felt decidedly permanent? A combination of grief and fear had caused his premonition—that was his diagnosis. The grief seemed logical. But the fear?

Thinking of it made him itch, a phenomenon he had yet to understand. He scratched the scar on his ear. And yes, it would have been simple to link it to Daffron Mears. After all, he'd inspired fear and its close cousin, hate, long before Monday when he'd first met him. And yes, the man was a known killer who could have killed his father, but Taylor had insisted that wasn't so. The matter was far too important for speculation. He wanted the truth.

Ahead, a car idled at the intersection, where the back road from Mam's cabin crossed the road from Promise's farm. Two weary beings looked his way, both waving, one more enthusiastically than the other. As the wagon drew closer, Andrew stepped out of his car, exchanged a few words with Ellen, and hurried toward him.

Unlike Andrew, who tended toward a confining tidiness, the car was heaped with grips, trunks, and bags positioned every which way. Andrew's usual fussiness curdled the joy from farm activities, squeezed spontaneity dry, and left Fletch wondering how Promise could entertain thoughts of marriage, despite what Taylor had asked her to do.

Andrew's clothing was the picture of limp perfection, but his breathless speech sounded disheveled and shaky. "We're off to Savannah, Fletch. I know it's not far from here, though I doubt we would get there if I hadn't seen you. Ellen is beside herself. Oh, the things a fellow must do for the women in his life."

He stepped into the shade of the wagon and dabbed his forehead with his handkerchief. "I'd forgotten how miserably flat these islands are. They barely look like islands, and every road looks like the next." His insulting tone suddenly expanded into shameful joy. "Look at that skyline, will you? It swallows the horizon, makes a man with no sense of direction feel," he kneaded his eyebrows with his fingertips and squinted up at Fletch, "ridiculously lost."

"You're leaving? Why?" Worried that something had happened at the farm, Fletch scrambled down from the wagon.

"Since Ellen had that tiff with your mother, things haven't been right." Andrew lowered his voice "By the way, I apologize for my sister. She tends to take her responsibilities a little too seriously."

Relieved this wasn't about Daffron, Fletch recalled Mam's rendition of Ellen's outburst. With it came another worry. "That would certainly change your offer for me to stay with you in Boston, wouldn't it?"

Andrew studied his dusty shoes. "Oh, having a medical student as a boarder will appeal to the teacher in Ellen." His voice had stopped quavering.

"The student part doesn't worry me. What about living under the same roof with a colored man?"

"Give her a chance, Fletch. My sister thinks of herself as a broad-minded woman. One who thrives on helping a person in need, especially a student. Besides," he lowered his voice to a whisper, "Promise and I have come to an agreement about our future arrangements."

"I don't understand what that's got to do with me."

"We've made some changes." Andrew paused.

Fletch put his hand on his wagon. "I have to go, I'll be late for work."

Andrew stepped between him and the wagon. "You're not going to need that job. Your attendance at Harvard will be entirely financed. I'm also going to introduce you to Dr. Robert Benson, one of the most excellent doctors in Boston, and my closest friend. You'll work with Dr. Benson. When he travels to France to lecture, you'll travel as his assistant.

Meanwhile, Promise wants to stay at Mearswood to raise the racehorses I ship there. The farm will change somewhat without disturbing the families Promise has been so concerned about. This arrangement will suit all our needs. You'll get a marvelous education, Promise can continue to work with her beloved horses, and no one will endure the burden of an unwanted marriage." Andrew's glee reflected a man who'd brokered a better deal than he deserved.

"Sorry for the shabby outline of something so dear to you. I've boiled the details into the essentials. Blame it on years of reporting—"

Ellen stuck her head out the car window and shouted, "Andrew, it's hot in here. Let's go!" Andrew shrugged. "And my impatient sister. You can see the pressure I'm under."

Fletch glanced at Ellen, who'd stopped fanning herself and was gesturing for Andrew to return. "You'd best be on your way."

"One moment," Andrew called, then turned and edged closer, squinting as men will do before unloading an awkward confidence. "We'd had such a good rapport, you and I. I'd have thought you would have said something about Promise."

Fletch clenched his fists, pulled himself up straight. "Then something has happened. Was it Daffron?"

Andrew shook his head. "She must have felt guilty about her secret, which, by the way, explains her behavior these past few days. We were discussing a date for our wedding when she told me."

An indignant huff gathered in Fletch's chest. Why would Promise tell Andrew, of all people, about their foiled coupling? "Exactly what did she tell you?" he demanded and, sensing the strain in Andrew, softened his tone. "What did she say?"

Andrew looked puzzled. Almost incredulous. "That she's part colored, of course. That she's your half-sister."

His off-handed announcement landed with the precision of Burnsie's ice pick. Fletch struggled to keep from gagging. He closed one eye and stared at the rivulet of sweat dribbling down Andrew's jaw, where he'd nicked himself shaving. Fletch gnawed on his lower lip. Ramifications cascaded one after the other, adding to his confusion. Not wanting Andrew to see his astonishment for what it was, he picked at the hangnail on the index finger of his right hand, the one with which he'd written his lessons detail by detail so as to consider all evidence before drawing conclusions.

His thoughts turned to Taylor, who'd treated him as his stepson. Questions once hard as tabby dissolved into answers. In those shadowed days after his own father's death when his family had lived with Taylor, Mam became Promise's mother. Taylor Crawford, that brilliant rogue, was Promise's father. The changes Andrew had described were beginning to make sense. Fletch parted his lips into an approving smile, which he hoped would conceal his surprise. "I figured when you agreed to marry Promise that you knew."

"Andrew, please!" The nasal insistence prompted Andrew to start walking backward.

"Got to go, Fletch."

Fletch pointed in the direction of Savannah. "That way, Mr. Andrew." That was the first he'd used this appellation with Andrew.

Andrew started but his response vanished so quickly, had Fletch been less confident, he would have overlooked the wrenching truth. This was a side of Andrew he'd not seen. Had Promise's assertion unmasked Andrew's attitude or had something else happened, something more dire?

Thankfully, Taylor wasn't here. With the faith he'd placed in Andrew, the disappointment would have been too much for him to bear. Fletch hardly knew how to reconcile this himself. Where would he start?

With the notion that today was Promise's lucky day. That Andrew wasn't the man for the woman he'd referred to as Fletch's close relation. The irony of Andrew setting off under a brown man's guidance pleased Fletch. The westerly direction in which he'd pointed would take Andrew from the singular insulated flatness of the islands toward Savannah's Victory Drive, where he would travel along its double thoroughfare, a parkway of stately palms, brilliant azaleas, and mirages of the white man's superiority.

Fletch headed Cassiopeia in the opposite direction over the chattering wooden bridge across the Mears River toward the ocean. Egrets shuffling through the water's edge squawked and beat their wings in protest. He pictured the whites-only beach in front of the Grand Mitreanna, the pulsing motion of the waves working endlessly to scrub this blight from the innocent sand. The idea that Promise would be forbidden from that piece of God's earth dispirited him.

Andrew had been so flustered he'd run off before Fletch could offer his thanks. Gratitude, as Mam would say, shows humility without which we are nothing. He owed Andrew more than he'd ever be able to repay—he'd brought him a step closer to making a plan.

Once he'd ensured Promise's safety, he'd ask her about the bargain she'd struck with Andrew, gather the facts, and weigh them carefully. Then and only then would he decide whether or not to accept its terms. He stopped to savor the satisfaction welling within him.

In his first bout of clear thinking since he'd cut Trivett from the tree, he understood that his presence as the only male on the farm—a black male instilled with authority—posed an enormous threat to Daffron. And that Daffron hadn't intended to kill a man he'd never met. With Taylor's death, Promise's acquiescence, and his mother's disintegration, he was the one person left between Daffron and Mearswood. He suspected there was something else behind Daffron's motivations, although this early hypothesis was a decent enough start. As with any new way of looking at a problem, the details would come to him later.

For now, he understood he was the man for whom Trivett's noose had been intended. Now he knew what he needed to do.

CHAPTER 33

Were a person of courage ever conceived within woman's womb, now, as the hour intones its desperate chimes, hear mankind implore you, "Step forward."

Taylor Crawford, *My Life in Georgia*, 1929

Daffron turned as though nothing had happened. "I tell you what, Promise." He pointed to the limp yellow dress on the porch floor. "How about showing me your grown-up things, so's I can pick a sweet something for you to wear to supper?" The rooster crowed loud and shrill causing the frenzied flutter in the barnyard to blot out the afternoon drone of insects.

"Where's Beatie?" Promise asked as he trailed her back to the cabin.

With one hand on the small of her back, he tried to guide her across the porch, but she stepped aside. He went on ahead of her. "Nice of you to fuss over her. My girl's doing what she was told—getting a little nap. She'll be just fine, so long as you get yourself prettied up the way I like."

He scooped up the dress and opened the door. "Tonight, I'm showing you off to my friends." The screen door slammed once as he let himself in and a second time as she tore in after him.

The clock chimed half-past three. Daffron nodded, his timing couldn't be better: Fletch was on his way to the Grand Mitreanna, and Mother Hart had arrived at that Cornelia woman's, where she was likely to stay for supper. And the steady drip of ice melting in the icebox reminded him that Burnsie had already delivered ice for the week. If he wasn't mistaken, the only sound left was the one he couldn't hear—little missy's heart slamming against her ribcage. Things were going as he'd planned. By week's end, he would clear the farm of everyone except him and one hell of a gutsy woman.

"You're going to want a fire," he said.

"Not when it's this hot, I won't." She dragged Taylor's rocker between them and pushed it back and forth, making the grit on the floor crackle as though she knew not a hint of her parentage. For, had she entertained the threat Daffron presented to the person she actually was, that person would have run screaming from the cabin. Instead, she forced herself into the calculated calm she used when facing a wild horse. That didn't stop damp moons from forming around her armpits.

Daffron took note of her nervousness and smiled. "You need to heat water so's you can take a bath."

"There'll be no bathing in this kitchen."

"Out in the pond, then, where I can help scrub your back?" She stepped one thigh in close to the other. His lusty laughter rumbled into the room. "That's what I thought. Best make yourself a nice fire."

"I'll have to get more wood," she said, heading for the kitchen door.

He peeked around the stove at the tinder and logs standing upright in a cracked copper boiler on the floor. Though hardly full, it held enough wood for his purposes. "Don't go any farther, Missy. This wood will start a real hot fire."

He let her glare a hard second or two, after which he nodded in the direction of the stove. Oh, she fussed all right. Drew a breath to show him how put out she was. Little by little she unwrapped her fingers from around the door handle and stomped back to the stove without him having to drag her there.

She shoved wood into the belly of the cook stove, leaned against the counter and pretended she was out of breath. Daffron smirked. Imagine a farm girl like her, losing her breath. Did she think he hadn't seen her hefting hay up into the loft without so much as a gasp? Did she think he was stupid? She'd learn soon enough that things were finally the way they were supposed to be, with him giving the orders. He clicked his tongue so she would understand he'd caught on to her playacting.

He removed the round burners from the top of the stove and piled them on the floor out of reach. No way was he going to chance her hauling off with one of those iron plates and knocking him out cold. "Just because I've not been schooled, doesn't mean I can't think," he said. "Thinking is something I've done plenty of, especially when it came to getting my daddy's property back for my little girl. Many a time I worried I'd never see the little things that would make this day worthwhile. That box of matches shaking in your hand is one."

Match after match sputtered and died. "Stall all you want, we've got plenty of time. Fletch won't get that stupid sandcastle built till way past dark. Soon as the guests at the Mitreanna collect their bets, Cooper'll arrest Fletch. You know," he made his eyes dance with their friendliest twinkle, "a hefty share of the profit from gambling finds its way into

Cooper's pocket, too. Matter of fact, Cooper is so beholding to that extra cash, it took me a few rounds to get him to agree to dredge up a charge against your nigger."

Daffron wiped the sweat from his forehead. A new resolve settled into his expression, a determination to take what he considered his. He looked Promise up and down. "Don't get me wrong. All this business with your boy doesn't mean I can't have myself some fun, too. That's why I'm bringing you."

"Matches won't light, they're too damp. You try."

"If you put your mind to it, you'll do just fine. That's what my daddy used to say just before he beat me silly."

She caught on right quick to his threat, wiped her hands on her overalls, then dragged the crusty match so hard against the side of the box, it exploded into an angry flame. The extra chunks of kindling she tossed on the fire scattered embers into a fury, after which Daffron replaced the burners.

"See? This is gonna work out real good with you and me. Long as you don't fuss."

While he pumped the water, she balanced the boiler over the sink and stared out the window. Daffron studied her as she refused to give him the courtesy of her gaze. You'll pay for being so uppity, he thought. When the boiler was full, she wrapped her arms around it in readiness to lift. He slammed his hand on her shoulder. "No use straining. I'll do that." He hefted it onto the stove. Water sloshed onto the hot surface with a hiss.

He ripped a dishcloth from the rack and mopped his face. "A lady ought to save her strength for making herself pleasing for her man."

"I'm not much of a lady, and you're not my man."

He let out a healthy snort, yanked the ribbon from around her head, brought it to his nose and sniffed. Seeing her draw back in horror turned her aroma all the sweeter. "I seen a lady in town with her hair piled atop her head, like this." He gathered her shoulder-length waves and pulled them up, a little too hard.

Like a flock of startled doves, her forearms flew up, caught his, and swooped them to his sides. That was the third time today she'd done that—you'd best believe he was counting. His sunburned face lit with realization, his eyes narrowed, and like that, he changed so fast, only a complete moron would miss the other creature that emerged fearsome and inhumane from beneath his skin. There was no denying what he was telling her: he could overpower her if and when he chose to. Clever as they'd been, her attempts to distract him paled when it came to what she would soon learn about him. She needed to stop.

Tensing, she drew back from what the foolish girl believed would be a crushing slap. But that wasn't his style. Believe it or not, he did have some subtlety. He strolled to the mantle and fingered Taylor's corncob pipe. Instinctively, she started toward him. She halted so fast, if he didn't know better, he would have thought he'd flattened his hand against her maidenly chest. Then she clamped her hands over her ears. The high-pitched squeal of the pipe stem being twisted back and forth hurt even his ears. Slowly, he turned the bowl upside down and stopped when she finally grimaced. One tap and the tobacco burst from the bowl, scattered on the floor, and released its stale scent.

"I don't like anyone touching me or my things," she blurted.

But she was too late. He snapped the stem in two. Other than covering her mouth with her hand, she didn't budge.

Daffron scanned the room. Rockers. Trunk. Piano. Table and chairs. Sewing machine. He ran his fingers over the hard quartz in the fireplace. “Me neither. I hate anyone taking my things.” He moved closer. “That’s why I come back. You can keep all this,” he pivoted, waving his arm in a broad sweep. “But this...” his jaw tightened, and he stamped his foot, “this farm belongs to me.”

Her cheeks burned crimson, the color of a roadside bloom he’d once picked. The clock’s ticking filled the room.

She looked him in the eye. “You’re shaping facts to fit whatever version of the story you fancy. Who gave you that right? Can you answer that?”

“Tantrum make you feel better, Missy? Best not wear yourself out. I got lots more surprises for you.”

Picking his teeth with a splintered match, he nodded in the direction of her bedroom. “How about you showing me your dresses?”

“I don’t have many dresses,” was her defiant answer. He caught her looking beyond him toward the piano for her Winchester, but it was gone; he’d seen to that. He smiled at the horror replacing her sun-tinged flush.

He bunched a piece of purple material on her sewing machine in his hand. “What do you call this?”

“The sleeve...to a dress.” She could hardly breathe.

He rubbed the fabric against his cheek. “Too fancy for farm work. What’s it for?”

She mumbled, “My wedding,” and turned away.

“You see what I’m saying, Promise? Your Mr. Andrew isn’t going to want to live back here in the woods. He’s city folk. You’re going to have to live with him up North.” He lowered himself into Taylor’s rocker. “A good bride follows her husband, ain’t that so?”

She hurried into the bedroom and tugged so hard on her dresses that their wooden hangers popped off their pegs and clattered to the floor.

"You keep me here much longer, and I won't have time to clean the inside of the shed before Beatie wakes up. You wouldn't want her to catch a scare, now would you?"

It was obvious Promise didn't understand what he was babbling about—nor would she until later when she found the nooses he'd hung from the rafters in the shed. True, he would admit later when she asked, he needed only one, but he enjoyed practicing his knots, looping the rope in and out and around, making a thick knot that glided up and down, smooth and easy, like his daddy taught him.

He leaned his elbows on the arm of the chair, rested his chin on his folded hands and sat back.

"Hurry now, before I lose my temper."

Promise arranged the loose blue pinafore Mother had made for her to wear during humid Sunday services and draped it over the back of the chair, taking time to smooth the fabric, so the buttons ran straight down the front.

Daffron shooed it away. "Got enough material in that thing for two ladies. Let's see the other one." He made a scooping gesture that imitated the dress's neckline low on his chest. She swallowed hard.

Fumbling, she dropped the dress on the floor and, bending as with an eighty-year-old spine, lifted and shook it several times before finally pressing the neckline to her chin with its back facing him.

Daffron waved a limp wrist at her. "Ugh, ugh. Stop right there, I know what you're doing. My Margaret sewed herself a dress like that. Now hold it up with the..." he patted the sides of his chest, "in the front." He grinned from ear to lopsided ear; her squirming made him feel powerful good. "That's the one you'll wear to supper." He pushed himself out of the rocker and towards Promise. "With your hair piled up, so's to show off your pretty neck."

She clutched the dress to her chest and stepped backward, but he caught her by the elbow. Running his finger down her silky neck, he registered her tremble. Nothing big, just a slight tremor, but coming from this steely lady it was the most he could expect. "Now you get yourself a nice bath."

He pushed his face into a kindly smile like he'd done for all the other ladies he'd terrified into pleasing him. Such a little gesture; it was the least he could do to make a lady comfortable. The second she understood he meant her no harm—not yet anyway—his crazy man's grin broke through, and he breathed into her ear: "And don't worry about me watching. I won't bother with you until after I take care of Fletch."

CHAPTER 34

I have extracted promises that are intolerable yet necessary given the gravity of our circumstances. Having to withhold specifics from my dear ones is a sorry business. I trust time will render the fulfillment of their pledges less burdensome than the consequences of inaction. These are the hopes that console a dying man.

Taylor Crawford, journal entry, March 1930

Daffron had stolen her rifle, and with it, another piece of her life. Had her thoughts not turned to Fletch, she would have lapsed into helplessness. Promise grabbed her shears from the sewing machine drawer, bunched the fabric for her wedding dress under her arm, and hurried into the bedroom.

On the bed lay the quilt Mother Hart had sewn for her when she was a child. Back then, Promise made a game of counting the swatches: solid blues with diagonal white lines, orange-flowered prints too fragile for a real garden, faded green ticking, yellow plaids with stars, and her favorite—the lavender dotted Swiss she'd grown so fond of she'd chosen it for her wedding dress. The patterns were too unrelated to form a picture, yet Mother had arranged them into a little girl on a swing. Before stitching the pieces into a whole, she stitched a heart on the girl's pinafore. On the bottom along the border, she embroidered blue curlicue letters: Promise Mears Crawford.

Mother Hart and Taylor had taught the girl with the orange-yellow braids that effort and imagination, the very forces with which they had kept her safe, had the power to stitch the most improbable notions into a coherent whole. She considered what she'd learned about Daffron. Could she find a pattern that would help her understand such a creature?

No matter how she thought about him, one thing was clear: he terrified her. But if she pumped hard on the swing Mother and Taylor had left for her, her lungs might fill with courage enough to protect Fletch. Playing along with Daffron—only because she had no better choice—to trick him into thinking he was in charge was crucial. Do whatever you must, she reminded herself, to keep Daffron away from Fletch.

She yanked the sheet from her double bed and placed it over the lavender dotted Swiss that would never become her wedding dress and cut. Sharp steel edges sheared the layered fibers. If she could keep her pulsing emotions under her tightest, most unyielding control, this evening would lead to the thread that would keep her life from fraying.

She dropped the long broad strips to her feet, where they gathered into a lush soundless pile. She selected a strip of sheeting, lashed it twice around her chest, and fastened it with a safety pin. Then, she tied that end to the next piece of dotted Swiss. Holding a portion of fabric at arm's length, she pivoted in a half-circle, passed the strip to her other hand, and continued to twirl like an awkward ballerina intent on swathing full breasts into dense flat mounds. Mounds that would protect her heart from the cruelty she'd read in Daffron's eyes.

By the time she looped the end of the last strip in on itself, she'd encased her chest and waist in several layers of fabric. She proceeded to armor the round of her hips, and across her most private place, encircling her thighs down to her knees, the way nurses at insane asylums were said to do, swaddling themselves so male inmates who'd raped other women wouldn't be able to reach them. Just thinking about the possibility set her heart to wobbling. As she stopped to ease her breath into a steadier rhythm, she fiddled with a gaggle of useless threads. She snipped at one section, then the other and, in her nervousness, nicked the back of her thigh.

Droplets of blood formed a thin line. "See what you've done." Her eyes welled with frustration. Having held such tight reins on her rage, she was afraid of what would happen if it erupted. "It's just a scratch," she scolded herself in her firmest horse trainer's voice.

Stiffened with fabric, she tried to pick up a leftover piece of fabric but couldn't bend. She steadied herself on the bureau, lowered her south end to her heels, grabbed the cloth, and pulled herself up.

She allowed herself two sniffles. Only two. One as she bandaged her cut and the other when she finished. At which point, she forced herself to set her anger aside. After taking a few deep breaths, her ability to reason returned. She pointed her index finger at her chest. *Stay calm and keep thinking. Do what you've always done—put what you know about the situation to use—and you'll find the corral built especially for Daffron.*

She pulled the scoop-necked dress over her head but couldn't squeeze it past her shoulders. Damn! It was too tight. *Sometimes it's necessary to take puzzles apart in order to see how the pieces fit together*, she recalled Taylor saying. Ripping at the side seams, the stitches popped one by one, releasing its tension. By letting the sides luff, she managed to stuff herself into the sleeves and fasten the buttons. The dress fit tighter than she'd wanted, but why shouldn't it? Everything about this evening felt suffocating.

Standing in front of the mirror, she arranged her hair. "Ready for supper?" The thought of being seen in public with Daffron made her queasy, but the lumpy woman peering back from the mirror scoffed at her cowardice. She mashed her hands onto her padded hips, cocked her head and reminded herself, *Playing along is the best way to reckon with him. For now.*

If her impressions were accurate, Daffron believed he'd left her no choice but to gussy herself up for him. And that she was afraid of him. She'd been under similar pressure when she'd tamed an unruly stallion. She didn't argue with the animal; she let him believe he was intimidating her. As he tired, she introduced him to her expectations. She intended to do the same with Daffron.

"Remember, be as docile as possible. Force yourself," she told the woman in the mirror whose plucky little grin gave her enough spit to get about her business. She had expectations to deliver.

She trudged up the path toward the barn. The soles of her brogans slapped along the pebbles, while their leather tongues waved at her scuffed toes. The primping ritual and her home-styled corset made her feel clumsy inside and out. Sweat dribbled under her hair, down the back of her neck, and smothered what little skin she'd left exposed. She adjusted her hairpins, prying them open with her front teeth, sliding a handful of hair up and off her neck, and pinning it in place.

Ellen had forgotten a pair of two-inch sandals under her bed and, on her bureau a scattering of hairpins. Had Ellen stayed, she would have been horrified by the way Promise had mangled her life. But Ellen hadn't, and that was the point: Promise was as alone as she could be. If Daffron had any inkling of touching her, he'd have to work damned hard before he laid his paws on anything that mattered. Taylor's adage, "Tough thoughts form the pillars against which to fix one's fears," came to mind along with the truth of the matter: The tougher the thoughts, the greater the fears. Now that she knew she was Fletch's half-sister, hers were among the greatest.

A pair of swifts looped and darted toward one another. Their intricate pattern reminded her of the affectionate games Daffron had played with Beatie, then drizzled into nothingness with the image of Trivett's pin. Her plan had grave limitations. She weighed the risks of leaving to warn Fletch against what might happen to Beatie if she left the child alone with her father. Despite his malevolence toward other creatures, Daffron seemed to love that little girl with a devotion as constant as evening birdsong. Of the two—Fletch or Beatie—Daffron was least likely to harm his own daughter.

Just as Promise veered into the woods toward the path for the Mitreanna, Daffron's cursing cut the air, "Good for nothing son of a whore," then something crashed against the barn wall. Beatie screamed and the critters Promise had been counting on fell silent.

Cambridge snorted with distress. There'd be no leaving now; besides, chances of getting far before Daffron realized where she was headed were poor at best. She was trapped, Fletch was on his own, and Beatie needed protection. She summoned her toughest voice from deep inside: Keep Daffron occupied, and Fletch and Beatie will be safe.

She stepped inside the barn. Between the swearing and stomping, her insides quivered along with the barn. What if... She searched the barn for Beatie. Not finding her, she was about to accuse Daffron of hurting his little girl when Beatie tore out from Cambridge's empty stall and flung her small arms around Promise's knees, inadvertently smearing poultice over her bare calves.

Promise wiped the child's tears; Beatie was more vulnerable than she'd thought. And that inspired her—Beatie was the key to overcoming her dread of Daffron. If she focused on the harm he might do to this little girl, she would get so angry she would forget about herself. She took a long, deep breath.

Now she was ready.

Somehow Daffron had managed to get the short lead on Cambridge. Although it should have made the horse easier to control, it wasn't clear which of the two was in charge. Cambridge flattened his ears against his head and bared his huge rectangular teeth. Never a good sign. Seeing her, he pulled his head up, forcing Daffron to his toes. Being forced to carve canals in the dirt floor with his boot toes didn't keep him from sneering, "Don't you go riling Beatie, you hear? She and me already had it out about that dress you gave her." By the time Cambridge backed up toward Promise, Daffron was out of breath.

She lifted Beatie and twirled her around slow and easy. The child shrieked with pleasure.

As if to annoy Daffron, Cambridge moved faster. "Give me a hand here, will you?"

"This supper business was your idea, not mine."

"You sure that other horse of yours won't make it from here to the roadhouse?"

"Not a chance. If you'd brought the vet, we'd be talking a different story."

She twirled Beatie a few more times. After stopping, she smoothed the child's tangled hair. "Beatie and I are going to the cabin to comb her hair."

Cambridge perked his ears in her direction and lowered his head. Daffron took advantage of Cambridge's momentary cooperation and positioned him in front of the wagon. "You stay put, Missy. Damn horse acts a sight better when you're around."

She strolled into the barn's musty shadows and searched for her Winchester. Seconds after Daffron had bullied his way into her sitting room, she'd noticed it was missing. His message was clear: he intended to have a woman, disarmed and inept, by his side. In that, she intended to oblige him. Up to a point.

Cambridge twisted his head toward her as if to ask why she was watching Daffron bumble when she could hitch him faster and gentler. What was it like for a man who feared horses to feel Cambridge's hot breath on the back of his neck? Having a known horsewoman gawk while he struggled with the harness surely made the task harder. Humiliating as it was for this man to learn a woman had inherited the remains of his grandfather's plantation, what would he say if she were to tell him his grandfather's farm was owned not by one but by two women? Two Negro women. The smug sense that she finally knew to whom she belonged tugged her lips into a secret smile.

The potency of secrets with their many indiscernible shapes now appealed to her. Excluded for years from their inner workings, she'd railed against them. But having discovered their potency and the courage needed to maintain them had filled her with awe. To think two people had molded their lives on her account. She had yet to absorb it all. Once the secret behind the secrets, now their caretaker. Her heart pounded with wonder. Prior to their unmasking, she'd envied the invisible line secluding Mother and Taylor from her. Privy to the reason they'd conjured their secret into being, she now understood; secrets protect as only secrets can.

Daffron fit the traces into the collar and fastened them to the whiffletree, shifting a step to the left, another to the right and back. His eyes darted between the traces and Cambridge's hooves. The steel in the traces scuffed and clanked with each uneasy movement. Fitting could be dangerous. Any moment Cambridge might raise his thick hooves and lower them on Daffron. Even though he'd grown up around horses, he'd never cottoned to them or their language. Had he been less fearful, he would have understood the reason for Cambridge's stomping. But Cambridge's movements flustered Daffron into a distracted thoughtlessness. He wiped his forehead and jumped again.

His twitching gave Promise such shameful pleasure she couldn't bring herself to tell him Cambridge was merely rubbing the flies from his legs. Whenever the blacksmith came, his apprentice, a young Negro boy, swished a swamp-rush broom around Cambridge's belly and thighs. Comfortable, Cambridge stood motionless and let the blacksmith do his work. There was so much Daffron didn't understand.

Think like a horse, she would have offered, had he been the kind of man to whom such instruction would have mattered. *Think how much a horse hates being tied.* That being tethered is the same as being trapped. If there is one thing a horse wants to know, it's that it's free to go when it wants.

Done at last, Daffron wiped his face on the sleeve of his collarless shirt. A wide skunk-stripe soaked the middle of his back. He scooped Beatie into his arms and crushed her to his chest. Her expression changed from wary delight to terror. He climbed onto the wagon and lowered her, whimpering, to the wagon bench. Rather than console her, he clicked his tongue and snapped the reins. Cambridge hauled the wagon from the barn into the evening light.

Daffron peered down at Promise, clomping angrily alongside the wagon. "You're not wearing those things in front of my friends." His tone was quiet, his threat, clear.

She glanced at her brogans, then up at him. "This is what a farm girl wears whether she eats at home or out."

He glowered. "What about your hair? I showed you what I wanted you to do with it." She peered into his scummy gray eyes. "The mirror of the soul," Taylor used to say.

"Go fix your hair, change those shoes, and get that yellow slime you smeared on my Beatie off your legs. Make yourself decent. A fella deserves to be seen with a good-looking woman every once in a while." He put his arm around Beatie and gave the child a squeeze. "I consider myself fortunate to have at least one."

Promise slammed the cabin door on Daffron's braying for her to hurry. The shoes she could manage, she decided, slipping her bare feet into the creamy T-strapped heels Ellen had abandoned. She studied herself in the dusky light. The figure standing in front of the mirror was taller than ever. This new height added an imposing quality that might come in handy.

But the hair. No way would she sweep it up into the provocative style Daffron demanded. She plucked the hairpins from behind her ears, gathered her shoulder-length waves into her fist at the base of her neck. With a little effort, she could position it at her crown, tie it with Ellen's green ribbon, and secure the unruly ends with hairpins. She glanced at the small metal nuisances Ellen had left. The satiny green ribbon lay flatter than a garden snake beneath her black-handled shears.

"Get it moving, Missy Promise, night's closing in." Daffron's voice turned her heart inside out.

She grabbed the scissors, fit its cold sharp steel against the back of her head, then bore down hard. The blades strained to cut her bundled hair. She pressed harder. Strand by strand, their slicing registered more violently than gunshot.

When she'd finished, she clutched her limp waves with one hand and patted the hacked remains at the nape of her neck with the other. Real or imagined, the loss of the mass she'd lived with her entire life threw her off-balance. She steadied herself on the edge of the bureau and moved her head back and forth. With the air flowing over her neck, she might as well have been naked.

"Don't make me come in after you."

A shiver bolted up her spine. She set her harvested hair down on the ribbon that would never again hold her tresses together. Grabbing hold of a straw gardening hat and pulling it down on her head steadied her hands. She took one last look around the room—at threads scattered across the circular pattern of the rag rug she'd made with Mother's help; at the tattered remnants of her wedding dress; at her ruined sheeting and lifeless hair, the one feature she considered pretty and had never told anyone, not even Mother.

If Daffron thought she was fool enough to make herself alluring, he was mistaken. Nonetheless, she cringed when he said, "You farm girls don't know lick about making yourselves up for a man." She tucked her skirt beneath her as she seated herself on the wagon bench and pulled her back up tall. He wasn't going to get to her, no matter what.

She stared out over the pasture at Taylor's grave. He'd known about Daffron all along and had done everything he could to protect her from him. As a child, she'd overheard whispered tales of the man who, wrapped in a cloak of righteousness, had tortured his victims, many of whom were whiter than she would ever be. A merciless man, remote and unfeeling, he laughed at the tortured screams of those he disemboweled—whites who'd helped the blacks. Having blood that ran in both worlds, she had more to fear than Fletch and Beatie together. Should Daffron discover her secret, hers would be an unimaginable death.

"Take it off."

"You'll be late for dinner. Best move on." She nodded in the direction of the road that would take her from the world that had kept her safe. Her strategy of making him believe he was in charge was more important than ever.

"Did you hear me, Missy?" Daffron leaned over Beatie's small body and looked her up and down.

"Beatie, help Miss Promise take off her hat. Do that for your old daddy, will you?" The child pressed her face against Promise's bare arm. "You like that sweaty old hat?" He took Beatie's jawbone in his fingers and turned her toward him. "Is that what you're telling me, Beatie?"

The child drew her fists to her throat and cowered at his cruel tone, the monster she'd known when she was very small, the one that had gobbled her words.

Daffron reached behind Beatie, took a fistful of Promise's straw hat, and yanked. He whipped the hat to the ground and hawked a wad of tobacco-stained spit splat on its brim. He arranged himself sideways and eyed her straight on. "Let me take a gander at what you've done," he said, motioning for her to twist her head toward the cabin.

When he'd had enough, he picked up the reins and kicked the brake free. Quiet as the aftermath of a spring storm, he said, "I know it's a hard lesson for a woman uppity as you, but you'd best learn to do what I say. You hear?"

Soft though it was, his was the most malicious sound Promise had ever heard. Until he hauled off and cuffed Beatie on the side of her head.

CHAPTER 35

Consequences are the scars that form after loathsome forces have coupled.

Taylor Crawford, *My Life in Georgia*, 1929

Cooper Peall was fastening the buckle on his gun belt when Aville Louise burst through the dining room door into the kitchen. The door's pivoting created a determined breeze, the kind that comes up fast just before a storm. "Now you've done it," his wife said, lowering a fistful of damp bandages into the trash pail and grinding the enamel lid soundlessly into place. The thunderclap in her voice was almost as painful as watching the flesh under her arm jiggle with self-righteous fury.

What disturbed him more than his wife's unspoken accusation was the anguish on Suzanne's bandaged face when he'd told her he'd arranged for her to take the teaching job in Whispering Willows. Her silence made him so uncomfortable he found himself adding, "Until I get enough money to rebuild your schoolhouse."

No sooner had the news of her banishment taken hold than her eyes welled. And Aville Louise's little lips began slashing: "Once you start, you can't stop, can you?"

He'd taken her question to mean once he started destroying he couldn't stop. First the schoolhouse—oh yes, Aville Louise knew all right. Understanding had seeped into her eyes last night just before he'd gone into Suzanne's bedroom. She'd sniffed it out; this smoldering mess had something to do with his cousin's coming home to roost. And she was right. The fire had Daffron's scent sprayed all over it. And bizarre as it seemed, Taylor Crawford's, too.

The other day Cooper returned to his office after lunch to find a sealed envelope on his desk. Pinned to the envelope, a note from Promise apologizing for not having delivered it sooner. She'd had the crumpled envelope since Taylor had died and was so preoccupied, she'd almost forgotten about it.

In it, a letter from that bastard, Taylor, saying he'd given an "unnamed" party the details about Suzanne's real birth mother, along with instructions to make them public should any harm come after his death to those living on his farm or their families. Cooper's brain swelled thicker than a bale of cotton in a rainstorm, so crushing hard he thought his head would blow right off his shoulders. If he let himself go, he'd likely kill someone.

The question of what to do next tortured him all night as he lay alone in his and Aville Louise's bed, staring at the ceiling. His bumbling mind tripped him sure as a prankster's foot. But then, he'd always had trouble juggling two things at once.

Aville Louise eyed the gun weighting his holster into the cock-eyed angle of authority. "Where are you going?" Her simple words failed to mask her distrust.

Tiptoeing into their room last night to get her pillow and the extra quilt from her wallpapered closet, she let him know she wasn't interested in his explaining what had prompted Daffron to destroy the love of his daughter's life.

"I'm going to sleep in Suzanne's room in case she needs me." Her announcement stretched beyond her seemingly simple message to tell him he was incapable of caring for anyone other than himself.

But that wasn't so.

Hard as it was to believe, he had been thinking of Suzanne. Protecting her was always on his mind. Sure, he had thought of the humiliation he'd face if Daffron learned about her having a Negro mama, but that worry was second to his concern for Suzanne. He rubbed his chin against his shoulder and snuffed that possibility from his thoughts. Daffron would never learn about Suzanne. Not after tonight.

Aville Louise wore the ruffled look that pleated her peach-sized face whenever he took too long to answer one of her questions. "Where am I going?" he repeated by way of reminding himself not to say too much or too little. "I'm going to see Patrick Latt over at the Dry Goods Store. He has a friend who's offered to sell me lumber at a good price."

She cocked her head like a hungry bird deciding whether to swallow a stingy worm. "Why the store, why not his house?"

"Because that's where Latt told me to meet him." His words bubbled close to a boil. She shifted her eyes from him to the gray night sky on the other side of the window above her bloodstained sink.

He felt sorry for her not grasping all he'd had to do these many years to keep her and Suzanne safe.

"When will you start rebuilding?"

"Soon as the smoldering stops." She chewed on his answer for a while. It wasn't the talk he'd aimed on having tonight, but if it got him out of the house without more questions or those tears that made his knees buckle, he'd scare up the damn lumber somehow.

"I can still smell it, can't you?"

"Soon as the wind comes up, it'll blow away. Takes a while to get rid of the stink." He was trying to steer the conversation away from the fire in case she asked about Daffron. He dredged up his gentlest tone: "Come with me, I have something for you."

She hesitated, crossed her arms over her bathrobed chest, and followed just like he told her. He opened the cabinet door in the pantry, pushed the jars around on the lower shelf until he found the one he wanted, and set it on the counter. Sometimes a man has to remind his wife he's the authority in the family. He was as tired of her acting like she was the plantation queen and he was her slave as he was of Daffron's pretending to be so nigger-killing all mighty. He took a tablespoon from the drawer, and filled it with a mouthful of white lightning.

"Open." He dropped his lower jaw and stretched his mouth wide in case she didn't understand. And when she did the same, he spilled the glistening clear liquid into her mouth and covered it with his three-fingered hand so that she couldn't spit it back in his face.

She gagged, but at least he'd managed to pour most of it down her throat before she started choking. She pushed past him into the kitchen, her tears raining on his arms. From the sounds of the water running free, then being interrupted before gushing again, he figured she was drinking straight from the faucet—an offense she regularly scolded him for. "Oh, oh," she gasped softly. Finally, her coughing let up.

One of these days, Cooper would add this little incident to the others he hated himself for. But right now, he had her interests in mind when he'd shared a mouthful of his best liquor. She would have to trust him, that was all there was to it. He wouldn't be able to do what he had to if he knew she was in a lather. Why, he'd never killed one of his own before and, later tonight, when he'd finally get Daffron alone, he'd need to have one thing taking up his thoughts, and that was doing away with his cousin.

It wouldn't have been so bad if he'd been able to figure out whom Taylor Crawford had entrusted with the information about Suzanne. He'd wager the last three fingers on his left hand, if he knew someone held a sealed letter from Taylor, Daffron had figured it out, too. The man was foxy like that. And that probably prompted Daffron's torching the school. The fire was a warning, that was how Daffron worked.

Cooper reviewed the persons Taylor might have conned into continuing the blackmail scheme he'd started twenty years earlier: Mother Hart was out; she knew all there was to know about everyone in Martonsville and never let on, nor would she. That was the kind of person she was and everyone, including Taylor, understood it better than God's own truth. Promise would have been a possibility if her temper didn't flare faster than—he hated the thought—fire. Why, as a kid she'd badmouthed Taylor to him and Aville Louise whenever the poor man nettled her. Fletcher Hart? Taylor had put a wagon load of effort into him. The man had a certain air about him, a decency that left Cooper wishing he could find a young white man like him for Suzanne, though he'd slit his own throat before letting on he admired a nigger.

Cooper listened for Aville Louise in the kitchen. She was getting a glass from the china closet. There comes a time when a man has to give up the best of his thinking and put his hands to the situation. He'd gone back and forth, trying to figure out a simpler way of dealing with Daffron. Even tried to talk himself into believing he had no need to kill him. But that notion didn't settle. Since he had no way of finding out who, as Taylor's note from the grave had explained, held his family's life in their hands, he had to act to protect his daughter the best he was able. He had no choice but take each problem one at a time, starting with the biggest.

Suzanne came first. He'd give his life so she could have hers. There was no question about it. That's how he felt. He tossed a mouthful of liquor down his gullet, smacked his lips, and slid the jar into the darkest corner of the shelf.

He joined Aville Louise by the sink. "You all right?"

She took a sip from her water glass and nodded. "What's going to happen to that boy, Francis Dobles?"

"Pucker Face? For now, he's safest in jail. I'll find a reason to set him free, once everything quiets down."

"You mean when the smoldering stops?"

Then it occurred to Cooper: he could tell everyone he discovered Daffron had started the fire, and when he cornered him, the guy jumped him, they got to fighting, and he had no choice but fire his gun. Self-protection, that's what he'd say. Surely, no one would think he'd kill one of his own if the man hadn't gone crazy out of his mind. Cooper smiled. The first that parted his lips in many an hour tingled with satisfaction, not to mention relief. By God, he could juggle two things at once.

CHAPTER 36

I brought her to my bed to remind her,
despite man's brutalities, love exists.

Taylor Crawford, journal entry, August 1909

His eyes. Peering from trees crippled with rot, through knotted vines and dripping moss, darting ahead through the woods. Each time Mother Hart thought she spotted them, they disappeared. Once or twice his smell, a sickening mix of bottled fragrance and his body's secretions, drifted more foul than she remembered up her nostrils. She'd know it anywhere. It had surrounded her the night he killed Will Hart: the odor Daffron left behind after he'd raped her.

Her birthing bag bounced faster and faster against her thigh, scissors and jars colliding. Shatter, smash, crush. This chorus pounded her thoughts. Had this been an ordinary evening, she would have cushioned her herb jars with compresses and wrapped the scissors in cloth before leaving Cornelia's.

But she hadn't.

Not tonight. Not when all she could think of was getting home. Hers was an urge strong as childbirth and just as demanding. Its quick pulse had taken command of her body while she was examining Cornelia and the new baby. The contractions in Mother Hart's chest told her she was needed. Get back, get back, they insisted.

A gust of wind caught her skirt and filled it to billowing. She set her back to the bluster, slapped her skirt down between her knees, and locked them tight, as she should have after Will had dropped into lifelessness. The wind shifted, and she pivoted onto the path and continued on.

Earlier that evening, Cornelia noticed Mother's preoccupation. The moment Mother finished checking Whittling, Cornelia took the fussing infant. Alarm rippled across her honey-brown face. "Phua, something bothering you besides the fire?" By then, Cornelia had heard about Trivett. Her soft way of asking was not lost on Mother.

She gathered her things from the bed and with nervous slaps tidied the quilt. Cornelia had been pregnant with Lilly when ghost riders stormed past her place south of Martonsville. Two days of walking later, Cornelia and Thaddeus showed up at Taylor's, frightened and exhausted, carrying half a stale biscuit in a sack.

Mother took one last pass at the quilt, then flicked her hand in the direction of Cornelia's window. "Nothing that won't soon be fixed," she said on her way into the kitchen, where steam from the iron fry pan formed a cloud around Lilly's head.

Memories of the horrors Daffron had already inflicted on her family made Mother Hart tremble with an anger that, if she weren't mindful, would become its own steam cloud. Whenever she'd turned a spade of earth, she pretended to lay another shard of anger to rest. That was her answer then.

But now, her vengeful thoughts roiled with frightening satisfaction. That she, who'd dedicated herself to bringing life into the world, should be possessed by this desire to kill meant her most awful self had broken through the walls of her heart and was about to spew. This time, she would do nothing to suppress her revenge. Not with Daffron closing in on what was left of her family.

Lilly had pointed proudly to the stew. "Papa made sausage to thank you for delivering baby Whittling."

Mother had no choice. She stayed for supper, though her contractions continued: Get back, get back. Explaining that she needed to tend to something at home would have unleashed questions that would tax her growing impatience. Thaddeus would press her for details, insist on helping. That was unthinkable; the next act belonged to her and her alone.

Plates of roasted oysters, boiled corn, sausage, and okra were jockeyed back and forth. "Mama, you ought to have a baby more often," Randolph, the second oldest, said, stuffing his mouth with oysters that reminded Mother Hart of boils. How the sparkling-eyed boy could love them, she'd never understand.

She tilted her head back and sent a shimmering oyster slithering down her throat. One would be enough to show her gratitude. She forced herself to swallow without chewing, then stifled a salty gag. She balanced the ridged shells, flaky as her granddaddy's toenails, on the pile in the center of the table and leaned back. She'd always kept her distance from slimy creatures. But one, in particular, hadn't kept his distance from her. Then or now.

Haunted by the vision of Daffron dragging Will off, she plowed faster through the woods. Will called from the great beyond for her to be careful, then vanished. She moved swiftly over the uneven ground and was tempted to run, but held back. No sense tripping in the smoky darkness. If she got home—no—when she got home, she'd grab the rifle from behind the kitchen door. The idea of shooting Daffron pleased her in a desperate sort of way.

Eventually, a rat ventures from its hole. She'd waited all these years for him to come after her and, for the first time that evening, could actually hear him crushing twigs, heaving branches, snorting, and snarling. Still reeking of roasted oysters, she clamped her hand over her mouth to keep from screaming. She chanted her quiet prayer: No panicking. Say it again, Phua, even though he's near. No!

Her arms flailed against the rough hands that grabbed her from behind. Wrenching herself free, she pounded and pushed against his hard body, one that, despite his years, had grown stronger than two grown men and a horse. Fool that he was, he grunted her name. Was he mad? Did he think that would make her stop? She kicked hard with the heel of her boot as she should have over twenty years ago when he forced her knees apart.

He yelped. She pulled her leg back for a second kick, aimed this time for his groin. A branch sprung from the shadows and whipped across her face. A sharp pain. The devil himself had bitten a chunk from her right eye. The more she tried to open her eyelid, the faster it ballooned. Seen through one eye and a slit, the woods were choked with a darker shade of fear.

He kept saying her name over and again. He made no sense. Not if he was going to drag her to the nearest tree and hang her like he'd done to Will. The fiend. She took another swipe at him, her most powerful so far.

"You started to run away from me..." He clamped one arm across her chest and gripped her forearm while his free hand stroked her wet cheek.

She'd hated the press of his body then; she hated it now.

"Give me your bag." Without waiting for her to move, he wrestled the bag from her hand.

She gawked at his blurry figure hunched in front of her. "Oh no," she murmured as the difference between the specter and reality of the man struck her. "What are you doing here?"

He took a compress from her birthing bag, patted the blood oozing from the gash above her eye, then folded the soft cloth in two and worked his way down her cheek. "Didn't mean to upset you. I mean, I knew I was going to upset you, no matter what, but I never…"

Her cut stung. Her eye throbbed. His chatter annoyed. "I thought you were..." she murmured. She peered as best she could at his face. The sad look had returned to his sweet blue eyes. They'd not twitched like this since he was a small boy.

"For a minute, I thought you were mad at me." He wrinkled his nose and swallowed hard. He looked like he was about to cry.

She picked her bag up from the ground, brushed it off, and looped it over her arm. "I can't dawdle, Acey. I have to get home."

"No, ma'am, Mother Hart, you need to come with me."

The strain in his voice drew her close enough to feel the warmth of his panting.

What's happened?" She touched his arm. "Is it Margaret?"

He shook his head. "I heard something. Something real bad." His lips quivered. "Makes me want to throw up."

A prickling sensation traveled down Mother's arms to the tips of her fingers. Her breath exited in stingy puffs. She guessed at the misery Acey had overheard and couldn't bring himself to repeat. "Tell me."

His eyes welled. "You'll hate me."

"It's my boy, Fletch, isn't it?"

"Daffron's going to—" Acey's hand went to his throat.

"When? Did he say?"

"Tonight. After Fletch is done at the Mitreanna. Sheriff Peall's going to arrest him, then Daffron's going to—"

She felt herself fading to the color of sand.

"You going to faint, Mother Hart?" He reached out for her, but it was too late. She'd already started through the woods.

"Mother Hart? Wait, I want to help you."

"Hurry," was all she said.

CHAPTER 37

Memory, the father of heartbreak, snares us all.

Taylor Crawford, *My Life in Georgia*, 1929

Crack! Daffron's whip cut the air. Promise held her breath, willed herself not to cringe but worried he would soon turn it on her. So much had happened in the three eternal days since he'd unpacked his white box into her life. To think that the box that had served as her childhood talisman also symbolized Daffron's desperate scheme. But he'd failed to understand that the moment she'd inherited the farm, she became as much an obstacle to his plans as Taylor had been, if not more so. Reckless as it was, she intended to teach this man a lesson.

He struck Cambridge again. Her skin smarted as though she'd been lashed, too. Cambridge burst into a powerful gallop that rattled the wagon and pulverized shells along the road. Spit and snot spewed past his haunches toward Daffron. Promise silently cheered.

Daffron mushed his face into his shirtsleeve, wiped himself clean. He withdrew into an unnerving silence that put her on edge. She inched as far from him as she could without dislodging Beatie, but this paltry distance did little to dispel the sense that a longtime connection existed between her and this man.

Twice her age, he was old enough to have fathered her. Careful not to tip his hand, he had avoided telling her the true origin of his white box. When she'd asked, he'd made up a story, claiming her mother lived with her drunken father upstairs from the bowling alley, earned money on weekends playing piano for the Baptists, and on her way home, let Daffron buy her a cherry cola. Ellen had dismissed the significance of his white box, but Mother Hart had reacted differently.

Between the box, the uncharacteristic qualities of the letter Taylor had written to her, and Daffron's having been with Mother Hart the night of Will Hart's lynching—an unmistakable twenty-years-and-nine-months to the day before her birth—the ghastly possibility that Daffron was her father seemed more probable than not. Add the fact that she shared Daffron's height, his slender build, and red hair, bleached from the sun, that the unholy likelihood of her being his daughter hadn't occurred to anyone, and the pieces of her puzzle were coming together.

But the next part made no sense: Mother Hart *was* her mother, of that Promise was certain. If Daffron had sired her—she couldn't help but think of him in animal terms—he would have had to take Mother Hart by force, which was a real possibility.

Promise thought back: Mother, who was never curt, had snapped at her when she'd threatened to ask Daffron about his white box. And she'd purposely kept the identity of Will Hart's killer from Fletch, leading him to believe his father's killer had never been near enough for her to glimpse his face beneath his hood, when he'd actually been revoltingly close.

Furthermore, if Mother had become pregnant by him, she would have known he wouldn't have tolerated a drizzle of Negro blood in his line. That in itself would have prompted her to keep the pregnancy to herself. Will's death provided her with a ready excuse to withdraw for an extended period of mourning and became her ready excuse to stop delivering babies. No one would have suspected she was pregnant. No one but Taylor.

Taylor had spoken about the time he'd chased "that man" out of Martonsville. This started around the time Taylor had adopted her. A matter of coincidence? She didn't think so. The puzzle he'd left for her was coming together one horror after the other.

Her adoption would have been in keeping with Taylor's notions of mixing the races. Not only was her Negro blood irrelevant, he would have celebrated the opportunity to perpetuate his theory. In the midst of what had begun as a social experiment, he came to love Phua and her little girl as though she'd been his. Promise closed her eyes and rocked in slow keening movements.

"What's the matter, you got to go?" Daffron asked.

Yes, thought Promise, *I need to go somewhere to forget who you are and what you've done to my family.*

Daffron ignored her silence. His hand burrowed beneath his shirt into his trousers. Father or not, if he made the slightest move to unbuckle his belt, she would ram him off the wagon, where, if she were lucky, a tree trunk would put an end to his hatefulness.

She concentrated on protecting Fletch. This would be her gift to Taylor and Mother. Call it a type of repayment. Her eyes darted from the reassuring quiver of Cambridge's haunches to Daffron's fumbling fingers. He peered into the darkness. Gone was his smug expression. In its place, the forbidding picture of a man who had lost his soul.

She checked Beatie. Lulled by the wagon's jostling, the child had fallen into a fitful sleep. Slumped, the only thing fixing her to the seat was Promise's arm. Beatie had pressed as far from her father as space allowed. If his daughter could distance herself from him, why should she feel guilty for her revulsion?

She rotated her shoulder, slid her tingling arm up and down to keep it from becoming a useless glob, and flexed her fingers to get the blood moving.

"Something got you to jumping?" Daffron asked.

His snarl jarred her back to his unfastened belt and wandering fingers. She couldn't bring herself to look. Loosening her grip on Beatie, she shook the life back into her arm. If he were about to do what she thought, she'd need both arms—one to keep Beatie from falling and the other to shove Daffron to the ground. Don't get squeamish now, she chided herself.

She'd barely swallowed the queasiness in her throat when he tossed his head back and gulped from a small flat bottle. He nudged her, murmuring, "Tight quarters," straightened his leg, and dropped a cork into his right pocket. "Don't imagine you want any." He offered her the bottle, holding out the label side for her to read. She shook her head.

"This here is for medicinal purposes." He wedged the bottle between his knees, then reached into his back pocket, and pulled out a wrinkled paper. "See for yourself."

Original Prescription Form for Medicinal Liquor, F281776. Extract of Vanilla, take as needed for pain. Dr. Hovner's signature had been penned in scratchy script beside a fingerprinted blot of ink. The pharmacist's record of sale had yet to be detached.

She eyed him. "That prescription's had a life of its own."

He wiggled his shoulders against the seat by way of scratching his back and nodded knowingly. "So, you're a dry, are you?"

She swept his hand away and pulled away. "It's getting dark, but I know corn whiskey when I smell it."

"One mouthful would do wonders for your disposition." He checked her over from head to backside. She braced for his next remark, 'But not your looks,' which he didn't deliver. He was too busy slugging back another mouthful, no longer paying a lick of attention to her. Or his driving.

Upset that the reins were being yanked about, Cambridge jerked back. "Take it easy, big fella." Daffron rearranged the reins in his hands. The new tension signaled Cambridge that something had changed, and the horse reared its head. "You'd best behave," Daffron hollered. Promise folded her smile into her mouth.

Muffled wails of music, jittery and impatient, seeped through the woods from the roadhouse. Daffron nudged her, asked if she'd fish the cork from his pocket.

"Get it yourself. Better yet, pour that stuff out. You want to get caught with that?"

"Who's to say what can or can't heal a man's wounds?" He took a pull from the bottle, dug the cork from his pocket, and was about to close it when he glanced at her. She lowered her eyes.

"You have the same disgusted look my Margaret has when she calls me a shameful child of a whore," he slurred. Another pull, another swallow. He let out a cross between a chuckle and a cackle. "Know what I like about you? You're full of vinegar. Reminds me of my Margaret, 'cept your dare-me-you-bastard look is meaner."

He lapsed into silence for a few moments, then bellowed his drunken imitation of a railway conductor, "Slow down for the Road House Grill."

Slits of yellow lights flooded the space where shutters ended and window frames began, giving the grill an eerie disjointed appearance. Cars parked front to side reminded Promise of the haphazard order of tilted grave markers.

"You damned dries did this to Sawtooth," Daffron muttered. "Turned him dishonest."

"What did you say?" Not that she cared. She was busy worrying about what Cambridge would do when he realized he was surrounded by automobiles with odd-sounding names like coupes. Loud churning engines spooked him, made him act as crazy as Daffron.

With automobiles prowling the roads, she had to be cautious whenever she rode Cambridge. At the first rumble, she'd turn him in the other direction. Even then, he would toss his head, stomp and snort until normal sounds—the trill of the red-winged blackbird or the call of the snowy white egret—returned. She wasn't sure how he'd react if they stayed on the road because she'd never been foolish enough to test his fear. Most of the time, making sure he was free to escape the noise was enough to keep him calm. Luckily, none of the cars by the grill were running. As long as their engines were silent, Cambridge was safe.

Daffron drove toward the grill's side entrance beside an ancient red cedar. An archway had been hacked out of its midsection and new bark had grown over old, forming a brutal scar. Daffron pointed to Cambridge's tail swishing nervously. "Talk your heart out to your horse. When he hears your voice, he minds," he said, climbing down from the wagon.

She did her best to dredge the scoffing lilt from her voice. "Everything is all right, Cambridge. About as all right as it can be."

Daffron tied the reins around a branch and walked, tucking his shirt under his galluses and into his baggy brown trousers, as far from Cambridge as he could.

Beatie rubbed her eyes. "We're at the grill. We're going to have some supper," Promise said in the same steady voice that soothed Cambridge.

When her father reached for her, Beatie scrambled onto the bench and flung her arms around Promise's neck. "Your pa is going to help you down," she said. The child tightened her grip. "Beatie? What are you doing?" She looked up.

The child had worked her little hand up Promise's neck into her hair and was running a few hacked strands between her fingers. Tears dribbled down her cheeks.

CHAPTER 38

Though the eyes are said to mirror the soul, the most telling reflection of one's inner being lies in actions performed while weighted with life's disappointments.

Taylor Crawford, *My Life in Georgia, 1929*

Promise and Beatie walked hand in hand in front of Daffron toward the grill. At the stairway, the child scampered ahead. How Promise wished she could grab her and help her escape! Branches from beneath the shadows clawed at the expensive sandals that left all but the bottoms of her feet unprotected and that were the one item of her outfit that appeased Daffron. She steadied herself on the railing and climbed the stairs on the balls of her feet; *I've made it this far, I'm not about to let a pair of skimpy high-heels throw me off-balance.*

Inside, draped on the wall behind the bar, a faded Confederate flag. Cobwebs lined the shelf once occupied by distilled spirits. Pleased that Georgia had stamped out this blight, Promise nodded her approval. Nearby, a couple sat forehead to forehead, fingers intertwined. Startled, they looked up and, seeing Daffron, relaxed back into their conversation. The scent of frying grease clotted the air.

Promise cleared her throat and headed to the table farthest from the bar.

"Not here. We're going somewhere special." Daffron pointed to the door opposite the bar, then rested his hands on her waist. Before she could push them off, he tapped her dress with its many layers of cotton. "You, of all ladies, don't need a corset, Promise."

Not wanting to chance a conversation about what caused her to bind herself, she put her hands on Beatie's shoulders and waited. Unfazed by her silence, Daffron shrugged, drew a key from his pocket, and unlocked the door. This caught her off-guard. The man who'd been banished from Martonsville these past twenty years had been coming here all along! He slipped the key back into his pocket, turned to her and sneered, "You didn't expect me to spend all my time in a dry town like Tilden, did you?"

The door opened into a smoky crowded room. Women with scarlet nails and plucked eyebrows rested their elbows on the backs of their chairs. Cigarette bobbing between her oxblood red lips, one woman leaned into a waiting match. In the narrow aisles, painted toenails crisscrossed by strips of leather bounced to the rhythm of the music. The saxophone wailed while band members, eyes closed in ecstasy, ran plaid handkerchiefs over sweaty necks. Skirts twirling along the edge of the dance floor slapped Promise's thigh as she worked her way toward the last available table. A premonition loomed over her, a sense that Taylor had dedicated his life to grooming her for this very evening.

Daffron nudged her into the seat between him and Beatie. And though every moment she spent with Daffron felt like an hour, in reality, he'd wormed their way into this hideous place in a very short time. *Fletch is in danger,* she reminded herself. *And Beatie needs you, too.* Focusing on them made this time with Daffron bearable. The longer she managed to keep him here, the longer Fletch and Beatie would be safe. Besides, being wedged within this crowd would keep her safe, too.

A man with a patch over his eye called to Daffron, "Got yourself one pretty companion." As he approached, the man's wooden leg, painted with the likeness of the rebel flag about to unfurl, thumped along the floorboards. Promise needed no introduction; she recognized his voice: he'd driven the sheriff's car the night she pumped a bullet into its bumper.

Daffron sat up tall. "Yeah, Sawtooth, my daughter's a looker."

"Daughter" ripped at her. She was about to push herself up from the table, grab Beatie, and run when she realized these two weren't smiling at her; they were smiling at Beatie. She blushed with relief and embarrassment. What was it about Daffron that inclined her to believe he could be her father?

Brackish yellow points protruded through Sawtooth's gums. "What'll it be?" he asked and, without hesitating, slipped Daffron a beer.

"Another beer for me and one for the lady here and a cola for my little one."

Sawtooth winked. "Right away."

Promise popped her hand up. "Just a minute." The music had stopped and members of the band—a sax player, two trumpeters, one guitarist, and a drummer—were talking with a waitress in a low-cut pink blouse.

"Ma'am?" Sawtooth sidled closer.

She drew back toward Beatie. "Do you have lemonade?"

"Sure do, but it's sweetened. Everything in the back room is sweetened." The leer in his voice told her this wasn't what she wanted.

She glanced at Beatie, then at Daffron. "I'll have what the little girl is having."

"Yes, ma'am." Sawtooth raised a bushy eyebrow and whispered in Daffron's ear. Daffron's graying red hair quivered with each nod. Sawtooth patted his shoulder and hobbled off.

Daffron fixed his eyes on her. "Got to have your way, don't you, missy? You've gone preacher on me, just like my Margaret. Not smart, missy, not smart."

The room was hot, and the smoke made her eyes water. Pretending to study the long cardboard menu, she dabbed at the sweat dribbling down her neck, then jerked the menu closer. Holding it like a shield, she scooted her chair against Beatie's and began reading the list of offerings. "Show me when you find something you want."

Before Promise had read the first item, Beatie pointed to the chicken offering. Daffron had taken the child here often enough for her to memorize the menu! Promise ran furrows through her desperately hacked up hair; jagged as it was, it was nothing compared to her heart. *Margaret, Margaret, where are you*, ran through her mind. If only Beatie were home with her mother, she would have had a warm bath, clean nightgown, and the calm rendering of a bedtime story. But here she was, in this awful cave, completely at ease with her father's routine.

Promise gave her a hug. "That looks good," she said sadly.

A demanding tug drew her attention to the top of her menu, where Daffron bore down, forcing her to clutch it with both hands. "Just what do you think you're doing, taking Beatie here?" she asked a little too loud.

People at nearby tables stared. Some seemed startled. Others, alerted to the possibility of a drama that might enliven their dull lives, watched through puffs of woozy boredom. Daffron dismissed them with a wave. "My old lady's uppity tonight. Quick, someone get her a drink."

"Get 'er one yourself." The floppy drunks at the next table clinked glasses and guzzled them dry. A burst of coarse laughter rekindled the chatter.

Seconds later, the room buzzed. A woman wearing a hat with a huge feather that bounced across her forehead slapped the man beside her and began kissing his surprised face. Everyone laughed.

Sawtooth made a lassoing motion above his head. The band members manned their instruments, then started playing an insane tune that spiraled upward, deferred to the trumpets, and skittered out of the sax. Chairs scraped the sandy floor as couples wiggled to their feet and toward the dance floor.

The place felt as if it were about to explode. Sawtooth hobbled over, lowered a beer in front of Daffron, and slid the colas across the table.

Someone yelled over the music, "What 'cha doing with two dry ones, Daffron?"

Daffron stood and pushed out his chest. "One's my sweet daughter—"

She winced. Hearing him utter that word terrified her; what if this was his way of telling her he thought she might just be...

Daffron whirled around and pointed a finger at the man. "You keep your hands off her, you hear?" The man guffawed. Then Daffron pointed at Promise. "But if you're interested in this one..." She winced again. More hoots and whistles. And to her embarrassment, "Naw, you can keep 'er." Heat flooded her cheeks. She wished she'd run away when she had had the chance.

Daffron raised his shoulders in an exaggerated shrug, sat down, finished his first beer, drained his second beer, then slammed his glass on the table. "Now, what were we doing?"

"I was helping Beatie with the menu."

"Never mind," Daffron slurred, motioning Sawtooth to the table. "We'll have three specials." Sawtooth nodded, replaced Daffron's empty glasses with another beer, and headed toward the kitchen.

What manner of man readies himself for the act of killing by eating a meal with his child? Promise shuddered. She envisioned depositing Daffron in a place of his own. One so deep he would forever endure the sensation of falling. Narrow jagged walls would scrape his elbows raw. So cold his only protection would be a layer of mottled mold. One color would surround him in this cavern—that of his hate. Bitter charred gray? Heavy-hearted crimson? Blinding venom green? The last fit best.

Steadying himself on Promise's shoulder, Daffron stood and pointed to the lady in the feathered hat. "Honey-Bunches, come here, will you?"

The woman wiggled over, slid her arm around his neck, and planted her cheek beside his. "I see you got yourself a new friend." She slapped her palm over the gaudy ruffles running down her chest. "Whatcha trying to do, Daffron, break my heart?" She clamped her hand on her hat, threw her curly head back, and laughed loud and crude.

He tickled her chin. "Don't go talking that way, Honey. This one's business, all business." Then he stroked her giddy throat.

"You better not be lying. You know I'm jealous as a she-cat." She winked at him. "Where you been hiding? I haven't seen you in a while."

He grabbed her by the ruffle and pulled her toward him. That hard look returned to his eyes. "You're not going to start in on me like my Margaret, are you?"

The woman's giddiness vanished. She put her hand over his and tried to pry his fist loose. "Course not, never."

Holding her at arm's length as though she were a dead raccoon, he took a long drink. "Good. I hate a woman who follows her man to work, hides in the bushes so she can watch him do what's needed to keep her safe, then looks down on him for it. You know what I mean, Honey? A woman ought to be happy her man is ridding the world of undeserving beings."

"You are so right."

He let her go. "Margaret used to call me her 'heart's light.'" His face softened, and for a second, his eyes welled. He scratched his chest as though he'd forgotten he was in the grill. "Yep, that's right. She made me feel seven feet tall. Whatever I did was the best, Margaret said so. I was her hero, till the other night when she started hating me."

Daffron rolled his head to one side and stared at Honey. "Do something for me? Take Beatie for a while? Like you did before? Me and the lady," he jerked his head in Promise's direction and snarled, "got an errand to run. I'll be done by the time Sawtooth sweeps the place clean."

The woman bobbed around the table and plunked a sloppy kiss on Beatie's forehead. Beatie's smile was as big and comfortable as the sagging divan in Mother Hart's sitting room. "I'd love to keep Beatie with me. We had loads of fun last time. Danced like the fools, didn't we?" Beatie answered with a wordless laugh.

Promise recalled helping Mother Hart deliver Beatie. What had that been like for Mother, after what Daffron had done to her husband, to tend to the wife of the man who had probably raped her? Did her hands shake and her voice quiver? What about her poor terror-stricken heart? "Lean closer," Promise told the little girl who might be her half-sister. And when Beatie did, she scrubbed the oxblood red lipstick from her forehead.

Sawtooth lowered a plate of steaming special in front of each of them, pulled forks and knives from his back pocket, and tossed them into the middle of the table. They landed with a clatter. "More to drink?"

Daffron waved him off. "Naw, gotta work tonight." A knowing expression came over Sawtooth's grizzled face. He patted Daffron's shoulder and turned to the next table. Daffron dragged a fork to his plate and stuffed a hunk of dripping brown meat into his mouth. Disgusting as that morsel looked, between it and Daffron, dinner was the more attractive view.

Promise sawed through whatever was smothered in the gravy, making each piece small enough for Beatie to chew. In between cuts, Beatie popped a bite into her mouth.

Daffron put his elbow on the table and leaned his head on his hand. "You'll make a good mother one of these days."

His offhanded remark didn't smack of his usual bile. He seemed to have fallen into a drunken trance. She studied him—not a ripple of unkindness marred his face.

Then he smirked, "That is if anyone will have you, what with what you've done to yourself."

"I keep wanting to find good in you, but you make it impossible."

"Let that be a lesson to you. A man's word lasts as long as the breath that carried it."

"No, Daffron, *yours* does." She placed Beatie's plate in front of her and handed her a fork. She began cutting her dinner like she'd done for Beatie, only slower. If she could keep Daffron at the grill long enough, Fletch would finish his work and leave. Hopefully, by the time she and Daffron arrived at the Mitreanna, she'd find Sheriff Peall, who was known to frequent the resort. Surely the man would help. Someone had to.

She watched Beatie, who had gathered menus from nearby tables and was balancing one across two others to make a cardboard house. She fretted about what Beatie would see when she was alone with that drunken woman. About Fletch having trudged through horse manure for Daffron's benefit. About inviting Ellen to Mother's without thinking of Mother's grief. About stealing Mother's key and accusing her of hiding the identity of her father. About Mother seeing how shaken she was to learn they shared the same blood. About using her newfound identity to draw Andrew into agreeing to the compromise she'd shaped.

With time, she would repair the hurt she'd caused. Acknowledging her wrongdoing was the first step. One by one, she'd right all her wrongs, except one: that of being Daffron's daughter. She could no longer deny the truth. Mother Hart would never have concocted such an elaborate scheme if she weren't hiding a secret more precious than her own life. Her throat welled to think that her mother had loved her in secret. She pretended to gag and, for Daffron's benefit, dislodged a chunk of gristle.

Busily mopping the gravy from his plate with the last of the biscuits, Daffron ignored her coughing. She thought back to the ways in which she'd disappointed herself these past few days, especially when she'd found the mother she'd longed for. Then she'd hacked off her hair and made herself ugly. Under the guise of self-protection, she'd brutalized herself. Truth was, she hated that she'd hated what she'd learned about the color of her skin.

Daffron was standing now, waving at the woman in the feathered hat, shouting that he was leaving Beatie with her. Without waiting for Honey-Bunches to wind her way through the crowd, he shook Promise's chair and said, "Let's go, it's getting late."

She stood. He was right; it was getting late. Everyone had had plenty to drink, and the crowd was noisier than ever. Music pulsed, chairs scraped, women hooted, and men guffawed. But as Daffron poked her toward the door, the sound of Beatie screaming, "Promise" was the only sound she heard.

CHAPTER 39

Each generation has the duty to instill in the next values permeated with goodwill. So crucial is this responsibility, if we fail in its propagation, we compromise our hopes for humanity's betterment.

Taylor Crawford, journal entry, September 11, 1910

Torchlight shimmering along the veranda of the Grand Mitreanna outlined the base of the three-story hotel from the dance pavilion along its southernmost railing to the crimson-carpeted boardwalk snaking around the bathhouse toward the whites-only beach. That Fletch Hart stood mere yards from the bold sign crying out against his presence created a sensational attraction. From behind the railing, the Mitreanna's patronesses watched with attentive yet discreet Southern interest as he staged their evening's entertainment.

Naked to the waist and perspired from hoisting shovel after shovel of damp sand into the forms he'd made especially for this show, Fletch's muscular body glistened. He pulled a rag from his back pocket and mopped his face from the widow's peak on his broad forehead over the round of his cheeks. While he dared not look directly at the women, he could feel them staring.

From the corner of his eye, he watched them lean into one another, point their gloved hands and whisper. He guessed at the heartless insinuations they were making through their muffled giggles, their imaginations replacing the tableau of a poor Georgian earning a night's wages with the spectacle of a lion in the throes of mating.

Heat surged across his chest, down his arms, and into his fingertips. He raised his shovel high and plunged it deeper than ever before. The women inhaled sharply as though—the thought was too terrifying to complete.

The hotel's owner, Mr. Fredrick, strode past the women, patted one gentleman on the shoulder, and called to another as he approached Fletch. "Sandy, my boy, you're late. People threatened to leave if you didn't show."

"Yes sir, I is," Fletch answered, hating his po' boy talk more than the circus name his employer had slapped on him.

Mr. Fredrick slid his tuxedo jacket aside and lodged his knuckles on his bulging hip. "Hotel's full up and tide's coming in fast," he said, his belly pushing against the black pearl buttons on his pleated white shirt. He returned his gaze to the veranda, where groups were seated around linen-draped tables.

Fletch swallowed. Mr. Fredrick was scanning the crowd for indications of boredom—the start of a quick game of cards, excessive drinking, women signaling their husbands for the keys to their rooms—any of which could sound the death knell for his act and the money he needed for school.

Brightening, Mr. Fredrick waved to a gentleman at the far end of the veranda, then looked up at Fletch and scowled. "You've never disappointed me before. What's happened to you, Sandy?"

Fletch respectfully averted his eyes; explaining the complexities of his life would only add to his troubles. "I be tryin' my best, sir."

"Make tonight better than your best." Mr. Fredrick brushed the sand from his cuffs and marched toward the boardwalk, shouting greetings as he went.

He climbed the staircase to the palm-lined entrance of his hotel to the center of its double doorway, where a glass bowl rested on a tabletop that rode the backs of two carved elephants. He turned and faced the crowd. "Ladies and gentlemen, tonight at the Grand Mitreanna we have a first—the highest tides so far in 1930 will wash our shores. There, Sandy the Sandman will attempt to outsmart the forces of Mother Nature." The crowd crooned in appreciation. "Yes, folks, tonight you will witness the Sandman attempt to build a three-story castle at the edge of the sea."

Necks craned toward Fletch, working on the beach. Mr. Fredrick stretched his arms wide. The whispering settled. "There's more. My bet says tonight's tide will destroy the Sandman's castle *before* he finishes it."

Nervous laughter rippled through the guests. Mr. Fredrick raised a five-dollar bill above his wispy hair, turned slowly to his left, then to his right. After the oohs and aahs had subsided, a tuxedoed waiter took the bill, set it in the bowl, and lifted a silver tray. He held the tray while Mr. Fredrick wrote his name in the register and beside it, his wager. The crowd applauded.

"Ladies and gentleman, the betting has officially opened: Sandy the Sandman versus the Mitreanna's moon tide." The waiter extended the tray to the first gentleman to step forward.

Most nights, Mr. Fredrick's familiar attempts to heighten the tension didn't worry Fletch. However, tonight, when he'd arrived, a young boy cried out from the edge of the veranda, "He's here, the Sandman's here." His urgent tone alarmed Fletch. As he unhitched his mule and hid her in the barn far from the shiny Model T's parked along the avenue, he tasted the dissatisfaction crackling in the air.

He usually arrived early, which gave him plenty of time to build a solid base for his castle. But this evening, he'd spent precious time sitting by the river, absorbing the implications of Taylor Crawford's death. Without a moment to waste, he tamped sand into the base form and filled the remaining gaps. He tightened his grip on the long handle of the tamping tool and leaned hard, forcing his weight downward onto the flat wooden square he'd attached for just this purpose. Satisfied that he'd compressed any air pockets that would cause the castle to collapse, he walked toward the boardwalk to get the forms for the second tier.

***

Two years ago, Fletch had calculated and tested the castle's dimensions. He'd built his forms on the far side of the pier beyond the skeletal remains of a ship, careful to confine his work within the Negroes-only section of the beach. He'd made several attempts at ungainly castles, all of which collapsed.

That afternoon, after he'd succeeded in building a three-story castle, he dug a moat to the water. Gentle waves washed hermit crabs, coquina, sponge, and feathery seaweed into the moat. Fletch arranged shells into a coat-of-arms in the wall of one of the turrets. After planting a small American flag on one side of the driftwood drawbridge and Georgia's state flag on the other, he dropped down onto the sand and admired his work.

His seven-foot castle drew the attention of the guests on the Grand Mitreanna side of the pier. Soon, Fletch was surrounded by a sea of admiring white faces. He dared not move.

Mr. Fredrick bustled through the crowd. "What's going on here?" he asked, rolling his shoulders in readiness to defend his patrons from this Negro annoyance. Taking note of their enchanted expressions, he changed his approach. "Ladies and gentlemen, I'm delighted to announce," he edged closer to Fletch, whose dark skin was sprinkled with sand, "I have arranged to hire the Sandman to build his extraordinary structures on our side of the beach."

The crowd broke into hearty applause. "A dollar says the tide takes the castle away by six o'clock," one ruddy-faced gentleman in a damp bathing costume shouted. "My dollar says six-fifteen," said another. Sandy the Sandman had been born.

***

Over time Fletch got caught up in the betting, too: if he finished before the tide destroyed his work, his take of the purse increased from five to ten percent. If not, his efforts went out to sea, a possibility he could scarce afford.

Tonight, the misty air distorted his vision. At first, he thought he recognized the black man running toward him, water jug clutched in one hand and small sack in the other. Whoever he was, the newcomer handed these items off to Fletch, huffed, "Sandwiches from Mr. Fredrick," and sprinted into the shadows.

Ladies in evening dresses and shawls twittered at this Negro marathon. Anxiety, the human version of thunderclaps before a storm, rippled through the crowd. What did they expect him to do? Tear into the sack with his teeth? The last he'd eaten was breakfast. Had this been a different crowd and another less delicate situation, he'd have reached into that sack and devoured this meal. Instead, he placed it to the side. Mr. Fredrick had never sent him food before, and this made him wary. After losing the inheritance Taylor Crawford had assured him of, he'd learned not to put a black man's hunger on display.

Just then, two young boys came running toward him, kicking and chasing a ball. The ball was skittering across the sand when a gust of wind sucked it toward his half-built castle. Seeing their predicament, the boys froze.

Fletch clutched a bucket of cold wet sand to his chest and climbed the ladder to the second tier. From the upper rung, he could watch the children without being obvious. God forbid anyone were to catch him looking at a white child; its hysterical mother would rile the crowd and create a deadly situation for a nigger. In no time, enforcers, men who'd stored their white robes in the back of their shiny coupes and on the floorboards of their trucks, would engage him in a different kind of amusement. After all, what would be more entertaining than a moon tide lynching?

The wind teased the blond boy's curls, while the other boy's straight dark hair stood on end. Lips separated into a snarl, the dark-haired boy spoke a few words to his companion, then nudged his ribs. The fair-haired child yanked off his jacket and, with the flair of a circus clown entering center ring, spun it in the air and released it. He glanced at his friend, took three dramatic breaths, and burst into a run. Sand sprayed from the soles of his small churning feet.

Fletch checked the high-watermark on the breakwater. Waves crashed and exploded into walls of white spray. The tide was moving fast. If he worked steadily, he'd finish before it destroyed the castle.

The little boy kept running head down into the wind directly toward Fletch. His friend had, no doubt, dared him to retrieve his ball before the Sandman snatched and buried it, and him, within his castle.

Sand swooshed from Fletch's upturned bucket into the second tier. With any luck, he'd soon plant the flag of the proud state of Georgia in the top turret, and the crowd would cheer. Not for him, but for Georgia, and themselves. He, Fletcher William Hart, was a mere fly that happened to hatch in the crowd's midst. He needed to keep that in mind. He banned all thoughts of his brilliance, of reading and writing at the age of three, and later secretly studying philosophy, history, literature, and mathematics with Taylor Crawford. Stifling his smile, he leaped to the ground and grabbed the tamping tool.

The crowd gasped. Ladies covered their mouths, eyes widened with horror. A distraught woman—most likely the blond boy's mother—pounded her husband's arm and sent him sprinting toward the boardwalk to the beach. A woman in a shimmering dress put her arm around the boy's mother.

Little actions had taken on enormous meanings. Fletch quickly dropped his tamping tool, so he wouldn't be seen as armed. Another ripple rose from the crowd. He rubbed his back, picked up his dinner sack, and ambled toward the breakwater. The crowd released an audible sigh of relief.

He made a show of plunging his big dark sandy hand into the sack. His rustling could never compete with the crashing of the waves or the men, hanging over the handrail on the boardwalk, shouting madly, urging the boy to give up his trajectory.

"Take off your shoes, so you can run," a woman screamed to the father.

Even with Fletch chomping on his sandwich, the father closing in on his son, the boy heading toward his father's rescuing arms, the boy's mother grew more hysterical.

Sensing his mother's concern, the boy became concerned, too. He raced even faster toward his father, far from whatever was terrifying his mother. The father reached for the boy and swung him around, while the boy squealed with relief, "Papa, put me down." After wiggling from his father's grip, he retrieved his ball and sped toward his sobbing mother.

The mother clutched her son to her breast, and the crowd's cheering funneled into a raucous obscene roar. By then the other boy had, at the frantic urging of his parents, abandoned his friend, and returned to the safety of the boardwalk.

See how it starts, Fletch thought, angry with these whites for sowing seeds of contamination in yet another generation, angrier with himself for being a part of it. That the crowd showed no interest in examining the senselessness of the drama they'd witnessed exhausted him. He brushed his forearm over his nose, lest anyone accuse him of weeping.

Another realization rippled through him. He stuffed the remainder of his sandwich into the sack and hurried back to his castle. There was no way, no way in hell, he'd let people such as these derail his dream. He patted his back pocket.

Fletch worked quickly, tamping and filling the gaps in the second and third tiers. The tide was in closer than ever. He gouged out a moat, poked his torches into the sand, one at each side, and lit them. The crowd crooned, releasing something he'd thought them incapable of: A gentle new force billowed over the railings of the veranda and floated on the moon tide wind.

Fearful lest he misinterpret it, Fletch hesitated before acknowledging the crowd's admiration with a bow. Not that it was intended for a black man or a man born white but for accomplishment, that of a fellow human being. His eyes blurred as he fashioned turrets and crowned them with the flags that represented them all. He savored the kindness of the moment, willed it into his memory, so he could call on it when he needed soothing.

From somewhere on the veranda, a thunderclap startled the crowd: "Pay up, the nigger's won."

Fletch's stomach muscles contracted. His bitter victory was another reminder that, despite the acceptance letter in his back pocket, he would never be one of the select.

The little blond-haired boy's mother joined others, clamoring after Mr. Fredrick, who tried frantically to reassure them, "I've lost, too."

The boy stepped away from his mother. Without drawing attention to himself, he turned toward Fletch, slipped his small hand into the air, and waved. Fletch lowered his eyes, but not before catching sight of the boy's father, elbowing his way through the angry crowd. Had he been able to run without causing a panic, he would have let his legs take him far away, for the boy's father was hoisting the Confederate flag. Worse yet, he was whistling "Dixie."

CHAPTER 40

Evil in its most fearsome form finds its equal in the awakening of the good.

Taylor Crawford, journal entry, undated

The barn loomed large and lonesome on the outermost edge of the Mitreanna property. Distant waves rinsed the shore, cleansing it of footprints, broken shells and sandcastles, those created during an afternoon of play and the one Fletch was building by torchlight's glow. Mother Hart trembled as she drew closer to her son.

Though she and Acey were the only ones traveling, she started at the smallest unexpected sound. "Acey, did you hear that?" she whispered, twisting around to check the back of the wagon. Other than a mound of burlap bags lumped in the corner, it was empty.

"Hear what?"

She searched the blur of blue-gray dunes and found nothing unusual. "I'm jumpier tonight than ever."

Acey nodded. "Me, too. And scared."

"You'd best leave me off and get home. If Daffron sees you with me—"

"What he thinks don't matter anymore. Soon as I find a place to leave the wagon..." Acey paused. Mother followed his gaze to automobiles parked like crooked teeth along the railroad bed. "There's no room. I'll have to head back to the bridge. This may take a while."

"Then I best get off."

Noise from the crowd on the veranda of the Grand Mitreanna drifted across the beach toward them. He glanced from the barn to Mother. "You sure this is where Fletch leaves Cassiopeia?"

Velvety perspiration coated his peach of a face and though Acey was still young, having overheard Daffron plot against Fletch propelled him closer to manhood. The aimless energy that had taken hold of him after his mother abandoned the family was less prominent now. In its place, a new steadiness, that of a young man who'd made a grave decision. One that would cost him plenty.

Mother touched her fingers to his damp cheek. "I'm sure. Cassiopeia's too jittery to stay outside in the wind. There's Fletch's wagon, see?" She pointed to the side of the barn.

"I can see, but can you?" He leaned toward her. "Your eye stop swelling?"

His tenderness helped quell the pain. She touched the side of her face and drew her hand away. "I'm fine," she lied. Using the wagon's gritty boards as a guide, she eased her feet over the side, rested them on the step-off, clutched the wheel's dusty spokes and lowered herself to the ground. Relying on one eye was going to be hard.

***

She waited inside the small door at the rear of the barn until her eyes grew accustomed to the flat darkness. The swelling had narrowed her vision to a slice that began at the bridge of her nose, burrowed into a stingy tunnel and faded. To her relief, shadows emerged, allowing her to discern nearby poles, beams, and stalls.

Cassiopeia stood in the corner stall by the door, tack neatly draped by the gate. Mother shuffled over the soft sand and scratched behind the mule's ears. She seemed as glad for Mam's touch as for the carrot she pulled from her pocket. In turn, the animal's familiar smell made Mother feel closer to Fletch who was, at this late hour, finishing his castle.

The image of Sheriff Peall waiting to arrest her son came upon her so clearly, the reflection of torch light from his badge pained her good eye. Dear Lord, keep Fletch from harm, she prayed. Sounds of talking and laughing drifted her way. Fletch's show must be close to ending.

She quickened her steps into the belly of the barn. After unlatching the double doors at the far end, she would lead Cassiopeia outside and hitch her to Fletch's wagon. By the time she finished, Acey would return. They'd drive together down Relter Avenue and find Fletch. From there, they would hurry home, where she'd pack Fletch's clothing, borrow Cambridge from Promise so Fletch would have a fresh mount, and send him to Trivett's home in Atlanta. Her plan was coming together.

Now that she thought of it, she was glad Acey had offered to stay. If needed, he could go among the crowd along the whites-only beach. So far, the details and her vision were still fuzzy. But they'd come into focus soon enough. They always did.

Hearing voices just outside the barn, she felt her way back to Cassiopeia's stall and hid, hoping her heart's hammering wouldn't give her away.

The oversized double doors at the far end of the barn opened into the night's gray light. A plump woman in a dress led a skittish horse inside. Partway in, the woman unhitched the horse from its wagon. A man tottered out from behind and helped close the doors. The couple disappeared for a few moments, then returned, arguing. The man slurred his words, and from what Mother could make out, was angry with the woman for unhitching the horse.

"The wagon stays outside. And stop riling Cambridge. Are you trying to force him into a panic? Are you looking for him to get hurt?"

By then she realized the woman was Promise and, for some unknown reason, she was wearing a dress, a garment she avoided except for a few hours on Sunday. Though Mother could distinguish only her outline, she looked different. Heavier by ten pounds. Gone was the flow of her pretty hair.

"Touch me again, and I'll—" Promise said, shoving the tipsy man. Mother covered her mouth to keep from crying out.

"What? You gonna kill me?" Daffron cackled as he slammed into the wall. Sliding to the ground, he chastised her for tossing his medicine into the marsh.

Promise patted her Belgian's nose and hurried out of the barn saying, "Cambridge needs water. I'll be right back."

Worried that Cambridge would trot over and nudge her pocket to see if she'd given away all her carrots, Mother withdrew into the stall. Her spine ached as she flattened it against the rough wall. Of the two, the roughness in Promise's voice hurt more.

Once soft as wind-rustled leaves in spring, her daughter's voice shrilled as ear piercing as Daffron's the night he'd raped her. Though the possibility chilled her soul, Promise might be right—Daffron *could* be her father. Mother had no way of knowing.

Over the last twenty years, she'd spoken privately with Taylor about Promise as though she was theirs. After the child dropped off to sleep, they'd meet halfway between their cabins to discuss her scrapes and rashes; whether sending her to Boston each winter was good for her; what might happen if they routed her friend, Suzanne Peall, from her life. With each conversation, Mother sewed another stitch around Taylor's belief that he was Promise's father and pulled as tight as her thread allowed.

Taylor must have suspected something was amiss when she'd crawled into his bed so soon after Will's death. Fearing she might already be pregnant by Daffron and unable to face the horror of raising his offspring, she purposely confused the possibility, for her sake and for the child's. As for her, during those precious moments in which their lovemaking blossomed, Taylor gave her the gift of taking her outside her failures as a wife who failed to protect her husband, to remind her that, rape be damned, she was and had always been a woman who lived life with all her being, and who treasured the comfort of holding him deep within her. If Taylor had known, he never let on. That being so, she owed him far more gratitude than she'd shown. He'd been a truly generous man, the kind you encounter once in a lifetime, should the good Lord choose to crack you a smile.

***

Cambridge perked his ears at Promise's footsteps. She set a bucket in front of him. "For my good boy." His slurping echoed throughout the barn.

She gathered a tangled rope from the ground and started looping it from her palm to her elbow, until Cambridge nudged her and knocked the rope to the ground. "This is a lead, nothing more." The horse snorted as if in disbelief. She glanced at Daffron slumped against the wall and back at Cambridge. "Don't worry, no one will tether my boy."

"If you'd left him hitched to the wagon, we wouldn't be in this disgusting barn." Daffron studied the pole closest to him from its sandy base to the rafters and shivered. "I hate barns."

"You didn't have to follow me in here."

"Who said you could help yourself to my rope?"

"Fletch's show will be over soon—" she started to say. Daffron's mouth twitched into a wicked smile. "I mean, *the* show's almost done. When those automobiles start, Cambridge will panic. I'm going to let him run, then bring him back with this." She finished winding the rope and set it by her feet.

Daffron groaned as he hauled himself up from the ground. "That rope ain't for your horse."

He reminded Mother of the old Negro men who spent their days in front of the dry goods store, talking about how, once Fletch became a doctor, he'd soothe their aches and cure their ills. They were counting on Fletch. She hoped Promise remembered that, and the agreement she'd made with Taylor to keep her half-brother safe.

Promise fiddled with her sandals seemingly oblivious to Daffron moving closer. To Mother's horror, she scooped up the rope and heaved it, knocking him to the ground. For a moment, he was stunned, until Promise pounced. He jerked away, then grabbed her across her chest. She struggled to pry herself free, but he slung his legs over and through hers.

Mother realized Promise's added weight protected her to a point. But the moves Promise had learned from wrestling with Fletch and Trivett—punches, fakes, slides, pushes, elbows—didn't make a speck of difference. Her blows glanced off the hard little man, who had no idea the woman he was intent on injuring might be his.

He landed a crack to the side of Promise's head. She gazed at him for a moment and collapsed into a motionless mound.

Daffron gathered his rope and pushed himself up. Mother hoped her blurry vision was misleading her, but from the way he caressed that rope, she feared his smile was born of a twisted brand of pleasure. He looped the rope into a noose, slid it over Promise's head, and pulled it around her neck.

"What a night. Two-for-one. Wait until the boys see you flapping aside a nigger, their eyes are gonna bulge clear out of their heads," he muttered.

Mother landed a tremendous thwack on his back. Fierce as a bobcat, she sank her fingers into his sunburned skin.

"God sakes, nigger, what you doing?"

She hadn't been this close to this vermin since the night he'd pinned her down and hoisted himself onto her. Into her. After years of washing, you'd have thought the man's sour smell would have changed, but it hadn't. He still stunk. But that was of no concern, not like twenty-one years back when he was jam-fracturing himself against what was left of her heart.

And now, for one jaw-clenching moment, while he was bending her fingers in the direction the good Lord hadn't intended them to go, she told herself he'd hurt her so much, there was nothing more he could do. But she'd been wrong. He'd hurt her plenty the second he hurt Promise. The memories she'd kept locked inside came tearing out raw as her wounds the day he'd torn her apart. For a blessed blank moment, she forgot he was climbing on top of her again, straddling her right then and there, hurting her something awful because, as he pressed her swollen eye into the sand, all she could see was the slumped body of her baby girl with a noose around her neck.

She cried out as he pushed her mouth into the grit. But she didn't let that stop her. What did it matter if she lost her eyesight or hearing in the ear he pounded, she refused to let him hurt one more of her precious ones. As she begged Jesus to ride his chariot down from heaven and strike Daffron dead, a burst of strength so enormous she was sure it was her last cut through her.

She screamed his name, and he flinched, yielding enough for her to toss a fistful of sand in his face, and sink her nails into his scalp. Digging her toes into the sand, she arched her back and tugged on his hair. Once for Will. Once for her adopted Trivett. Twice for her Promise.

He twisted her over. Just as he was raising his fists to set them square in her face, a land-me-dead-in-my-tracks look took hold of him. He froze.

CHAPTER 41

Grand instrument, the mind; kind beyond measure,
capable of burying tortured recollections
within the mist of time.

Taylor Crawford, journal entry
On the anniversary of Will Hart's death

At first, "Dixie" tripped haltingly from the man's lips at the Mitreanna, toward Fletch. Then, as the man gained control over his breath, more forcefully. With menace. And while the man never looked directly at him, Fletch got his message: this tune was meant for him.

Sharper than a new nail, the tune pierced Fletch's memory of being three years old, of two men holding his arms and legs, while a third locked his head between a pair of scratchy knees. He recalled the men's robes, the foul smell of their burlap, and the fiery itching of the fabric against his face. One of the men snarled, "Forget trying to scratch, coon boy." He whipped out a knife and sliced Fletch's earlobe in two.

Fletch clamped his sandy hand over his ear, thinking his blood was oozing warm and salty as it had when he'd screamed, "Pa!" He could feel the filthy corner of the man's robe being stuffed into his small boy's mouth, taste its foulness. The man pressed his face close to Fletch's bloody ear and hissed, "Stop your hollerin' so's you can see what's gonna happen to you one day."

The man pried his eyelids open and forced him to watch a ghost-like figure slip a noose around his father's neck. Sour notes from the figure whistling "Dixie" writhed in the damp night air, along with his father.

Fletch released a warm trickle down his leg, over the men's hands. "Little bastard," one of them cried. Fletch started retching, and the men released him so he could vomit.

A white woman whisked him away, cleaned his face, and wrapped him in a blanket. He'd not remembered her until now and didn't know who she was. The thanks he owed her for saving him was overshadowed by another realization: the man who'd killed his father took a perverse joy in whistling "Dixie."

Fletch understood: The reactions he'd been having to Daffron Mears were those of that three-year-old boy. Throughout his life, he'd smothered this memory by devouring every piece of knowledge Taylor fed him. Taylor had known his tutelage would help a brilliant young boy find healing. History, mathematics, and similar tomes became the tombs in which Fletch buried his horror.

Fletch's hand, fisted like a little boy's, traveled over his damp cheeks and stopped at his chin. His heart thrilled; the insanity Daffron Mears inspired wasn't as irrational as he'd feared. He released a shaky sigh; he wasn't going mad. But he had reason a-plenty to be scared.

CHAPTER 42

Last requests, promises invoked by the dying,
tax the spirits of those left behind.

Taylor Crawford, journal entry, February 7, 1930

A woman's low growl accompanied the metallic release of a trigger. "You leave Mother Hart alone, you hear?"

Daffron lowered his fists.

"Get off her," Margaret Baldwin Mears hissed, aiming a rifle at his temple. He swung his leg cur-like into the air and landed on his butt. "Unfasten that noose from around Promise's neck."

Promise moaned, rolling her head back and forth. Daffron slipped off the noose.

"Now, untie that knot. Do your best, don't disappoint."

With her eyes on her husband, finger on the trigger, Margaret spoke to Mother Hart. "Can you imagine the night he tied one of those around our little Beatie's neck? He did, all right, that and more. I seen him. Only with what he did to my hands and feet, I couldn't get at him like I wanted. All I could do was scream. Even then, he beat me bloody. All with my little girl watching."

"How'd you get here, Margaret? You're supposed to be sick."

"Hitched a ride on an unsuspecting wagon, is how."

"Whose?"

"None of your concern."

"You need help, Mrs. Mears?"

What Mother failed to put into words set Margaret's voice to cracking. "You feeling up to it, I'd appreciate your tying Daffron's hands and feet. We can't have him rushing off. Not just yet."

From the corner of her good eye, Mother watched Promise steady herself against Cambridge and pull herself to standing. Seeing her child upright gave Mother the strength to go on. She picked up the rope.

The look in Daffron's eyes was more hateful than Mother remembered. She stepped back and, with the same studied motion she'd used hours after welcoming a baby into this world, held the rope at arm's length and looped it into a slipknot that could sever that baby from its life-giving cord. One little tug and her handiwork would cut the baby off. Same thing would happen tonight. She gazed at her noose, the one she'd dangled over Daffron countless times in her dreams. "Hands together."

"I don't take orders from no nigger-woman."

Margaret pushed the barrel of her rifle closer to his skull. "Do what this fine lady tells you."

As Daffron slapped his palms together in mock prayer, his face went mean spitting hard.

Mother pulled the noose tight around his wrists and fastened a length around his ankles.

When Mother had finished, Margaret planted her foot on Daffron's side, then rolled him over, took his knife from his pocket, and cut him from the remainder of the rope.

"Wouldn't this piece look handsome dangling from the tree in front of our house? What do you say, Daffron? Just you and me, the rope, and that big ol' tree?"

She paused to let her husband's face sink into a scowl. "I watched you kick the bench from under the feet of that poor Trivett fellow. Before I left home tonight, I set our bench out by the tree so you'd have something to step up on. Seems fair, don't you think?"

Mother Hart whirled on her heel. "You saw him?" She wanted to slap and hug Margaret at the same time, but pulled back. An unholy relief flooded her: Now she had proof for what she'd always suspected: *Daffron had killed my Trivett.* Had her heart beat more generously, she would have left him writhing on the ground. But that same heart, from which had come every good act, was no longer whole.

She took the rope from Margaret and tied a slipknot, then lowered the noose over Daffron's head. Margaret's thin pale face flushed a hellish shade of crimson. Mother yanked the noose, and he gagged like any man whose windpipe was being crushed. She peered into his spiteful eyes. "Fits real nice."

Outside, engines started and automobiles drove, headlights leading the way onto the road by the barn. Slices of ghost-like light appeared and disappeared through the cracks in the walls. Cambridge swung his head toward the lights and back as if to check for a cue to take refuge in the woods.

Voices shouted. Horns honked. Men gaffawed. The sandman had finished his show. Bets had been paid off. Any minute now, Fletch would return to the barn, pockets stuffed with the devil's lure. He'd hitch Cassiopeia to his wagon. Then they would ride home. Together.

Mother had to hurry. She quickly looped the end of the rope through Cambridge's harness. The horse's eyes widened with panic.

"NO! You warned me headstrong women can be tricked into unlocking hatred's door. Kill him and that's just what will happen—Daffron will win," Promise screamed, pushing Mother off balance and lunging for the noose. She'd almost freed Daffron when Mother spun her around.

"Don't be foolish, child, he's not your father, Taylor Crawford is. I ought to know!" Mother shoved her daughter to the ground. For one ugly moment, she hoped Promise would pass out.

Daffron lifted his face from the sand. "Far be it from me to interrupt, but would you do me a favor? A dying man's last wish?" Mother hesitated. Lord knows she'd made enough promises for one lifetime. She wasn't about to make another.

"Watch me die?"

The snap of Daffron Mears' neck would undo her forever, render the hands that had coaxed life from the laboring unworthy to catch slippery babes, squirming hot from the womb. She folded her hands on her chest over the rippling deep within her spirit and wondered how much longer she could endure. Taylor's words returned to her: *Punishment reflects the sin we choose to commit.*

Since Will's death, she'd strained against the insanity burrowing in her mind, dark thoughts that teased her with promises of release from vengeance-seekers' hell. She'd turned to lulling teas and numbing tinctures to silence the voices that accompanied those lies. When she neglected a dosage, she trembled. Whatever right-mindedness she'd once had now struck back for having pushed it too far, doling out the punishment she deserved for what she was about to do. She groaned with weariness. Far be it to give her conscience a voice now, not when she was about to fulfill her vow to rid the world of Daffron Mears. Will and Trivett deserved this comfort, nothing less.

Nodding, she granted Daffron's request to watch him die. "With pleasure."

Her gift to him—a promise she had no intention of keeping. All she had to do was slap Cambridge's rump into a gallop and listen for the snap.

CHAPTER 43

Of life's many burdens,
honoring another man's secrets
is the most solemn.

From Taylor Crawford's journal

Hours earlier, in what seemed a lifetime ago, the possibility of being unable to right herself had never occurred to Promise. Truth be known, she'd intended to face Daffron with all the spit she had in her and, in so doing, make up for the fight Trivett would have delivered had he not been outnumbered. There was no question about it; this confrontation would be her last. During those frightened moments in her bedroom when she'd shrouded herself within yards of protective fabric, her energy pulsed so furiously that she tied hard knots, impenetrable nuggets that would repulse Daffron.

Now, splayed on her stomach, she wished she'd fashioned a more flexible armor, one with ample room for breathing. Had her mother not been about to deliver Daffron's brand of justice, she would have gladly slipped into unconsciousness. She curled her toes under and, despite her stiff bodice, forced herself to stand. She tottered. Her arms flailed in an effort to stop the barn from spinning. When it refused, she spread her feet and steadied herself best she could. She'd almost found her balance atop her high-heeled sandals when the left heel twisted out from under her.

Unable to bend at the waist, she folded at the hip and fumbled with the buckle. Between this awkward stance and her fingers sweating, the buckle slipped, not once but several times. She did what she should have done precious seconds earlier—snatched Daffron's pocketknife from the sand and slit Ellen's expensive leather strap.

One was enough; there was no time to slice the other sandal strap. Though it hobbled her, as long as one foot landed firmly on the ground, she could get around. Lopsided as her mother's judgment, she limped toward her, reaching her just as she finished attaching the rope from Daffron's noose to Cambridge's harness.

"Mother?" Promise peered into her swollen sand-speckled face. No answer. Not a flicker of recognition, just wild-eyed concentration. Promise's chest tightened; her mother seemed lost.

Tail flicking with uncertainty, ears flattened to his head, Cambridge stepped forward, drawing the rope to Daffron's neck into a taut line. On the edge of becoming thoroughly spooked, the horse stumbled farther from Daffron, who followed like a tethered worm, arching his middle, drawing his knees to his chin, then straightening.

Cambridge twisted around to see what was happening. Daffron stopped crawling. More confused than ever, Cambridge took a few steps forward, and Daffron crept after him. This death-dance continued a few excruciating seconds more until at last Cambridge stood still. Promise grabbed the rope and started cutting.

"You trying to get yourself killed? Get away from there." She scarcely recognized her mother's snarl.

"Easy, Mother, go easy," she crooned, hoping to calm her and Cambridge while she struggled to keep the blade on the rope. She edged her shoulders between the rope and Mam, pivoting to herd her away. She stretched her arms as far as they could reach, pressed hard on the rope and sawed furiously. Frightened, Cambridge stepped back. The rope sagged.

Meanwhile, automobile engines revved one after the other. Lights shined through the cracks in the barn walls. Not knowing where to go, Cambridge shifted from side to side, forward and back.

"Run, you fool, run," Mam shouted.

Promise wished she were shouting at her. She repositioned the knife on the rope and cut until Cambridge stepped backwards. "Steady," she crooned one of the commands she'd taught him in another lifetime, in the days when the farm and all living there sparkled with contentment. But he reversed his direction and stepped forward. She gripped the gritty rope between her teeth, held it eighteen inches from her face and sliced.

Mam lunged for Margaret's rifle. "Make her stop, make her stop." Margaret scuffled with Mam. "Promise doesn't know what she's doing. She's making a mistake," Mam sobbed.

The one clump of hair Promise had failed to cut tumbled over her eyes. She jerked it aside and continued sawing. Bundle after bundle of yellow fibers sprang free. The rope snapped in two. Daffron's head bounced on the sand. Cambridge crashed out the barn doors. Women screamed. Horns blared. Men swore.

Promise pressed her ear to the ground and listened to Cambridge's hooves, pounding down the beach. Satisfied he was safe, she crawled to Daffron.

"Promise, no," Mam moaned. But too late. Promise had already loosened Daffron's noose.

Mam's begging rolled into a defeated keening. A whooshing noise, the rage of hell's breath withdrawing, retreating to its pit.

Beneath Promise's ribcage, a stabbing pain—grief at having witnessed her mother succumb to her own. The nagging recollection that she, too, had considered murdering Daffron danced in the shadows. She wobbled forward, struck by how alike she and her mother were.

A strong hand gripped her elbow and steadied her. Expecting Fletch, she looked up into Cooper Peall's round sweating face. She let him hold her long enough to yank off her lone sandal and shrugged away. He sank his hands into his belt and caressed his handcuffs with unmistakable strokes. Those of long-awaited lust.

She heaved her sandal at Daffron when she really wanted to fling it at the sheriff. If he arrested Mam, he would set off the biggest scandal in Martonsville. Mam would go to jail, and, if lucky, be subjected to a trial. What if—the thought was too hideous for words. She searched the excitement shivering in the sheriff's eyes. He wasn't concerned with Mam; the path he was heading down led to her.

"Funny what a man can learn when he hides in a barn. Never thought I'd overhear that Taylor and Mother Hart..." he licked his bottom lip, savoring every last crumb of this long-awaited morsel, "but since I have, I must say I'm pleased I decided to show up. Very pleased."

Promise had yet to catch her breath. What she was about to do filled her with fear and an audacious sense of hope. She leaned close to the sheriff's ear and whispered, "We all have—our secrets—don't we—Sheriff Peall?"

He swallowed his ape of a grin. His face drooped. He understood clear as the dawn after a cleansing rain that she'd read every word in the letter he'd received from Taylor. The one containing his secret about Suzanne. The secret she now possessed.

At first, he seemed dismayed, then a bit baffled. To her amazement, his face brightened with—dare she believe it? Admiration. He looped his thumbs into his trouser pockets and let his arms hang limp.

"I came here to arrest Daffron. Instead, you're arresting me. I can hardly believe I'm beholden to Taylor's girl. You do your father proud." His ruddy complexion blanched. "It's amusing, in a sickening sort of way."

"You see that man, Sheriff Peall?" She nodded toward the lump, not far from her feet.

The sheriff snorted. "He's hard to miss."

She glanced at Margaret, cradling her rifle like a stillborn child, at Mam, shaking with terror at what she'd almost done, and hoped she wouldn't regret what she was about to say. "Your job, Sheriff Peall, is to get this man out of Georgia. Don't let him sully our soil again."

"Smart girl, you kept your Mother Hart from getting herself in a pile of trouble."

She searched the sheriff's sweaty face. Was he toying with her, reminding her he held her secret, too? Would she be forced to tell him she'd shared his secret with her former fiancé, the accomplice who, if needed, would ruin the sheriff, his career, and his family?

She imagined Taylor's frustration when the barrier surrounding his precious farm had showed its first signs of rot. Maintaining his beloved dream had rounded his shoulders into a stoic stoop; one day she would wake to the honor of being bowed like him. Barefoot on the split rail fence he had built long ago, her heart's weight shifted to accommodate its new sense of balance.

Unable to fathom all she'd learned about the manner in which Taylor embodied his love, she trusted she would eventually repair, rebuild, and replace her orphan's memories with those of a much-loved child, one who would silence the thrum of *there's more*. The gentleness of this promise helped reposition her thoughts on the post that had hinged their lives together.

Mother and the others would depend on her ability to dance along the weathered edges of Taylor's fence. No tincture, poultice or tea would loosen the layers of secrets corralled within that enclosure. Bonded to the secrets she'd added, they bordered the family she now claimed as her own.

Her mother came to her side. Promise took her hand. Slowly, cautiously, they started toward the door to join Fletch who had just arrived, bewildered but safe.

EPILOGUE

Within the arena of human discourse,
endings give way to beginnings.

From Promise Mears Crawford's journal

When Promise's children visit her in the Berkshires, where she has made her home these many years, they beg her not to repeat stories from her ninety-year-old past. She smiles at their teasing and reminds them it was only shortly before they were born that she had discovered her true origins. They insist the face of Jim Crow has changed since 1930, and she respectfully corrects them, reminds them that because no reporter from their hometown presses chooses to write about lynchings doesn't mean the executions have stopped. Some, occurring in a private grove no one cares to visit, are exercises in bloody torture; some take place at a kitchen table while neighbors sip bitter coffee, others in the boss's office. She reminds them of their youthful years and how angered they'd been whenever fellow pedestrians scurried to the other side of the street after catching sight of four exuberant black teenagers.

Inevitably, when she speaks too plainly about such things, cellular phones beckon her sweet adult children. They entertain calls from the administrative assistant at the integrated school district where her son is its first black superintendent, the university publishing her other son's genetic research, the veterinary hospital confirming the surgery her daughter is scheduled to perform the following morning, and the farm, not far from here, where her youngest daughter breeds horses. Not that they're dismissing her. No, they're not like that but just the same, they welcome these distractions. Seems once this new millennium arrived, they rely on them to palliate the sting of having attended segregated schools, and of watching footage of others being held at bay by tear gas, fire hoses, and yes, modern day lynchings.

How she wishes Taylor had brought his vision of a gentler world to life for them. But people are people, she reminds herself. Most delude themselves into thinking the sun will always toast their backs when, in truth, it charms them with a meager slice of warmth, enough to comfort them through one upset before launching the next.

She understands her children's reluctance to revisit their memories: Since that defining upset in 1930, she'd padlocked the door to her three days with Daffron, but not their lessons. Over the years, she had pried it open with the help of a special few: her friend, Suzanne Peall, Margaret and Beatie Mears, and Acey Baldwin, often muddled with drink. At first, they'd been unable to wrap their minds around the horrors Daffron had inflicted. But her half-brother, Dr. Fletcher William Hart, helped them express their just outrage.

During the rare occasions when Mam had regained her lucidity, she, too, revisited the days that forever changed her life. During those times, she spoke to Promise through a favored Bible verse: "In you, the orphan finds compassion." In her inimitable way, she ultimately asked Promise's forgiveness with, "I should have entrusted you with your father's identity." That father, she continued to insist, was none other than Taylor.

Occasionally, when certain her mother could handle a question, Promise had asked if it was possible that Daffron might be her father. She let out a sleepy yawn. Her hazel eyes fluttered and her chin fell to her chest. Promise smiled. Her mother had yet to give up her secret.

Some days Promise chooses to believe her. Other times, she doubts. Truth is, she doesn't know. Right or wrong, Taylor succumbed to the paradox of all paradoxes by hiding her, the embodiment of his hope that race would have little sway in our dealings with one another, within the utopia he'd created at Mearswood Farm. To honor his memory, she often waded through the possibility that he was her father.

Then Daffron creeps into her thoughts. For some unexplainable reason, seconds before he was hauled off, Promise asked for a lock of his hair. To this day, it remains in her carved white box. Her children urge her to submit that faded shock of graying bronze hair to a laboratory for a series of DNA tests. "That way you'll know for certain whether he was your father."

She hesitates. "Why pursue the matter at this late date?" After befriending her uncertainty these many years, she's not eager to part with it. After dwelling in the ashen region, where her questions remain crusty and stale, she no longer needs the truth. Had she not achieved the goal she'd set out when she was very young—that of cherishing the finest she'd learned from Taylor and discarding the rest—she wouldn't have felt this way. To that end, she succeeded, of that she is certain.

"Look at yourselves," she says, sweeping a gnarled forefinger past her bevy of stunning adult children—dark, light, and in-between—offspring of her marriage to a loving but short-lived Negro veterinarian. "I find comfort in concluding that Taylor had acted as only a father would. I need no more."

She wishes she could say the same for her mother. Sadly, as years passed, the intervals between Mam's lucidity and her mind's confusion grew further apart. Had Promise not witnessed her coax squirming babes into this world and later, heal their cuts and bruises, she'd never have believed her capable of such powers. Ultimately, Mam found more comfort in joining Will and Taylor and Trivett than in remaining on this side with Promise and her great grandchildren.

"Before I join her," Promise confesses to her children, "there's something else I need to confess." Here, her children's hazel-hued eyes, stamped with smile lines common to all parents, grow as wide as the gap between the fine afternoon and the time their bodies fit snugly on her lap. "Yes, there is one more part to my story."

Right or wrong, decades passed during which she chose not to burden Suzanne, Margaret, or Beatie, now a remarkable woman with children of her own, with this occurrence. Though in retrospect, had she been more forthright, her mother might have tasted contentment before she died. In leading her to believe that she'd handed Daffron over to Sheriff Peall to do away with, she'd added to her madness. For Mam had never intended her daughter to execute the revenge she had planned. "The weight of that act belonged to me and me alone," she'd told her.

Spurred by her natural inclination to do the unheard of, after nearly being killed seventy years ago, she followed

Sheriff Peall and his prisoner, Daffron, out of town. With the help of a borrowed rifle, she waylaid them and insisted they accompany her to the psychiatric hospital in Milledgeville. The facility, reputed to be a veritable hell-on-earth, employed horrific procedures to "cure" its patients. If the patients didn't succumb to the cure, those tortured souls unfolded their days within moldy institutional walls, listening to fellow inmates' screams.

Had Daffron and Promise been alone when Milledgeville's bow-tied superintendent met with them, he would probably have sent them away. However, a white sheriff, committing a raving white pauper, lent an undeniable credence to Promise's pleas for assistance. One gesture from the superintendent and two men who were hired, no doubt, for their girth, accompanied the flailing Daffron down a dark corridor, shaved his madman's head, bathed him in icy water, and tucked him into a locked room. The guard handed her a lock of Daffron's hair, and the tension that had dogged the sheriff eased. She had to admit—she shared the sheriff's relief, she did. For Suzanne, the woman they both loved, was safe at last.

During the intervening years, as Promise reconstructed the pieces to her story, she visited Daffron at Milledgeville. She wanted him to see her auburn hair streaked with gray and hoped this quiet reminder would bring him back to the suffering many had endured at his hand. The last time she sat across a table from him, his was a decrepit shadow of a man, worn thin with age.

"I don't believe I have much time left," he said.

"That being so, there's something I need to tell you."

He cocked his head to the side, as he'd done when he'd first arrived on her farm, and leaned back to take her in from the peak of her new felt hat to the toes of her navy blue pumps. “You look like you done fine for yourself. What do you want with an old madman like me, Missy Promise?” Denser than hate, his anger hadn’t changed.

She curled her gloved fingers under the hard wooden seat of the chair on which she sat and drew her bowed back straight as age would allow. “I’ve been led to believe you killed Will Hart and raped his widow. Would that be true?”

His expression curdled. “That’s old news. What’s that to you?” was his ignorant question.

Her anger welled. All those years of surrounding herself with a husband, and babies, and a home full of love did little to offset his ugliness. A pain jabbed her chest with such fierceness she feared it would swallow her then and there. She rubbed her thumb knuckle round and round. Setting her forearms on the table over the gouged words LOVE IS ALL, she whispered, “I was born of that rape.”

From the revulsion registering on his face, anyone in that foul little visitors’ room might have assumed she’d reached across that table and slapped him hard. She took a deep breath and stood. “I thought you ought to know,” she said, and turned to leave.

“Wait,” Daffron said.

She started walking and kept on as she should have long ago.

Dr. Fletcher William Hart, renowned in his field of psychiatry, later told her Daffron had hanged himself in his room at the asylum. Fletch fingered the scar on his ear and called this “justice,” while Promise felt guilt, not for Daffron’s undoing, but for the decision she had made that set all of them on this path. Had she been able to roust Daffron out before Taylor had died, Trivett and Lizbeth would have shared the joy of hearing their son play the very trumpet with which Trivett had enthralled folks. Not that Fletch wasn’t a wonder of a husband to Lizbeth and father to Junior, for Fletch's enormous intelligence had combined with Mam's generous heart and yes, Taylor's inescapable wisdom. Had she landed Daffron early on, Trivett would have lived, and she would have pried her spectacular mother from the smothering soil of despair.

As it was, they all lost too much too soon. In winter 1965, shortly after their respective husbands died, Suzanne and Promise returned with Fletch and Lizbeth to Mearswood Farm—renamed Mearswood-Gills Thoroughbred Racing Center—where, when sober, Acey worked as a farrier. With special permission from Andrew Gills, they laid Mam alongside Will Hart, a glance from Taylor's grave.

Mam's solid granite headstone matched Will's and Taylor's in its simple dignity but not in color, Promise saw to that. Theirs were an immutable gray, hers a mottled combination of light and dark earthy brown. While wrestling with the inscription for her headstone, deciding upon the words that best captured all Promise held in her heart, she felt the hush of her mother's presence. To think she'd thought herself an orphan long before life handed her her real orphanhood. At that point inspiration graced her:

Mother Phua Semra Hart
February 17, 1880 to December 1, 1965
Found too late. Lost too soon. Forever loved.

ACKNOWLEDGMENTS

In 2004, Richard.P. Burnham, editor of the literary journal, *The Long Story*, honored me by publishing my 10,000-word story, "Seduction." Shortly thereafter, a subscriber to *The Long Story*, literary agent Nat Sobel of Sobel Weber Associates, Inc., contacted me and asked if "Seduction" was part of a novel. While I yet to commit to writing that novel, that was the moment at which I embraced this project. I am grateful to Richard and Nat for having motivated me to do so. The roots of *Sunday's Orphan* lie deep within the early publication of that story.

Thanks go out to Katherine Oxnard, talented author and writing instructor, whose wise advice has guided me along my writing journey. Through Katherine, I met Carol Semple and Frazier Meade, my trusted critics and writing partners of close to twenty years. Animated discussions about our characters often sounded as though we were gossiping about raising cherished but troublesome children. We fretted over their backyard brawls, marveled at their resiliency, and loved who they were becoming, revision after dogged revision. Thank you, Carol and Frazier, for being there as I raised my orphan.

Monica Wood, acclaimed novelist and playwright, mentor and friend, your incisive eye has reviewed numerous iterations of this novel. Thanks, Monica, for thoughts shared over many a fine glass of writer's inspiration!

Fred and Mary Bowers, I delighted in your equine expertise and the opportunity to watch you in your barn, playing and working with your stately horses. Besides your hospitality—you fed the horses, then fed my husband and me —you reviewed my manuscript to make sure I got my lessons right. You are the best!

Cherished memories hail from writing sessions spent in the home of elegant fiction writer, Janet Albright, and that of Jean Aberlin, accomplished devotee of non-fiction. Your reactions to my fiction gave me impetus to forge on. Thank you, Jean for introducing me to Gerard Van der Luen, whose comments on the emerging voice of Promise helped me flesh her into the orphaned protagonist.

Longtime friend Maureen Eberly, neighbor and fellow book lover Nan Kneckt, dear ones Joan Erickson and Mary McMorrow, and fellow writers, Lisa Hayden, Phyllis Chinlund, and Joan Dempsey delved into sections of this novel as though it were their own. I wonder if you'll recognize the forms your suggestions have taken?

Editors Anne Wood, Amy Congdon, Betty Darby, and Ariel Felton, thank you for your thought-provoking insights. Your fresh perspectives instilled me with energy and much creative joy.

Angela and Richard Hoy, Ali Hibberts, Brian Whiddon, Todd Engel, and all the team at Booklocker, your expertise and support has been invaluable.

My warmest appreciation to my talented publicist, Caitlin Hamilton Summie, a woman of thoughtful creativity and patience.

My thanks to Jeremiah Conway, whose interpretation of the subtext within the orphan's story, and John Collins, whose lectures on Flannery O'Connor's work, persuaded me that there is a place in the world for a novel about the impact of prejudice on the human spirit.

The librarian at the Tybee Library in Georgia, graciously located every reference I asked for and more. Tireless, she bookmarked sections in tomes that answered my questions with remarkable precision. I neglected to ask your name but haven't forgotten you.

I could not have reviewed all the materials the librarian provided without the help of my capable research assistant, devoted reader, sounding board, enthusiast, and husband, Mike. The orphan wouldn't have made it off my hard drive if not for your loving encouragement. Big forever hug!

Scott Irving, without your generous technical support, this manuscript would never have found its way to print. I mean that literally! Thank you, Scott, for sharing your knowledge of the binary world.

To those I should have acknowledged and have inadvertently overlooked, I offer apologies and gratitude for your gracious tolerance.

About the Author

Photo by Leslie MacVane.

Catherine Gentile's fiction received the Dana Award for Short Fiction. In 2020, her collection of short stories, *Small Lies* was published. Her debut novel, *The Quiet Roar of a Hummingbird*, achieved Finalist Status in the Eric Hoffer Novel Award for Excellence in Independent Publishing. Her nonfiction covers a variety of topics and has appeared in *Writers' Market*, *North Dakota Quarterly*, *Down East*, and *Maine Magazine*. She currently edits and publishes a monthly ezine entitled *Together With Alzheimer's*, which has subscribers throughout the United States. A native of Hartford, Connecticut, Catherine lives with her husband and muse on a small island off the coast of Maine. You are invited to explore her website: www.catherinegentile.com.

CPSIA information can be obtained
at www.ICGtesting.com
Printed in the USA
FSHW012334080721
82926FS